DEAD Ringer

By Robyn Nyx

2024

Butterworth Books is a different breed of publishing house. It's a home for Indies, for independent authors who take great pride in their work and produce top quality books for readers who deserve the best. Professional editing, professional cover design, professional proof reading, professional book production—you get the idea. As Individual as the Indie authors we're proud to work with, we're Butterworths and we're *different*.

Authors currently publishing with us:

E.V. Bancroft
Valden Bush
Addison M Conley
Jo Fletcher
Helena Harte
Lee Haven
Karen Klyne
AJ Mason
Ally McGuire
James Merrick
Robyn Nyx
Simon Smalley
JJ Taylor
Brey Willows

For more information visit www.butterworthbooks.co.uk

CATALOGING INFORMATION
ISBN: 978-1-915009-53-1
CREDITS
Editor: Victoria Villaseñor
Cover Design: Nicci Robinson
Production Design: Global Wordsmiths

Acknowledgements

A huge thank you and love to my editor and wife, Victoria Villaseñor, who reads my books chapter by chapter and is always demanding more. If only I could write as fast as you, my love. Margaret Burris, my proof reader, continues to do a marvellous job of correcting my Britishisms, but I dare to dream that I'm getting better and reducing her workload!
To the amazing readers in my ARC team: thank you so much for agreeing to read my book babies and being so kind with your reviews. I'm grateful for your time and care.
And of course, to all those fantastic readers out there who have demanded the return of Dak and CJ: this story is for you. I hope you enjoy their continuing journey, and yes, they'll be back in another volume soon enough. Thank you reading me and for taking the time to review and rate too—your engagement means the world to me.

Dedication

To my beautiful wife,
who never questions where I
get my inspiration for serial killers...

Chapter One

Have you ever woken up from a dream, and an idea has been so solid, so complete in your mind, it's as if you've been God-touched, or there's been some divine intervention? Or if you're not a particularly religious person (Who can tell? I have no idea who might eventually read this), then it might feel like the Universe has conspired to work through you in some small way.

Well, whether you have or not, *I* had that experience this morning. I don't usually remember my dreams clearly, even the really good ones that are incredibly vivid and as real as if one is truly inhabiting the situation. You know the ones; you feel every touch, you sense danger and excitement hiding just around the corner of your active subconscious mind; the ones where you wake and try to claw the memories back to you, but it's as futile as trying to hold armfuls of sand. And all of it simply slips away, forever lost to that greedy, immature part of your brain that doesn't like to share with anyone or anything.

But I remember every detail of this dream, though it wasn't a dream as such. It was more of a question posed and a path to the answer illuminated. I woke plagued by the concept of nature versus nurture. However, it wasn't a general rumination on the vast topic. My interest was very specifically about the act of killing, and even more specifically, about killing people. Not singular, not a crime of passion or revenge, but repeated killing. The question of whether a serial killer is born that way or molded through experience has become of great interest to me.

What was also in place when I woke, was the methodology with which to run the experiment. Of course, it would be wonderful to run a national, or even international, search for subjects whom I could direct. People all across the world who would commit multiple murders and record their findings. Was the fifth murder harder than the first? By the tenth dead body, did the process become rote? At what number corpse did it begin to excite you, if at all? And was that excitement sexual? I've read the books and watched myriad movies and TV episodes where the killers are profiled and the raison d'etre emerges as sexual and almost always related to childhood trauma. I'm sure you have too, so maybe your mind has posed the same question to you...but you've ignored it, for one reason or another. Perhaps you think yourself too decent a person to go around slaughtering people for the sake of science. I wonder if you're the kind of person who thinks it's okay to do that to animals for the sake of a kiss-proof lipstick though? Or maybe you just like the quiet life, and the thought of being the subject of a person-hunt (Not a manhunt, no. Gender specificity is so limiting) is terrifying. But these are my pages, about me and what I think, and I'm not interested in you and your thoughts—unless you're a serial killer. Then I'd love to talk to you. Do get in touch if I'm still alive when you read this.

Since an international search for like-minded, inquisitive individuals seems ill-advised for this particular conundrum, I'm forced to investigate alone. Which, I confess, is quite the way I like it. People are irritating and needy. They're skin-sacks stuffed to the brim with unnecessary emotions, illogical anxieties, and overly complicated desires. People ruin perfectly serviceable opportunities to engage and interact with other people. I am yet to find my peer, though perhaps if I were able to advertise this incredible opportunity to answer an age-old question, I might find one. However, I'm not one to dwell on things beyond my control, so I'll content myself to run a solo experiment, and should the results of said experiment eventually find their way into a scientific journal, perhaps then, things will change for future trailblazing thinkers.

For now, I will color within my own lines of morality and confine myself to a single researcher. I have never had the urge to kill, torture, or maim. I believe all of those things require a level of emotional investment with which I am not equipped. I thus believe myself to be a perfect person to carry out this experiment to discover if, after executing, say, ten people, I will become a killer. A killer who *needs* to hunt in order to live, to truly breathe. And before you bleat about the ethics and inherent risks of *creating* another murderer when there are already hundreds of them operating worldwide at any one time, I will have a way to reverse the process should I succeed. Please imagine a dramatic eye roll and deep, exasperated sigh at your incessant questioning.

Anyhow, I have lots to do, and there's much to prepare. How exciting. I haven't had a project for a while, and my brain has been fermenting in its own brilliance. To be busy is to be at peace. First, I need to define my core text. I don't believe the *Big Book of Serial Killers* exists, but I'm sure there must be something similar from which to draw. To get a broad base of data, I'll follow in the footsteps of established serial killers, mimicking their modus operandi. It seems like it would be a waste of my energy to reinvent the wheel when there is such a rich and imaginative tapestry of murderous culture to choose from. I wonder, though, if I should make contact with anyone still alive to explain what I'm doing. I'd hate them to think I was tampering with their legacy or disrespecting their life's work in some way. On the contrary, I'll be paying them homage and recognizing their excellence in this particular field. Perhaps someone who was particularly successful...until they weren't.

Location, location, location. I believe the crass saying about not defecating where you dine applies here. So of course, I won't do that. I shall plan a lengthy research trip to an old colonial hunting ground. The ironically monikered City of Angels seems like a fine place to set up base. Drug gangs, human trafficking organizations, and vice dens all conspire to provide the LAPD a veritable treasure trove of work to keep them busy. My little research project should fly nicely beneath their radar, and I shall be careful not to overstay my welcome. Once I have my source text, I'll create my research schedule. Perhaps I might even consider LA my first data set. There are so many cities in the world drowning in a sea of crime...

We shall see. I leave you now and task myself to the planning phase of my project.

Chapter Two

Nerves weren't something Dak Farrell was particularly familiar with, but tonight, they were painful needle jabs to her brain. And worse than the nerves was the indecision and doubt plaguing her. Both were irrational; she knew damn well how strongly she felt about CJ. If her duel with death thanks to a knife wound and a gunshot on the same day had taught her anything, it was that her life could be over any second, and life-changing decisions shouldn't be delayed for fear of making mistakes. When she'd been lying on the floor, bleeding out from where the Artist had strategically stabbed her, Dak's strength to push through the pain had come by focusing on CJ. She'd wanted, more than anything, to save her from the clutches of a crazed serial killer. She'd needed to rescue CJ so they could have a life together.

So here she was, with the ring box still nestled in her jacket pocket, pressing against her chest, daring her to take the plunge. Marriage had never been something she'd thought much about before, but in the past three months of rest and recovery, it had been one of the things on her mind the most. Sure, Walker had been in contact regularly to check on Dak's progress and to find out when she'd be able to return to active duty, and those check-ins had been weekly since she'd moved to LA. And yeah, Dak had idly perused the homicide advisories that came into VICAP daily, but for the first time in her life, her job hadn't been front and center. That position had been fulfilled by CJ and their future together.

"Are you okay?" CJ placed her hand over Dak's. "If you're not feeling well, we can go home."

"I'm fine." Dak smiled. CJ had wanted to come to this restaurant since she'd gotten back to LA a month ago, but Dak hadn't felt up to venturing out in public. If she were honest, she'd been licking her wounds and re-hashing all the decisions she'd made and the clues she'd missed that had allowed the Artist to kidnap CJ. It was guilt she'd have to learn to live with because letting it go was proving impossible.

CJ didn't look convinced. "Your face is telling a different story."

"There's something wrong with my face?"

"Not wrong, no." CJ traced the central vein running across the back of Dak's hand. "You just don't look like you want to be here."

Dak turned her hand over and interlocked their fingers. "I'm sorry. I definitely want to be here." She raised her wine glass with her other hand. "Let's celebrate."

CJ clinked her glass to Dak's. "Happy to. What exactly are we celebrating?"

"Being alive, for starters."

CJ arched her eyebrow. "That's a little too close to the bone, isn't it?"

Dak shrugged. "I know we've talked some about this before, but do you think what happened in Salt Lake changed you?"

CJ took a long drink of her wine then nodded. "How could it not?"

"True." Dak waited to continue when their waiter came to the door of the private dining igloo with their entrees. He laid them on the table, topped up their glasses, and retreated, closing the door behind him softly. "Overall, would you say it had a positive or negative effect long-term?"

CJ was silent for a moment, clearly contemplating her response. "A little of both, but mostly positive, I think. On the negative side, I'm still a little jumpy even now, and I'm ultra-aware of my surroundings. At home, I still check to make sure no one's in the closets or the bathroom when I go into the bedroom." She tilted her head slightly. "Just like you check every room in the house whenever we get home."

Dak bit her lip. "No points for subtlety then?" She'd tried to do their house sweep without CJ noticing. She didn't want her to feel unsafe in her own home.

"Subtlety isn't one of your strong suits, my love—which is one of the things I love about you, before you defend yourself." CJ sliced into her vegetarian lasagna and moaned quietly. "Mm, so good. Do you want to try?"

Dak waved the offer away and cut off a chunk of pinky-red wagyu steak. "I'll stick with this, thanks."

"Going back to your question though, it's also strengthened my belief in myself. I didn't panic or cry or break down; I tried to buy you time by talking to him." She smiled, her love crystal clear in her eyes. "I knew you'd find me."

Dak returned the smile *and* the love. "I'll always find you." At the time though, given how careful the Artist had been throughout their investigation, she hadn't shared CJ's confidence. It was only when he'd allowed his ego to get involved that he'd tripped up. But thankfully, that had been enough to find him.

"It's been a hot minute since we talked about this," CJ said. "Is there something on your mind that's prompted it?"

Dak nodded. She stared deep into CJ's gorgeous eyes, and her niggling doubts melted away. She loved her in a way she'd never thought possible, in a way so deep that it was almost as painful as it was pleasurable. Whatever the rest of Dak's life held, she wanted CJ in it. "My dance with the metaphorical Devil has mostly made me grateful for the gift of life. And I don't want to waste a millisecond of it. I've never been one for rash decisions; I like to gather all the information and process every tiny piece of it before I set off on a course of action. And for the past twenty years," she swallowed hard, "ever since Dad died, I've been obsessed with my work to the exclusion of everything else, including the family I had left." She took CJ's hand and kissed her fingers. "I'd also never been in anything more than lust, which was invariably transient. But then you came along, and you've shown me what love is, and what it's like to love another human being more than life itself."

Dak released CJ's hand, then pulled out the ring box from her inside pocket as she pushed away from the table and took a knee. "So I've been thinking about what I want for the rest of my time on Earth. And what I want—what I need—most of all...is you, CJ." She flipped the box open to reveal the diamond engagement ring, and her heart expanded in her chest at CJ's obvious delight. "There's no timetable for marriage, and there's no pressure on you at all, but I need you to know that you're the woman I want to spend the rest of my life with. You're the woman I want by my side through whatever this world gifts us or throws at us. The good, the bad, and everything in between, I want to face it with you as my wife." Dak took the ring from its velvet cushion. "Will you marry me?"

CJ offered her left hand and blinked back tears. "I would love to."

Dak exhaled, the release of tension a physical relief. She hadn't wanted to entertain the possibility that CJ might turn her down, that she might think it was way too early for lifetime commitment, but the potential had been at the back of her mind, quietly taunting her.

She slipped the ring onto CJ's finger. "Do you like it?" She rose and retook her seat.

CJ splayed her fingers and appraised the rock. "I love it. It's beautiful..."

She pressed her lips together and wrinkled her nose, something Dak discovered that CJ did when she was unsure how to ask or say something. Dak quelled the slow rise of panic. *She said yes. Relax.* "But?"

CJ shook her head. "No buts, silly. I was just wondering if you had any help choosing it."

Dak laughed. "Not that you know me, but since you're *wondering*, yeah, my mom offered her invaluable input. But I'd already narrowed it down to two, and this one was my favorite." She puffed out her chest some, wanting credit where it was due.

CJ ran her hand across Dak's cheek. "It's gorgeous, baby. I

adore it. You and your mom have exquisite taste."

Dak leaned into CJ's touch, and the gold band pressed against her lip. A strange sense of belonging swept over her. CJ wore *her* ring.

"So where's yours? People should know you're mine too," CJ said as if pulling Dak's thoughts from her mind.

Dak pulled the velvet lining from the ring box and flipped it over. "Here."

CJ took the simple, thick gold band and pushed her chair back. Dak frowned as CJ went down to one knee, then sighed as the full-length slit along the side of CJ's dress split to reveal her smooth thigh.

"I didn't know love until I found you either," CJ said. "You've changed my life, and my world is so much richer with you in it. I don't ever want to think about an existence without you by my side, and whatever we face, we'll do it together. I love you, Dak."

CJ held out the ring and Dak, baffled by CJ's impromptu proposal, extended her hand.

She slid the ring onto Dak's finger and kissed her knuckles. "I can't wait to call you my wife."

Dak got up and gently pulled CJ to her feet. "How come your proposal was so beautiful when you hadn't prepared it?"

CJ nibbled Dak's lip then kissed her softly. "Who said I hadn't prepared it?"

Dak wrapped her arms around CJ's waist and pressed their bodies together, needing the closeness and intimacy that proximity provided. "You've been thinking about marrying me?"

"Only every day since I realized I was in love with you."

Dak pressed her lips to CJ's and kissed her hard and deep, trying to compress everything she felt in her heart and mind, and express it through the melding of their mouths. She didn't know what she'd done to deserve this kind of love, but she was going to grab it with both hands and never let go. CJ was hers, and Dak, totally and completely, belonged to CJ.

Chapter Three

AIR TRAVEL ISN'T WHAT it used to be. Post-COVID, it seems as though companies have decided to charge more and deliver less. Smaller food portions, smaller seats. Surprising, since people have gotten bigger, are eating more, and taking up more space. Customer service has declined dramatically, and people are even more self-centered than ever before. On the hellish eleven-hour flight from London to Los Angeles, I encountered dozens of people who not only fit the bill for my experiment but who were also rather deserving of a grizzly end to their pitiful lives. Most of them seemed to be existing vicariously through their screens rather than actually living. I would've done most of them a favor, I'm sure. Then the end of their lives would have appeared on someone else's screen for avid consumption.

But all the ants emptied from the plane and scattered far and wide, barging past each other to scamper through security as if what awaited them on the other side of those gun-protected gates was somehow worthwhile, and that it couldn't possibly wait the precious moment it would take to assist that octogenarian with their luggage in the overhead locker. In a rare moment of empathy, mixed with mild rage at the disrespect shown by multiple people to the old guy, I assisted. On multiple levels, my interference was ill-advised. For the purpose of my visit, it's essential that I become an *everyman*, blending into the background unnoticed. I must minimize all quirks and foibles that might otherwise identify me and make me stand out from the crowd. I must epitomize Mr. Average in every way and not draw attention to myself lest I be identified and my research project be cut short.

Since I am anything *but* average, I expect this might prove to be most challenging. I suppose that the *average* person might find the actual killing of another human being—multiple human beings—to be the hardest part, but as I have taken on the persona of scientist for this endeavor, I shall be depersonalizing the individuals whom I will select. Additionally, other human beings are generally loathsome parasites, and the world is due a cull. The recent global pandemic didn't do the job that was needed, and a world war would most likely result in the absolute end to humanity (not necessarily a bad thing, though I'd rather that waited until my time was up). Whilst my efforts are but a drop in the ocean, fewer humans consuming finite resources seems like a good thing, and every little helps, as one of our grocery stores in the UK is so inexplicably fond of reminding us.

However, in a sprawling metropolis like LA, with a populace most interested in the young and beautiful, I believe I will have no trouble at all operating under the radar, especially if I disguise my Englishness. The place is crawling with tourists, executives, and would-be starlets of all presentations, and I can play the traveling businessman in my sleep. I'm sure you're wondering exactly who I am, especially if you've discovered this literary and scientific opus in a trunk in someone's attic. Perhaps I'm your great uncle or a distant cousin seventeen times removed. Does it scare or excite you that you might be just a little like me? I could even be your grandfather since I'm in the habit of depositing my seed to a very exclusive fertility clinic. Before you roll your eyes and comment, I realize that you might view my donations as folly and vanity, and that my willingness to provide fifty percent of multiple human beings for decades to come with my DNA rather flies in the face of my earlier assertion that the end of humanity wouldn't necessarily be a negative outcome, especially with my superior genetics. However, I'm working on the basis that the annihilation of the entire world may never come to pass. In which case, the aim is for my DNA to dilute the general inanity of the current pool. Of course, I have strict stipulations on the potential parents of my progeny—no one with an IQ of less than 140, no genetic defects, a minimum of three languages spoken, and no fans of rap music.

And if you continue to wonder: tough. I'm not about to waste precious ink and paper recording my life story thus far when I have important empirical evidence to gather. And anyhow, it's more likely that you think you know exactly who I am if my writings have been discovered and made public. Psychiatrists and profilers galore will no doubt have poured over my history, my family situation, and my childhood, desperate to put meaning and motivation to the actions which you are currently reading and I am currently living (in a kind of clever time travel phenomenon). You might consider me a monster, but I hope that you will eventually see the truth and know that I was simply inquisitive. What is it to be human if we have no interest in what goes on around us? Who knows what experiment I might conduct next? I suppose it will depend on how this one goes. So, settle in for the ride; I have some supply shopping and reconnaissance to complete.

Chapter Four

Dak threw a large towel onto the seat and dropped onto the outdoor couch, then nearly bounced back up off the giant, plump cushion. She wriggled backward and folded her legs in front of her. The patio in front of CJ's rented house was twice the square footage of anywhere Dak had lived since her childhood home, and the infinity pool was half the size of an Olympic pool. She yawned and extended her arms high, feeling the new skin over her wounds stretch. She'd rinse off the sweat from her workout and get in the water to loosen up in a few minutes, as her physiotherapist had advised, but first, she wanted to appreciate the view.

It was far from beautiful; the sprawling expanse of skyscrapers half-hidden in a haze of pollution looked like something from a science fiction novel, and though Dak hadn't previously spent much time thinking about what her idea of a perfect view might look like while relaxing, this wasn't it. Putting this rental high in the mountains of Spain, overlooking the vast, far-reaching deep azures of the Mediterranean would fit the bill. But still, there was something iconic and classic about the vista that stretched before her, and at the very least, she appreciated being alive to see it.

Since Dak had proposed, CJ had bombarded her with images of stunning villas in glamorous countries and sophisticated locations Dak had only ever seen in movies or read about in books. Their short visit home to see her mom and Ward had mostly been consumed with wedding and honeymoon planning: suits and dresses, cake and menu options, invitations and omissions. Dak's mom was delighted that she would get to see her married, and before they'd even left, she'd arranged a visit to LA for what she'd called "serious planning time." When Dak had asked CJ to marry her, she'd had no idea things would move so fast.

That wasn't a problem, of course, and honestly, having her mom help with preparations was very welcome. Her future with CJ was taken care of, and that gave Dak the time and space to think about her career. She pushed up from the sofa, pulled off her shorts and tank, and after washing the sweat off with a quick outdoor shower, she dove into the pool. After thirty laps, she got out and sat on the edge of the pool, dangling her legs in the chilly water, a pleasant contrast to the dry heat of midday. She stared at the gentle ripples of energy she'd created in the clear blue surface; it felt good to be breathing hard from the exertion and feeling the burn in her muscles. After the inertia of the initial recovery period, Dak had reveled in the extensive free time she had to get back to peak physical shape. But thoughts of her work were never far from her mind, and as her strength returned, so did the desire to get back to it. She just wasn't sure what form that might take.

"Hey, babe."

Dak looked up at the sweet sound of CJ's voice. "Hey, beautiful. I wasn't expecting you back so soon."

CJ kicked off her heels and lowered herself to Dak's side at the pool. She dipped her toes in then pulled them out instantly. "Have you turned off the heat again?"

Dak nodded. "I need cold water for my recovery."

CJ raised her eyebrow. "I don't think you get to use your heroic wounds to justify your weird obsession with swimming in ice-cold water."

Dak lay back on the terrazzo tiling and looked up into the bluebird sky. "I think I should be able to use my heroic wounds to justify anything for another couple of months, minimum."

CJ gently kissed each of the scars that looked like macabre bookends on Dak's abs, which were thankfully making a strong reappearance now that she was back to a regular diet and plenty of strenuous exercise, including sex with her gorgeous fiancée.

. "If that's the case, do I get to use my traumatic kidnapping to justify random and expensive purchases?" CJ fluttered her eyelashes.

Dak groaned. CJ had been trying to curb her consumerism since returning to work. Three solid years of work with only a hot sports car and a ridiculous amount of clothes was far from a 401k plan. "What did you buy?"

CJ trailed her finger along the edge of Dak's briefs and looked up at her, feigning an innocence long gone. "Something pretty."

Dak arched her eyebrow. "Pretty and returnable?" She was teasing, though. Their incomes were their own, and Dak had no designs on controlling CJ's finances or any other part of her life.

"Half of it *was* returnable," she said as she slipped her hand under the waistband of Dak's underwear. "But now that I'm wearing it, I can't return any of it." She pressed her finger lightly on Dak's clit, eliciting a deep, guttural moan.

"I've seen that dress before," Dak whispered, her words harder to come by now that CJ's fingers had slipped between the lips of her pussy.

CJ pushed inside, slow and deep. "But you haven't seen what's underneath it."

Dak clasped her hands behind her head and settled into the moment; the intense heat from the sun warmed and dried her skin, while a very different heat created by the insistent motion of CJ's finger made every nerve in her body tingle. "Do I get to see it?"

CJ pushed a little deeper. "Only if you give yourself to me now."

Dak grunted and said, "As if I wouldn't."

"Mm." CJ pressed her thumb to Dak's clit. "Sometimes your mind can be on other things..."

Dak reached out and wrapped her hand around the back of CJ's neck. "My mind is only ever on you when you touch me like this. Let me see..."

CJ smiled mischievously and shook her head. "Not until you've given me what I need."

Dak's breath caught when CJ thrust deeper and faster.

"And like I said, what I need is for you to give yourself to me," CJ whispered, her voice husky.

She used her other hand to push Dak's sports bra over her breasts then lowered her mouth to Dak's nipple. She sucked and nibbled as Dak lifted her hips to meet CJ's rhythm.

"Haven't I done that already?" Dak said when she could find her breath.

CJ looked up. "Because you're going to be my wife?"

"Yes." She gasped when CJ quickened her pace.

"The title doesn't mean *anything* if it doesn't come with *everything*." CJ ran her tongue across Dak's chest. "I want your mind, your soul, and your body." She emphasized each word with a hard thrust of her fingers.

Dak swallowed hard. She was losing her ability to focus on anything other than the intense pleasure building inside her. "You've got all of me. And you always will."

CJ grinned and pressed her finger to Dak's lips. "Stop talking. I just want you to feel me."

Dak did as she was bid and let her head rest on the hard ground. CJ continued her steady motion as Dak's pleasure rose, and she sucked Dak's nipple into her mouth again. Dak moaned and grasped the back of CJ's neck when CJ nibbled her lightly. She ground her hips against CJ's hand and closed her eyes, drawing every sensation into her mind. After a while, Dak placed her hand over CJ's and looked down at her.

CJ nodded, understanding that Dak wouldn't come from touch alone. She licked her lips and wiggled her eyebrows. "Can I have the good stuff then?"

Dak laughed quietly. "You can have whatever you want."

CJ withdrew her fingers and slipped into the pool fully clothed, gasping as she submerged to her shoulders. "If that's true, I want the heating back on in the pool, so I don't freeze to death sucking you off."

"You're not worried about your dress?" When CJ shook her head, Dak motioned toward the house. "We can go inside if you'd be more comfortable."

CJ shivered but waved Dak's suggestion away. "I'll cope. I need you in my mouth right now."

Dak put her feet on the edge of the pool for CJ to tug off her briefs. She tossed them away and CJ pushed Dak's thighs apart before lowering her head. Dak sucked in a breath as CJ pulled her clit into her mouth and began perfect circles with her tongue while sucking at the same time. CJ slipped a single finger back inside Dak but didn't move it, allowing Dak to concentrate fully on the insanely pleasurable sensation of CJ's mouth on her. Because CJ knew that Dak was only able to orgasm this way, she was able to totally relax and let go.

CJ wrapped one arm over Dak's thigh and pressed her hand against Dak's hip to keep her in place. With the added stimulus of CJ's finger deep inside, Dak's crash came even quicker than usual. Every muscle tensed as she rode the wave against CJ's mouth. Dak sighed contentedly and glanced down at CJ smiling and looking particularly pleased with herself.

"That might be a personal best." CJ lifted herself from the water and laid on her back beside Dak.

"I'll play harder to get next time." Dak shifted onto her side and pushed up on her elbow. She slid her finger beneath the strap of CJ's dress, which now stuck to every curve of her beautiful body. "Do I get to see now?"

CJ batted Dak's hand away. "I never realized you were so impatient."

"Usually, I'm not." Dak ran her hand along the soft curve of CJ's breast. "But I can't help myself when it comes to you."

CJ made a gagging noise and laughed. "That's a terrible line. Lucky for you, you don't need them anymore."

"I think I do." Dak squeezed CJ's breast gently, feeling the unmistakable outline of lace beneath the sheer material of the wet dress. "I'm not going to be one of those spouses who stops seducing their partner just because they're married."

CJ chuckled. "You better not be." She took Dak's hand from her breast and guided it downward.

Dak happily took the hint and began to slowly pull CJ's dress up, wanting to build the anticipation. When she'd raised the material to the top of CJ's thighs, Dak focused on what was beneath the dress: jet black lace panties. "Are they—"

"They are."

Dak gulped at the uninterrupted view of CJ's sex through the crotchless lace. "They're filthy."

"I know." CJ grinned wickedly. "You like?"

Dak shook her head and slipped her fingers between CJ's wet lips. "I *love*."

Chapter Five

BIND. TORTURE. KILL. THE BTK killer. Don't you find it fascinating how serial killers get their names? Some are far more imaginative and catchier than others. When I began reading about prolific serial killers of the twentieth century, Dennis Rader caught my eye and simply had to be the first murderer whom I would imitate as part of my research. It turned out to be happy coincidence that he was also the first serial killer in the book I'm using as my step-by-step guide. I've developed such a fascination with him that I might have had to find another book if that wasn't the case. I find the juxtaposition between the self-control he displayed around his urges and his egotistical desire for attention incredibly interesting. He, too, seemed fascinated with the murderous moniker he would be assigned, going so far as to suggest his own. And he looked so ordinary, so bland and unassuming, like an accountant. Receding hairline, eyebrows that resemble slugs, a mustache like a walrus, and unflattering glasses. Isn't he just the antithesis of handsome?

What do you think it was about his method of killing that he loved so much? The very act of murder stops someone breathing, but Dennis seemed obsessed with the physical act of the cessation of breath, strangling or suffocating each of his victims. And I have to wonder how he selected his victims. From what I've been reading, most serial killers have a particular type; their victims fit a mold. Something about their appearance excites them, or in some way, they remind the killer of their father or mother, someone they're repeatedly playing out their fantasy of killing because they never summoned the courage to do the deed to the real object of their hatred. But Dennis seemed to have no such limitations.

His youngest was nine years old and his oldest sixty-two. An entire family, a couple, and an old woman. Male and female. But again, I won't waste my ink and paper with unnecessary detail of his repertoire; there are quite literally hundreds of books devoted to the man and his work—hobby?—and if you're truly interested in him, you can do your own research. Consider it suggested further reading. Depending on when you've found this, he might still be alive. Perhaps you could write to him, as I did.

But I digress. His modus operandi gave me free rein to select my first subject, which was both slightly overwhelming as well as exciting. I might liken it to the proverbial child in a candy store. Here I am, out in the wilds of America, and every single person around me is a potential victim to whom I can apply Rader's methodology. Oh, the possibilities. A veritable lottery of death you wouldn't want to win. So many people have been in my space and had no idea that they were close to becoming an unwitting non-volunteer in my experiment.

I know that you're desperate to know which sweet I selected from the shop. Guy Keyes was a particularly attractive older man who carried himself with the confidence born from years of adoration and love. I suspect that his parents verily doted on him. Possibly he was a miracle child, birthed after years of his parents trying unsuccessfully and multiple miscarriages. I wager he was intellectually above average and had been gainfully employed his whole adult life. He wore a Patek Philippe Nautilus and a quite beautiful and intricately etched wedding band. The ring's silvery-white hue leads me to think that it was palladium, another indicator of his wealth and success. Rader, as with lots of mass murderers, liked to take souvenirs from his kills, though he often chose underwear. Since I had no desire to see the inside of Keye's Boss briefs—comparison is the death of happiness—I took the wedding band. The only part of Rader's crimes that I couldn't quite bring myself to imitate was the masturbation at the scene.

No. As you jump to conclusions in trying to dissect this particular omission, it was not because I am in any way sexually inhibited. You should remember that I have no problem at all handling myself since I do it consistently for the fertility clinic. I consider the regularity of this practice solely for my pleasure irrelevant to the topic at hand. My solo sexual practices and those I engage in with others have no bearing whatsoever on my motivation for this experiment.

Now that's understood, the actual reason for not leaving my semen at the crime scene was that I don't want to leave a single trace of my DNA. Whilst I'm not on any of the US or even international criminal databases, and thus, nor is my DNA, I don't wish to chance my luck with discovery at this early stage or indeed any stage at all over the coming months. In making this decision, I don't believe I've compromised the integrity of the experiment. There has to be an element of self-preservation at play here, as well as sound application of logic and risk assessment, while still adhering to the basic principle of each murderer. Hence, the care I take in making certain I use gloves and all the other paraphernalia I'd use in a laboratory experiment. I'm sure that makes sense to you.

LA had an average of only one murder per day last year. Since I have no idea when in time you might be reading this, you might think that rather high or surprisingly low. I thought it would be far higher and have to admit to being a tad disappointed. Though it *is* satisfying to know that I've doubled the statistic today. I shall be scouring the media to see where and how my murder is reported, and I feel that I can say with almost absolute certainty that no one in the local police or sheriff's department will join the dots and link it with Rader's body of work. Which is exactly what I need: for the murder to be just one of many in this city. And as homicide detectives scrabble around the crime scene looking for motive, perhaps they'll discover that Keyes was involved in some dealings which would logically lead to his murder. Perhaps it will seem like a mindless and particularly violent crime. It matters not to me, as long as there's no way to connect me to it. All I care about is that my research project is off to a wonderful start, and I have the first set of qualitative and quantitative data to record while it's deliciously fresh in my mind.

Chapter Six

CJ LOOKED AT THE spread of six cities across the States she'd be visiting for six episodes of *Dead Pretty*. Each of them was marked with a neon pink skull and crossbones. "Is this your idea of a joke?" she asked Emily, her best friend from college and now assistant to her agent, Paige.

Emily scrunched her nose. "Is it too much?"

"*I* think it's hilarious, but I'm not sure Netflix will agree that they set the right respectful tone." CJ lifted one from the board then replaced it. "Nice touch that they're magnetic. I'll take them home to Dak; she can use them on her murder board."

"Murder board..." Emily wrinkled her nose. "Dak and neon pink? Doesn't seem likely."

"You'd be surprised. Secretly, I think it might be her favorite color." CJ winked, belying the twinge of fear that registered in her gut. Though they hadn't talked about it yet, it seemed that Dak's involvement in the Artist killers' case had reignited her passion for current murderers and stemmed her obsession with cold cases, if the new information on the board was any indication. If Dak made the decision to officially join the LA field office, it would put her firmly back in the line of fire, something CJ was trying to reconcile. "How's Paige treating you? Any regrets?" CJ moved back to a topic that didn't chill her soul.

"She's working me hard, but I love it." Emily shrugged. "And you know I wanted a new start after the divorce. Relocating here is exactly what I needed." She put her arm around CJ's shoulders and gave her a quick embrace. "I can't thank you enough for suggesting Paige give me a chance."

"So everything's working out?"

"Absolutely. Paige's client list is growing exponentially—a good number of which have been attracted by the publicity of you being kidnapped by the Artist—so she says I couldn't have come along at a more perfect time." Emily gestured to the large boardroom, yet to be filled with Netflix representatives. "I'm able to babysit clients at meetings like this, leaving Paige to attend the more glamorous and aggressive engagements."

"Two of her favorite things." CJ gave a wan smile. "I'm not sure I appreciate the 'babysit' term though."

"You know what I mean. Paige has done all the hard work, getting you the deal you deserve. All of this is just strategy and planning—two of *my* favorite things." Emily began to pick off the skull magnets and replace them with a simple black sticky dot. "These are so boring though. You really don't think they'll have a sense of humor about these?"

"I'm pretty sure the director was drawn to this project because of a personal situation with a deceased partner." CJ gathered the bright little magnets into a pile when Emily had pulled off all six and dropped them into her tote bag.

"Speaking of personal situations, how are your wedding plans going?"

CJ laughed, pulled out a soft leather chair and sat down. "Subtle, Emily. Very subtle."

Emily clasped her hand to her chest. "I'm sure I don't know what you mean." She perched on the edge of the giant table beside CJ. "But since the topic has come up..."

CJ didn't respond. Instead, she removed her iPad from her bag and opened a file ready to make notes. She waved the Apple pencil toward the wall-mounted map. "It's interesting that most of the cities they've chosen are on the East Coast, don't you think?"

Emily sighed dramatically and dropped into the chair adjacent to CJ. "They said they were trying to minimize the travel while still representing a varied picture of the States with the highest murder rates."

"I see." It was logical that Netflix would want to capitalize on CJ's encounter with a serial killer and focus on "fixing" murder victims for the show, making it look like they hadn't suffered some horrific thing right before they'd died. For whatever reasons, mass murderers fascinated the average person, and she supposed she should be grateful for that. It had gotten her back in front of the camera, which had been all she'd wanted when she'd headed home to Salt Lake City to lick her wounds. But she'd ended up with the love of her life first—then nearly lost her. She shuddered and shoved the intrusion away. *Think nice thoughts*.

"My mom said that your mom has been telling everyone who'll listen all about you and your impending nuptials."

CJ laughed at Emily's persistence, but she wasn't about to put her mind at ease just yet. "Really?" Version 2.0 of her parents was taking some getting used to. The amazing studio they'd equipped for her at home, the daily text messages, the weekly phone calls... It was all still very new and alien.

Emily drummed her nails on the glass tabletop. "Really. All the ladies at the golf course have been getting involved."

That felt like a step too far. "I hope not," CJ said. "Ruth is flying in from Boston next week, and I'm pretty sure she's got a lot of ideas too. I'm happy for the parents to be involved, but I don't want random strangers offering their 'expert' advice on all things bridal. And I bet they're all straight women who wouldn't have a clue about organizing a lesbian wedding."

Emily nodded. "I bet you're right. You know what you need? Someone to run interference on nonsense like that. Someone who totally gets you *and* understands who Dak is too. Someone who's known you for years and who you can shout and rant at, but they won't get upset or offended."

"Mm. That sounds like exactly what I need." CJ tapped her finger to her lips. "If only such an angel existed."

Emily swatted CJ's shoulder. *"Rude.* I'm *right here."*

"*Oh*, you mean you're the angel? I did *not* get that!" CJ laughed and squeezed Emily's forearm. "In that case... Emily, would you do me the great favor of being my maid of honor?"

Emily pulled her into a bone-crushing hug. "I would love to!"

"Are you sure?" CJ asked. "I don't want to impose."

Emily held her at arm's length and arched her eyebrow. "You're such a tease."

"So Dak tells me," she said and grinned.

The meeting room door opened, and the Netflix team filed in, led by the director Patricia Wolf, whom CJ recognized from her IMDb profile. "Hi, Ms. Wolf." She walked around the table to shake hands. "I'm so excited to work with you." Her comment wasn't regular Hollywood bullshit; Pat and Rix Reardon had co-directed *The Extractor*, one of CJ's favorite TV shows, and she couldn't wait to work with her.

Pat's grip was extraordinarily firm, and CJ flexed her hand when she finally released it.

"And I'm looking forward to working with you too. I think your work is spectacular. Please call me Pat though," she said. "This is my team."

Pat pointed to each person and introduced them, along with their pronouns. CJ grabbed her iPad and scribbled them all down. She was hopeless with names, so she sketched a small picture alongside each name or noted a couple of physical characteristics she could use to identify everyone in the first few days of working together.

After everyone got themselves drinks from the long table that held every sort of flavored water, tea, hydrating liquid, and specialty coffee, they all sat, with Pat claiming the seat at the head of the table.

"Okay, CJ. We're going to be working closely with each other, but before we start getting to know each other, let's get into the meat of the program. We've got two weeks of prep and six weeks of filming. The families of all twelve murder victims have agreed to the cryo-freezing process—"

"Twelve?" Emily said. "We were under the impression each episode would be dedicated to a single victim."

"Yes, yes," Pat said and tapped the end of her pen repeatedly on the notepad in front of her. "But our content scout has selected two from each location so that CJ has a choice of who she'd like to work on."

"Will I be making the choice before filming begins, or will that be part of the show?" CJ was vaguely relieved she'd be the one with the final choice. But did twice as many victims mean some kind of macabre live voting fiasco?

Pat raised her eyebrows as if she hadn't yet decided which of those options she'd be going with. "Which would you prefer?"

"Which would play better?" Emily asked before CJ could respond.

"Good question," Pat said. "Maybe we could do some last-minute audience canvassing to see which the audience would prefer."

CJ had always spoken with the families of every dead person she'd worked on in the previous three seasons, and she never stopped being surprised by the abundance of people willing to put themselves and their loved ones through the public scrutiny of the show. Of course, she was glad to have their consent or her show wouldn't exist, but still, she liked to talk to them personally before filming began to ensure they were fully aware of everything being involved entailed. How would it feel though, to be discarded as if their loved one wasn't worthy of being featured on the show? "I'm not sure I'm comfortable with either option," CJ said and explained her thinking.

"What do you suggest instead?" Pat asked. "The bodies are rather varied and all very challenging. We thought this aspect would enhance the interest for your existing audience and fan base, as well as being an attraction for a new audience."

CJ frowned at Pat's apparent defensiveness. Maybe she'd

misheard that Pat wanted to be involved in *Dead Pretty* because of a personal tragedy. She only seemed interested in treating this like any other reality TV show, focusing on ratings and gimmicks instead of realizing the respect that was required in dealing with such a taboo subject. CJ took a deep breath. Perhaps she was being too hard on Pat; she had to make the show a success after it had been dropped, and that required a fresh approach. CJ hadn't chosen who she would or wouldn't work on for the previous three seasons; the TV cameras had simply rolled on her daily work at four of the biggest funeral homes in the LA area, so that had been easy. The media interest in the Artist and CJ had revived the show, and Pat was working with that prompt. "I'd be happier if they were randomly selected. I really don't want the responsibility of choosing who may or may not 'play' to the audience." She glanced at Emily, thinking that they should've been briefed about this aspect so they were on the same page. "And I definitely don't want to do that and then have to speak to the family whose murdered loved one wasn't chosen."

Pat nodded and looked thoughtful. "Okay. I can work with that."

She jutted her chin at her assistant, and they tapped away furiously on their laptop for more time than CJ judged necessary for such a small detail.

"We'll be keeping the filming locations top secret," Pat said. "The last thing we want to incite are murderers who want to see their handiwork on TV being fixed." She looked pointedly at CJ. "And you know firsthand how that can go bad if they don't appreciate the interference."

CJ tilted her head slightly and offered a small smile, slightly uncomfortable at the casual way which Pat had raised her recent kidnapping. Her statement made it seem trivial and yet sensationalistic at the same time.

"We could announce that all the people in the show had already been selected," Emily said. "That would prevent that from happening, wouldn't it?"

CJ nodded, liking the suggestion. The notion that her reality show could inspire or prompt murder for the sake of it—and messy murder at that—was abhorrent.

Pat nodded. "I guess we could make that happen."

Her muted reaction to Emily's solution seemed juxtaposed to her previous statement that she *didn't* want to incite murderers. CJ felt her perceived control over the content of her own show slipping away and with it, her excitement to get back in front of the camera. Things weren't feeling as respectful as she wanted them to be, as they'd always been.

With this director in place, the next few months began to look less and less appealing.

Chapter Seven

DAK POURED A LARGE glass of water then headed to the office for her weekly check-in with Walker. Their relationship had been strained since Walker had "loaned" Dak to Salt Lake PD for the Artist killers' case without talking to her first, and these regular little meetings were beginning to grate too. Being on the road for the past five years had given her a sense of autonomy that was deceiving, like being a special agent with special dispensation to do what the hell she pleased as long as she was getting results.

And she had been. All over the States, she'd closed cold cases that everyone else had thought unsolvable, and that had gone a long way to fulfilling the reason she'd joined the FBI in the first place. She adjusted the family photo that she always carried with her, making sure she had a good view of her dad as well as the computer screen where Walker's face would soon appear. Goddamn, Dak still missed him every day, but her grief had been assuaged somewhat now that she had begun to repair her neglected relationships with her mom and her brother, Ward. Reconnecting with them was yet another benefit of being with CJ, who was also in the process of repairing her own family ties, though Dak felt CJ's estranged relationship with her parents had been justified in a way her own never had been.

She clicked to enter the encrypted meeting at 8:59 a.m. and waited for Walker to join her. Dak had never liked wasting time traveling to and from the office for meetings, so the increase in virtual meetings during the pandemic suited her just fine. It had the added bonus of decreasing the wear and tear on Betty, the old truck that had been her last project with her dad.

"Farrell," Walker said as she appeared on the huge screen of CJ's iMac.

"Good morning." Dak gave a curt nod.

"How's the rehab going?"

"Good." She instinctively touched the site of her knife wound and then that of the bullet wound. The stitches had been out a while now and the elasticity of her skin had returned, but there was still some tenderness around both. She suspected that had more to do with tissue memory than actual tenderness.

"I've instructed the LA office to expect you within the week to begin assessment. Getting you back in the field is my priority right now." Walker tilted her head slightly. "Is it still yours?"

Dak clenched her jaw at the insinuation she'd been distracted by the change in the relationship status she'd advised them of after her proposal. Walker certainly wouldn't be making the wedding invitation list. "Of course," she said, marshaling her tone. "Why wouldn't it be?" She made sure her face revealed nothing, but internally she'd irritated herself by reacting to the cattle prod question. She should know better.

Walker's expression made it clear that the answer was painfully obvious to anyone who cared to look. "You've always been such a good agent because your sole focus has been the job. That's changed, so it's natural for me to wonder if you've changed along with it."

Dak bit her tongue before answering. Walker's implication was clear: she would no longer be as efficient with the distraction of a beautiful wife. "Aren't you married?" she asked instead of directly defending herself.

"Hamilton's application is on the fast track due to your recommendation," Walker said, clearly choosing not to engage.

Finally, Walker had something positive to offer her. Dak had encouraged Hamilton to take the leap; his natural aptitude and talent for homicide detective work were wasted in Salt Lake City, where last year's murder total was just 1.3 per month. After working with Dak and closing a few cold cases, including collaring Atkins for the infamous Rats case, there was no way he'd be content staying where he was. And he'd said as much himself, especially after Dak had floated the idea that she thought he was ready to become a special agent. "That's good news."

"I thought you'd be pleased. He passed the writing assessment and takes his physical fitness tests in two days."

"Excellent." That information was a little surprising. She would've expected him to reach out and maybe ask questions about what the written and physical tests entailed. Almost immediately, she dismissed her surprise. Of course he wouldn't do any of that. He'd want to pass all of it without any assistance to prove to himself that he was worthy of her faith in him. She couldn't resist a small smile. Her pride in him hadn't worn off even though they were no longer working together.

"And if he gets in, you're sure that you want him as your partner?"

"*When* he gets in, yes, I still want him as my partner."

"Seems like a strange choice after not working with anyone for five years," Walker said. "Are you ready for that?"

Dak fought not to roll her eyes at Walker's clumsy attempt to analyze her. "It's time," she said simply. Walker had never been someone Dak had been inclined to use as a sounding board or confidante, and that prospect had disappeared completely after Walker's lack of communication with her working the Artist case. The only person she wanted to talk to about Hamilton or Ben, her dead partner, was CJ. Now that Dak had fully committed to their relationship, her decisions affected them both, and she knew that she had to discuss every work decision with her. That seemed to apply two-fold for Dak's current dilemma of whether to go back to cold cases or return to current field work. CJ's kidnapping notwithstanding, the thrill of a live hunt had relit the original fire that burned beneath her motivation for becoming an FBI agent. But with that choice came an inherent risk that was all but invisible when it came to cold cases, and CJ would be the one at home or on set, wondering if Dak would come home every night.

"Is Hamilton that special?"

"I believe he is, yes. Shouldn't you be happy that I want to take on a rookie as a partner? No seasoned agent enjoys teaching a newbie the ropes. At least, very few of them do."

Walker shrugged. "I guess I should be pleased that you want to take on a partner at all..."

Dak didn't fill the pregnant pause Walker left for her to fill with more justification. She'd made her wishes clear, and that should be enough. Walker had the power to assign anyone she wanted to Dak, even if she didn't want anyone, so maybe Dak should be playing a little nicer, but the charm currency she usually held in reserve for her superiors had diminished. Walker would have to earn it back if she wanted more than the bare minimum from her.

"Have you seen anything of interest in the VICAP advisories this week?"

"Mostly drug-related and domestic violence," Dak said, glad to get back on track with the part of the meeting she was most interested in. "But one report caught my eye. Forty-year-old white male, no ties to any criminal activities, no reasons to suspect the wife. Victim was bound before strangulation by hands—big hands, so our killer is most likely male and taller than six feet. There was no sign of sexual violence, and the victim wasn't mutilated post-mortem. There wasn't much else to go on in the report. I know a lot of cops find the advisories a pain in the ass to complete because we ask for so much detail. I'm going to the station tomorrow to see if..." she scanned the copy of the report she'd printed out, "Detective Miller can give me any other information that he didn't put down here."

"You don't think it's random?" Walker asked.

"I don't know yet. I need to see the crime scene photographs and the video walkthrough, talk to Miller and see if he's got any feeling about it." Dak shrugged. "It could be nothing." But it didn't feel like nothing. It very much felt like something, the *start* of something. She hadn't seen anything else out of the ordinary in the whole of LA county for the past two months. Or maybe she simply wanted to see something in the murder because she was getting bored hanging around this rented mansion, working on her fitness and by default, her tan. "I'm going to search other cities for similar murders over the past couple of months because this doesn't feel like a first kill... Maybe our guy wanted a change of scenery. But like I said, it could be nothing. I'll know more after talking to Miller."

"Okay. Tread lightly." Walker affected an expression like she had a bad smell under her nose. "You know how cops get about their jurisdiction, and it'll be a gray area since you're not on active duty yet... Maybe you should wait to talk to the investigating officer until you've been cleared to return."

Dak shook her head. "I don't think it'll be a problem. I'm just making some inquiries, and I do know how to be subtle when I want to be." Though she used her height and stature wherever she needed to.

Walker laughed, and it sounded genuine. "You're known for a lot of things, but that's not one of them."

She tilted her head and gave a small smile. "I guess not."

"What are you? A hundred and sixty pounds?"

"Something like that." She hadn't weighed in for a couple of weeks. She'd dropped way too much muscle in the recovery process, and now she was shoveling in the protein and red meat to get it back. Dak didn't feel like herself if she wasn't in shape, and her confidence suffered as a result. Not that she'd share that with Walker. Or anyone.

"Exactly. You scare the shit out of our agents; what chance does a city cop have?"

"You want me to drop to a size zero, so I don't intimidate insecure men?"

Walker laughed again. "As if someone like you would even consider that. But no, I don't. One of the little joys in life is knowing you're out there making supercilious assholes a little more aware of their fragility and of strong women."

Dak raised her eyebrows, surprised at the vague praise and show of solidarity. It went some way to making amends. "So I'm good to see Miller tomorrow as planned?"

"Okay. I'm sure I don't have to tell you not to wear your gun."

Dak curled her lip and didn't hide her disgust at the *not telling but still telling* comment. "No, you really don't."

Walker held up her hand. "I know, I know. I'm just covering myself."

Dak's hackles settled. Walker was a woman in a traditionally male position, and she had to be seen doing everything by the book even when her male counterpart might do things differently and get away with it. Someday she hoped that would change. The Bureau was getting there; it was just taking way too long for Dak's liking. "Okay. I get it."

"Good," Walker said. "If you do discover something unusual about your vic's case, what do you want to do about it? It's far from a cold case unless you find a whole load of similar unsolved murders across the country that span decades."

"You want to know if I'm going back to my cold cases or if I want to go back to the job I was doing five years ago?"

"I do." Walker's expression remained neutral. "If you're going back to cold cases, you already have your schedule in place for at least the next year. If you want to return to live cases, we need to talk about which field office you'd prefer. And then we need to make sure there's an opening. Plus, if you're really serious about taking Hamilton as your partner, that field office has to know you come with a plus-one."

Dak nodded thoughtfully. It was a perfectly valid question, but it took them back to Dak's personal situation as a newly minted fiancée, something she didn't want to discuss. And she certainly wasn't about to say that she needed to talk it over with CJ before she made a final decision... even though she kind of had. She *did* want to be back in a busy field office, but she couldn't ignore whatever feelings CJ might have on the matter either. "Can you give me until the end of the week? I've been so focused on rehabilitation that I haven't thought about my future all that much."

Walker arched her eyebrows, and a hint of a smile twitched her lips. She could clearly smell bullshit even without being in the room. "The end of the week," Walker said. "Let me know how it goes with Miller."

She nodded, and Walker ended the meeting. Dak glanced at her cell to see a message from CJ.

I'm going to need a drink after this meeting. Wanna go out tonight? X

Dak sighed. If CJ wasn't happy before she even got home, how would she react to Dak wanting to get back in the thick of the action? CJ had known what she was getting herself involved in when they got together, but the near-death experiences for them both might have reduced her level of comfort with that fact. But Walker had given Dak a deadline, and she could no longer put off *the talk*.

Sure. I need to talk to you about getting back to work too. Walker's given me until the end of the week x

Dak watched the bubbles on her screen to show CJ was responding.

Okay, babe. I'll be home early evening x

Dak got up and headed to the bedroom to change into her workout gear. She wanted to pass the physical the first time and be ready for active duty. After working out, she'd have a couple of hours to dive back into the VICAP reports to see if anything matched the Keyes murder, and pumping iron would get her mentally and physically prepped. She hoped it might also build her resolve to face CJ. It felt strange to have to seek someone else's opinion and permission on her career choices—something she hadn't done since 9/11 and the subsequent discussion with her dad—but that's what choosing to share her life with another person meant: sharing all the decisions too. She just had to get used to it.

Chapter Eight

CJ PULLED INTO THE space at the top of the driveway, cut the engine, and smiled. Dak was waiting in the doorway, dressed to kill, and looking good enough to eat. If CJ could clear her head of the eight-hour long meeting she'd just had, she'd make sure she did exactly that, either before they went out or when they got home. Or both if Dak could "recharge," as she called it, that quickly.

Dak opened the car door and offered her hand. "Hey, beautiful."

CJ climbed out of her car, as elegantly as anyone in four-inch pumps could climb out of a Ferrari, and into Dak's arms. As CJ responded to Dak's hungry kiss, she felt the drab effects of the day begin to ebb away and pool at her feet. "I want you, right now." Burying herself between Dak's legs, she decided, would be the perfect way to forget about the day's events, at least for a while.

Dak lifted CJ off her feet. "I was hoping you might say that."

CJ placed her hand on Dak's chest. "Are you sure you should be straining yourself like this already?"

Dak grinned and walked toward the house. "Why do you think I've been working so hard at my rehabilitation?"

"I thought it might be so you could get back to work." She ran her hand along Dak's strong jaw and raked her nail over Dak's lower lip.

"Let's not talk about that just yet." Dak crossed the threshold and shut the door with her butt.

CJ tugged on Dak's tie. "It's almost a shame to undress you."

"I don't need to undress to give you what you want." Dak gently placed CJ on the couch in the living room.

"Then you don't know what I want." She flicked her gaze

downward and licked her lips, not feeling even slightly coy or interested in being subtle.

Dak shook her head. "You can have me when we get home. Right now, all I want is to fuck you hard and fast."

"You say the most romantic things, Special Agent Farrell." CJ hitched her skirt up over her hips and opened her legs. "I do love that about you." A rough quickie would do just as well to get her mind off her work.

"What else do you love about me?" Dak whispered as she pushed her fingers deep inside CJ.

As Dak fucked her exactly the way they both liked it, CJ gasped out all the things she loved about her wife-to-be.

After CJ came, Dak pulled her close and held her so tight, CJ thought her ribs might crack. "Ease up, baby. You're crushing me."

Dak loosened her arms and kissed CJ's neck. "Sometimes I just can't get close enough."

CJ sighed deeply. "Do you think you'll always feel that way?"

Dak tipped CJ's chin so she could look into her eyes. "Yes. Always."

She liked how instant Dak's response was and kissed her softly. "How do you know?"

"I can feel it." Dak took CJ's hand and pressed it to her chest. "Here. You can feel it too."

"I can feel the beating of your heart, steady and strong." A strange melancholy settled despite the deeply satisfying orgasm Dak had just given her. "That just tells me you're alive and healthy."

Dak gave her a half smile and tsked. "It tells me that I can't wait to see your face again from the moment you leave every morning. And it tells me that my life is sweeter every day because you're in it." She wiggled her eyebrows. "And it tells me that I want to make you come that hard every day for the rest of my days."

CJ swatted her chest. "Always back to the sex with you, isn't it?"

Dak shrugged and planted a kiss on CJ's nose. "It's how we started. I figure it's how we should stay. You're the one who jumped my bones the first chance you got. If I don't keep it up, I might lose you."

CJ wrapped her arms around Dak's neck. "I'm not going anywhere... Hot sex and super cuddles are a tough combination to find." She remembered Dak's text about needing to talk about work. She should be the one scared that Dak wouldn't come home one day. She extricated herself from Dak's arms and sat cross-legged, facing Dak. "So your boss has given you until the end of the week to decide what you want to do... Have you already made up your mind?"

Dak took CJ's hands in hers and rubbed her thumb across CJ's knuckles. "I know what I'd like to do, but no, I haven't made a decision yet. You're going to be my wife, and that means I don't make unilateral decisions anymore."

"And how do you feel about that change? You haven't had anyone to think about but yourself for a long time." She caught Dak's gaze. "I didn't mean that to come out as harshly as it did. It's a genuine question, without judgment, I promise."

Dak wrinkled her nose. "I know you didn't, but you're right. I haven't had a partner of any kind for five years, and I've never had a partner to share my life with." She glanced away, looking mildly guilty. "It *is* going to take me some time to get used to, but I want to. I want everything that comes with building a life with you. How do I feel about that change? I'm excited for all the possibilities, and I'm nervous about how all of it will work." She bit her bottom lip and raised her eyebrows. "Does that make sense?"

CJ nodded. She'd only been in relatively transient relationships too, and she'd never truly considered what the other person might want from a life together because she hadn't seen the possibility of that life. Until she met Dak. "It makes perfect sense. And I feel the same way. I just think that maybe the decisions you bring to the table are a lot heavier than mine."

Dak frowned. "What do you mean?"

CJ gestured toward the view of LA through the giant

floor-to-ceiling windows. "What I'm doing with my life and career doesn't have the impact of what you do with yours. You have the capacity to save lives, hundreds of lives. I'm just giving people access to something that maybe shouldn't be on TV."

Patricia Wolf's behavior throughout the meeting had never taken the more respectful turn CJ had hoped for. And it had soured CJ's outlook completely. What was she really achieving by making dead people pretty again? Was she just pandering to a population's macabre obsession with death? Who cared what they looked like when they were going six feet under or into an incinerator?

"Where's this coming from?" Dak asked. "I thought you couldn't wait to get back to filming?"

CJ shrugged. "I can't wait to get back to the challenging cases, to helping people say goodbye to their loved ones as they knew them in life. And that's what being on this show gives me easy access to. But I'm not sure I'm happy with the tone my new director wants to go with." She waved her hand as if her problems were taking up space in the air between them. "But let's talk about that later. You're on a deadline, and I want to know what you need from me." *Like masking my total panic that you won't come home one night because someone has succeeded where the Artist failed.*

Dak narrowed her eyes. "Okay, but we'll pick this up later."

CJ nodded. "After a few drinks, yes. Talk to me about Walker." She listened to Dak catch her up on her boss's demands and the case she thought might be the work of a serial killer. And she couldn't miss the way Dak's demeanor altered, the way her features animated with the thrill of the possible chase. It was clear what Dak wanted to tell Walker. "And?" she asked when Dak had finished and gone silent. "I want to know exactly the same thing as your boss; do you want hot or cold cases?"

Dak chuckled. "We don't call them hot."

"I don't care what you call them, you know what I mean." She gave Dak a light shove then placed her hand on her chest again.

"What does your heart want to do since it talks to you so much?"

Dak rolled her eyes. "You're making fun of me."

"Stop avoiding the question and just tell me."

"I want to go back to the real-time cases," Dak said and was silent for a moment, clearly summoning the courage to share something difficult. "When Ben took a bullet for me and died because of it, I threw myself into cold cases and couldn't ever imagine doing anything else. But after taking the bullet that would've killed Hamilton, it kind of feels like I've redressed the balance...even though it could never bring Ben back. But I'm reinvested, and I want to return from the cold of cold cases. I joined the FBI because I wanted to make a difference; I wanted to save lives. I can do that better if I'm working on killers who are active now and who would go on to murder more people. Cold cases give people peace, but they don't make a difference in the here and now." She took a breath and her chest heaved with the emotion of it all. "What do you think?"

Despite the weight of their conversation topic, CJ couldn't help but smile at Dak's gentle question. Every day, Dak was letting her see more of her true self, more of the person she kept hidden from the rest of the world for fear of her vulnerability being seen as weakness. CJ fought her own gender battle to be taken seriously in the TV studio, but Dak's battle was so much more pronounced. Dak couldn't show any emotions, or she'd be seen as just some woman who couldn't control herself around a crime scene.

But as their relationship grew, Dak was allowing CJ to understand her and what made her tick. CJ couldn't be more grateful for the strength it took for Dak to lay that vulnerability bare. In turn, she had to show her own. "I think it scares the shit out of me."

Dak's hopeful expression fell, and she ran her hand through her hair, sighing deeply. "There was a 30% increase in homicides in the first year of the pand—"

CJ pressed her fingers to Dak's lips and shook her head. "Don't.

Don't quote statistics at me. My heart doesn't care about numbers, about the faceless people in danger all over the country. It only cares about you and what might happen when you're chasing these murderous bastards." She trailed her fingers from Dak's lips, down the line between her pecs, and to the site where the Artist had left his mark, the scar CJ would know the location of in the dark with a blindfold on. "You were lucky last time. The bullet didn't cause any intro-abdominal injury. But you would've bled out from the knife wound if you hadn't gotten to the phone."

Dak tilted her head slightly and frowned. "You were lucky too. If you hadn't managed to get him to talk, he might've killed you before we could locate you. I recall asking you to take a step back from *your* job, and you refused... Are you saying you want *me* to stick with the safety of cold cases because—"

"Because I'm afraid that you might not come home one day?" CJ dropped her hand to Dak's thigh and squeezed gently. "I'm not just afraid; I'm terrified. What we have together is nothing short of a gift from the Universe. I'm not religious or all that spiritual, but I'm grateful for every moment I get to spend with you. The thought of those moments being finite because of the danger your job puts you in makes it hard to breathe."

"I know."

"No, you don't know," CJ said. "You're big and tough, and you can take care of yourself—Christ, you're more powerful than most men—but I'm relatively helpless. And I'd be even more helpless if anything happened to you. That isn't what worries me, though. What worries me is having to face the rest of my life without you by my side."

Dak glanced away, looking defeated and exasperated at the same time. "So what does all that mean?"

"It means I have to learn to live with a certain level of terror when you're on the hunt." It helped to think of Dak as a hunter, on top of the food chain with serial killers below her, and victims below them. Dak was king of the jungle and that's how CJ wanted it to stay.

Dak's eyes brightened, and it looked like she had to fight off a giant grin. "I can tell Walker that I'm done with cold cases?"

CJ nodded. "But we're going to need some serious ground rules about communication. I'll need regular texts, calls, and updates. You don't get to leave me at home panicking unnecessarily, okay?"

Dak pulled CJ into her arms and kissed her, and CJ felt the tension slip from Dak's shoulders.

"Anything you need, I'll do it," Dak said, breaking from their breathless kiss. "I'll need the same thing from you when you're filming all over the country, you know?"

CJ's self-worth blossomed. She was loved, and that was the most awesome feeling in the world. That she was loved by a woman as incredible as Dak was even more astounding, but she'd take as much of it as she could get. "Nothing bad happens on TV sets. You don't need to worry."

Dak took CJ's face in her hands. "I'll worry as much as I damn well please, thank you very much. You're my life, and you're safest when I'm by your side. I'm always going to worry about you, so you better get used to it."

CJ ran her tongue over Dak's bottom lip then sucked it into her mouth. "Same goes for you, handsome." She slipped her tongue between Dak's lips and sighed when Dak did the same. She briefly thought about her previous wish to go out for drinks to forget the day she'd had, and then she looked into Dak's eyes, dark with desire and promising her more of what she really needed. "Maybe we could stay home tonight," she said and began to slowly unravel Dak's tie.

"Yeah?" Dak asked, her voice husky. "And what would we do if we stayed home?"

CJ slid off the sofa, positioned herself between Dak's legs, and began to unbutton her shirt. She took a deep breath as she revealed Dak's muscular chest; the Hollywood tan suited her and made her even more attractive, if that was possible. She tugged

Dak's shirt from her jeans and shook her head slightly at the abs Dak had been working so hard to get back. "Goddamn, you're so fucking sexy."

"I'm glad you approve. But you haven't answered my question." Dak placed her finger beneath CJ's chin and tilted it so they could lock gazes. "If we're staying in, what do you want to do?"

CJ grinned wickedly and yanked open Dak's belt. "You."

Chapter Nine

MAYBE WALKER WAS RIGHT; subtlety wasn't Dak's strongest trait. It had taken less than ten minutes for her patience to fade once she was in a room with *Detective* Miller. As far as Dak was concerned, he didn't deserve the title and should have been pounding the sidewalk, handing out traffic violations. She'd seen more professionalism in the barista who'd prepared her coffee. He clearly suffered from the outdated obsession with jurisdiction and so far, her polite requests for anything from files to videos to extra detail had been met with Neanderthal-like grunts before he reluctantly lumbered off to retrieve whatever she'd asked for.

Suffice it to say that it was not going well three hours later.

The door to the briefing room swung open, and an androgynous officer younger than Miller by at least three decades entered with the box of evidence collected from the Keyes crime scene.

"Detective Miller asked me to take over. He's going for some fresh air."

Dak rolled her eyes. Miller's addiction explained his irritability in part; she'd spotted the nicotine patches at the edge of his short-sleeved shirt, as well as his sweat-stained pits. She wondered how long it'd been since his last cigarette and what exactly she'd done to push him to break his run. She tried hard not to judge other officers of the law—everyone had their way of coping with the stresses and rigors of the job—but she couldn't abide apathy and laziness disguised as jaded experience. "And you are?"

"Detective Weaver, at your service, Special Agent Farrell. I videoed the walk-through and attended the crime scene alongside Detective Miller. I should be able to answer all of your questions—"

Weaver stopped abruptly as if they might say something derogatory about Miller.

"You can speak freely, Detective." Dak suspected that Weaver held their colleague in as high regard as she did.

They looked hesitant and glanced over their shoulder while kicking the door closed. "I should be able to answer your questions better than Detective Miller."

"And why would that be?" Dak kept her tone light.

"Because I did most of the work."

"Yet it was Miller who completed the VICAP report."

Weaver nodded. "I wanted to do it. I like all the detail and all the questions, but he insisted." They glanced out the window and into the bullpen again. "I don't think he wants to be shown up by a woman. He's old school homicide. Thinks we don't belong here."

Dak nodded, taking in Weaver's self-identification and her show of solidarity. Dak knew that sentiment all too well. She already knew she liked Weaver and would much rather work with her, especially if she had more information than Miller did.

Dak beckoned her over. Weaver put the box on one of the tables and then came to stand across the desk from her. Dak slid a copy of the VICAP report to her. "How about you fill in the details now?"

Weaver's face lit up. "Are you sure that's okay? I've only just joined the department from vice, and I'm trying to keep my head down and take all the shit. I don't want to get on Miller's bad side. He's been here a long time, and he can make things a lot worse for me."

Dak clenched her jaw. Miller's attitude was beginning to make even more sense. In addition to his anger at the Bureau's involvement, he was a misogynistic prick. Weaver was going through the same rite of passage every female officer unjustly had to endure, and it pissed Dak off. "That's not the original, so you won't be altering any work done by Miller. And as a Federal Agent, though I'm asking you to do it, it's fine if you want to call it an order."

Weaver nodded and took a seat. She pulled the pen protruding from the top pocket of her stylish pinstripe vest, and as she pulled the top from it and got to work, Dak noted it wasn't a cheap ballpoint but a sleek, silver-barreled fountain pen. It seemed a little fussy for a cop, especially one who hadn't yet earned the right to complete reports, not that anyone did them by hand anymore. Maybe that's why it looked so new. "Don't see many of those in a city PD," she said, gesturing toward Weaver's pen.

Weaver looked at it, her expression softened even more, and she looked wistful. "It was my father's." She opened the report booklet and folded the cover page over, running her fingers over the paper to sharpen the crease.

So not new, just well taken care of. "Was he a cop too?" It was almost too easy to recognize the sign of the generations of cops in Weaver's family, as well as her clear desperation to make them proud.

Weaver's frown was fleeting before she smiled proudly. "He was a captain in this department."

Was. Dak decided not to press, but her obvious love for her father enhanced Dak's opinion and gave them something else in common. She knew enough about Weaver now to know that the rest of her visit would run smoothly, though she had to wonder if Miller had worked with Weaver's father. And if so, maybe their working relationship had been fractious, giving Miller even more reason to be harsh with Weaver. "How many homicides have you worked?"

Weaver focused on the report and didn't meet Dak's eyes. "This is my second. I've only been here a few months."

Dak suppressed a smile at Weaver's discomfort with her level of homicide experience. She remembered her own early years, desperate to get as many cases under her belt as possible and be taken seriously. Dak's physical presence had given her an advantage in that regard, which was something she and Weaver did *not* share. Weaver looked like she'd barely make a hundred pounds fully clothed and soaking wet. She was a couple of inches shorter than Dak and combined with her lack of weight, a strong breeze was likely a serious adversary.

"But I read all my dad's case files," she said when Dak had let the silence sit for a while. "Even though I probably shouldn't have—I used to sneak into his home office and study them." She smiled, revealing a small gap between her front teeth. "He caught me when I was fifteen, but then he started letting me go over them with him."

Dak held back her frown and judgment. Crime scene photos weren't appropriate material for quality daddy-daughter time at that age. But it didn't seem to have done Weaver any harm. At least it had pushed her toward the right side of the law instead of inspiring a murder spree. Weaver's willingness to share personal details without being prompted was interesting. Dak looked out into the offices and saw only men. Weaver's loose tongue seemed understandable.

"And I've read a lot of books. I'm always checking across other cities for interesting murders." She glanced up at Dak, clearly hoping for approval. "I want to be the best I can be."

Dak nodded. "It sounds like you're on the right path. What was your first case?"

Weaver wrinkled her nose. "Run of the mill gang execution."

Again, Dak held in a smile at Weaver's enthusiasm. She only hoped Weaver could hold onto that for the decades to come, especially as she fought her way to a promotion. "What do you think of this one?" Dak pointed to the various photos of Keyes, the murder victim.

Weaver placed her pen on the report and touched each of the images as if she were divining some information by osmosis. "There's nothing run of the mill about it, that's for sure."

"What makes you say that?"

"Keyes was a clean-living, family man." Weaver inched forward to the edge of her chair. "He had a beautiful wife and a cute kid.

He was a physical therapist, and everyone at his clinic had only great things to say about him." She pulled an internet article from a pile of nearby papers and pushed it to Dak. "He ran marathons for charity, and he volunteered at his church. His finances are in order: no debt, no gambling problems, nothing out of the ordinary. He had a small circle of friends, and they occasionally had boys' trips, but even they were just fishing weekends and not wild adventures in Vegas." She pushed back in her chair and sighed. "We can't find a single motive, and he seems like the least likely murder vic you could come across. I don't want this to stay red on the board, but right now, we've got nothing to go on. The rope that the killer used to bind Keyes is standard Home Depot supply, sold to thousands of customers, and there's no DNA evidence... It's like the killer was dressed in a hermetically sealed hazmat suit."

"And he was killed at his home?" Dak skimmed through the article Weaver had slid over. It was one of many accounts of Keyes' charity runs.

"Yep."

"Where were his wife and kid at the time?"

Weaver tapped a wedding photo taken from his home. "Visiting her parents for the weekend. They live in Tacoma."

"Alibi for the wife?"

"The whole set of in-laws, flight attendants on their plane, waitstaff at various restaurants—take your pick. She's got plenty, and they all checked out." Weaver pressed her lips together hard enough for the color to disappear momentarily. "And she was a mess. Unless she's an Oscar-winning actress like Elodie Fontaine, she loved him something fierce. She was devastated with a capital D."

Dak studied the wedding photo and didn't look at Weaver, who might blow a gasket with the sudden overload of female powerhouses in her orbit if she knew that CJ had invited Elodie Fontaine and Madison Ford, her Pulitzer prize-winning journalist wife, over for dinner next week. "Anything unusual with the kid?"

she asked, hoping for a negative response. If there was anything she found hard to stomach, it was child molesters. But with the wife and kid safely in Tacoma, it'd be easy for an older brother to seek retribution.

"Well-adjusted. Excelling at school. Solid friendship group. Nothing suspicious at all."

Dak paced the relatively small briefing room. Ten paces and she was turning around again. She liked that Weaver had done the work and had it stored in her mind too. She had the makings of a good homicide detective, unlike Miller, who burst back into the room looking even sweatier and more harangued than before.

He focused on the report in front of Weaver. "I've already filled one of those in. Why are you wasting her time making her do it again?"

Dak crossed the room and stopped directly opposite Weaver, close enough to Miller to make him take a half-step back. "It wasn't adequately completed." She held his combative gaze until he wavered and gestured back toward Weaver.

"And what makes you think she can do a better job?"

His movement sent the stench of his body odor tumbling through the air, and Dak flared a breath down her nostrils to keep from inhaling it. "Detective Weaver has already provided some very helpful information that wasn't on the report. As I told you before, I'm interested in gathering as much intelligence as possible on this case. I assumed you sent her in because you believed she had something to offer that you couldn't, which I very much appreciate." She made sure her expression matched the blandness of her words. She wanted him gone, and fast. In her peripheral vision, Dak could see Weaver faltering, uncertain whether she should excuse herself or stay put, and Dak very much needed her to remain exactly where she was so they could continue their illuminating conversation. She took the last few steps toward him and extended her hand. "Thank you for your help so far; I don't want to waste any more of your valuable time when your partner is more than equipped to answer my remaining questions."

His eyes flicked to Dak's hand, back to her eyes, and then to Weaver. When he finally took her hand, his palm felt clammy and cold, which was strange since he was slick with sweat on every other part of his body that she could see. He was probably weeks from a heart attack. Then Weaver wouldn't have to deal with him at all. She squeezed his hand firmly and watched his brow twitch in pain at the pressure. *Weak bones as well as a weak work ethic.*

Miller glanced at his watch then tapped it. "I've got a thing to get to anyway." He backed up, fumbling for the door handle. "If you stay beyond shift end, it's not authorized overtime," he said to Weaver.

"No problem," she said.

Dak liked that Weaver's voice was firm and steady, even though it was clear, if only to Dak, that she was struggling. Miller grunted and retreated out of the room, closing the door behind him.

He'd been gone a few seconds when Weaver whistled. "Wow. Just, wow. That was amazing."

Dak turned to face Weaver and tilted her head. "What was?"

"That!" Weaver pointed toward the door. "How you handled Miller." She shook her head and grinned widely. "I've never seen him like that before. He practically crawled out of the room."

Dak shrugged. "You'll learn to deal with people like that eventually. And it *is* all people, not just men. Women and non-binary folk can be assholes too; they're just not as prevalent."

Weaver fiddled with her pen. "It's a shame you're not going to be around for me to learn from you."

Dak smiled. "You never know. Maybe this case will turn out to be something we're interested in." What was it with the young cops she kept running into who wanted her as a mentor? First Hamilton and now this one. Had she reached that age when she was seen as the experienced font of all knowledge? It gave her an alternative career if she ever grew tired of the action, she supposed, but that wasn't looking likely for another fifteen years minimum. The thought that she looked past her prime and old enough for a grizzled mentor role was less than comforting.

Weaver glanced around the room, looking everywhere but at Dak. "If that happened, do you request to work with certain officers? Or do you just take the case and all the evidence to the local field office?"

"Depends on the case." She watched Weaver deflate slightly. "I've got officers looking for similar cases across the country over the past few months since there's nothing in LA County that raises any flags."

Weaver looked up. "You think Keyes was the victim of a serial killer?"

If she was trying to hide her excitement, she failed. She'd have to learn to school her emotions better if she was going to thrive in homicide. And Dak wasn't sure how she felt about Weaver's enthusiasm for the possibility of multiple victims. But she was fresh to the department, and her thirst for interesting cases was bound to be pronounced. "I didn't say that."

"Okay." Weaver tapped her pen to her chin repeatedly and didn't say anything for a few moments. "The crime scene was very neat, like the killer knew exactly what he wanted to do, and everything went according to plan."

Dak came back around the table and took a seat opposite Weaver. She picked up one of the photos of the basement, where Keyes was found. "The houses in this area, do they all have basements?"

Weaver nodded. "Why?"

"Are they visible from the sidewalk?" Dak asked. "Is the basement obvious?"

"Yeah." Weaver flipped through another pile of photographs and laid one of the house's exterior on the table in front of Dak. Then she tapped on each of the three skinny rectangular windows visible below the ground floor. "The driveways are about thirty feet long, so yeah, if you were looking, you'd see these from the sidewalk."

"Estimated time of death was between two and three a.m.?"

"Correct. The CSU techs are piloting the new motion photogrammetry methods, so the death window is short. Sinead, Keyes' wife, said that they were having their usual pre-sleep text conversation around ten thirty, but Keyes didn't respond to her final message. She assumed he'd fallen asleep and didn't call to check on him. The timestamp from her last message on his cell was 10:27 p.m."

"So our killer spent a few hours with Keyes before murdering him..." Dak closed her eyes and ran through the video walkthrough but couldn't see the detail she needed. "Were there any lights on in the house?"

Weaver frowned. "I don't recall because it was nearly noon when Miller and I were called to the scene. Let me check my notes." She got up and left the room.

Dak continued to look at the spread of photos focused on the basement. Weaver was right; the scene was meticulously neat, almost as if the killer had tidied up any mess he might've made—and not because he didn't want to leave any clues but because he couldn't abide disorder. What was it about Keyes that caught the killer's attention?

Weaver returned quickly and retook her seat. She flipped through her notepad and chewed on her bottom lip. "Here. Lights were on in the living room, hallway, and basement. Nowhere else."

"The drapes weren't closed. The blinds were, but they were pale so it would be easy to see the light on from the sidewalk," Dak said, mentally walking through the living room. "The killer would be able to see Keyes' shadow moving around in the house. He had to know that Keyes was alone, which means he watched his victim for a while, probably even saw the wife and kid leave with luggage... But how could he have done that in a neighborhood like this? The resident busybody was only five houses down. He would've noticed a car that didn't belong if it hung around."

"Oh shit," Weaver said.

She pushed out of her chair and grabbed the open laptop at the far end of the table. She tapped furiously, then her eyes widened, and she turned the computer toward Dak.

"That's on the same street?" Dak looked at the house for sale, almost identical to the victim's.

"Not just the same street—it's opposite Keyes' house."

"You should contact the realtor and explain we need access to the house today because we think the killer used it to stalk his victim. We'll check it out, and if we suspect the killer was there, you'll need a CSU team to sweep for potential DNA evidence."

Weaver was on her feet and almost to the door before Dak had finished talking. "Can I drive?"

It was a strange question given the myriad of others she could've asked. Dak shot her a questioning look. "Why?"

"Miller says I haven't earned driving rights yet." Weaver dropped her shoulders. "And it'd be my pleasure to play chauffeur to a special agent."

"Sure." It wasn't just Weaver's grin that made Dak acquiesce. The LA traffic was hellish, and Weaver would know shortcuts and routes far better than she did. The rush of adrenaline from the thrill of the chase had been sorely lacking over the past couple of months, but now it was coursing through her veins, pushing her forward in pursuit of another killer. Technically, she shouldn't get involved. She had nothing but a gut feeling that this could be the work of a serial killer, and she wasn't yet cleared for active duty. But Weaver was carrying, and the house would be empty. There were no risks, really. She'd gleaned most of what she could from the physical evidence. The rest was in Weaver's brain. This was more for Weaver's benefit than Dak's, since she seemed so eager to spend more time in Dak's presence. Yeah, it was a nice, steady reintroduction to the job. Exactly what she needed.

Chapter Ten

SINCE I'VE SET MY schedule to allow maximum time for experiment, reporting, and contemplation, I have forty-eight hours between the closure of one sample murder and the beginnings of preparation for the next. As I've said, it's my intention to maintain a low profile, but I have needs, just like any other human being. Indulging this particular one isn't as tedious as the others can be. Quite the opposite, actually, and it's something I divine more than just physical pleasure from.

So I got in my recently acquired second-hand truck (with tinted windows and a flatbed complete with tarpaulin for the murders that require privacy and for me to transport the bodies of my experiments), and headed to another large and anonymous city to scratch my itch: San Francisco. The couple who entertained me would have made perfect subjects for Joseph Paul Franklin, since the woman was white and her husband was Black. Thankfully, Franklin wasn't featured in *Close to Death*, but I would have dismissed him as a potential killer to copy since I don't agree with his politics and abhorrent racism, and whilst I must remain objective and detached, I'm afraid I won't compromise my central belief system even for this endeavor. And yes, you're correct, I *am* indifferent to the human race generally, but differentiating between skin colors, genders, sexualities, etcetera makes no sense. It's completely illogical, and that's what irritates me most about it. By all means, be prejudiced against stupidity (which is something that can be lessened, if one is so inclined. Free courses abound to expand one's mind and understanding), but discriminating on the basis of characteristics a person cannot change? Folly and nonsense.

Additionally, you must understand that at my core, I'm a scientist, and I'm engaging in this murderous experiment for the good of humanity. It's not a selfish venture to satisfy any need other than curiosity, and I'll thank you to remember that as you continue to read my study. And yes, I know that I said it had to be a solo experiment, but that doesn't make me selfish; it makes the present scientific world short-sighted. Perhaps it makes me a little impatient, I'll give you that much. I suppose I could have spent some time on the dark web gathering like-minded souls, but I was eager to begin. After this initial series of experiments, I might do just that. But for now, I'll content myself—and thus you must also be content—with my efforts alone. I wonder if you might be the kind of person who would have made a good companion if only our paths had crossed. I can only assume that we haven't, but should you be so inclined, you might wish to make this study the basis for your own investigation...

But I digress. If there's one thing I do enjoy about current culture, it's the sexual availability of people in general. Of course, the prudish minority remain, but the expansiveness of sexuality and gender nowadays make for a wonderful soup of seduction for someone with all tastes and proclivities. I've thoroughly enjoyed watching this particular phase in the evolution of humanity, and I admit that it does offer a modicum of hope for the future of the species. That hope, however, is tempered by the insane and illogical actions of those who find this development somehow threatening to their ridiculously boring status quo. If the opportunity arises, I shall be allowing a measure of subjectivity to slip into my subject choice. If I'm able to rid the world of a few bigots during the course of my study, I feel I will be killing two birds with one stone, or knife, or whatever other method I might employ.

I met my entertaining couple in a sex club on Diamond Street in the Castro. I'd only been at the bar a few minutes before they approached with a delightful proposition. I find sadomasochistic sex to be particularly stimulating for the mind and, given that I am striving to be at the very zenith of my intellectual game for the duration of my study, it seemed not just pleasurable but also necessary for me to engage in the couple's elaborate scenario. Moreover, since they wanted me to wear a beautifully crafted volto (Venetian mask, if you didn't know), it made the evening less risky to my being identified. This way, I could make my mark, both metaphorically and literally, without chancing either of them remembering my face.

Usually, this kind of couple fantasy goes a certain way: the man wants to be forced to watch another man take his woman. What intrigued me about this pair was that they wanted it the other way around. I expect that's why they chose me almost as soon as I walked in. Her husband was a tall, well-built specimen, and a quick scan of the club floor revealed I was the only one present who could credibly overcome him. I enjoy a good Greco-Roman scuffle, and he put up an impressive fight, but overcome I did. And enjoy him thoroughly, I also did. In fact, I got so carried away with whipping and fucking him that I failed to notice she had escaped her bindings until I felt the cool steel of a large blade against my ribs.

Had they not provided me with the Cliff notes of their script, I might've seen fit to try to defend myself, but the next part of their fantasy was quite the cherry on top. A woman in control sexually is a glorious thing to behold, and while I played the part of the man unwilling to be used as a sex toy while bound to a chair, inner me was joyful as could be. I don't know who *you* are or how you identify, but I thoroughly recommend you experiment extensively. Monogamy is an unnatural social concept made to keep people in line, in cages, in unhealthy relationships that don't allow for the true expression of all the myriad selves we can be. I don't believe that humans are built for such monotony. And we're certainly not meant to taste only part of the rainbow. Play with women, non-binary, trans people, and men, and any other kind of people there are by the time you read this. Test the limits of your body. You never know who you can be until you've given all of your control to someone and until you've been in complete control of another person...

Suitably satiated and intellectually inspired, I returned from the Golden City raring to continue my experiment and seek out my second subject. An in-depth perusal of the media seems to indicate that I've achieved my objective of operating under the radar with my virgin flight. The police have no leads in the murder of Guy Keyes, which is both a good and bad thing. With nothing nefarious in his life, the killing seems random and senseless, and that can sometimes stimulate a more intense investigation. Also, the victim's family and loved ones tend to be more demanding of the police to solve the crime, but I believe the LAPD have far too much on their proverbial plate with organized crime to concern themselves too much with this. As a learning point, perhaps I should be more careful when I select my subjects. Had Keyes been a person of particular note, filthy rich or high-profile, I might have inadvertently caused a media storm, the likes of which I do not wish to become the eye of.

I want to emulate the selection process of the killers I'm imitating, but I can't let that cause unnecessary risk which might jeopardize my study. Ted Bundy is the next chapter in the book I'm following, so when it comes to selecting the woman, I will endeavor to do a little more research into her background before I strike.

Chapter Eleven

DAK TOOK A DEEP breath and concentrated on the target twenty-five yards away. She drew her Glock and fired four times before dropping to her knee and discharging a further four rounds. She holstered her weapon, jogged to the next target at fifteen yards, and waited for the buzzer before she pulled her gun and fired three times. She paused before shooting another three rounds. She ran through the three remaining targets at seven, five, and three yards then grabbed a drink.

"This is your last run-through before the assessment."

Roach, the agent in full SWAT gear, eyeballed her, and she met his gaze until he glanced away.

"Damn it, Farrell. Can't you let me win just one time?"

"What fun would that be?" Dak placed her plastic cup on the shooting table. It had taken longer than she'd expected to get back to the same kind of scores she used to get when she was partnering with Ben. The element of friendly competition between them always pushed her to do better. Without that, and without the need to fire a gun for the past five years, she'd become predictably rusty. But she knew Roach from their time together at Quantico, and it'd been a relief when she'd discovered he would be the one to take her through practice and assessment. Along with Ben, Roach had been one of the few guys from the Academy who'd enjoyed competing against her instead of seeing her as either an anomaly or an enemy.

"Tanner said you were taking on a rookie as a partner." He beckoned her to join him as he reset the targets. "Does the poor schmuck know what he's in for?"

Dak followed him. "It's been a long time since we trained together. I've mellowed."

Roach chuckled. "That's not what I've heard. You've been terrorizing police departments all over the country for the past five years." He turned and gestured in her direction. "And you're still built like a brick shithouse."

"I can be mellow and still bench press a hundred and thirty."

He whistled. "Christ. That's more than most of the guys here." Roach went to the next target and swapped it out for a fresh one.

Even though she hadn't seen Roach for over a decade, she could still tell when he was holding something back. "Is there something else you want to say?"

He glanced at her and rolled his eyes. "I suppose I shouldn't be surprised that you'd know that. Guess that's why you've been so prolific with the Bureau."

"Spit it out, Roach."

"I wanted to say I was sorry. About Ben. I know you guys were more than just partners."

Dak swallowed and clenched her jaw. It still wasn't easy to talk about her old partner and especially not their friendship. But Roach and Ben had been buddies during their training too. "You said sorry at the funeral," she said, assuming he had. She couldn't know for sure since she could barely remember much of that day. Or the days immediately after.

He tilted his head slightly before ambling to the next target. "I wasn't sure you'd heard me. It seemed like you were checked out that day."

This time she couldn't hold his gaze. She'd been more than checked out; she'd been numb. Losing her dad and then Ben had kicked all of the emotion out of her. It was only when CJ came into her orbit that everything began to change again. And if she were honest, Hamilton had been a part of that transformation too. He reminded her of Wade, who she'd more or less abandoned along with their mom after her dad had died. She sighed. "You're right.

Ben's death hit me hard."

Roach stopped working and looked like he might come in for a bro hug but then seemed to stop himself.

"I couldn't handle it," he said quietly. "The field work. Not after Ben died. It's one of the reasons I ended up here. No risks other than rookies shooting themselves in the leg."

Dak acknowledged the courage it had taken to make that admission. She had no idea anyone other than herself at the Bureau had been affected by Ben's death. His honesty made her wish she'd been mentally present at the funeral; maybe she would've recognized his grief too, and they could've helped each other through it.

"It's good that you're ready for another partner," Roach said as they approached the start line again after a short period of silence. "I've got a buddy at Salt Lake PD, and he only had good things to say about your new boy."

A sense of unease set in, making her want to get on with the assessment and get the hell out of there. Roach was clearly trying to be encouraging, but he'd only managed to disturb her peace by bringing up Hamilton in the same conversation as Ben. Was she making a mistake? Was she better off alone and back working the cold cases, out of danger?

Dak wrapped her hand around the hilt of her gun and squeezed until her knuckles ached. She shook off the doubt and stretched out her fingers. She wanted this, and she was ready, and having Hamilton as her partner was the right course of action. She felt it in her gut, and her dad had taught her to always trust her instincts.

"I heard from that same buddy that it was your new boy you took a bullet for. Is that true?" Roach asked.

"It's true, yeah." Instinctively, she touched her fingers to where she'd been shot.

Roach shook his head and whistled again. "You're an impressive woman."

She arched her eyebrow. "I'm an impressive agent," Dak said, instantly bristling at the inherent surprise that someone of her gender could garner respect for her performance.

He held up his hands. "Apologies. I should know better. But still, getting in the path of a bullet..." He blew out a long breath.

"It's just what you do for your partner."

Roach gestured to the course. "That's why I chose this as my partner."

"Field work changes you." She checked her watch. "Speaking of, I need to get this done and go home." If she was late for CJ's big dinner date with Elodie and Madison, there'd be trouble. Roach looked like he might have something else to say, but Dak didn't have the time. "We should go out for drinks soon. We can talk more." She wondered if she meant it. Talking had never been her thing, whether it was with family or co-workers. Ben had been an exception. And now CJ had crowbarred herself in there, and her mom and brother, *and* Hamilton too. Dak didn't think she had room for more.

Roach pressed his lips together and nodded slowly, as if he'd recognized the brush-off. "Okay. Let's get you back to active duty."

He slipped back into professional mode, which Dak was grateful for, and she readied her Glock and herself for the assessment. She hadn't experienced this kind of pressure for a while, but she welcomed it and took a steadying breath. She had CJ's blessing to get back to work. Now all she needed was to pass this final test.

***

Her score of ninety-one wasn't a personal best, but it was eleven points over the minimum and enough to become an instructor, which Roach overeagerly reminded her of numerous times before she left. He said he didn't want a partner, but Dak got the distinct feeling he was lonely even though he saw plenty of agents daily. She'd just given him her cell number when her phone rang. "I've got to take this. Call me for drinks," she said, with more conviction this time. She strode away from the firing course and headed inside before she answered. "You shouldn't be wasting time making personal phone calls, Hamilton."

"It's good to hear from you, Hamilton. Thanks for checking in, Hamilton," he parroted.

"You've got way too much sass for a rookie. I'll beat it out of you if they don't."

"You heard I got into Quantico?"

"I did." Dak found a quiet corner in the main concourse and dropped into an empty chair. She had some paperwork to complete before she left, but she had a few minutes to chat with her partner-to-be.

"You're not mad that I didn't talk to you before I applied?"

She smiled at the instant change from cocky to contrite. "Of course I'm mad, but I'll kick your ass for it next time I see you."

"Ah, Farrell, I'm sorry," he said. "I wanted to get through and make you proud without you feeling like you had to pull any strings for me... Shit."

She laughed lightly. "I'm fucking with you, Hamilton. I'm not mad. I *am* kind of proud, which is weird."

His raucous laugh nearly deafened her, and she pulled the phone away from her ear until he'd stopped.

"It's not weird!" Hamilton said, sounding ecstatic. "It's because we're connected now. Blood brothers. You know I've got your bullet on a necklace?"

"You already told me that, and it's dumb." Which it wasn't; she had the bullet Ben took for her too. She hadn't made jewelry from it, but she did shove it deep into her pocket every morning.

"I was kidding back then...but it's on my keychain."

She shook her head. "Why would they give that to you?"

"Because I asked for it right after your surgery."

"And they agreed?"

"Uh-huh." He chuckled. "The nurse couldn't resist my charm."

"I bet your girlfriend loves you charming other women."

"We've split up, so she doesn't care what I do now," he said.

From the obvious sadness in his voice, Dak assumed it had been her decision. "She dumped you? Did she get tired of washing the donut jelly from your ties?"

"It was mutual. I don't know where I'll be going after training—could be anywhere—and Susie doesn't want to move from Salt Lake." A heavy silence filled the air for a few moments. "And I want to give a hundred percent to my career right now."

Dak flexed her left hand and stared at her engagement ring. She'd given everything to her career for a long time too, so she understood the sentiment. And she'd never expected to find love as she'd crisscrossed the country in Betty. She knew she should have some words of comfort for Hamilton, but she was still getting used to this talking shit and vapid platitudes escaped her. "You're coming here, if you really want to know." She couldn't talk relationships, but she could talk about work.

"To LA? So it's true?" His words practically effervesced from the phone. "Walker said that you'd requested to take me under your wing when I graduate from Quantico, but I didn't really believe it. I can't even begin to tell you—"

"Then don't," Dak said. "Show me how much it means when we start working together by paying close attention and not screwing up." She shook her head at her word choice. Maybe she should read a couple of mentoring books. Though Hamilton had done well enough with her tough love approach so far.

"Okay."

"Forget screwing up," she said. "I know you're not going to screw up." Dak sighed. *Jesus, was it supposed to be this hard?* "I mean, pay attention and don't be cocky." That didn't sound much better. "Just get through training, and we'll figure everything else out. You're going to make a great agent. I'm sure of it."

"Thanks, Farrell," he said softly.

She cleared her throat, and he coughed. CJ would be laughing at their discomfort with the emotion of the situation, Dak thought.

"What's going on in the City of Angels?" Hamilton asked. "Are you back on active duty yet?"

Thankful to be back on a topic she found far easier to handle, Dak filled him in on how she'd kept herself busy with VICAP reports and how it had led her to taking a closer look at the Keyes case.

"Did you find anything at the vacant house?" he asked.

"We got some hair samples. LAPD are busy matching them to anyone who visited the house recently. But the place had been bleached clean. We did get a tire tread in some dirt in the driveway. It's not much, but maybe it narrows down the vehicles the killer could be driving."

"If the house is for sale, how come they hadn't had an open house or any showings while your guy was in residence for a few days?"

"The owner was on vacation for a week and didn't want anyone in the house without him there." She sat back in the chair and thought about the sweep she'd done with Weaver. "I look at the circumstances, and I see a series of random decisions resulting in bad luck for Keyes."

"You don't think he was targeted for a reason?" Hamilton asked.

"I don't." She looked across the concourse and watched agents, analysts, and administrative workers move from place to place. A pretty woman with long hair caught her gaze and gave Dak the kind of smile that would normally have her easing up from the chair and sauntering over to introduce herself for an evening of fun. Dak returned the greeting but not with the same sentiment. She touched her fingers to her engagement ring, its solidity providing a pleasant reminder of the beautiful woman who had agreed to be her wife. The exchange highlighted the unpredictable nature of connection; waking up in the morning, it was impossible to know who you might meet during the course of the day. "I think Keyes was selected at random when he simply caught the eye of the killer."

"I thought you said there was no sign of rape?" Hamilton asked.

"There wasn't, and I didn't mean it in that way. Suppose Keyes simply crossed paths with the killer in a coffee house or at the gym, and that was enough to seal his fate. Our unsub was looking for his next victim, and Keyes was in the right place at the right time—"

"Or the wrong place at the wrong time, depending on your perspective."

Dak ran her hand across the back of her head, as if she could massage a theory into being. "Keyes was selected arbitrarily. Literally anyone could have appealed to the killer. I can feel it. I just can't prove it."

"Maybe the killer uses houses for sale to find his victims," Hamilton said.

"Could be. And maybe he was lucky that this owner had suspended viewings, giving him a nice, comfortable place to surveil Keyes and assess his suitability, assess the risk." Her phone buzzed, and she checked the screen to see a text from CJ. She was running out of time to get home and cleaned up before their guests arrived, and she still had the admin side of the visit to attend to. Another few minutes, then she'd wrap this conversation up.

"But you haven't found any other unsolved murders like this in the VICAP reports?" Hamilton asked.

"Not with this MO," she said. "And I'm also certain Keyes wasn't his first victim. Everything was too ordered, too clean. There was no frenzy, no excitement, no mistakes. This guy knew exactly what he wanted to do, and he did it. Meticulously. There's almost always something at the scene of a first-timer that indicates their inexperience. There are occasionally exceptions to the rule, sure. Restrained and intensely calm individuals who operate clinically, but they're unusual."

"Did he take a souvenir?"

"A very expensive palladium wedding band." Dak twisted her own ring again. "His wife said that it was the only thing missing."

"So he could have taken it to sell it?"

"I don't think so. Keyes was wearing an even more ridiculously expensive watch, and he had a whole collection in their bedroom—all untouched." She recalled the photos of his watch box that Weaver had shown her. Dak would've loved to own just one of the ten or so timepieces Keyes had. But the choice of souvenir perhaps indicated the killer's motive. "Maybe the unsub is someone who covets good marriages or perfect-looking families. Maybe he saw Keyes with his gorgeous wife and child, and he wanted to end that."

"So the killer is divorced and misses his kid?"

"Maybe. But all we've got are maybes." Dak checked her watch again. "I have to go, Hamilton. Keep up the good work at the Academy and stay in touch."

"Sure thing... And thanks again, Farrell. For everything."

Dak grumbled and ended the call before getting up to finish off her assessment paperwork. CJ's text asked how everything had gone, and if she'd still be back for dinner. She quickly thumbed a response and slipped her phone back in her pocket. Once again, she twisted her ring around her finger and thought about the significance of the killer's souvenir choice. She'd revisit the VICAP reports in the morning to see if that added detail drew any hits in the database, and she'd check in with Weaver to see if she'd had any luck with a palladium ring turning up at local pawn shops. Dak doubted it. The question was if the ring might lead her to the killer and kickstart her return to live cases at the same time.

Chapter Twelve

CJ SURVEYED THE BOMB site that had once been her kitchen and questioned her sanity in asking Elodie Fontaine and her wife over for dinner. They should've just met at one of the many discreet restaurants in the city that catered to superstars like her. Elodie wasn't like many other actors; she had a strong physique that probably meant lots of protein and not much fat. She wasn't built like Dak, who probably had twenty pounds of muscle over Elodie, but she was in exceptional shape. CJ figured it was a throwback to Elodie's days in the military.

Madison, her wife, was far easier to cater to. She was someone who wasn't Hollywood-skinny and, given her career as an investigative journalist, there was no reason at all for her to aspire to the ridiculous standards set by the men in charge of the major studios. Though CJ had to wonder if Madison was threatened by the many women surrounding Elodie on movie sets all over the world who did fit the current socially accepted ideal of what a woman was supposed to look like. But they'd been married for a couple of years now, and there'd been none of the kiss and tell stories that had previously been weekly occurrences for the Oscar-winning actor.

Paige, her agent and Elodie's, had been useful in providing a possible menu, and CJ's dad had been strangely helpful in providing recipes, even offering to Zoom with CJ while she cooked. But CJ was still getting used to the new, improved version of him, and being supervised while she attempted a three-course meal didn't appeal at all.

So it wasn't a total surprise that she'd managed to burn and overcook *everything*. Luckily, Paige had then provided the name and number of Elodie and Madison's favorite restaurant, and a Thai meal was on its way even as CJ unsuccessfully tried to scrape away the gravy that had welded itself onto the bottom of a pot.

She heard Dak come down the stairs before she saw her peek around the edge of the kitchen door.

"Is it safe to come in?" Dak asked.

"Only if you're wearing a mask." CJ gestured to the mountain of mess, and soapy bubbles flew off her rubber gloves. "You might get lung damage from smoke inhalation."

Dak grinned. "You haven't inherited your parents' cooking skills then?"

CJ narrowed her eyes. "When I was a kid, I never had meals like the ones they made for you. I told you that." She stuck out her bottom lip.

"Have I told you that you're adorable when you pout?"

CJ leaned back against the sink and peeled off her gloves. The kitchen from hell would have to wait. "Yes. But you can tell me again."

Dak ventured into the kitchen and placed her hands on CJ's hips. "Do we have time for me to tell you again?" She wiggled her eyebrows.

CJ wrapped her hand around Dak's neck and pulled her in for a long, deep kiss, the kind that made her feel slightly weightless and giddy. She reluctantly broke away. "No, we don't. I still have to change." She ran her fingers over Dak's soft black tie and sighed happily. "You look good enough to eat."

Dak glanced around. "You may just have to do that. I don't see dinner anywhere."

CJ slapped Dak's chest. "And what would our guests eat? And don't be rude. Marriage has changed Elodie, so I doubt she or Madison would be interested."

Dak raised her eyebrow. "Good. Because I only have an appetite for you."

CJ maneuvered from Dak's gentle grip. "Enough. You're beating the metaphor to death. The food delivery should be here soon." She walked to the door then turned. "And don't follow me, or I'll never get ready."

"Spoilsport."

"I'll make it up to you when our guests have gone." She blew Dak a kiss and gave her best seductive look before she headed up to their bedroom.

When she returned downstairs thirty minutes later, Dak had already taken delivery of dinner and had laid it out on the table in the pots with tealights beneath them to keep the food warm. CJ indulged in another sigh-inducing kiss but was interrupted by the doorbell. "Okay. Remember not to stare or ask for an autograph."

Dak curled her lip. "Please. Give me some credit..."

"I'll give you something later."

"Tease." Dak took CJ's hand and accompanied her to the door.

CJ paused and took a deep breath. Elodie Fontaine was behind that door!

"Are you okay?" Dak squeezed her hand.

CJ nodded. "Just taking a moment to appreciate what's happening. It's a bit overwhelming."

Dak smiled and kissed CJ's forehead. "It's okay. I'm right here."

CJ relaxed, and some of the tension ebbed from her shoulders. As long as Dak was beside her, everything would be all right—even dinner with Hollywood royalty and an award-winning investigative journalist. She took the remaining steps to the door confidently and opened it. Elodie looked stunning in a trouser, shirt, and tie combo not dissimilar to Dak's outfit, though thankfully not in the same color palette. CJ swooned a little inside and didn't reprimand herself for it. Whose knees didn't go weak for Elodie Fontaine? Probably not Dak's, she suspected, who had made it clear that long-haired women in skirts and heels were her weakness. Which led CJ to take in Madison's understated beauty in a calf-length flowing silk dress, her blond hair cascading over her shoulders like all the beautiful women in the hair commercials. God, they were a gorgeous couple, and both such powerful, independent, and successful women in their own right. CJ might have to be the one careful not to stare, not Dak.

"Hi. We're so glad you could make it." CJ air-kissed them both then stepped aside to let them in.

Dak shook Elodie's hand and greeted Madison in the same way as CJ had. "Hi. I'm Dak."

"There's a name that has to have a story behind it," Madison said, following CJ into the dining room.

"It's not an interesting one, I'm afraid," Dak said. "Can I get you both something to drink?"

Elodie offered Dak the large gift bag she was holding. "We've brought a few bottles of chardonnay. Paige told us that's what you like. Did she get it right? She often doesn't."

CJ tilted her head as Dak took the bag. "Surprisingly, yes. And it'll go perfectly with dinner." Heat rose to her cheeks and the need to confess her kitchen disaster was strong. "I had to order dinner from the restaurant Paige said was your favorite, because I had a total disaster in the kitchen." She wafted her hand in front of her nose. "Which you can probably still smell over the many scented candles I had to light."

Elodie and Madison's genuine laughter instantly put CJ at ease, and she motioned for them to sit.

"I can't smell anything other than Christmas," Elodie said, pulling out a chair for Madison before taking the seat beside her.

"And I can smell very little since getting COVID a few months ago." Madison shook her head and looked rueful.

"That must be awful." CJ didn't want to imagine what life might be like if she could no longer appreciate Dak's natural scent or the woody, rugged perfumes she wore that drove her wild.

"It's coming back slowly." Madison placed her hand over Elodie's. "Thankfully."

Madison obviously had a similar thought process to CJ, who

didn't miss the naughty twinkle in her eyes when she gazed at Elodie. Nor did she miss the return look of total adoration. *That's why there'd been a dearth of gossip stories;* Elodie was clearly very much in love with her wife and didn't care who knew it. How many millions of hearts had Madison broken when she claimed Elodie?

"Domaine Romanet Montra— Nope, I'll stop there," Dak said after pulling a bottle from the bag. "I don't know French any more than I know wine."

"Neither do I, but my buddy just came back from a long engagement in France, and she assured me it was a quality wine, and that I had to get some." Elodie shrugged. "Though she's more of a whisky woman, so I guess we'll just have to try it and find out."

"This is a lot of food," Madison said. "Are we your only guests?"

CJ sat opposite Madison and wrinkled her nose. "Is it too much? Dak has a huge appetite, and I had no idea what you might want to eat. Paige gave the restaurant name, but she didn't respond when I asked about your favorite dishes."

Elodie jutted her chin toward Dak uncorking the wine, which was making her biceps strain against the seams of her shirt. "Maintaining a physique like yours must take some fuel."

Dak's smile showed that she enjoyed Elodie's platonic appreciation of her body. "Same goes for you."

Elodie chuckled. "That's nice of you to say, but your forearms are the size of my biceps."

Madison rolled her eyes in CJ's direction. "Instant bro-love. This could well be the first of many, many evenings together."

CJ liked the sound of that. She was no longer the party girl she'd been before she'd briefly left LA last year, and her circle of friends had shrunk to the one she'd brought back with her. It turned out that all the people she'd thought were friends had simply been hangers-on, only interested in what CJ had to offer as a celebrity. Now that she wasn't throwing all-weekend soirees, they'd disappeared. Having dinner regularly with a couple of friends seemed like something she and Dak should be doing.

Elodie nudged her gently. "You shouldn't mock. You know how hard it is for me to make real friends."

"I get that," CJ said. "I mean, I don't get it on *your* level, but it's amazing the amount of people who call themselves your friend until the ride ends."

Elodie nodded. "I've got one good buddy, and I've got Madison. Everyone else is a colleague or an acquaintance. Except maybe Brad Carlton; he's somewhere between a colleague and a friend."

"*Babe*," Madison said, her eyes wide.

They exchanged a brief look that said more than words ever could, and it made CJ grateful that she'd found Dak, someone she could have that kind of communication with.

"Sorry." Elodie looked suitably chastised. "I wasn't referring to you two. We're looking forward to getting to know you both."

Madison shook her head slowly. "That didn't make it any better." She pushed a dish of fish cakes toward Elodie. "Eat. Then you can't offend anyone."

Elodie grinned and began to load her plate, prompting the rest of them to do the same. The conversation flowed organically from topic to topic. CJ found Madison's intelligence and passion intimidating and inspiring at the same time, and it was easy to see why Elodie had fallen for her. She wasn't CJ's type at all—CJ was marrying the epitome of her type—but Madison's appeal was clear, and CJ was ashamed to admit that the attentive way Dak was listening to Madison's epic tales of her global investigations sparked her jealousy.

"I feel like I'm hogging the conversation," Madison said. "Tell me about the Artist. I've read that Dak rescued you," she turned and kissed Elodie, "just like Elodie rescued me."

Elodie winked and tucked a stray slip of curls over Madison's ear. "I had some help from my buddy."

Dak waved her hand, seemingly dismissing the chance to tell their story. "There's nothing much to tell other than what you've read."

Elodie looked at Dak and raised her eyebrows. "I bet that's not true. And I've hardly read anything about it, so I want to know."

CJ nudged Dak's shoulder. She liked that a Pulitzer-winning investigative journalist wanted to know *their* story. "If you don't tell it, I will, and my stories are way more meandering and long-winded than your versions."

Dak groaned playfully. "Fine." She took a sip of wine. "This tastes fantastic, by the way."

CJ slapped her shoulder lightly. "Stop stalling."

She listened intently as Dak retold the details of her investigation, CJ's kidnapping, and the discovery of the Artist and his twin brother. God, she loved looking at Dak's face and listening to her talk. The way her lips moved; how her eyes conveyed every emotion she expressed; her deep, gravelly voice. *Everything* about her was so incredibly sexy. CJ couldn't believe Dak had asked her to be her *wife*. She'd said it would be forever, forever. Music to her ears and her heart.

"You took a bullet for your partner." Elodie's words were a statement rather than a question, and she was clearly impressed. "What was his name again?"

"Hamilton," Dak said.

Elodie and Madison shared another communicative glance, and Elodie shook her head almost imperceptibly. CJ would've loved to have known what they were talking-not-talking about.

Dak spooned some massaman curry onto her plate, making CJ wish she had a metabolism like hers.

"He was part of the team I trained to work their cold cases, but I could see he had potential," Dak said as she dished up the rice. "That hunger, you know?"

Dak's question was aimed at only Elodie, who nodded. CJ assumed the "hunger" was something specific to the military and law enforcement agencies.

"He's working his way through the Academy at Quantico now, and when he graduates, he'll be my new partner."

Though Dak would probably deny it, it was clear that she was proud of Hamilton. CJ was grateful that Dak had been able to put the guilt about her old partner in the past and was taking on a protégé. "Dak's going back to work on live cases. It makes me feel slightly safer that she won't be doing that alone." She'd only meant to *think* those words, not say them out loud.

"Cold cases *are* invariably safer," Madison said. "Being with someone who regularly faces danger can be difficult."

CJ appreciated Madison's sympathetic look, but Elodie only faced stage guns in her work now. Madison was the one who might not return home from an investigation. "How do you handle it?" she asked Elodie.

"I'm sure Madison would say I don't handle it that well. When we first met, Madison was investigating an organ trafficking gang, and my way of 'handling it' was to ask my buddy to tail her and keep her safe."

Madison arched her eyebrow. "*Without* my knowledge."

Elodie took Madison's face in her hands and kissed her forehead. "I've apologized for that, but also, if she hadn't, we may never have found you."

"Is that the rescue Madison mentioned earlier?" Dak asked.
Madison nodded.

"I read your article about the gang, but you didn't go into much detail about your escape."

Madison tilted her head toward Elodie. "My wife and her best friend wanted it that way. Elodie doesn't like *that* kind of publicity, and her friend doesn't do publicity at all."

CJ might not be an investigative journalist, but the way both Madison and Elodie had been careful not to mention the name of Elodie's buddy made CJ suspect that she was still active in the military or a government agency.

"Suffice it to say that while I wouldn't want to be kidnapped again, it was a huge benefit to have a girlfriend with special forces training."

"Would you rather she stuck with the celebrity memoirs like Troy Donovan's?" CJ asked.

Elodie placed her hand over her heart. "I'm pleading the fifth. I want to keep my wife happy."

The look of pure love they exchanged would've made CJ jealous again if it wasn't the same joy she felt every time she gazed into Dak's eyes.

"Elodie knew who I was and what I did when we got together, and she admired that. She might not be at her happiest when I'm on the hunt for a special story, but she wouldn't ask me to stop doing what I loved."

The sentiment echoed in CJ's mind. She felt the same, but that wouldn't ease her anxiety whenever Dak was in the field chasing down killers.

"Would you ever go back into the military?" Dak asked.

Elodie's eyes went flint-hard, and her jawbone twitched. "No."

Madison put her hand over Elodie's. "I'm sorry, guys. That period of her life isn't something Elodie likes to talk about."

Dak raised her hand. "Sorry, man. I didn't mean to make you uncomfortable."

Elodie waved Dak's apology away. "It's fine."

It clearly wasn't fine. CJ wished Paige had mentioned that detail, because an awkward silence enveloped the table, and she half-expected them to get up and leave. So much for the insta-bro love and future couples' dinners. "Do you have a story you've covered that really sticks with you? Not like a favorite, because that would be a weird way to describe it, given the serious nature of what you do, but you know, something that you hold onto."

"Mm, good question." Madison looked up to the ceiling as if she were searching a visual library of her articles. "The partial destruction of the Vatican would probably be up there—for obvious reasons."

Everyone laughed lightly, including Elodie, thankfully.

"And I rather enjoyed interviewing Sage Samara last month.

She's so young and idealistic. That kind of innocence mixed with activism is rare these days." Madison shrugged elegantly. "I don't know, honestly. My most recent story is often the one that sticks with me until I cover something else."

Elodie draped her arm around the back of Madison's chair. "My favorite would be the one of me. Not because I'm egotistical but because it set us on our path together."

CJ put her hand over her heart. "Aw, that's so romantic." She turned to Dak. "I don't know about all the cases you've investigated over the years, but even if I did, my favorite would still be The Artist for the same reason."

"Is that right?" Dak narrowed her eyes and gave a wicked grin. "You're not giving credit to your dad for that?"

"Do tell," Madison said.

"We first met when I was greased up under the hood of her father's Shelby GT-500."

Elodie whistled. "Nice car."

"Right?" Dak grinned. "But I think it was what was under *my* hood that got this one going."

CJ swatted Dak's shoulder, and the hardness of it reminded her of their initial encounter. She looked to Madison for backup and grasped Dak's bicep. "How was I supposed to resist this in a tight white tee, ripped jeans, and work boots? It was like someone had delved into my fantasies and built her just for me."

Madison covered her eyes. "I can't respond in case my wife gets jealous."

Elodie tilted her head slightly and wrinkled her nose. "You can appreciate Dak as much as you want so long as you go home with me."

Madison ran her hand through Elodie's platinum blond hair. "You know you never have to worry about that. *You're* my home."

CJ smiled, grateful that easy conversation had resumed. "You two are like a Hallmark movie. It's beautiful."

"I'm a lucky woman."

Elodie gazed at Madison lovingly, and CJ turned away to look at Dak, her own happy ending. She couldn't wait to marry Dak and be known as her wife. And if they had even half of what Elodie and Madison had, she'd consider herself a lucky woman too.

Chapter Thirteen

Ted Bundy was an interesting fellow, particularly with regard to my study. To all intents and purposes, there seemed to be no pathological motivation for his obsession with the subjugation and murder of women. He provided so much fascination to experts that they removed his brain for study in an attempt to understand what drove him to his spree killings, asking essentially the same question I'm addressing in this study. Their analysis proved fruitless; there was nothing abnormal about Ted's brain, and that in itself adds fuel to the fire of my own quest. Given that traditional methods of inquiry have yielded no solid results, does that not make my experiment even more essential? Let's consider that I do develop a taste for murder, and I then reverse engineer my metamorphosis. Imagine the applications and the capacity for rehabilitation. Compelling, don't you think? Perhaps that's why you're still reading my journal now. Perhaps you have your own cravings. Perhaps you control them. Or not. Are you hoping that I can help you? Or don't you want help? Are you perfectly content torturing and killing your victims?

I will likely never know. We shall probably never cross paths. Does that irk you? I'll wager you want to meet me really, don't you? I *am* fascinating, in an altogether far more remarkable way than ninety-nine percent of the population. I wouldn't blame you at all. Curiosity is what brought me here too.

But I digress into self-indulgent verbal masturbation. Back to the matter in hand, the brain matter, as it happens. Ted strangled or bludgeoned his victims to death with a crowbar, and since I'd already strangled Keyes, it made sense to try a different method of taking a life. Goodness, it was messy. I can understand why that fictional chap Dexter always covered his kill rooms in plastic for easier clean-up. I made sure to keep my mouth closed, and I wore protective clothing and glasses. I don't have the time to check the general health of my subjects, so I can't know whether any of them have any infectious diseases. The last thing I want is for the person I'm killing to contaminate my blood with an illness that would go on to kill me. That would be irony in peak form (ten thousand spoons when all you need is a different piece of cutlery is *not* irony, it's bad luck).

I couldn't bring myself to keep the body and certainly not to perform any sex acts on her after I'd killed her—the one I had to do while she was still breathing was hard enough. Remember that I'm interested in whether a murderer can be created, and Ted's actions post-mortem don't form part of this study. They would be the fodder for an entirely separate line of investigation, one that holds no interest for me at all. Perhaps as I progress with my subjects, my tolerance level will increase, and the lines I am willing to cross will recede into an immoral distance. That will mark an interesting deviation and a change in my moral code. It would be a surefire check in the argument for nurturing a killer to fruition, would it not? But I also didn't do any of those things because I can't risk being caught at this, or any other, stage of my experiment. Two killings do not make a killer, methinks. I have a plan, and I shall be sticking to it. Providing the police with DNA evidence and hanging onto body parts are not the emblems of a sophisticated or accomplished killer. Or one in complete control.

Actually, that's not strictly true. Ted did all of that and still evaded capture until the time his ex-girlfriend gave him up. Nonetheless, I won't gamble unnecessarily with my freedom or this scientific endeavor, and copulating with a corpse would most certainly be hazardous to both my continued experimentation and, I'm inclined to believe, my mental health. I didn't take a souvenir from this one, though I know that's what most killers do. I find that need to revisit the kill through a memento rather fascinating, if not predictable. For me though, Keyes' wedding ring will suffice as a treasured memory of this whole experiment.

I wonder how Ted felt as he was being strapped down like an animal before execution. Do you think he was angry that he hadn't been allowed to continue his work? I would have liked to meet him. He seemed like quite a fascinating chap. I think he led the various psychiatrists who tried to evaluate him a merry dance in an effort to evade the death penalty. I believe that despite his thirty-plus murders, the thought of dying himself was abhorrent, and he couldn't handle it. But I suppose how he felt is irrelevant to me now. This is about how I feel each time I act like a serial killer, and if the act will eventually become my nature.

At this stage, it's far too early to draw a solid conclusion. There's something god-like about ending a person's life, of course, and I can certainly see how that might become addictive, if one had that personality type. It doesn't feel satisfying, nor have I been sexually aroused. At most, and particularly with Evelyn, I've been rather disgusted by the mess created by the whole debacle. If this experiment does indeed succeed in turning me into a serial killer, I'm quite sure that my subsequent murders—before I successfully reverse the process, as that will take time—will be neat and tidy affairs. No blood spatter to analyze nor brain matter to wash from my clothes. By the end of my study, I will have decided upon my ideal modus operandi, and I'll document it in detail as an appendix. It could serve as *your* guide if you're so inclined, and I'll guarantee that if you follow it to the letter, you will avoid capture by the authorities. Do not be tempted to rush. <u>No!</u> Don't skip to the end. This isn't a buffet of brutality and can't be consumed in non-sequential segments. A linear approach is required and will stand you in good stead should you choose to follow my guide, because the steps to successful and guilt-free killing will also have to be followed in a linear fashion. If you could see me now, you'd know that I'm shaking my head. Your urge to skip to the conclusion is indicative of the instantaneous gratification culture I told you I loathed in an earlier section. And yes, you can go *back* and reread, especially if my principles have yet to penetrate your skull and sink into the depths of your brain, subconscious or not. But really, if that is the case, perhaps you should simply put this journal down and find more suitable reading material. Like *Sports Illustrated* or *Vogue*.

Anyway, as I was saying, I'm yet to find myself indoctrinated to killing, but my experiment is still young. I have no investment either way, of course. I am but a vessel in the quest for scientific knowledge to fill me up. Another of the elements of Ted's murders that I found difficult to emulate was to feign the need for help. Donning an arm cast and luring Evelyn to help me load furniture on the truck was particularly alien (Bless her, she seemed rather dumbfounded at my predicament but came to help anyway). I have always prided myself on my self-sufficiency, and thus, the vulnerability grated despite it being disingenuous. The rather unnecessary and elaborate ploy also slowed me down and increased the potential for passers-by to take note and possibly even offer their assistance. Given that I was targeting a young woman, the likelihood of interference from some dinosaur of a man who thinks himself a gentleman rushing to the aid of the weaker and fairer sex was dangerously high. Hence the need to strike in the early hours after closing time of a bar in a relatively quiet neighborhood. I'm confident that choice limited my being exposed, but I suppose you never know who's peeping through curtains and watching you, do you?

Chapter Fourteen

Walker had assured Dak that her meeting with the Assistant Director in Charge of the LA field office was a mere formality, but she dressed like it was an interview anyway. Her mom had always reinforced that you only got one chance to make a first impression, and Dak, after initial skepticism, was now inclined to agree. She assessed people the moment she met them, and her initial analysis and conclusions were invariably correct. In fact, her mom's rule had become an integral part of Dak's practice when profiling people as soon as she started work with the Bureau.

Because she'd dressed in a smart suit and tie, Dak had barely made it out of the house on time. CJ's appreciation of her in that attire had yet to dampen. Long may that continue—lesbian bed death was an affliction Dak wanted none of. Though given their relationship had started on such a sexual basis, she figured they had a pretty good chance of not succumbing to it. Leaving CJ sated on the sofa before Dak straightened her tie to leave was a welcome benefit to having a long-term partner, something she never thought she'd have. She was hoping to pick up where they left off, once CJ was back from another meeting with her new Netflix team. Dak had a feeling married life would suit her just as well as it had her parents.

She patted Betty's dash affectionately as memories of her dad inevitably flooded her mind. The old girl was the last project they'd worked on together before his body, ravaged from years of abuse through and after the Vietnam war, finally gave up, and Betty was still going strong. She'd be no use in a high-speed pursuit, but cruising was something she excelled at. Which was useful in

LA, since twenty miles per hour had been her average pace since they'd moved here. She hoped her dad would be proud of her career. When he'd unsuccessfully tried to return to service after 9/11, Dak had promised him she'd take up the baton and serve her country instead of taking over the family's auto repair business. Solving serial murder cases wasn't exactly what they'd had in mind, but Dak had an affinity for it more than chasing terrorists.

And what would he think of her impending wedding? She'd never thought about tying the knot before, so she hadn't had to face the prospect of walking down the aisle without him by her side. She blew out a long breath and blinked away the possibility of tears. Sure, the pain of grief had lessened, but the loss still stung like a motherfucker. She was grateful when her GPS announced she'd arrived at her destination, and she shook off the blanket of melancholy to focus on her imminent meeting.

Dak took a left onto Veteran Avenue and then a right into the parking lot for the Wilshire Federal Building, which was a strange beast. The central tower looked like a stunt ramp, imposing on the landscape around it and lumbering above the freeway.

She parked her truck in a spot farthest from the entrance with no one on either side of her. The paint job she and her dad had done on Betty was something Dak wanted to keep pristine. She passed through building security and accessed the FBI's dedicated, high-speed elevator up to the sixteenth floor before going through more stringent FBI security protocols so she could go up one more floor to the very top, where the ADIC's office was. The acronym was certainly true of the New York field office's assistant director in charge, but she hoped it wouldn't be the same for Evan Charnwood. Dak had enjoyed the relative autonomy she'd had roaming around the country's police departments, solving cold cases that everyone else had long abandoned. Coming back to work under closer purview of any boss was going to be a challenge. It'd be even worse if that new boss was a complete asshole.

She was only halfway to Charnwood's office, located at the

end of the long corridor, when the door swung open to reveal the man himself. She recognized him from the small amount of stalking she'd done through the Bureau's intranet. She hadn't done too much digging since she didn't want her initial impressions colored by someone else's lens, but she had a thing about knowing what someone looked like before she met them if the meeting was unusual or important in some way. And this was important to her continued career and how well she would be able to do her job under new *supervision*. God, she hated that word. It almost made her consider becoming a consulting specialist, the type Elodie had mentioned FlatLine Studios was looking for. The insanely high salary had raised Dak's eyebrows and made CJ splutter wine down her chin, but that prospect was a couple of decades away. Dak was in her line of work for the reward of the work itself, and no amount of eyelash fluttering from CJ would tear her away from it just yet.

"Special Agent Dak Farrell, I presume?" Charnwood extended his hand as he approached.

So he'd done his own homework. Dak was marginally impressed by the just-right pressure of the handshake. A lot of men squeezed too hard, trying to intimidate or infer some kind of superiority over her. It never worked. "Assistant Director," she said as she walked alongside him back to his office.

"Please, just call me Charnwood." He closed the door behind them and gestured for her to take a seat. "I served in the Army for fifteen years before I worked my way up to this. I prefer the informality."

"Okay." *That* was different too. Anyone in the senior positions, regardless of gender, usually liked others to use their correct title. And why not? Most of them had worked damned hard to get where they were and deserved the recognition. She liked hearing CJ call her Special Agent Farrell, but that served an entirely *different* purpose.

"I'm sure ADIC Walker reinforced that this meeting *isn't* an interview?"

She'd noticed the way his glance had swept over her as they met in the corridor, but then she'd done the same to him. And though she didn't know high-end fashion, she knew the cut of a quality suit when she saw one. Clearly, he did too. "She did, but I'm old-fashioned when it comes to meeting my boss, especially for the first time. Something my parents taught me."

Charnwood nodded. "Your father was a military man, wasn't he?"

"Yes, he was." He hadn't come away from it quite as healthily as Charnwood obviously had.

"When Walker called to ask if I'd be amenable to you joining my field office, it wasn't a hard decision." Charnwood leaned back in his comfortable-looking chair and steepled his fingers. "Your closing percentage is...incredible. There's no other way to say it."

Dak inclined her head slightly at the unexpected and entirely genuine compliment. If this level of mutual respect could be maintained, working here would turn out just fine. "Thank you. I appreciate you saying that."

"And the partner you want—Hamilton—he seems like he has a good pedigree. All of his family members are in the military or another government agency of some kind."

She nodded, though she hadn't known that. Dak had known everything about Ben, including his family history, but really, she knew very little about Hamilton. She hadn't asked personal questions of any of her transient colleagues during her time with cold cases. She'd gotten out of practice. She resolved to rectify that as soon as they reconnected.

"But he was more or less coasting in a police department in a relatively low-crime area." Charnwood narrowed his eyes slightly. "What if he doesn't make it through the Academy?"

Dak arched her eyebrow. Charnwood's question was a logical one, and she detected no malice. "He'll make it."

"You're that confident?"

"I am." She smiled. "But if he doesn't, you can partner me with whoever you want." *Damn, Hamilton, you better come through.* The thought of playing partner Russian roulette was about as appealing as donning four-inch heels and a dress for her wedding. She could end up with any manner of asshole.

"It's a deal. But I promise I won't pair you with someone incompatible to your methods or personality."

Charnwood had clearly done more research into her than she had into him. Both of the things he mentioned had been cited before as a problem by other agents. Asshole agents, of course, but agents, nonetheless. "I'd appreciate that."

"You don't need to worry. We've got a lot of good agents. The top ten percent of Quantico graduates are split between here and the D.C. field office, as you know. I wasn't here back when you chose D.C. over us, so I'm not too sore about that, but I'm glad you've chosen us now. I think you're going to like it here."

Dak felt no need to point out that she'd been in the top one percent in her class. She suspected he'd already discovered that in his mini-investigation. Her cell vibrated loudly in her pocket, and she glanced at her smart watch. Officer Weaver was calling, which reminded her that she should get Charnwood up to speed on what she'd been doing with her time. She tapped the screen to divert Weaver to leave a message. "I've been reading a lot of VICAP reports while recuperating."

He laughed. "Just some light reading then. Walker said you weren't an agent who enjoyed time away from the job."

"Not so much." Though that had changed some since getting involved with CJ. Aside from wanting to keep apprised of America's violence, studying the reports had kept her busy between rehab and workouts, leaving less time to be alone and missing CJ. "There was a murder in Hollywood Hills that stood out." She gave Charnwood a rundown of the particulars, and he seemed to pay attention, nodding and asking supplementary questions in all the right places. "I've asked Detective Weaver of the LAPD to let me know if any subsequent murders strike her as similar." Dak tapped the phone in her pocket. "That was her calling. If it's okay with you, I'd like to continue monitoring the situation."

"You said you'd scoured the system for any similar serial killings across the country?"

Charnwood rubbed his left eyebrow, and Dak thought that might be an indication of discomfort or disagreement since he'd remained relatively motionless thus far in their conversation. "That's right, and nothing has jumped out at me. I know what I've got seems very thin. It's little more than a hunch, but my gut rarely lets me down."

"Okay." He nodded and looked to the right, as if he were formulating a plan. "Since your hunches are likely a direct correlation to your solve rate, you can keep your eye on any developments... But what I'd really like you to cast your expertise over is this." He picked up a manilla folder around two-inches thick and handed it to her.

The Rodeo Killer? She flicked through the index and discovered the press had birthed the tasteless moniker because the killer used a bullwhip on his victims. She nearly tossed the file back to Charnwood. "This is a cold case."

He shook his head. "Not cold: lukewarm. It's only been thirteen months since the last killing. The agent who was in charge of the investigation, Dave Kimbal, liked a guy called Magnus Street for it, but I think he spooked the suspect."

Dak looked at the profile of the potential killer but didn't comment on him using past tense for the agent. Was Charnwood the kind of boss who moved agents on to other field offices if they weren't getting results? "You think the murders have stopped so the heat can die down?" Dak asked, with only a hint of incredulity in her voice. It was a very rare serial killer who could control his urges that way.

"In a way. He's driven down to Mexico twice in the past year."

"Where he might've sated his need." That part would make

sense more than having the self-control to stop completely.

"There are so many people disappearing down there. The UN Committee for Enforced Disappearances conducted a tour of nearly half the states in the country a few years ago. The authorities aren't doing anything about it, and the situation's just getting worse. Seems like a perfect hunting ground for someone needing a fix. That means the case may not even be lukewarm. It could just be on a different burner."

She wouldn't argue with that logic. "Have you tracked him on one of these sojourns?"

"That's where it takes an even more sinister turn." Charnwood's lip curled in obvious disgust. "Special Agent Kimbal tailed Street to Culiacán—"

"Jesus. That's desperation." Her geography was a bit rusty, but she did know the state of Sinaloa was around a full day's drive from LA.

"Kimbal never came back," he said and ran his finger over his eyebrow again.

So she was half-right about the meaning of that piece of body language. Charnwood went silent, and his jaw worked furiously, easily visible since he had Desperate Dan features. His obvious distress at losing an agent cemented Dak's growing appreciation of the man and the way he supervised his team. "Either Street has a giant set of balls and took him out, or Special Agent Kimbal fell foul of a drug gang who might've realized what he was."

"Much as it pains me to give Street that kind of credit, the other option isn't likely. Kimbal had done years of undercover work, and he was damned good at it. No way he would've been randomly discovered by narcos." He dropped his hands into his lap and clenched his fists. "And he would've known to steer clear of the usual suspects in that neighborhood. Kimbal had interrogated Street, so he must've made the tail and dealt with it." Charnwood unclenched a fist long enough to gesture toward the folder Dak held. "Turns out that Street's got a military file. We didn't get that plum information until after Kimbal didn't return from Mexico."

Dak raised her eyebrows. "Why the delay?"

Charnwood interlaced his fingers and pushed back into his chair. "We discovered he was military by chance when one of our agents who's also a veteran saw his picture shortly before Kimbal trailed him on his first trip south. And the information request took a long time to progress through the chain of command due to the Navy having to redact the file before they issued it."

"And that red tape cost Special Agent Kimbal his life."

Charnwood nodded. "So you can see why I'm eager to have your take on this one. We're a collaborative bunch here. Practically family. We can't let one of ours die for nothing. Street has to pay."

There was something menacing about the way Charnwood delivered his final statement, and it made Dak a little itchy. He didn't scare her, of course. It was more the inference that he wanted Kimbal's death avenged rather than Street brought to justice that raised her concern. "Who's been working the case since?"

"Special Agent Garrity. I've briefed him that you'll be lending your assistance." He stood abruptly. "I'll show you to your office, and you can get comfortable. Garrity isn't in today, but I'd appreciate it if you could arrange to liaise ASAP and get up to speed."

"Of course." Dak pushed up from her chair and followed him back to the elevator and down one floor. She appreciated his hands-on approach to orienting her. Most people who headed up field offices delegated that work to their assistant or secretary. It was another check in his pros box. Charnwood was promising to be as good a supervisor as she could hope for.

After he'd shown her around and introduced her to a few other agents, Charnwood gave her access to her office. It wasn't particularly big, but it did have decent-sized windows, and it was front-facing rather than overlooking the parking lot. She dragged her finger over the dusty desk and dropped the Rodeo Killer file on it, trying to calculate how long it had been since she'd last had an office that was hers alone. It wouldn't last anyway. If she had to be bound to a physical space, she'd share it with Hamilton soon enough, just as she'd shared her previous office with Ben.

Dak dropped into her chair, noting it wasn't as plush nor as comfortable as Charnwood's seat had looked, but there had to be some perks to being chained to a desk and missing out on all the action. She pushed the file away and pulled out her phone, choosing to find out what Weaver had for her. She'd take the file home and—

No, she wouldn't. Dak had office space in their house, but she didn't want CJ seeing crime scene photos at any time, let alone a couple of months after she'd been part of one. She'd come in early tomorrow instead and absorb it all before arranging a meeting with Garrity. She liked Charnwood's ideal that his agents were collaborative, but that hadn't been her experience. Agents usually hated other agents helicoptering in with their unsolicited opinions. She resolved to keep an open mind. Charnwood had surpassed her low expectations quite spectacularly, so maybe Garrity and the rest of the agents here would too.

"Weaver."

"Hi, Weaver. It's Special Agent Farrell. I'm returning your call."

"Hey, that's great," Weaver said, sounding cheerful. "How are you?"

Dak rolled her eyes and sighed. Small talk. She hated small talk. "Has something interesting crossed your desk?"

Weaver coughed. "Oh, yeah. Sorry. Yeah. You asked me to call you if I caught any cases with similarities to the Keyes murder..."

Dak didn't fill the silence. She disliked repeating herself too. Weaver was likely just nervous, but Dak didn't have the time or inclination to coddle the baby detective. And wrapping her in cotton wool wouldn't help her case with her fellow detectives anyway. She had to toughen up and be ultra-professional if she wanted to make captain like her father.

"Yeah. Okay. We had a murder a couple of days ago."

Dak rubbed her hand across the back of her head. Why had

she waited? "A couple of days?"

"Yeah, I know. But I wanted to be sure. As sure as I could be because this one isn't similar in a lot of ways. And it's not as straightforward as it seems."

Dak bit her top lip. She'd thought Weaver had potential, for Christ's sake. Where was her confidence? "Tell me about the victim."

"Yeah, okay. Evelyn Berenger. Caucasian. Twenty-year-old college student working part-time at a bar. Good-looking. Slim. Five-four. Long, dark hair. She went missing a couple of days ago after a late shift. Her roommate reported her missing when Evelyn never made it home. Police found her car still in the staff parking lot where she worked. No CCTV in that area, so the last recorded images of her were as she left the bar."

Dak reprimanded herself for her earlier impatience. She began to suspect they'd only just found the body and confirmed an unnatural cause of death. "What time did she leave work?"

"One a.m."

"What about colleagues and patrons?"

"What about them?"

"Any altercations or disagreements of note? Did someone make advances that weren't welcome?" Dak asked.

"Oh, I see. Sorry. Not that anyone remembers, and none of her colleagues reported animosity between Evelyn and anyone else. She was well-liked, got on with her job, and didn't stand out."

Dak arched her eyebrow. "She stood out to the killer."

"Sure, of course." Weaver cleared her throat. "Evelyn went missing on Tuesday morning, and on Wednesday afternoon, a patrol found a lot of blood and brain matter at an abandoned warehouse close to Evelyn's bar. DNA was a match for hair pulled from a pillow in her room."

"No sign of the body?" Thus far, Dak couldn't see how this case bore any similarity to the Keyes murder.

"Not there, but a runner out at Ryan Mountain discovered a

body near the trailhead parking area at around eight thirty this morning. She'd been decapitated, and they found her head on the side of the road a few miles away. Riverside County Sheriff called us when they found Evelyn's ID and discovered she was a missing person."

"Where's Ryan Mountain?"

"Joshua Tree National Park, over a hundred and thirty miles away."

Dak pulled her leather notepad and miniature pen from her pocket and began to scribble some notes. "Cause of death?"

"Blunt force trauma."

Dak made some mental calculations. The victim must've been murdered soon after her abduction, and it was now Thursday morning. Depending on how long the killer spent with her and the time it took him to drive there, it had given the park's animal residents forty to forty-eight hours to aid the killer by devouring any trace evidence. "Any signs of sexual assault?"

There was an audible swallow on Weaver's end of the call. "Anal penetration."

She put the pen down. Whatever conclusions Weaver had drawn, Dak couldn't see the connection. "It's a nasty case, but where are the similarities to Keyes?"

"The crime scene had mostly been scrubbed clean."

Dak flicked open the Rodeo Killer file again. Maybe she would get up to speed on this now. "I thought you said that the uniforms found a lot of blood and brain matter. If that was the case, what makes you think the scene had been cleaned?"

"No blood spatter. What they found was in the corner of the warehouse. The kind of force it takes to smash a skull had to leave an arc spray, but there was nothing. Thirty feet from the scene, there was cobwebs, needles, bottles, all kinds of trash. But within that radius, the area was clean."

"But not clean because of the blood and brains in a small, specific area?"

"Exactly," Weaver said. "I think the killer left that on purpose."

"Why?"

"I don't know." Weaver went silent. After a few moments, she said, "It could be the same killer then?" she asked, sounding hopeful.

"The only apparent similarity is the tidiness of the scene." Dak shook her head. "That's pretty thin."

Weaver gave a defeated sigh. "A witness came forward yesterday. He described a guy a few inches over six feet tall."

"So the perpetrator is about the same height. It's not much to go on. Anything else?"

"He said the guy had an arm cast on, and he was unloading a big armchair, like a La-Z-Boy, into the parking lot at the back of the bar. He saw a woman fitting Evelyn's description helping him."

Dak almost dropped her cell phone. In capital letters at the top of a fresh page, she wrote TED BUNDY. A copycat killer? "I'd like to watch the interview video." What passed as interesting to her would simply pass most people by.

"Of course. If you can give me a time and day, I'll make sure I'm here. Miller... well, he's Miller, and he's got a bug up his ass about collaborating with the FBI. Something about it always being a one-way street."

"It's been known to be that way." Although things were changing, Miller's description of the flow of information and assistance was still pretty accurate. The Bureau took what it wanted and gave little back. Miller was old-school, and he remembered the old ways. It wasn't surprising that he'd be suspicious of her involvement, and cops tended to be territorial about their cases. If something could be solved, they wanted to be the ones to claim the credit. If things looked unsolvable, the FBI were welcome to engage. She tapped the LAPD HQ into her phone's GPS. "I can be there in about an hour." *Christ.* Fifty-four minutes for fifteen miles. Maybe she should invest in a motorcycle to cut through this heinous traffic.

"Okay, that's great. See you in a while."

"Sure." She hung up and laughed lightly at the instant uptick in Weaver's tone after Dak had said she wanted to watch the interview. She guessed it was a slight validation of Weaver's logic in connecting the two murders. Dak was yet to be fully convinced, but she knew to trust her own instincts. Though it currently seemed unlikely that these two crimes were perpetrated by the same killer, she wouldn't rule it out until she'd seen the crime scene photos and watched the witness video. And there were three important locations in this case that she wouldn't mind taking a look at.

She glanced back at her bold capitals. Ted Bundy? What about the Keyes murder? Different victim type. Different method of killing. Different location and selection method. Sexual assault. It took strength to smash someone's head in, and that fit with the size of the guy they were looking for with the Keyes murder, but that kind of killing was usually frenzied. And then there was the switch from a male to a female victim. There were a lot of differences between the two murders. Dak turned the notepad around and around, trying to make connections that didn't appear to be there. Perhaps her gut was out of practice. Still, it was worth working through her process to get back in the game. She began to scribble her train of thought into her notepad.

Keyes was nearly two hundred pounds. He would've taken far more effort to subdue than Evelyn. Was it because Keyes was difficult to take down that he turned to easier and weaker prey? But he'd bested Keyes, and it seemed like he'd managed that without much of a struggle, if the crime scene was anything to go by. No skin under Keyes' fingernails, no bruising on his knuckles, no sign of an altercation at all. After a success like that, surely an easier kill wouldn't be as satisfying or as much of a triumph.

Maybe the killer was escalating or experimenting. *He's drawn to kill but isn't quite sure what his ultimate fantasy is yet.* Copying the methods of killers who'd had a successful run... That could be his way of finding what really satisfied him without having to put too much effort into it. But that in itself didn't make sense. Nearly eighty percent of serial killers had been developing their fantasy since childhood and knew exactly what they wanted to achieve from the kill, even they weren't fully aware of why they were pulled to it, like metal shavings to a magnet, a fractured personality unable to stop themselves.

That left twenty percent of killers, but they were usually relatively easy to explain too. Pre-crime stressors such as job loss, a sexual partner leaving them, or an important family member dying all contributed to the literal straw that broke the back of their normal reality and sent them on a murderous rampage. Did this unsub lack imagination? He was obsessively neat and tidy, but creativity was chaos. Maybe he didn't have it in him to conjure up new and ingenious ways of taking a life. Maybe his internal rage was such that he didn't care who his victim was as long as he had one.

But if the murder of Evelyn *was* a dead ringer for Ted Bundy's kills, where did Keyes fit in? And how could that help Dak find him before he continued his devastating exploration? Lots of murderers bound and tortured their victims before killing them.

She looked at her notes, specifically at the last line she'd written and the order of her words. Bound. Tortured. Killing. *BTK*. Dennis Rader. Ted Bundy. It was like the alumni of serial killer school. And if that was her working theory, who was next?

Chapter Fifteen

"How was your flight, Ruth?" CJ asked while Dak loaded her mom's luggage into the back of Betty. CJ thought the name suited the truck and liked the idea of naming her own Ferrari, but inspiration had yet to strike. Dak said it meant that her car was currently soulless. Her fascination with giving an inanimate object a human moniker made CJ smile. It was another example of the playfulness she hid from most everyone else.

Ruth smiled. "I met some lovely people. It's amazing how much people love to talk about themselves and their family, isn't it?"

"Honestly, that's one of the reasons I like to drive everywhere." Dak slid behind the wheel and gave CJ's knee a gentle squeeze.

"What do you mean?" Ruth asked.

"Analyzing people is a massive part of my job." Dak maneuvered into the flow of traffic and rested her forearm on the edge of the rolled-down window. "I can't shut it down. So when anyone talks to me, that part of me immediately kicks in. Driving everywhere reduces those interactions and gives me a break from it."

"Oh, I see."

CJ glanced in her side mirror and caught Ruth's sad expression. Dak had been more or less absent from her mother's life. Ruth didn't really know her daughter at all, through no fault of her own. CJ and Dak were in similar positions, reconnecting with their family though CJ's parents openly bore the blame for the emotional and physical distance she'd put between them. She couldn't help but feel sorry for Ruth. She'd lost her husband, and it must've felt like her daughter had followed soon after.

But things were changing. Ruth was here now to help with their wedding preparations, giving her the opportunity to reacquaint herself with Dak. "What is it you like about meeting new people, Ruth?"

"They fascinate me," she said with some gusto. "You meet people you never would otherwise." She leaned forward and placed one hand on each of them. "And now I get to tell anyone who'll listen all about my daughter's upcoming marriage to a beautiful woman."

"You tell complete strangers about that?" Dak asked. "You probably shouldn't, Mom. You have no idea who you might be talking to. Bragging about us could put you in danger."

Ruth huffed. "Let them try. Your dad taught me a thing or two about defending myself, Daniella."

CJ stifled a laugh and didn't have to look at Dak to know she was rolling her eyes. Listening to Dak and her mom was adorably cute.

"I'm sure he did, Mom, but please be careful."

"I won't be bullied into being ashamed of my amazing daughter," Ruth said, clearly not ready to give it up.

"Now I see where you got your stubborn streak." CJ winked when Dak glanced at her, eyebrow arched high to show she was serious. All that did was make CJ giggle.

"If you think I'm stubborn, you should've met her father. Between the two of us, Daniella didn't stand a chance."

The affection shone in Ruth's tone, making CJ's heart ache that they were separated too early. CJ didn't want to think about growing old, ever, but since she couldn't avoid it, she wanted Dak by her side for the rest of her life. The thought of having her wrenched away before they'd had enough time choked her. She stared at Dak's profile and sighed. No matter how long they had together, it could never be enough to satisfy CJ.

"He would've loved you, CJ," Ruth said. "And he would've loved to walk you down the aisle, Daniella."

Dak's jaw clenched, and her chin wobbled almost imperceptibly. CJ bet that Dak was wishing she'd accepted CJ's offer to pick Ruth up so she could go to work. She glanced at Dak's cell mounted on the dash: another forty-five minutes to home. Ruth could fit a lot of emotional torture in that time, though she probably didn't realize she was doing it.

Dak glanced at CJ and gave her a sad smile before returning her gaze to the road. "Mom's right. He would've loved you *and* he was a stubborn mule."

Dak's laugh broke the light tension, which was a relief. After years of her own therapy for family issues, CJ considered herself an ipso facto expert. Dak would benefit from exposure to more of these interactions, even though they would be painful. She'd been avoiding them for too long and would have to pay the emotional price for that. Dak hadn't thanked her for the pop psychology when she'd offered that opinion.

In the silence that followed, the photos Pat Wolf had shown her of the people she'd been working on for the new series popped into her mind. That set her on a train of thought about her current ennui with the project though, and she didn't want to think about that right now. What she wanted was to enjoy time with her mother-in-law and Dak.

"How's Ward?" Dak asked.

"He still has a relatively healthy obsession with your fiancée." Ruth chuckled.

Dak grumbled. "I'm not sure any obsession can be called healthy."

CJ welcomed Dak's possessive touch on her thigh. While she'd never actively incur or encourage Dak's jealousy, she couldn't deny it was wonderful to be wanted this much. She would never think of herself as Dak's possession but equally, she wasn't averse to the thought of them belonging to each other.

"Honestly, I don't know about that boy. He's so desperate to fall in love and settle down," Ruth said. "He should be sowing his wild oats at his age."

"Ew, Mom." Dak wrinkled her nose. "I hope you haven't said

that to him."

Ruth gave the back of Dak's head a stern look. "Of course not."

CJ giggled at Ruth's indignance. Boy, she was a firecracker. CJ was going to enjoy being around while Dak and her mom got to know each other again. "Maybe he's not a wild oats kind of boy. Maybe he's old-fashioned...unlike his sister," she said and wiggled her eyebrows. Dak threw her a sidelong glance. Her narrowed eyes did little more than serve as encouragement to keep stoking the fire.

"There's a Starbucks." Dak gestured toward the iconic mermaid sign. "Maybe I could drop you off, and you can finish the conversation I don't want to be a part of."

"Are you trying to dump us, Special Agent Farrell?"

"And I've come such a long way to see you, honey." Ruth chuckled and tapped CJ's shoulder.

CJ placed her hand over Ruth's. "We're going to have so much fun while you're here, Ruth."

Dak groaned and shook her head.

Ruth squeezed CJ's shoulder. "Call me Mom. Then I can tell complete strangers I have *two* beautiful daughters."

CJ glanced at Dak in time to see her lip curl. Beautiful wasn't Dak's favorite adjective to describe herself. CJ tapped Dak's thigh and mouthed, "Handsome," when she met her gaze. She was rewarded with a sexy grin and a wink.

It was Ruth's first time to LA, so her attention quickly turned to the streets and landmarks that were familiar through TV and movies. Dak visibly relaxed and made good time across the city, with the only delay around the Santa Monica Freeway.

Ruth gasped when Dak rolled up their driveway. "Goodness, CJ. What a beautiful home."

Dak put the truck in park and dashed out to open their doors, something CJ never tired of even though she'd hate if anyone else did it for her. Dak went to help her mom out of the car, and Ruth batted her away.

"I'm not an old woman yet, Daniella. I can get out of the car myself."

Dak held up her hands. "Fine."

She went back to CJ, who gladly accepted Dak's strong hand. Getting out of Betty in four-inch heels was always a challenge. While Dak retrieved Ruth's luggage from the truck bed, CJ took Ruth into the house and began the tour. Dak joined them as CJ was showing Ruth one of the guest rooms.

"Oh, wonderful," Ruth said when she discovered the attached bathroom. "That'll save me wandering around the house in the middle of the night." She nudged CJ gently. "I can't wait to tell the girls about this. They'll be impressed."

CJ had met Ruth's girls—all of them over sixty—when she and Dak had visited last month. If she made it that long, she wanted to have that kind of vitality and a group of friends to share it with. "Why didn't you ask one of them to come with you? We've got plenty of room."

Ruth rolled her eyes. "And risk incurring the wrath of the ones left behind? Oh no, we don't have favorites."

CJ laughed. "In that case, I'm sorry we don't have a big enough house for you to have brought them all."

"That would've been total chaos for you, honey. And I didn't want to share you both either." Ruth smiled. "This is special family time, and I don't want to waste a second of it."

The implication that enough time had already been wasted wasn't lost on CJ, but Ruth's words held no malice.

"And I want to get to know your mom and dad too. Then we can share all sorts of stories."

CJ involuntarily bristled. She'd been enjoying this so much that she'd temporarily forgotten that her parents were joining them the next day.

Dak placed her mom's suitcase on the bed. "I have to go into the office, but I'll be back for dinner. We'll order in."

Clearly, she still hadn't forgotten CJ's last attempt at cooking for more than just the two of them.

"Nonsense." Ruth hooked her arm into CJ's. "I'll be cooking with my daughter-in-law in your glorious kitchen. I've always wanted an island. I'll feel like one of those celebrity chefs, without the potty mouth, of course. Do you know any of them, CJ?"

"I don't, and I have to admit that I'm a pretty terrible cook. My mom didn't really do home-cooked meals. Though my dad has now become quite the chef, hasn't he, Dak?" CJ recalled using her dad's chili as an excuse to go over to Dak's house when they first met.

Dak gave her mom a hug and kissed her forehead. "He's not bad, but he's got nothing on you, Mom." She gestured toward the door. "I really have to go."

"CJ said you're back on active duty..."

Dak took a deep breath in the silence Ruth left and strode toward the door. "We can talk about that tonight," she said over her shoulder.

Ruth grumbled, but Dak was already gone. Her truck rumbled out of the drive, and CJ sat beside Ruth's bag. "Would you like me to help you unpack? You must be tired after the long flight."

Ruth sat opposite CJ in the armchair at the side of her bed and looked at her seriously. "I worry about her, CJ. I wish she'd gone back to her cold cases. She went five years without any trouble, and the moment they pulled her back to a live case, she got stabbed *and* shot."

CJ clasped her hands in her lap and stared at them. Guilt snaked around her throat and choked her into a momentary silence. How CJ felt totally responsible for *both* of those injuries was the one thing she and Dak hadn't talked about in their many deconstructions of those events. She kept telling herself she'd raise the subject and get it out in the open. She was almost positive that Dak didn't blame her at all, but that little sliver of possibility that maybe she did... That was too much for CJ to contemplate right now. Because if she mentioned it, Dak might fixate on it and realize it *was* CJ's fault, and then she'd cancel not just their wedding, but also their relationship.

"CJ?"

She looked up and offered Ruth a tight-lipped smile. "I worry too, but this is what she wants. It took her a while to recover after her partner was shot and killed, and—"

"Her partner was killed?"

CJ frowned. Surely Dak had told her about the big things like that. "You didn't know?"

Ruth shook her head and let out a sigh that filled the room with its sheer volume of grief and melancholy. "When did it happen?"

"Just over five years ago." CJ didn't want to reveal more. It was Dak's story to share, and she had her reasons for not doing so. CJ couldn't fathom them, but she knew they existed.

Ruth closed her eyes and put her head in her hands. "She told me she'd changed departments and would be working cold cases because there are over a quarter of a million of them in the country." She dropped her hands and looked at CJ. "I remember the number because it seemed like such a lot, and it made me proud that she could bring peace to families who'd suffered so long. And I was happy because I knew that she wouldn't be in the line of fire anymore."

The reminder of Dak's recent wounds goaded CJ toward a confession, but she resisted. If and when she talked about it, it would be with Dak. That's what married couples were supposed to do: share their darkest secrets... Or maybe she'd talk to her therapist first. Dark secrets were their bread and butter, and she could give CJ some much-needed outside perspective and a dash of courage. "She was probably just trying to protect you and keep you from worrying about her." She couldn't think of any other reason for Dak's silence on a subject so deeply painful.

"Perhaps." Ruth rose and began to open her suitcase. "I wonder what else she's kept from me all these years."

CJ caught Ruth's wrist gently. "If there's one thing that I've learned from years of therapy, it's that the time ahead of you is what counts. If I focused only on the past, you wouldn't be meeting my parents tomorrow, and I certainly wouldn't have invited them to the wedding."

Ruth frowned. "Oh. I'm sorry, I didn't know."

CJ wrinkled her nose and shrugged. "It's not something I talk about." She saw the disappointment in Ruth's expression. Maybe talking about her demons might help Ruth overcome Dak's self-enforced separation from her mom and brother. "But after you've settled in, I could make some iced tea, and we could sit by the pool. I could tell you more...about me, about my childhood."

Ruth smiled, and her eyes brightened. She pulled CJ into a rib-crushing hug. "That would be perfect. I'd like to get to know you better. And I can share some stories of little Daniella." She released CJ, and now she was all but glowing.

"Little Daniella," CJ said. "I can't imagine Dak ever being little."

"Mm, I suppose she never was." Ruth pulled a folded skirt from her bag and shook it out. "Do you know, she was five weeks early and still weighed just over nine pounds."

CJ retrieved a hanger from the closet and handed it to Ruth. "Is that a good thing or a bad thing?" She'd never been interested in having a child and knew little of the finer details. All she knew was that she never wanted something baby-sized emerging from between her legs.

"That depends on your perspective," Ruth said. "A baby puts on the most weight in the last eight weeks of pregnancy. If she'd hung around in there for another five weeks, who knows how heavy she would've become."

CJ shuddered. "If you think about it that way, it was a very good thing for you that she came out early."

"You're not wrong!" Ruth laughed. "She was always a stocky girl. And I couldn't bribe her with anything to get her into a dress."

CJ giggled at the thought of her handsome and divinely butch special agent in a dress. "So you're not expecting Dak to walk down the aisle in a princess-like wedding gown?"

Ruth snorted. "Goodness, no." She touched CJ's forearm and winked conspiratorially. "But when she comes home, it might be fun if we pretend that I am. We should pick out the frilliest, fanciest gown in your bridal magazines. I bet I can keep a poker face for longer than you can."

"I don't doubt it." CJ continued to help Ruth unpack and make the guest room feel like home. She was glad that Ruth seemed able to turn off her justified sadness at the distance between her and Dak; it would make her stay far more joyful. And arranging a beautiful white wedding was bound to enhance that joy.

Her cell vibrated in her pocket, and she pulled it out to see her own mom had sent her a text. Before going home to Salt Lake a few months ago, CJ would've easily hit delete and never called back. But she had to practice what she'd just preached to Ruth. The past was just that, and the time to come included a wedding her parents wanted to be a big part of. She vaguely wondered if she and Dak should leave the two moms to plan the wedding and simply show up on the day.

The thought of Dak in a virginal white wedding dress popped back into her mind. *Maybe not.* CJ wanted to see Dak in a traditional, perfectly tailored three-piece suit as she walked down the aisle toward her. *That* thought made her respond very differently. No doubt the wedding would be amazing, but their wedding night? That was the part CJ couldn't wait for.

Chapter Sixteen

"IF YOU ASK ME, you're better off out of the way," Garrity said as he dropped into a chair. "Planning a wedding is stressful enough. Adding both parties' parents to that is self-inflicted torture."

Dak hadn't asked him, nor would she since they barely knew each other. But in her effort to ease back into being a team player, she'd answered him honestly when he asked why she'd gotten into the office later than planned. Now she wished she'd employed some subterfuge. She tapped her pen on the photo of the Rodeo Killer's third victim to shift the focus back to the case Charnwood wanted her to work. "Where was this girl's body found?"

"Malaga Cove, on the main trail. It's a way up from Rat Beach. The creek feeds directly into the ocean."

She scanned the photos of the surrounding area. "This looks like the Amazon rainforest. How far was the body from the nearest parking lot?"

"Over half a mile."

Jani Parks. Fifteen years old. Seventy-three pounds. Dark hair. Good looks. The other two girls on the murder board were similar, though the hair color varied in shades. "The murder sites have never been found... And the girl couldn't have walked to her death?"

Garrity shook his head. "There were a lot of prints on the trail, but none matched the shoes she was wearing. And there was only one set of boot prints off the trail leading up to the spot where Jani was found, apart from the hiker's prints, whose dog sniffed out the body. There was no sign that she was killed at the site."

"All the victims were found here, but the last one was found first, indicating that he got careless, or bold, or he wanted to be discovered... Or he was just running out of space."

Garrity scoffed as he doodled on a notepad. "Murderers like this don't ever want to stop."

Dak wouldn't argue that point. She'd spent hours combing over the case files and had concluded this was someone who would never stop. It wasn't in his DNA. Stopping would be like giving up, and giving up was failure. This man didn't like to fail, nor was he used to doing so. She took a seat opposite Garrity and skimmed through the profile her predecessor had written. "Magnus Street fits this profile perfectly. I can see why Special Agent Kimbal pursued him."

A twitch of Garrity's mustache was the only show of emotion he displayed at the mention of his former colleague. "Kimbal was a good agent. If he was convinced it's Street, then it probably is."

Dak ignored Garrity's defense of his colleague and zeroed in on the slight doubt in his voice. She hadn't seen another serious suspect mentioned in the files. Fathers, school friends and foes, old boyfriends, teachers, family friends: five hundred and sixty-four people had been interviewed over the course of the investigation, but all of them had been dismissed as potential murderers. "You picked up the case when Kimbal didn't return from Mexico?"

Garrity nodded and took a noisy slurp of whatever sludge was in his cup.

"You saw something else?" she asked. Garrity clearly respected the dead agent, but Dak had the growing feeling that he wasn't giving her the entire story. Loyalty could be a double-edged sword.

He wiped the corner of his mouth repeatedly with his knuckle. "One of the school security guards looked good for a while, a guy called Moreno, but Kimbal didn't think he had it in him. He thought he wasn't intelligent enough to pull off the complicated nature of the crime, and how and where the bodies were dumped was well-considered."

"But you do?"

Garrity shrugged. "He worked the two schools that the three victims attended, and his wife was his only alibi. A couple of the victims' friends said Moreno was creepy and had made inappropriate comments to all of them. I think he'd be worth looking at."

Dak narrowed her eyes. She had to admit to being a little confused. Garrity had been given the case, and Kimbal was dead. There was no need not to follow all lines of inquiry. Any new agent on an investigation, especially a cold one, would be expected to consider the evidence and information with a fresh perspective. "But you haven't?"

"Charnwood is convinced the killer is Street, so that's where I've been focusing my efforts."

Pressure from above. Now his reticence made sense. Sometimes an investigation could concentrate too intently on one subject to the exclusion of all others, leaving the actual suspect to avoid consideration and even give them time to escape altogether. That kind of thing was usually confined to local police forces though, not the Bureau. "And you've been getting nowhere with Street?"

He shook his head. "He seems to be behaving himself and keeping busy with the daily running of his security group."

"The same group that Moreno works for?"

Garrity nodded. "You got it."

Dak thought of the Hillside Strangler and how those murders had been perpetrated by a team of two. Inevitably, that led to her own case with the Artist and his twin brother. She'd almost been disappointed when that case turned out to be such a cliché. Twins shared a lot of traits, but murderous intent seemed like it should be a step too far. "Is it possible they're working together?"

Garrity raised his eyebrows then nodded slowly. "That's possible."

"Maybe there's a connection between Street and Moreno that's been missed. Maybe they served together. Was a thorough background check run on Moreno at the time?"

Garrity scribbled on his pad and looked a little more energized. "I don't think so."

Dak schooled her expression and didn't show her consternation at such a glaring omission. Fixating on one suspect was always detrimental to any investigation, but it certainly looked like Kimbal had done exactly that. "It could be there's nothing to connect them... Kimbal followed Street to Mexico though, and then he turns up dead in an alley. That's a hell of a coincidence if Street's not involved at all." She flipped through another file that detailed Street's movements through a period of surveillance that Kimbal had ordered. "I'm assuming we don't know where Moreno was while Kimbal was in Mexico?"

Garrity shook his head. "Aside from knowing Moreno had an alibi for when the third victim was abducted, we don't know anything about his movements. Because the other two victims were so badly decomposed, it was impossible to get a time of death. He could account for enough of the possible abduction time that it convinced the police he wasn't worth pursuing."

"Was it a solid alibi?"

"His wife."

A wife wasn't a solid alibi. No family member was. Usually, a wife who provided false information to the law would only do so if they were convinced their husband couldn't have been involved. And even then, they'd likely only do it once. Her cell vibrated on the table, and she glanced at it to see it was Detective Weaver. After talking to the witness for Evelyn Berenger's case, a strange theory had begun to present itself. She hadn't shared it with Weaver—it was too embryonic for that—and she also hadn't brought Garrity up to speed. But if he was going to be okay with her disappearing to look at local murders that might supplement her theory, she had to let him know what she was working on.

When she dismissed the call, Garrity chuckled. "Is that your wife-to-be already struggling with your mom?"

Dak frowned and stopped short of clenching her jaw. If she was going to be a useful, functioning part of a team again, she had to get used to talking about aspects of her personal life. "No. My mom's a peach." At least, that's what Dak believed. She hadn't been around her enough for too long to form a valid opinion yet. But that's what visits like this were for. "It's a homicide detective at LAPD." She painted an outline of her suspicions and filled it in with details from the two cases.

Garrity looked baffled. "I know you've got a reputation as a bit of a cold case savant, but..."

He blew out a long breath and paused, as if he was choosing his words carefully. He'd obviously heard about her reputation for being a hard ass too and clearly didn't want to offend her. This was their first meeting, and they'd be working together for a while. Bad blood borne of mistrust and ridicule wouldn't be a great start.

She held up her hand to keep him from developing an ulcer from the effort he was putting in to not call her crazy. "They found a witness, a homeless guy, on the second case. He saw a guy with his arm in a cast hanging around the parking lot, and he fits the basic description we have for Keyes' murderer. The witness wasn't able to provide enough information for a full sketch, but he put the guy at well over six feet tall."

Garrity fiddled with his pen but held her gaze. "That narrows it down to about fifteen percent of the population."

"One percent if he's over six-four." She shook her head. "But that's not the interesting detail. It's the arm cast and acting vulnerable to get the young woman to help him load a heavy piece of furniture into his truck."

"She had to be pretty gullible to fall for that," Garrity said. "Who buys furniture at one in the morning?"

Dak shrugged. That did seem naïve on Evelyn's part. "Maybe the guy is extremely charming."

"Huh." Garrity rolled his eyes. "Like Ted fucking Bundy."

Dak raised her eyebrows and nodded. "Exactly."

"What do you mean, 'exactly?' Last time I checked, Bundy fried nearly twenty-five years ago."

Dak pushed up from her chair. The energy fizzing through her made it impossible to remain seated. She paced around the table. "I think Evelyn's killer mimicked the MO of Ted Bundy, right down to his choice of victim: long dark hair, middle parting, young. He donned an arm cast to gain her trust. She was sexually assaulted and killed the same way, and her body was dumped—headless—in a similar fashion. I think he's a copycat killer, struggling to settle on his own fantasy."

Garrity shook his head slowly, remaining clearly unconvinced. "That's an over-reach, Farrell. Lots of killers rape their victims. Maybe Bundy's arm cast gig just inspired him. If I follow you, who was he imitating with the Keyes murder?"

"There are hallmarks of Dennis Rader."

"BTK?" Garrity huffed. "He's choosing the classics. Who's next? The Zodiac Killer? Or is he only copying murderers who were caught and punished?"

She'd expected Garrity's pessimism, especially at such an early stage in the development of her theory. She would've been the same if he'd brought the hypothesis to her. "There's no way of knowing who might be next. Unfortunately, it's something of a waiting game." Which was a terrible situation to be in. Her gut was telling her how the cases were connected but knowing that she couldn't move further forward until another body dropped was insufferable.

Garrity sighed. "Okay. Aside from the perpetrators in both cases being a similar height, what else is making you think they're related?"

Dak told him about the neatness of both scenes and how there was nothing in the VICAP reports for months prior that were similar cases. She still believed Keyes wasn't the murderer's first victim, but his excessive cleanliness indicated he might just be organized enough to have pulled off his first murder with exceptional planning.

The content of Weaver's latest message could be exactly what she needed to build on her theory.

He scribbled something on his pad. "I've had a couple of copycats in my time, but this is a fresh approach to being a copycat serial killer, if you're right. And it makes it damn hard to anticipate his next move."

"Right." Dak appreciated that Garrity was half-prepared to take the leap with her. If she had to have a temporary partner while she waited for Hamilton to graduate from Quantico, she needed one who would challenge her but still trust her.

He gestured to her phone. "You should check to see if that's the next piece in your puzzle."

Dak scooped up her cell and returned Weaver's call. "Hey, it's Farrell."

"Hey, Special Agent Farrell. Thank for getting back to me."

Dak took her notebook from her pocket and flipped to the back where she'd been keeping details of the Keyes and Berenger cases. "Do you have a new body?"

Chapter Seventeen

THE THIRTY-MILE DRIVE TO Cherry Canyon Park took twice as long as it should have, and Garrity complained all the way after realizing Dak's truck didn't have AC. By the time they got there, his light gray shirt had darkened considerably around his armpits and collar. He loosened his tie but didn't remove it, just as she hadn't. Dak's black shirt didn't betray her body's response to the searing heat, but she'd rolled her sleeves up as far as they'd go so that she didn't collapse from heat stroke. They'd burned through four bottles of ice-cold water from the cooler plugged into the car, and Garrity had rubbed several large ice cubes on his forehead.

She pulled into the shade beneath some giant trees, and Garrity practically burst from the truck.

"We'll take my car next time," he said and slammed the door.

"Hey, be careful." Dak got out and closed her door more carefully. "He didn't mean it, Betty," she muttered, too quietly for anyone else to hear. But he was right about needing AC. A Yeti full of water did little to cool their skin temperature. She'd gotten a quote for a system but didn't really want anyone else touching her. But her time for tinkering with Betty was severely limited now that she had a fiancée to play with.

"The M.E. is just finishing up," Weaver said as she approached them. She tilted her head toward Garrity. "Who's this?"

Garrity held out his hand. "Special Agent Garrity. Special Agent Farrell asked me to accompany her."

Weaver flicked her gaze from Garrity to Farrell and back again, like she was unsure about this new intruder.

Dak patted Garrity on the shoulder and smiled. "He's one of

the good guys."

Weaver smiled widely after Dak's seal of approval, and she shook Garrity's hand. "Good to know." She turned and headed into the trail. "Follow me."

Dak spotted Detective Miller sitting in an unmarked Dodge Charger, his stare less than friendly. She jutted her chin in his direction for Garrity's benefit. "She's got an asshole for a partner," she said, feeling the need to explain Weaver's suspicion.

Garrity nodded. "Understood."

She got the feeling that he actually did. So far, none of her new colleagues had shown themselves to be anything other than good people. She was bound to come across a few idiots like Miller eventually, but it didn't hurt for Weaver to see that there were men who enjoyed working with women. "What have you got?" she asked.

"Just up here."

Weaver pointed over the ridge, then led them past a smattering of uniformed cops scouring the area for clues. Dak noted the tire tracks going up then reversing down the incline. Cars didn't usually come this far up the trail, but the driver had a body to dump.

Dak was careful not to step on the flags marking evidence points. CSU were still busy with the scene, capturing every element of it on digital camera. They stopped at the body, already covered.

Weaver gently turned the sheet over to reveal the victim. "Jason Beasley. Fifty-six-year-old white male. Robbed and shot multiple times at close range. The tracks you saw just back there are from his car, which was found a few miles away a couple of days ago. License plate had been removed but was found close by, along with multiple cans of beer–"

"What kind of beer?" Dak asked, already running through her memory of serial killer cases and their many pertinent details. *If* this was her unsub, she had to figure out who he was imitating.

"Budweiser, I think. I'll double check," Weaver said.

"Anything else in the car?"

"More beer cans and a ripped condom wrapper. Unused."

"Maybe he was about to get down to business, but someone disturbed him," Garrity said. "Maybe he liked to jack off out here and had done it hundreds of times before. Our perp taps on the window, thinking he's got an easy target, but Beasley fights back, and our killer shoots him."

"*Nine* times?"

Weaver's expression made it clear what she thought of that theory. But she had to be objective, and it seemed like she was already rooting for this murder to be part of Dak's growing collection. Dak had stopped writing when the prophylactic came up. And the nine bullets reinforced the niggling memory. Taken in context, that detail meant it was all but impossible that this murder could be part of the copycat series. Looking at the basic sketch from the homeless guy, their unsub would have trouble passing as a woman. "What makes you think this could be the same killer as Keyes and Evelyn?"

"I'm not sure that it is, but you asked for any murders where little bits of detail didn't make sense."

Dak heard the lack of confidence in Weaver's voice and took a breath. She had to remember that Weaver was still new to this, and she was looking to Dak for guidance, regardless of Dak not really wanting another mentor role. "Okay, that's good. So what didn't make sense to you?"

"Obviously I wasn't called to the abandoned vehicle, and that's already been towed and impounded for evidence, but when I looked at the photos they took, that pattern of neatness struck me. There were no erratic tire marks or signs that the car had braked suddenly. It was parked in perfect alignment with the edge of the road even though there were no lines to park in. And there were prints all over, so it hadn't been wiped down. All of them have been accounted for as family. It was his wife's car, and she hardly used it. He was only using it because his car was in the shop."

"You're thinking the killer wore gloves?" Dak liked Weaver's path of logic and found it easy to walk alongside her now. Weaver nodded. "But the way the body was dumped and the frenzied nature of the death indicates an impromptu kill."

"Gloves say 'I'm prepared,' but the number of bullets used indicate it was almost a crime of passion or rage."

Dak squatted beside the body and checked his left hand. The white line on his otherwise tanned hand indicated the absence of a wedding ring. "Have you spoken to the wife?"

"Yeah. She hadn't reported him missing. She said that he travels a lot and often doesn't tell her when he'll be gone or when he's coming back."

Dak stood and stepped away from Beasley's body. "Do you believe her?"

"Do you mean, do I think she could've killed him?"

"That's what I'm asking, yes."

Weaver shook her head. "She was quiet as a mouse. She didn't strike me as a cold-blooded killer."

"But this doesn't look like a cold-blooded murder, does it?" Garrity asked, the challenge gentle but firm.

"No." Weaver rubbed her chin. "No, it doesn't. But she didn't seem like she'd be quick to anger either. And this is a secluded spot late at night. Driving out here indicates premeditation, doesn't it?"

Garrity shrugged. "Not if they came out here for a little role play or just some fresh air naughty sex to spice up their marriage. If things went wrong or got a little rough, she could've snapped."

"How tall would you say the victim is?" Dak asked, far more concerned with whether Beasley was her killer's third victim than she was with sex games gone awry.

Weaver swung her attention from Garrity to Dak then took the time to look at the body. "Pretty short. He looks about five-six to me."

Dak agreed. "Was the driver's seat in a position commensurate to the victim's height?" When Weaver didn't answer immediately,

Dak asked, "Was it pulled closer to the steering wheel for a shorter person or was it further away to indicate a much taller person?" However unlikely it was for this to be part of the series, Dak would still follow the clues.

Weaver looked up, as if she was visualizing the car's interior. "I guess it was quite far back. Why?"

"Far enough back for someone over six feet tall?"

"Ah, got it... Maybe. We've got photos back at the station, and you could take a look at the car yourself. It's in the impound yard."

Dak studied the drag marks: long stretches between stops, indicating strength and stamina. "Do you remember the height and build of Beasley's wife?"

Weaver frowned and nodded. "She was short. Five-two, probably, and painfully thin. I could see her collarbone and chest bones."

"Unlikely that she could pull him that far before taking a mini break then."

Weaver huffed. "Damn near impossible for her to pull him at all."

Dak motioned toward the trenches dug out by Beasley's heels as he'd been dragged from the car to the dump site. "The fact that there are just feet marks also indicate that the person pulling the body was tall and capable of bearing the brunt of the weight. Most people drag a dead body by its wrists, so the ground disturbance tends to be far wider."

"So it could definitely be someone big, like the killer we're looking for in the other two cases?" Weaver asked.

"It's too early to say that. I need to look at the car and where it was dumped." Dak exchanged a glance with Garrity, who looked mildly amused by Weaver's enthusiasm. She was just glad it wasn't irritation. A lot of the agents she'd worked with had little patience for anyone outside the Bureau but he seemed more inclined to humor Weaver. And better yet, he also seemed happy to ride along on Dak's intuition train without a sense of judgment.

"No problem." Weaver grinned. "Whenever you're done here,

I can take— Ah, crap."

"What?" Garrity asked.

She jutted her chin back down the way they'd come. "Miller's waiting in the car for me to go back to the station."

"I'm sure he wouldn't mind a couple of detours," Garrity said.

Dak tilted her head slightly. "Detective Miller isn't quite as happy as Detective Weaver that the FBI is showing an interest in this clutch of cases."

Garrity waved his hand dismissively, clearly pegging Miller as an asshole. "Do you want me to talk to him?"

She appreciated that he didn't just say that he *would* talk to Miller, which would've been dismissive of her ability to tackle him herself. "No, that's okay. I'll suggest he ride back alone. We'll go in my truck to where the car was dumped."

Garrity chuckled. "Sounds good to me—if you like riding in the fiery pits of Hell. Does that work for you, detective?"

Weaver was dumbstruck for a moment, obviously not used to being asked her opinion. "Uh, yeah. That'd be fine."

"Good. I'll talk to him when I'm done here." Dak turned back to study Beasley's body and to think about her theory. Including this body seemed crazy, even to her. But maybe it wasn't. Something was niggling at the back of her mind, wanting attention. The bullets. Aileen Wuornos had used an odd number of bullets when she'd killed her victims. And the order of the killings felt familiar rather than random *if* this was a copycat of Aileen Wuornos. But that was the stumbling block. Wuornos had killed men who used prostitutes, men who had gotten abusive. How could her unsub have lured Beasley into letting him into his car? Because she was pretty sure a relatively short guy like Beasley wouldn't be interested in paying for a six-foot-four inch drag queen. The other two victims fitted the preferred victim choice for both serial killers, which would mean Beasley had to have a vice habit. And not just a regular habit; he had to be known as someone who got violent or wanted more than he paid for. That was the kind of information prostitutes shared among themselves in an effort to keep each other safe.

Dak slowly returned her attention back to the moment and focused on Weaver. "We'll need to talk to vice. See if anyone recognizes Beasley. Check the known corners around where Beasley worked and maybe even where he lived. I want to know if any street workers know him, if he's a regular, and if he was, what kind of sex he was into."

Weaver nodded slowly, processing the information before it looked like she had a light bulb moment. "Because of the torn condom wrapper? You think a prostitute could've done this? So you don't think this could be the other killer?"

"I don't think a prostitute did this, no. I think it was done *for* a prostitute," Dak said. Both Weaver and Garrity looked puzzled, and with good reason. Her theory and the link between the three murders didn't fully make sense to her, so they didn't have a hope in hell of grasping it. "Take us to where the car was dumped. We'll talk about it more there."

Weaver and Garrity shrugged, and Weaver re-covered the body before they headed back down toward their cars. Dak made a quick detour to inform Miller of their plans and didn't hang around to entertain his predictable grumbling. When she rejoined Weaver and Garrity, she zoned out of their small talk. She had more important things to process. Like, if Keyes was a replica BTK victim, and Evelyn was a homage to Ted Bundy, and *if* Beasley was an Aileen Wuornos sacrifice, which killer was up next for this weird LA treatment? Dak couldn't shake the feeling that she should know the answer. She resolved to study her vast collection of serial killer and true crime books that she'd gotten out of storage now that she'd moved to a more permanent home. They were still in their cardboard boxes, awaiting placement on the bookshelves Dak had yet to build. CJ's dad, Roger, had said he'd like to help her with them while his wife, Nicole, helped CJ and Dak's mom with wedding plans. A few beers and playing with power tools sounded like a good way to spend a few hours over the weekend, and it would keep her away from the insanity that would inevitably ensue. There were only two decisions Dak cared about—her suit and the cake. She was happy to acquiesce to CJ's preference on everything else.

"Special Agent Farrell?"

Dak tuned back into Weaver's voice and realized they were back at her truck already. How had she drifted to thoughts of nuptial nonsense when she should be thinking about her unsub? Or three different killers if her theory was complete nonsense.

She practically heard her dad's voice in her head telling her to trust her gut. It had served her well this far, and she had a growing certainty that she'd find her answers within the pages of her books. "Jump in," she said to Weaver. "There's water in the cooler." Dak wiped the sweat from her brow, and the heat inside Betty evaporated her breath and dried her throat. "You're gonna need it."

"Jesus Christ." Weaver wound down the passenger window. "How have you not melted in this truck? How old is it to not have AC?"

Dak raised her eyebrow. "Younger is not always better." The moment the words hit her own ears, she groaned internally. God, she sounded old. If this was what being some sort of mentor figure was going to turn her into, she wanted none of it.

"You know you can get AC installed in classics like this, don't you?"

"That's what I told her," Garrity said from the back seat.

Dak half-smiled, noting Weaver's acknowledgment of Betty's inherent value. "I know." Maybe she and Roger could install one after they'd finished the bookshelves. She rolled her eyes. Now she was sounding domesticated as well as old.

She started the engine and threw Betty into reverse. "Tell me more about how you think these crimes could be related," she said, wanting to refocus.

Weaver turned side on to Dak, excitement effervescing from her. "I've been reading that book you recommended—"

That's it. Weaver hadn't finished her sentence, but Dak's familiarity with the sequence of these kills suddenly made sense. *Close to Death*, the book she'd recommended, was by an ex-FBI profiling expert who'd become a psychologist. Each chapter was dedicated to an infamous serial killer. Chapter one was BTK. Chapter two was Ted Bundy. And chapter three was Aileen Wuornos. The order couldn't possibly be a coincidence. Their new killer was using one of the best books on serial killers ever published to *become* a serial killer. There was a certain poetry to it. But better than that, it gave Dak a real foothold in the case. Chapter four would reveal this killer's MO, giving her and the LAPD a heads-up in what they were looking for. Instead of waiting for the next body to drop, they could actively predict the *exact* nature of the crime and narrow down the victim pool. In a city the size of LA, it didn't give them a whole lot, but it was a whole lot more than they'd had to that point.

"Have you gotten to chapter four yet?" Dak asked.

Weaver looked pleased with herself and nodded. "I'm at chapter nine. John Gacy, the killer clown."

"That's great." Dak stopped at the intersection and turned to Weaver, who was still looking like the teacher's pet. "Do you remember who the subject of chapter four was?"

Weaver grimaced. "Luis Garavito, La Bestia."

The traffic cleared, but Dak didn't move. Garavito's seven-year rampage haunted even the most hardened agent. "Jesus Christ."

Chapter Eighteen

OF THE BINARY OPTIONS that have long held humanity in its grip, I have always thought that women should be given the opportunity to rule the world over men. Centuries of unrest and war, primarily driven by religion and greed, have been led by men for the most part, so why not give women a crack at it? They're generally less aggressive and more inclined to diplomacy and democracy than men.

Thus, I consider myself something of a pro-feminist on those days when I care enough about the human race to think about it. But every day, I know that I receive the gifts bestowed upon me as a cis male, and they're so ingrained and innumerable to list that it's virtually impossible to reject them. Since I cannot remove myself from the power and privilege of being a man, I don't believe I can claim the actual title of feminist, but I'm conscious of their struggle. I wouldn't say I'm an active feminist because I interact so little with people that I'm not often in a position where I can change the inner workings of a patriarchal society from the inside. If you're a woman (cis or otherwise) reading this, I'm with you in spirit.

So now that you can claim to know me a little, I'm sure you can picture my delight when Aileen Wuornos was treated to her own chapter in my source book. Though there have been numerous female serial killers over the centuries, only Aileen has been profiled by the FBI—hence her auspicious appearance here. The author of my source text was an FBI agent-turned-psychologist, and he included cases that he was either personally involved in or ones that interested him over the course of his career. I have to admit that the number of blanket statements he employs troubles me. I suppose I *have* learned from him, but I have no doubt that he could learn from me. If I'm successful in turning myself into a murderer, if I develop my own fantasies of killing, and then I desensitize myself and reverse-engineer them... Imagine the possibilities. The author is adamant that rehabilitation is impossible. In a way, he's given up on humanity in much the same way as I have. But I disagree. Humans are as programmable as computer hardware. He was short-sighted. I'm not finished, but I have faith in my methodology: give me a murderer, and I'll return to you a regular citizen. He may still be an idiot and of no use to society, but to address that would be a whole new area of study.

And only murder interests me now.

The scientific community might have argued against me including Aileen in my experiment; clearly, I was unable to pass as a woman, and so the imitation couldn't be pure. However, the basis of this project is *not* to blindly copy the whole process, but to mimic the victim selection and the modus operandi of the murder. In this case, the victim selection posed a problem. I'm not part of the prostitution community in LA (or anywhere else in the world, should you be wondering), which made a consultation with a few working members a necessity.

I thought about this requirement long and hard. It had the potential to expose me if the police made a connection between my victim and his whoring, so I made my initial inquiries quite vague. In that little chat, the few women with whom I spoke were most worried that I was a vice cop, and they relaxed considerably when I assured them that I was nothing of the sort. They mentioned their two biggest concerns in their line of work were the police and "violent johns." Given that I wasn't the first and I wanted to reduce the number of the brethren in the second, I decided that consulting with these women was worth the risk. They were wary of me at first—my size can be intimidating—so I sat on a nearby bench to enable them to look down on me. I've read many psychology and behavioral books to understand the average person, their expectations, and their anxieties, and it can be exhausting pandering to them all, padding the actual topic with small talk and niceties and how's your family type questions? Such nonsense. But that's what is expected of polite society. And I needed information so I played nice.

I wonder about you, reader of my process; do you know what I'm talking about? Do people and their emotions baffle you? Do you wish they were easier to understand? Not to read—words can be misinterpreted, their meaning lost. And not when people speak, because they lie. Oh, how they lie. To cover inadequacies (perceived or real), to hide self-esteem issues, to disguise their darker side. Do you have a dark side? Is my experiment inspiring you to embark on your own project? Or perhaps you already have the perfect fantasy, and you're working yourself up to action. Or maybe you're an observer, a little like me, and the machinations of mankind fascinate you.

I'm both fascinated and appalled. I mentioned earlier in this journal that the human race would be best extinct, a relic. Such devastation we wreak upon the planet. And yes, I know there are some good people, like scientists trying to reverse the damage that hundreds of years of industrial, mechanical, and technical evolution has visited on this earth. But my ultimate question remains: is the human race worth saving?

Anyhoo, I continued to speak with them and asked if they had any regulars who were violent. After finding out the kind of horrors these poor women are subjugated to by the men they told me about, I have to admit that I was rather looking forward to the kill. Thanks to Aileen, I had a totally new method to try. I wonder whether I'll eventually become like a kid in a sadistic sweet shop who can't decide which murder method to use, but I suspect that my feverish anticipation was more to do with the stories I'd heard.

Beasley begged for his life and even used his wife and kids: *"The people I'll leave behind won't survive without me."* I suspect they'll do just fine, that they'll thrive without a grubby little man like him holding them back—if there even are kids. His wallet held no pictures of a family, nor did his phone. But since he was in a talkative mood, I took the opportunity to ask why he abused the street workers he paid. I'm sure you can imagine my eye roll when he came back with the highly unoriginal excuse that his wife was too frigid to experiment, and that he had needs that went beyond regular sex.

Nonsense. There are sex clubs for those activities, much like the one I visited in San Francisco, and there are role play partners he could've sought out. Beasley's violent interactions with these women were non-consensual, and that I cannot abide. His explanation, such that it was, made it easier to pull the trigger. Not just once, but nine times. Aileen varied the number of bullets she used, and I believe that it might have directly correlated to the level of rage she felt toward the men she murdered. Having spoken to the women Beasley took advantage of, my rage was particularly high, hence the nine bullets.

After Beasley, I'm at three murders. How do I feel? Ugh, what an airy-fairy question. If, after I've completed my research, my experiment is uncovered—perhaps even by you, depending on how you discovered the book you're now reading and whether you plan to experiment yourself—and my identity revealed, I wonder what the profilers and psychiatrists will make of my killing streak. I think I'm a few decades ahead of true acceptance and an open-minded scientific community, as much as they already purport to be that, so I don't suppose that I'll be lauded in the manner I should be. I expect they'll dig into my past, my life, and my childhood, desperately seeking the wrong answers to the wrong questions. No doubt they'll think they can solve me like I'm a simple puzzle, and that my relationship with my parents will explain why I've done what I have. Why I'm *driven* to murder, to bludgeon, and with my second subject, to rape. *That* part was abhorrent, if you're wondering, and I know you must be. Especially if you're a man. Though I suppose you might call me sexist—is there an antonym to misogyny? But the stats don't lie; men are the dominant perpetrator. But going back to how I feel, I don't believe this means that I'm not as detached as I ought to be. I think it's impossible to separate one's morals from one's actions, even in the pursuit of science.

Anyway, it was awful. Consent is king, or I should say, queen. A human's ability to have sex for the fun of it, rather than merely for procreation, is one of the few positives to the species. (And I have to reiterate, that the right to do so should be severely limited. Too many imbeciles, bigots, and Republicans have contributed to the over-population of a dying planet). And it's a pursuit I thoroughly enjoy with all manner of partners. But it is a privilege and a gift. It's not something to be taken from someone, and those people who are of a mind to do so should be rendered impotent by removal of their testicles. I'm not sure what the punishment should be for those without this equipment, but with the right motivation, I could think of something.

See? I told you I was a pro-feminist.

Chapter Nineteen

"You think these three cases are related, and the killer's next victim will be a young male between the ages of fifteen and twenty, in the style of Luis Garavito?" Charnwood sounded less than convinced.

"I'm aware the link might seem tenuous at first glance, and I haven't worked out his motivation yet, but you've got to admit there's something to it." Dak tapped the cover of Perry's book, *Close to Death*. "I've searched the VICAP reports over the past eighteen months, and yes, there are similar cases—there are only so many ways to kill someone—but this exact order has never occurred in one place. Until now."

"Didn't Garavito pose as a monk?" Charnwood leaned back in his chair and crossed his arms. "A monk would stand out in a crowd, even in this town."

"He dressed as a priest too." Dak picked up the book she'd put on Charnwood's desk along with the file she was compiling. She flicked through to chapter four. "This guy killed homeless kids. Nearly two hundred of them between the ages of six and sixteen. He raped, tortured, and—"

"I'm familiar with the case." He grimaced and shook his head. "I have a young son, Farrell."

He turned one of the photo frames on his desk so she could see it. Charnwood, a good-looking woman, and two kids: the quintessential all-American family. Dak pulled back a little; this job was hard enough without a family. She'd been devastated when CJ was in the Artist's clutches. She couldn't imagine having children, knowing the horrors they could face if fate struck.

"You know he'll probably be released this year." Charnwood's expression declared his disgust. "Sentenced to nearly two thousand years and ends up serving twenty-two. You've got to question the Colombian justice system's efficacy."

Dak nodded. "I want to reach out to his prison in Valledupar to see if he's corresponding with anyone, particularly anyone new in the past year. And I want to do the same with Rader at El Dorado."

"And Bundy and Wuornos? I'm not sure Hell will allow its inhabitants to cooperate with us." He gave a wry smile.

"Probably not. But the other two are worth looking at. It could be this new killer asked permission to copy their MO. His crime scenes suggest a certain politeness and order."

Charnwood frowned. "Order, I understand, but how do you get politeness from a crime scene?"

Dak shrugged. "It's a feeling. It's not so much the crime scene as the image of him building in my mind. Maybe politeness isn't the right word. He likes to follow rules, but I think they have to be the rules he chooses to adhere to."

Charnwood picked up her file and flicked through it slowly. "Where do you want to go with this?"

Dak acknowledged the hint of opportunity. "We've got a sketch worked up from the description given by the homeless guy at Evelyn Berenger's place of work. I want to distribute it to all the stations across the county and tell them to focus on the homeless populations in their area. Garavito only targeted street kids, and our killer likes to mimic the murder method as close as possible."

Charnwood raised his eyebrows. "You think he dressed up as a sex worker to entrap Beasley?"

Dak couldn't tell whether his question was serious or not. "I wouldn't think so, but I don't know what kind of women Beasley was into. Maybe tall, powerful women were his catnip. Maybe that's why our killer selected him. I'm waiting on information from Detective Weaver; she's trying to find Beasley's street corner of choice. Once I have that, I'm going to talk to the women there. If there was a six-foot-four inch guy hanging around but not buying anything, they would've noticed him."

Charnwood closed the file. "You mean, you'd *like* to talk to the women there? This isn't a confirmed case yet, Farrell. The Rodeo Killer is. We *know* the same guy has killed three kids and a federal agent. That's the case you were assigned." He handed her the file. "I want you to concentrate on finding *that* killer."

Dak clenched her jaw. The main reasons she'd enjoyed being on the road was that no one directed her energies or stopped her following her instincts. She didn't respond because what she wanted to say wasn't entirely respectful.

Charnwood sighed after a prolonged moment of silence. "You can put out the sketch but let Detective Weaver put in the groundwork with the prostitutes. Right now, you have nothing to place your sketch guy anywhere near this crime. Get me some solid evidence that your mystery killer was near Beasley's regular haunts, and I'll give you some latitude to pursue this."

Dak nodded, glad that she hadn't voiced her irritation. As her superior, he had every right to direct her work, but that didn't mean she had to like it. She appreciated the concession he was making but didn't think she could simply hope that Weaver would do the job for her. For now though, she'd take the minor win. "Thanks. That'd be good. And contacting the prisons?"

"Don't push it." He nodded toward the door. "Catch the Rodeo Killer first."

Dak headed out of Charnwood's office, already set on partially ignoring his instructions. She'd work that case with Garrity, as directed, but she'd reach out to the correctional facilities too. Her killer had struck every seven to ten days, and if she was right, they had a maximum of eight days before he emulated Garavito. The Rodeo Killer was currently dormant as far as they could tell, and that made Dak's case her priority.

But she had to play nice if she was going to make this field office her home. Dak knocked on Garrity's open door and walked in.

"How'd it go?" He gestured to the empty chair on the other

side of his desk.

Dak furnished Garrity with the Cliff notes of her meeting but kept out her intention to do what she thought was necessary in addition to Charnwood's instructions. Garrity seemed like a good agent, and she couldn't expect him to risk his career on her instinct when they barely knew each other.

"So what do you want to do next?"

"Let's pay Moreno a visit," Dak said. "But I want to observe him at work first, and I want to talk to him at home when his wife is there. Do you know if she works?"

"Let me check." He flipped through a stack of files on his desk and pulled one out.

Dak looked at her messages while she waited. One from CJ asked her to pick up some wine and beer on her way home. Their consumption of alcohol had increased along with the occupancy of the house, particularly now that CJ's parents had arrived, and Dak's desire to stay out of all the wedding preparations had grown stronger with even more opinions in the mix. She glanced at the time; it was already after six, so watching Moreno would have to wait until tomorrow. It wasn't that she didn't want to go home—she missed CJ—but the emotional chaos and delicate repair of broken relationships wasn't conducive to them spending quality time together. If CJ's heart wasn't set on a fancy wedding, Dak would happily drive to Vegas and elope. But she also knew her mom was looking forward to the whole thing, and after so much time was lost between them already, Dak didn't want to disappoint her either.

"I don't think the wife is working right now," Garrity said. "She was pregnant when detectives talked to her."

"Did he ask how far along she was?"

He consulted the file. "Doesn't say. Why?"

"If the timings were right, that might explain why there hasn't been a killing for a while."

Garrity frowned. "He stopped murdering local children so he could become a good dad?"

"Seems like a strong enough motive, don't you think? Can I take a look?" She held out her hand for Moreno's file then scanned through it again. "Did you find any connection between Moreno and Street?"

He shook his head. "Street is Moreno's boss. That's all we've got."

That's what she wanted to hear. After the Artist and his twin brother, another double team to hunt down didn't appeal. "Good."

"Is it? If Moreno turns out to be the killer, where does that leave us with Kimbal being murdered after tailing Street to Mexico?" He pulled another file from the stack and opened it to the morgue photos of Kimbal's body.

"All his valuables were stolen?" she asked, and he nodded. In addition to the fatal gunshot wounds to the head and chest, execution-style, Kimbal was covered in bruises and had multiple fractures, indicating he'd been severely beaten before being murdered, possibly for his bank information, possibly for sick fun. "Could be a terrible coincidence. Charnwood said Street had been to Mexico twice, including the time when Kimbal trailed him. That would mean he'll be going again the moment the urge grows too intense. If he's the killer. It could be that Kimbal was wrong, and Street's trips to Mexico were for something else entirely. And that could have gotten Kimbal killed too."

Garrity narrowed his eyes. "Yeah. What are you thinking?"

"The US side of Border Patrol will flag him if he leaves again?"

"That's right. We've instructed them to let him through and inform us immediately. Should I be packing for a trip?"

Dak nodded. "It wouldn't hurt to have an overnight bag here at the office in case we need to follow him." An uninvited thought popped into her head concerning CJ's reaction to that possibility. Considering other people's reactions to her movements had never been an issue before. It would take some getting used to, as would having to be at home certain times to have dinner with her mom and her in-laws. Conscious of the time, she eased out of the chair and walked to Garrity's door. "I'll pick you—"

"Oh no, you won't." Garrity shook his head and widened his eyes comically. "I'm not riding in your hotbox of a truck again until you get AC installed. I'll meet you in the parking lot or I can pick you up. What's your druthers?"

She didn't particularly want him at the house. Its location and value weren't commensurate to the salary of a federal agent, and though Garrity hadn't mentioned CJ yet, she didn't want to talk about her or her TV career. But the school Moreno was currently working at was closer to her than it was to this building. "Fine. Pick me up at my place at eight."

"I like the new school times being late; I get to sleep in," Garrity said.

"You've got kids?" Dak scanned his desk, but there were no photo frames.

"Triplets. Girls. Fourteen."

Dak laughed at the raging hormones that must be flying around his home. "That explains the bags under your eyes." And the fact that he looked fifty when his file said he was thirty-nine. He offered no explanation of the lack of photos, and he didn't pull his phone out to bore her with a thousand images, so she didn't push. He obviously had his reasons, and she didn't need to hear them.

"You have no idea." He shook his head slowly.

"And I don't want one."

"Sound decision."

"See you tomorrow." She tapped the doorjamb and left, pleasantly surprised that he hadn't asked if she wanted kids. She got back to her office and took her laptop out of standby to fire off the requests to Garavito and Rader's prisons, then she packed her leather bag and headed out to the parking lot.

Dak dropped in at a liquor store on the way home and stocked up on enough beer and wine for a month. She doubted it would last that long.

Roger's Shelby GT500 looked good in their driveway. As she

pulled in beside it, he popped up from behind the wing, polishing cloth in hand.

"Hey, Dak. I'm glad you made it. I'm outnumbered in there." He thumbed toward the house. "I had to come out here for some peace."

Dak climbed out of Betty, and he pulled her into a side hug and patted her back hard. "Is it that bad?" She extricated herself and grabbed a crate of beer from the truck bed.

"There are a *lot* of opinions and not much consensus." Roger lifted the case of wine. "This should come in handy, but I suggest we quietly drop it in there and leave them to it." He nodded at her truck. "Betty looks like she needs some love."

Betty did need some attention, including installing an AC unit. His suggestion was tempting. "As appealing as that sounds, I think they might notice our absence at dinner. Aren't you supposed to be cooking?"

"My signature chili is simmering on the stovetop, the cornbread is cooling, and the potato skins are keeping warm in the oven." He shrugged. "I really don't need to be in there."

"I'm hungry, and I've missed your chili. I'm gonna brave it. Come on." She stepped aside for him to lead the way.

Roger rolled his eyes and tsked. "Don't say I didn't warn you."

He trudged toward the front door, and Dak was about to follow him when a black SUV with tinted windows turned onto their driveway.

"Is that our backup?" he asked and chuckled. "I hope they're armed."

Dak didn't recognize the vehicle. She placed the beer on the ground to have the use of both hands, just in case. "You go in. I won't be long."

"If you hear me screaming, you'll come rescue me though, won't you?"

She shook her head. "You can take care of yourself, Roger."

The truck came to a stop, but no one emerged from it. When

Roger had closed the door behind him, the driver's door swung open, and a tall, strong-looking woman with dark hair tied back into a tight ponytail got out. She wore fucked-up jeans and a battered leather jacket, and when she pushed her door closed, Dak caught sight of a shoulder holster and gun.

Dak rested her hand on the butt of her own weapon and flicked the catch for a quick draw if the situation necessitated it. "Are you lost?"

"I've never been lost in my fucking life, Agent Farrell."

Dak's discomfort ratcheted up a notch. The woman's confidence and the way she held herself made it clear she was military or another government department, but Dak wasn't expecting any visitors, and her address wasn't public knowledge. "Is there something I can do for you?"

"Yeah, there is." She leaned against the hood of her Yukon. "I wanted to meet the person who convinced my little brother to join the Feds."

Dak frowned. "Your little brother?" She tightened her grip on her gun.

"Dee told me your new partner is going to be Liam Hamilton. I'm Ice, his big sister."

His much bigger sister, Dak thought. "Who's Dee?" she asked, though the pieces began to click together. "Hamilton never mentioned he had a sister."

Ice's eyebrow quirked, and she gave Dak a cocky grin. "That's because I'd have to kill you if he did." She glanced at Dak's hand on her weapon. "You can relax. I'm not here to fucking mess with you. And you probably know Dee as Elodie Fontaine, the big fucking movie star."

Dak didn't relax even with the name drop. Maybe Ice was the buddy Elodie had mentioned at dinner. "Do you have a license for your Sig?" she asked, flicking her glance to Ice's jacket.

Ice's grin widened. "I've got licenses for all sorts of fucking weapons. But if it helps you feel safe..." She placed her hands wide on the hood. "I've been trying to get Liam to fulfill his potential for years, but you convinced him in less than one. I figured you had to be something pretty fucking special, so I wanted to see for myself." She looked Dak up and down. "Dee was right; you're pretty big."

Dak didn't know what her size had to do with anything, but she and Ice were probably about the same build. She'd never felt threatened by a woman with long hair...until now. The uncomfortable feeling didn't sit right, and she bristled silently. Behind Ice's dark eyes lingered a sinister danger, the kind fostered from years of witnessing *and/or* perpetrating darker deeds. Everything Ice had said so far could've been discovered with some serious investigation, so Dak racked her brains for some personal snippet Hamilton had shared with her and that she'd miraculously hung onto in the depths of her memory. Once again, she made a note to change that once he became her official partner. He'd split with his girlfriend to pursue his career as an agent, and he'd only just mentioned her name when they last talked... *Susie!* "Have you met his wife?"

Ice chuckled. "That's a pretty blunt knife you're trying to use there, Agent Farrell. Liam isn't married. He just dumped his long-term girlfriend, Susie, so he could become *your* partner. Since you're not his type, and I'm pretty sure you only swing your bat one way, his motives aren't sexual." She narrowed her eyes. "And he really loved her, so again, you've got to be something special."

Dak wasn't about to invite Ice in, but she did appear to be who she said she was. She relaxed her hand. "I don't know what you want me to say."

"I don't need you to say anything. I do need to personally thank you for saving my little brother's life though."

Ice held out her right hand, which would've made it unwieldy for her to pull her weapon if Dak accepted the gesture, but it also meant Dak had to take her hand off her own gun. She knew how to fight, but she had a feeling Ice had forgotten more about self-defense disciplines than Dak would ever know. She stepped forward and shook Ice's hand. "You're welcome."

"Did you know the sentimental ass made that bullet into a keychain?"

Dak relaxed her shoulders and nodded. "He told me that, but I thought he might be joking."

Ice rolled her eyes. "Fucking softie." She gripped Dak's hand a little tighter. "That's why you need to take care of him. He might pretend he's a cigar-chomping man of the world, but he's still just a little squirt."

Despite Ice's vice-like grip, her eyes had softened, revealing her genuine concern for her brother, and Dak's tension fell away completely. "I don't know why he smokes those things. I think he's watched too many film noirs."

"You could be right." Ice released Dak's hand and turned away abruptly. "Thanks for the hospitality." She opened her truck door and got in. She hung partly out of the window and handed Dak a card. "If you need anything, *ever*, call me."

Dak looked at the card that only had a cell number printed on it. "I was expecting a bat signal," she said and tucked the card into her pocket.

"I think you've watched too many superhero movies." Ice started the engine. "But it's not like I haven't been told that before." She winked before pulling away.

Dak watched the Yukon pull away then she turned and picked up the crate of beer. She stopped at the door, already able to hear a heated discussion about something wedding-related, and half-wished she'd gotten into Ice's truck to have a few beers and hear some stories about Hamilton.

CJ opened the door. "Dad said you were hiding out here with a visitor. Have they gone?" She took Dak's arm and tugged her inside.

"Roger's a snitch." Dak put the beer down and kissed her. "And I think I just met Elodie's best buddy."

CJ frowned. "Did I miss Elodie?"

"Nope. She was alone. Turns out that she's Hamilton's big sister, and I mean *big*."

CJ slapped Dak's chest. "Are you body-shaming her?"

"Of course not. I mean big as in tall and muscular."

CJ grinned wickedly and wiggled her eyebrows. "*Oh... Nice. Why didn't you invite her in?*"

"Because of *that* reaction. I can't have your head turned by some butch superwoman."

CJ pushed Dak against the door and ran her nails along Dak's collarbone. "*You're* my butch superwoman." She crushed their lips together.

Dak wrapped her arms around CJ's waist and pulled her closer. "Tell everyone to go home. I want to take you upstairs and make love to you for a week," she said between kisses.

CJ broke away. "You'll get to do that on our honeymoon." She pushed away and called over her shoulder, "I promise I'll make it worth all this pain."

Dak took a moment to enjoy CJ's exaggerated hip sway before the thought of her current cases intruded. The wedding was over six months away, and she had two murderers to catch. *No pressure then.*

Chapter Twenty

CJ WOKE TO THE soft jingle of the alarm she'd set to make sure she and Dak could talk before Dak left for work. She was mentally exhausted from herding the three parents currently occupying their space. She bit her bottom lip at the unkind thought. She shouldn't think of their parents as Viking-like invaders. They were only trying to help. But they were also trying to make up for lost time, and *that* was tiring her out more than the wedding planning.

Ruth was lovely, but she was clearly struggling to reconcile all her lost mother-daughter time, and more than a few times, she'd emerged from her room with bloodshot eyes that indicated she'd been crying. It didn't help that Dak was working twelve hours a day, so she and Ruth only had a few hours together in the evening. And that left CJ with hardly any Dak time at all.

Which just wasn't acceptable. CJ had tried to console herself that it wouldn't always be this way, but life had a habit of getting in the way. Both their careers were demanding, and it was unlikely that their parents would let up now that they were all back in their lives. So CJ had to make time by getting up at the crack of a sparrow fart, which was a curious phrase she'd heard parroted from an Aussie TV show. Curious but catchy.

She turned over and bit her lip for an entirely different reason. Dak, being the inferno-hot-body that she was, had shoved away the bedsheet, and in her nocturnal tossing and turning, her tank top had ridden up and her bed shorts had ridden down, revealing the very top of her pubic hair. It wasn't something CJ had ever taken much notice of before, but on Dak, it was incredibly sexy. She supposed it had something to do with the L-shaped slabs of muscle that framed her abs and soared under her waistband like arrows pointing toward the good stuff.

CJ moved down the bed so she could run her tongue along the deep lines between the solid planes of musculature. She'd had no idea the effort it took to cultivate and maintain definition like this until she and Dak had moved in together, but now that she did, CJ sure appreciated the struggle. Dak's silken skin contrasted against the marble hardness beneath it, and the combination made CJ hot for her *all* the damn time.

Dak murmured and wrapped her hand in CJ's hair. "That's got to be one of the best ways to wake up in a morning."

"I'm only just getting started."

"What time is it?" Dak whispered.

"Time for me to get you off," CJ said, tugging down Dak's shorts. "I promise I won't make you late for work." She slid farther down the bed and maneuvered herself between Dak's legs. Her musky scent fueled CJ's ardor, and she wasted no time on foreplay. Instead, she took Dak into her mouth and garnered a quick but very satisfying orgasm. She climbed up and lay on the brick wall that was Dak's chest. "Morning, handsome."

"Morning, beautiful." Dak gave her a sleepy half-grin. "Thank you for that."

"My pleasure."

Dak glanced at the phone on her bedside table. "You're up super early. Couldn't you sleep?" She gently moved a few strands of CJ's hair from her face and kissed her nose.

"I wanted to talk to you." She gathered the courage it took to be honest and open. "I'm missing you. The wedding planning is bigger than I ever thought it would be. And this whole full-house thing is getting a little too much to cope with alone. It's like I'm caught in the middle of a tornado." CJ pressed her face against Dak's chest. She'd wanted to ease into the difficult part of the conversation, not blurt it out like a spoiled kid.

Dak eased her finger beneath CJ's chin and lifted gently to look at her. "Are you okay?"

CJ pushed up and sat back, tucking her legs underneath her. She shook her head and let out a sigh so big, it should've carried all her worries away with it. "Everybody has different ideas for our wedding. I'm leaving next weekend and probably won't see you for eight weeks. And you're shut down like a top-secret closed movie set."

Dak propped herself up on the pillow and placed her hand on CJ's knee. "Do you want to talk about those one at a time?"

She blinked back the soft burn of tears that resulted from Dak's tender response. "Okay. The wedding... You're working so much that I don't want to bother you with it when you get home. And you need to spend quality time with your mom while she's here. But the only thing you've offered any input on is the color of your suit. Our moms can't seem to agree on anything: the venue for the party or the ceremony, the menu, my dress."

"Whoa, baby." Dak caressed CJ's cheek. "This is *our* wedding. What do *you* want for all of those things?"

"Honestly? I'm overwhelmed by all the choices." She glanced along Dak's body and promptly pulled the sheet up to Dak's waist to limit her distraction. Even this upset, her overriding emotion faced with a half-naked Dak was still desperate desire.

Dak grinned and rolled her tank top down. "Do you *want* a big wedding?"

CJ shook her head. "This is supposed to be our special day, and the only people I want there are the ones who are special to us."

"Are the moms trying to force you into a big wedding?"

"No, not really." CJ blew out an exasperated breath. "I'm overreacting. I know I am. I just feel a bit out of control and a lot alone. I know you're busy getting back into work, but I can't deny that's part of the problem. There's a distance growing between us because you're not sharing anything with me anymore."

Dak frowned and shuffled along the bed so they were closer.

"You've switched topics." She held up her hand as CJ was about to defend herself. "But that's okay. We can flip between them all, baby." She drew lazy circles on CJ's thigh and looked at her seriously. "I haven't been talking about my work because we haven't had much time together. But that's not the main reason. After what happened in Salt Lake, I don't want to expose you to my cases. They're dark and monstrous. The stuff of nightmares. Accepting my marriage proposal doesn't mean that you have to hear all about the work I'm doing."

CJ arched her eyebrow. "You decided I needed protecting?" It was sweet, but it was also terrifically old-fashioned and unacceptable. "Me being a femme doesn't mean I'm a fragile flower. You should know that better than anyone, Dak."

Dak closed her eyes briefly and nodded, looking suitably chastised. "I know."

"We need to share it all, Dak, or I'm scared that we'll lose our connection."

Dak lifted her hips from the bed and wiggled her eyebrows. "I don't think there's any danger of that."

CJ swatted Dak's chest. "I'm being serious."

"I'm sorry. I'm just playing." She squeezed CJ's thigh. "How about we have some time to talk every night before we go to sleep? That should give you plenty of material for your nightmares."

"I think you forget that I work with dead bodies all the time."

Dak tilted her head slightly. "You *used* to, but—"

"But nothing. I do. And that's the other problem. I leave for eight weeks of filming soon, and I won't see you for fifty-six days."

Dak shrugged. "That's your career, baby, and I completely support you in that. It's something you want to do."

CJ wrinkled her nose. "That's another thing on my mind. I'm not sure that it is anymore. I just don't think I can get out of it, and I don't want to let Paige down. Or Emily. She's worked really hard on this." She looked up at Dak, who'd upended her life to join her too. "And then there's you."

"I don't understand." Dak took CJ's hand and intertwined their fingers. "I thought you came back here for exactly that reason. To do the job you love."

There didn't seem to be any hint of frustration in Dak's words, but if there had been, CJ wouldn't blame her. Dak had loved her life on the road, something which CJ already worried about without adding her indecision to the mix. "I did, but Netflix and its director are taking the show in a direction I'm not happy with, and Emily hasn't been able to negotiate any compromise."

"What would you want to do if you didn't do *Dead Pretty*?"

CJ smiled and brought Dak's fingers to her lips. She hadn't expected Dak to be so philosophical about her flip-flopping, and her support brought tears to CJ's eyes. "You're so wonderful."

Dak wrinkled her nose. "I love you, CJ. I want you to be happy. So what do you really want to be doing?"

The prompt brightened her mood considerably. "If I could do anything in the world?"

Dak nodded. "The world's your oyster, yep."

"I want to get back to sculpture. The studio Mom and Dad created for me lit that match again. But I also like connecting with the wide audience TV gives me. Somehow, I'd like to combine the two. Maybe get a group of artists together who can mentor contestants, like that tattoo show you like that's being going for a hundred seasons. If Paige can sell something like that."

"*Ink Master*. Great show." Dak raised her eyebrow and grinned. "Sounds like you've spent a lot of time thinking about this..." Her expression darkened a little. "I'm sorry that you felt you couldn't talk to me about it."

CJ wrapped Dak's hand in hers. "We're just starting out. We've got to find our rhythm, and I know there's so much going on right now."

Dak pressed her finger to CJ's lips. "No. There'll probably *always* be a lot going on, babe. You're right about us having to find a rhythm...and balance too. But we can only do that if we talk to each other." Dak squeezed her eyes shut briefly and shook her head. "And I haven't been here for us to do that."

"You're here now."

"So what are you going to do about Netflix?" Dak asked. "Whatever you decide, I'll support you."

"You promise?"

Dak lifted CJ's chin so their eyes met. "You doubt my word?"

"No, of course not. It's just a lot to ask after you've already uprooted your life for me. The show might not work out, and Netflix might sue me for breach of contract. I might end up teaching art in a community college. Or embalming to funeral home students."

"Whatever happens, we'll figure it out." Dak pressed her lips to CJ's head. "What about everything else?"

"I feel selfish for being jealous of the time you're spending with your mom." CJ glanced away, unable to hold Dak's gaze. "You've got a lot to figure out."

"We do, yeah. But not at the expense of us." Dak wrapped her hand around CJ's shoulder and pulled her in to rest against her chest. "And I can't fix two decades in one week. It's going to take time."

CJ ran her fingers along the ribs of Dak's tank top. "And there's always so much of that available."

Dak's chuckle reverberated against CJ's head.

"I know, baby."

CJ relaxed further when Dak tightened her hug. God, this was her happy place. The steady and dependable thudding of Dak's heart, strong in her ear. Dak's protective arms holding her, safe and secure. Their bodies pressed so close together, the thinnest sheet of silk couldn't separate them. It was as if the whole world slipped away, and nothing could hurt them. Sure, CJ had been alone long enough that she'd become self-sufficient, but there was really nothing like this connection. Needing *this* didn't lessen her fortitude; if anything, it increased it, increased her self-belief. In Dak's arms, or with Dak by her side, the world could challenge her however it wanted, and she knew they'd overcome it together.

"Will you find time to help me with the wedding?" she asked and softly kissed Dak's pecs.

"I will. And I'll do whatever work from home I can this week to help you out with all the parents." Dak traced a tantalizing pattern on CJ's shoulder. "And if you decide you want to say screw it and elope, say the word, and we'll jump in Betty and drive to Vegas."

"And you'll talk to me about work too?"

"If that's what you want, yeah, I will. I've got a really interesting case already. Want to hear about it?"

CJ smiled widely and nodded. She shuffled down the bed and lay with her head on Dak's stomach so she could look at her while she was talking. Dak began to regale her with the details of the case and instantly animated in a totally different way than when she was excited or interested in anything else. This was what CJ wanted. They'd shared the Artist case in a far too visceral and realistic way—CJ could live without that kind of proximity, thanks— but listening to Dak enthuse about the possibilities of her current hunt was what she needed. It wouldn't matter if Dak was a mall cop relaying tales of zitty, thieving teens or cute, lost children. It wasn't the subject that made this exchange important, it was the connection. And that was something CJ just couldn't get enough of.

Chapter Twenty-One

DAK SHOVELED A FORKFUL of omelet into her mouth, then took a big gulp of the special coffee CJ had brewed, a mix of cinnamon and pecan she was trialing. After the very early sex and her regular morning workout, she was hungrier than usual and had asked her mom to use five eggs instead of three. CJ's parents were still in bed, so Dak's mom had taken great delight in commandeering the kitchen to make them some food.

"What's on your docket today, Mom?"

Her mom's eyes lit up, and she jiggled her stomach with both hands. "Cake tasting. We're trying to get as much done as possible this week since CJ is going to be filming for the next two months." She smeared the smashed avocado on two seeded pieces of toast and slid them across the kitchen counter to Dak. "Is red velvet still your favorite?"

Dak nodded. She couldn't remember the last time she'd had cake, but red velvet was a safe bet given that she still had a sweet tooth. "The wedding is six months away, Mom. We've got lots of time."

Her mom arched her eyebrow and looked across at CJ. "I see what you're dealing with now, honey." She glanced back at Dak. "Daniella, there are so many moving parts and so much you have to organize months in advance. *Most* people take two years to organize their wedding."

"We're not most people." Dak closed her hand over CJ's. "Is there anything I can do to help?"

"Actually, yes." Her mom turned away for a moment and slipped the sizzling hot pan into the sink. "It would be good if we could finalize the guest list. Can you have your list of people ready tonight?"

"Sure, Mom." That wouldn't take long at all. Or would it? Should she invite Hamilton? And where would their fledgling friendship with Elodie and Madison be in six months? Would it be weird to invite them now in the hope that they'd grown to be great friends by then? She shoved another chunk of omelet into her mouth and looked to CJ for help.

"We can it do together, babe." CJ's smile indicated that she instinctively understood the issue.

Dak drew her close and kissed her softly. "What would I do without you?"

"You're never going to find out."

A car horn broke the moment, and Dak looked at the kitchen clock. It could only be Garrity, but he was fifteen minutes early. Her cell buzzed with a text confirming he was outside. "Damn it."

"Your new partner?" CJ asked.

"Temporary partner, but yeah." She speared what remained of the omelet and squished it into her mouth. The piece was so big that it was almost impossible to chew. Almost.

"I'll invite him in," her mom said. "He might like some breakfast."

Dak shook her head and swallowed her half-chewed food. "No. He'll be fine." It was going to take time to get used to having a partner again, and she was nowhere near ready to invite him into her sanctuary. She made a sandwich from the two pieces of toast, picked up a napkin, and got up from her stool. "I love you." She kissed CJ and her mom goodbye, grabbed her bag, and headed out. By the time she got to Garrity's car, she was down to the last bite.

"None for me?" he asked as Dak got in the passenger side.

"I didn't think you'd want food in your fancy car."

"I'm early." He motioned toward the front door. "I could've come in." His expression as he looked at the house spoke volumes, even though he didn't say anything about it.

Dak raised her eyebrows and gave a half-laugh. "You don't get access to my house until the six-month mark."

"So never, given that you've already got your rookie lined up when he finishes his training."

Dak shrugged. "You never know. You may just make the cut."

Garrity rolled his eyes and drove back to the road. "So you want to observe Moreno at work to decide if he's our killer?"

"Not exactly." Dak balled up her napkin and shoved it in her bag in the footwell. "I want to see how he interacts with the kids and the parents. I want to get a sense of how he holds himself, what kind of a man he is. It might not tell us anything at all."

"Or it might tell us everything."

"Maybe."

They fell into an easy silence, punctuated with Garrity's occasional attempts at small talk. As much as she hated it, she humored him. He was trying to get to know her, like colleagues are supposed to do. He was a nice enough guy, and she'd liked the way he'd interacted with Weaver at the Beasley crime scene.

The LA traffic tripled the time to cover the distance between her house and the school Moreno was working at, and by the time they arrived, Dak had a complete family rundown, Garrity's entire work history, and the background to his latent ambitions to be a movie director, which was the only tangential reference he'd made to her being with CJ. He liked to talk so much that Dak had gotten away with sharing very little.

Garrity parked close enough for them to observe Moreno through binoculars and far enough away not to attract attention. People usually recognized government plates and tended not to ask questions, but they were outside a school, and parents could get understandably paranoid about strange vehicles lurking too close to their children.

Dak quickly identified Moreno from his mugshot. At his size, he'd be hard to miss, and he was positioned at the main gate in front of the metal detector. *Metal detector.* They'd become as much a part of a school's fabric as math class and prom nights. Dak was pretty hardened, but news of any school shooting always froze her blood. The previous year, there'd been almost fifty school massacres, a statistic that made her sick, and one that had steadily increased the use of security guards or police officers to seventy-five percent of schools over the past two decades. Which made Moreno's potential guilt even more distressing: the person hired to protect the kids was another person they were at risk from.

The angle at which they were parked made it easy to see Moreno's face, while he swept the street and the approaching children with their parents and caretakers like clockwork, scanning for ten seconds in each forty-five-degree area. He smiled intermittently but mostly schooled his expression to a neutral mask. Until the older girls started to arrive. Then he became more animated. The change was too dramatic to be innocent.

"You sick fuck."

Garrity's outburst made Dak lower her binoculars. "See something you don't like?"

He shook his head, and his nostrils flared. "I knew we should've looked at this guy more seriously."

"Relax. We're looking at him now." She refocused on Moreno.

He grunted. "What if he's killed again?"

"As far as we know, he hasn't," Dak said. "And no kids have gone missing in the area. Remember our working theory is that he's taken a hiatus since his wife got pregnant. We don't know how long that might last, but now that he's in our sights, we can ruffle his feathers." She thought about his alibi. "It's likely the wife will be the weak link. If she's got any suspicions at all, she's *got* to be frightened for the life of their child. Or more likely, her own life. Look at the size of him. If he's threatened her into providing his alibi, she'll be terrified. If we're right, we'll see that today when we visit their home."

Garrity sighed. "I hope you're right. Charnwood still thinks Street is our man."

Dak shook her head. "I don't think the evidence bears that out.

Maybe Street is up to something else, and maybe Kimbal's death is related to that. Street has no connection to the girls, whereas Moreno does. Street might be an asshole on other counts, but I have a feeling this isn't one of them. Which is why Kimbal couldn't make a case against him and had to chase him all the way to Mexico. Like I said before, those two things could be totally unrelated." She gestured toward Moreno. "But we're here to find the guy who murdered those children, and what little evidence we have points to this guy."

"I bet he's feeling pretty fucking smug about getting away with it."

"*If* he's our killer, he won't be getting away with it much longer," she said.

They watched him for the next hour as the entire student population entered. His behavior and body language strongly suggested that his thoughts towards the young girls were far from pure. Dak didn't know the gender of the child his wife had just given birth to, but if it was a girl, it would be something she could use to get the wife to crack.

Moreno secured the gates and after a brief conversation with his colleague, he headed up the street toward them. Dak and Garrity lowered their binoculars. Moreno got into his truck a few vehicles down from them and drove away.

Garrity waited a few moments before pulling out to tail him. "Looks like he's heading home," he said.

"Good. After exposure to that kind of temptation, he might be a bit reckless." Dak shoved their binoculars in the glove compartment. "Kimbal didn't interview the wife, did he?"

He shook his head. "It was done by a detective on the case. Carver, I think. Why?"

She recalled the notes on the woman's testimony or rather, the sparsity of them. "She didn't seem to say much."

"As far as Carver was concerned, nothing stood out as unusual." Garrity slowed down to keep the distance between them and Moreno. "I don't think he paid much attention because Kimbal had already worked up a profile on Street, and the police were on board with it. I think they thought following up on Moreno was a waste of their time."

Dak didn't respond. An FBI agent getting fixated on one suspect was incredibly unusual. That was something small-town detectives or those with little experience fell prey to, not a relatively distinguished agent like Kimbal. "Close the gap," Dak said when they were less than a half mile from Moreno's house.

Moreno swung into the driveway of a modest place with a tidy yard, and Garrity pulled up curbside. They'd gotten out and were halfway up to Moreno's house before he pushed his truck door open and joined them.

He tilted his head to the side, taking more time to appraise Dak in particular, though his expression remained neutral. "Can I help you?"

Dak offered her badge for inspection, as did Garrity. "We'd like to chat with you and your wife about the Rodeo killings." She watched his body language and saw an almost imperceptible jaw clench.

"I've already told the cops I had nothing to do with that." He began to walk away. "And there's been no more murders, so what are you bothering me for?"

They followed him to the door. "You seem quite convinced about that," Dak said. "How do you know?"

He turned at the door, almost filling the frame. "I ain't seen anything on the news about any more prick-teasing jailbait being found dead."

Dak didn't have to look at Garrity to know that comment hit too close to home. His own triplets were in the Rodeo Killer's victim parameters. But he remained steady. "You think those three girls deserved to die?"

Moreno opened his mouth then seemed to catch his response. "I don't know anything about them."

Dak could partially see why Kimbal had dismissed this guy as a suspect. He didn't seem anywhere near as in control as the killer's profile suggested. Which was why any profile should only ever be a guideline rather than a map taken as gospel. "That's not true though, is it, Mr. Moreno? You worked at both of the schools the victims attended."

He shrugged. "I've worked at a lot of schools over the past few years. I don't remember any of the kids."

She doubted that from the way he'd looked at way too many of the teenagers going into the school half an hour ago. The door opened from the inside, and Moreno half-turned to reveal his wife holding their baby.

"What's going on, Ike?" Her eyes flitted from Dak to Garrity nervously, and she adjusted her embrace around the child.

"Nothing. Go inside and shut the door."

She lowered her eyes and bowed her head at the command, and Dak instantly recognized the signs of an abused wife. "Actually, we'd like to talk to you too, Mrs. Moreno."

"Why?" Her eyes widened, and she took a half-step back. "Why would you want to talk to me?"

"We have some questions about the Rodeo Killer case." Dak shifted to look around Moreno's bulk. "You provided an alibi for your husband for the time of death of the third victim, Jani Parks." She flipped open the file they'd brought with gruesome crime scene photographs and held aloft one of Jani's half-buried body. Mrs. Moreno clapped her hand over her mouth and gasped, making it clear the previous interviewing detective hadn't done the same.

"Jesus. What the hell?" Moreno snatched at the picture, but Dak pulled it away.

Garrity stepped between them and put his hand against Moreno's chest. "Take it easy, Moreno. Do you want to be arrested for assaulting a federal agent?"

Moreno curled his lip into a sneer. "I didn't touch her."

"Let's keep it that way." Garrity motioned to the yard across the street. "Looks like your neighbors are interested in what's going on. Let's go inside."

Moreno puffed out his chest. He tugged his wife's arm to move her out of the way, and she winced. Dak would bet money on that same area being bruised beneath her long-sleeved cotton shirt.

"I've got nothing to say to you people, and if you want inside my house, get a warrant." He crossed his arms, making his forearms bulge.

Garrity looked to Dak for guidance on how she wanted to proceed. She held up her hands and backed away, gesturing for Garrity to follow. "I just have one question. If you've stopped murdering young girls because you've got a kid now, what are you doing for your twisted kicks?"

His left eye twitched, and for a fleeting moment, a startled expression crossed his face. "I don't know what you're talking about."

"No?" Dak shrugged. "We'll see." She turned and walked away, knowing that Garrity had followed.

He unlocked the car, dropped into his seat, and chuckled. "That was a bold move."

"I wanted to see his reaction." She closed her door and looked back up the driveway. Moreno had already disappeared into the house.

"And?"

"And I think you're right; he's our killer."

Garrity smacked the steering wheel. "I knew it."

Dak clicked her belt into place and took another long look at the house. The blinds shifted in one of the upstairs rooms. Mrs. Moreno, probably. How many times had she been forced to lie to cover up her vicious husband's actions?

"What are we going to do about it? No judge is going to give us a warrant when we've got nothing to link Moreno to the crimes." Garrity pulled out into the road. "I can't believe someone like that isn't in our database."

"He's been careful. He's far more intelligent than Kimbal gave him credit for, likely than anyone gives him credit for. Which is what makes him so deadly. But I think we can convince his wife that we can stop his reign of terror over her."

Garrity frowned. "I pegged her as abused too, but they've been married for fourteen years, and she's never called the cops on him. Why would she start now?"

Dak recalled the way Mrs. Moreno had tried to shield her child from Moreno's touch. "She's a mother now. It's not just about her anymore. And there's not much a good mother won't do to protect her child."

Chapter Twenty-Two

GARRITY SHOOK HIS HEAD slowly. "I don't think this is a good idea."

Dak waved him away. "It's a great idea. Division of labor. You watch Moreno, I talk to sex workers. We need to figure out the best place and time to approach Mrs. Moreno. Just because Moreno is at work doesn't mean he doesn't have some way of keeping an eye on her. There could be CCTV all over the house and a tracker on her phone. Men like him want total control of their women, and we have no idea what measures he has in place to achieve that." She thought again of the way Mrs. Moreno had flinched and cowed in her husband's presence. Putting him away would be a double win, ending the possibility of more young girls being murdered and his spousal abuse. "We don't want to be responsible for putting her in more danger."

"I get that. I do. But Charnwood wants *this* case closed. If he finds out you're working another case, he'll have your ass."

"Closing this case might not solve Kimbal's murder like he's hoping it will." Dak shrugged on her jacket and picked up her keys. "And it doesn't take two of us to watch the house and shepherd your junior agents."

"That's another thing. I get to roast in the car while they get fresh air at the park or knocking on Moreno's door."

Dak smiled. "I'd have sympathy if you were in my truck, but you've got AC."

"I can't believe you still haven't fixed that damn thing. You must lose ten pounds of water on your daily commute."

Dak didn't bother responding. She'd talked more about her AC in the last week than she had in a decade. "Look. I'm going to talk to street workers who get more than their fill of men every day, and I'm going with Weaver. They'll be squirrelly enough with the two of us. Three is overkill." She tried to keep her tone even. Having to justify her movements to anyone didn't sit well. She liked Garrity, but his desire to follow protocol and not rock the boat with Charnwood was prohibitive. Coloring outside the lines was part of the job for her, and more and more, it was becoming clear that Garrity didn't share that proclivity. Hamilton's time at the Academy couldn't pass by fast enough. He'd shown that he was more than happy to follow her lead.

"What am I supposed to tell Charnwood if he asks for an update?"

She grabbed her bag and headed to her office door. "The truth. We're laying the groundwork to flip the wife. It's a delicate situation, which will take finesse and time." She shrugged. "Besides, the tire tracks came back from near where Beasley's car was dumped. They were a match for the ones at the empty house opposite the Keyes' home—"

"Tires which could be from several thousand trucks. It's thin, Farrell."

Dak sighed and clenched her jaw, aware that every minute she spent explaining her actions became ten minutes in hellish traffic. "Just do it. Blame me. Do whatever you have to do, but I'm going to follow up on this lead." She yanked open the door. "I'll see you tomorrow."

She managed to exit the building without getting accosted by Charnwood or anyone else and headed out of the parking lot with all the windows down. Roger had picked up the AC unit a couple of days ago. Now all she had to do was find the time to install it between murder cases and marriage preparations.

She pulled into the station to pick up Weaver, who was already waiting on the front steps even though Dak had managed to get there two minutes early despite Garrity's irritating delay.

Weaver jumped into the passenger side. "Hi, Agent Farrell.

How're you doing?"

"Fine. You?"

"Miller's on my ass. Nothing new there. He says your theory is horseshit, and that I'm wasting my time." Weaver rubbed the top of her head like it was a lucky charm.

"And what do you think?" Dak didn't give a rat's ass for Miller's opinion—he was a poor excuse for a cop—but she did vaguely hope her instincts about Weaver being a good detective proved to be correct.

"I think it's a great theory. And I can't wait to help you prove it, wrap it in barb wire, and shove it up Miller's ass sideways."

As unprofessional as it was, Dak couldn't hold back a chuckle at Weaver's visceral imagery. "Solving the case will be vindication enough," she said, though Miller probably deserved it given the way Weaver had described his treatment of her.

As they talked over details of the three cases, Weaver provided a twisting route around private roads and neighborhoods that got them to the street corner Beasley had patronized fifteen minutes faster than Dak's GPS. She'd promised to do her best to be home by nine for dinner and family time, a concept so alien that a small part of her almost wanted to work late. The biggest part of her however wanted to please CJ and to spend some quality time with her, something that was proving to be the most difficult thing to achieve now that she was fully back at work.

Dak and Weaver got out of the truck and wandered toward the small group of women already gathered on and around the benches at the edge of the park.

One of the women looked over Dak and Weaver and smiled. "Aren't you two handsome? You're like bite-size and jumbo versions, huh?"

"We were hoping you could help us with some questions," Dak said.

The woman's eyes narrowed, and the rest of the streetworkers seemed to turn their attention to Dak and Weaver. "Are you...the *police?"* she asked, her expression incredulous.

"Hey." One of the other women got up from a bench and swished her way toward them on dangerously high heels. "I know you, don't I?" she asked, focusing on Weaver.

"Hi, Cherry," Weaver said.

Something about the vaguely squirrelly way Weaver responded, both in words and body language, alerted Dak to a story deeper than Weaver busting Cherry when she worked vice. Dak couldn't see Weaver ever working undercover, so what was it?

"We haven't seen you around here in a while."

Cherry insinuated herself close to Weaver, and the intrigue ramped up a notch. Had they slept together?

"I'm working homicide now, Cherry."

Cherry nodded slowly and moved her head from side to side, as if appraising Weaver for any change she could observe. She dusted the shoulders of Weaver's cotton shirt. "I like the new look. The uniform never quite did you justice."

"I don't think anyone looks good in our uniform," Weaver said and took a half-step back.

Cherry looked amused by Weaver's discomfort. "Do you like your new department?" She glanced at Dak, raised her eyebrows, and blew her a kiss before turning back to Weaver. "Looks like you keep far better company now."

"Thank you." Dak returned Cherry's smile and leaned against a parking meter to watch the scene unfold.

"Unfortunately, the bar was set very low," Cherry said. "Wasn't it, Detective Weaver?"

Weaver looked at Dak like she could bail her out of whatever this situation was, but Dak wasn't about to do anything of the sort. Whatever their history was, it wasn't acrimonious so it could only help their inquiries.

Cherry ran her long, bloodred fingernail over her bottom lip then licked her top lip provocatively. Goddamn, Dak wanted to know what the hell their story was, but for now, she was more interested in getting answers to her case. Weaver needed to regain control of the conversation and take back the lead, but Dak couldn't hurry that and risk alienating the women.

"Can we skip that part of a catch-up, Cherry?" Weaver asked.

"Sure." Cherry fluttered her eyelashes. "If you're not here to talk about the past, Detective Weaver, why are you here?"

Weaver pulled a photograph of Jason Beasley from the slingshot satchel slung over her shoulder. "We've been told this guy was a regular around here. Do you recognize him?"

Cherry's scarlet lips curled into a sneer worthy of Cruella de Ville after a bunch of Dalmatian pups used her fur for a pee blanket. "I do."

A few of the others glanced at the picture and had similar reactions.

"We haven't seen him in a week or so, if that's your next question." Cherry put her hand on her hip.

"And we don't care if we never see him again," another woman said.

Cherry tsked. "Tulip."

Dak stepped to Cherry's side so she could see Tulip. "Why is that?" she asked gently.

Tulip grimaced. "He was rough with the girls, especially the new ones."

"Rough?" To provoke the reaction Beasley's photograph had, there had to be more to it. Plenty of consenting adults liked it rough. It was obvious the guy went a lot further than a touch of kink.

"We can't call it rape and assault if they've paid, can we?" Tulip glared at Dak, her anger evident.

"Actually, yeah, you can," Dak said.

Tulip and the other women laughed. "Yeah, well, we don't get justice. We warn others about him and the rest of them like him—there are plenty—but some of these girls are desperate, and they put up with a lot of things they shouldn't just so they can survive."

Dak nodded slowly. She'd seen far too many instances of violent men's entitlement with sex workers. The things these women were forced to do sickened her. "I'm not going to say I understand or know, because I can't imagine being in your position. Is it okay to say that?" She waited for Tulip's slight shrug and tilt of her head in acknowledgment. "We need to ask if anyone else has been asking you questions about Beasley." Dak indicated the picture still in Weaver's hand when Tulip looked blank.

Tulip frowned. "Why?"

"So someone *has* been asking questions?"

Tulip shook her head. "Not about that guy specifically, no."

Cherry sidestepped between Tulip and Dak. "What *exactly* is this about?"

"We'd like to know if anyone has been hanging around, being helpful with violent clients."

"You mean like the way a pimp is *helpful*?" Cherry asked. "We don't have pimps on this corner. We're our own co-op. We protect each other—"

"Except when you can't." Dak nodded toward a young girl hiding in the shadows. Dak had caught a look at her bruised face and busted lip when the girl had slowly emerged from behind a tree as the conversation progressed.

Cherry turned to follow Dak's gaze, and her jaw tightened. "Except when we can't, yes."

The sassy edge to her voice had dropped, her concern for the girl's welfare obvious. Cherry looked like she might be the oldest of the young women and girls that were gathered and was likely the organizer of their little co-op, something Dak admired her for. But while she was quite tall, she was also of slight build and could probably do very little to stop any actual violence unless she was armed. Dak briefly considered the possibility that Cherry could have ended Beasley's life, but she was nowhere strong enough to have dragged his body into the woods. Cherry didn't look like she'd ever worn a pair of heavy hiking or work boots in her life either, and they were the only tracks around the body.

"I can understand you being reluctant to tell us anything." Dak focused her attention on Cherry. "But there might be innocent lives at risk."

Cherry scoffed. "You think Beasley was innocent?"

Dak raised her hands. "No. Definitely not. I'm not talking about the people you have to deal with."

Cherry lifted her chin and narrowed her eyes. "Why don't you put your cards on the table? And then maybe I can help your hand."

Dak had to admire Cherry's street smarts. "Okay." She pulled her badge from her back pocket. "I'm a federal agent, and I'm investigating the possibility of a serial killer."

Cherry glanced at Weaver. "You really *are* keeping better company." She laughed. "But if your serial killer is murdering bastards like—"

"He isn't." She had to marshal the information she released, but the likelihood that any of these women would talk to the press was slim to none. She decided to keep it vague. "His other victims were a female student and a happily married father of one. His next victim is likely to be a homeless boy between the age of six and sixteen. After that, he'll be looking for a young couple." Dak didn't mention that, if left uncaught, his victims would include a prostitute. She suspected Cherry would be far less cooperative if she thought that the killer might come after her for giving the cops information.

Cherry raised her eyebrows. "That's a very...eclectic killer you've got there. But what does that have to do with that abusive asshole?" She nodded toward Beasley's photograph again.

"He was found dead in Cherry Canyon Park. Shot nine times in the chest and face."

Cherry's brow furrowed. "Nine times?"

"Nine times. And while you and your friends aren't going to miss Beasley, the killer wasn't doing you a favor. He's serving his own purpose, and his next victim is going to be a kid."

Cherry narrowed her eyes. "How do you know who his next victim is going to be?"

"I'm sorry. I can't say anything else about that particular aspect of the case. You already know more than anyone outside me, Weaver, and two other agents." Dak pulled her phone from her pocket and opened the hidden folder with the crime scene photographs from this case. She flipped to one of Evelyn Berenger's severed head. "I'm not showing you this to shock you, Cherry," she said before turning the screen to her. "I just need you to see that this guy isn't on your side. If you don't tell us anything about the guy we're looking for, you're not protecting your guardian angel, you're protecting a vicious murderer."

Cherry clasped her hand over her mouth, and Dak quickly pocketed her phone before any of the other women caught sight of it. "She was twenty-two." Dak gestured to the young women behind Cherry, who were of a similar age or younger.

She nodded and swallowed hard as if she might be quashing the need to vomit. Some of the color had drained from her face, visible even behind the extensive mask of makeup she wore.

"There was a guy that came around here last Thursday night," Cherry said. "He said he'd pay money to anyone who could help find someone he was looking for. He said he didn't have a name or a description, but he knew that he abused women like us." She shrugged. "It sounded weird, but he pulled a stack of fifty-dollar bills from his pocket and handed me a chunk without even counting it." She blew out a breath and shook her head. "It was eight hundred and fifty dollars. I've done weirder things for a lot less. The notes were crisp though. And sequential. I asked if they were real, and he laughed, saying he had plenty of money and wouldn't dream of giving us fake notes."

Dak got her leather notebook from her back pocket and opened it to a blank page. "Do you have any of that money left?" She knew the likely answer but thought it was worth asking. New and sequential notes were issued by ATMs, banks, lots of places. It was a long shot, but if she could get a serial number, it might be possible to get a location. Better yet, they might be able to lift a fingerprint.

Cherry chuckled. "What do you think? I gave most of it to our landlord, and he's got a gambling problem, so it could be anywhere by now... But I did stash a couple of hundred in my rainy-day fund."

Dak looked up from notebook, a little stunned. There was no way she could ask for it for evidence though. "Any chance I could swap your two hundred with my cash?"

Cherry arched her eyebrows. "It's tempting to charge you an exchange fee, but I won't." She glanced again at Weaver. "As long as it's Detective Weaver who comes to my place to pick it up."

Dak couldn't interpret the way Cherry's lips quirked. Was she just amused, or was there some sexual attraction there? "I'm sure the detective wouldn't mind doing that, right, Weaver?" She didn't care if Weaver did mind. The notes could be important evidence, and the clock was ticking on the next murder victim.

Weaver nodded. "Absolutely. When do you want me to swing by?"

"Tomorrow, before ten," Cherry said. "I'm still at the same place."

"You got it." Weaver looked somewhat guilty about knowing Cherry's address.

"What did this guy look like?" Dak asked. Whatever their history was, it was helping her case, so she felt no motivation to judge.

Cherry held her hand above her head to indicate height. "He was really tall, like six foot four. Would've made a good basketball player. And he looked powerful and strong."

Dak's heart rate quickened. Cherry had met their unsub and lived to give them their first real description. Her theory was becoming more solid. Charnwood would have to give her the time to investigate it officially. Then maybe Garrity could relax too. "He was muscular?"

"I don't know. He was wearing a loose-fitting shirt." Cherry looked up as if she was trying to recall his image. "He had big hands and long, thick fingers. I noticed those when he pulled out his cash. And he was pale. Whitest white man I've ever seen. But they don't get much sun in England, do they?"

Dak stopped making notes and looked up at the casual way Cherry had just dropped such a huge piece of information. "He was English?"

"I think so. He tried to do an American accent, but he ended up sounding like a Texan redneck, and that didn't go with the rest of him. I didn't say anything about it. I assumed he had his reasons. I might've thought he was Australian if it hadn't been for how white he was. No one from that country could be that pale unless they were afraid to go outside."

Dak glanced at Weaver. She'd also stopped making notes and had looked up, open-mouthed. "Anything else you can tell us about his appearance?"

"Yeah. He was average-looking. Not so handsome that he'd turn heads but not plain either."

"Hair color?"

"Dark brown and short. Clipped neat but not military short."

"Any facial hair?"

Cherry shook her head. "He was clean shaven, no sign of stubble at all, and I think his eyes were brown."

"Any scars or tattoos that you could see?"

"No. Like I said, he was wearing a long-sleeved shirt, so he didn't have much skin on show. But his hands… Mm, his hands were lovely and soft, like he'd never done a day's manual labor in his life."

"What was he wearing, other than the shirt?"

"Boat shoes, dark trousers, and a light brown jacket. Nothing fancy, but it all matched and looked expensive. He had an LA Lakers baseball cap on too. Didn't really go with his outfit."

"The Lakers? Their colors are purple and yellow, right?" Whoever thought that combination was a winner had particularly bad taste.

"That's right. It was purple with a yellow bill." She sighed. "That's about everything."

"That's incredible, Cherry. Do you think you could come in and do all that with a sketch artist at Weaver's station?"

Cherry shook her head. "If I'm not working, I'm sleeping, honey. I don't have time to waste making trips to the places I want to go, let alone the places I'd rather never go."

Dak glanced at Weaver as she took the photo of Beasley from Weaver's hand. "Can we get one of the artists to come down here?"

Weaver frowned. "I guess so. Miller won't like it, so it's got to be worth doing."

"Would that be okay, Cherry?" Dak knew she was pushing Cherry's goodwill. Having any kind of law enforcement around, even if they were just artists, wasn't great for business.

Cherry glanced at Weaver again, and Dak saw how her eyes softened.

"It'd take a couple of hours, but you could do it in that diner over there, with lunch courtesy of the LAPD. And you can still keep an eye on things over here. If you tell me when you usually take a break, Weaver can have them here at that exact time."

Cherry kept her gaze on Weaver. "That would mean I don't owe you anymore, huh?"

Weaver looked everywhere but in Dak's direction. "You don't owe me anything, Cherry. We'd just really appreciate your help with this."

Cherry huffed. "Okay, I'll do it. Your Picasso can buy me brunch at eleven tomorrow. You can give me a ride when you pick up the cash."

"No problem," Weaver said.

"So how did you point him to Beasley?" Dak asked as Weaver made a note of Cherry's demand.

"He said he was going to hang around, and he wanted me to give him a signal if anyone came by that fit the type of john he'd described."

"Did he sit on any of these benches?" Dak asked. She couldn't imagine how many hundreds of people had used them in over a week, but all it would take was one hair to match the sample that was unaccounted for in the empty house opposite the Keyes residence. Then she'd have another connection between the two crimes.

Cherry shook her head and dashed Dak's brief flicker of hope. "No. He was parked down that alley in a truck."

Bingo. "Did you see the color or make of the truck?"

"It was a dark color. It was night, and you can see there are no streetlights around there. And trucks look the same to me. I didn't even notice him leave, so I think he reversed and went out the other side. I looked over a little while after Beasley left alone, but he was gone."

"So you only gave the signal for Beasley?" Dak asked.

"Yeah. Beasley showed up about two hours after the guy had talked to me, and I gave him the signal, which was just a twirl. Then he was gone, so I figured Beasley was the guy he was looking for."

Dak pocketed her notebook. "Thank you, Cherry. We really appreciate your help." She handed Beasley's picture back to Weaver, who deposited it in her folder.

"See you soon, Detective Weaver," Cherry called after them.

"What's the story with you two?" Dak asked as she headed toward the alley where the killer had been parked. It was a longshot that there'd been any tire tracks—the alley was concrete—but putting the same tires at this scene would be helpful.

"It's nothing."

Dak scanned the area for CCTV but unsurprisingly, there wasn't any. Weaver could check the street cams, but Dak suspected their guy knew what he was doing and had purchased the baseball cap to hide his face. And since he'd driven there, it was unlikely he'd bought it from any of the shops along this boulevard. She walked farther up the alley, but it yielded only an assault on her nose from the number of people who'd used it for a bathroom. "Let's go. I think we're wasting our time here. I'll give you a ride back to the station, and you can tell me all about nothing."

"I want to tell you." Weaver followed Dak back onto the main street and along to her truck. "But I'm not sure how you'll react... I like working with you." She pulled open the passenger door and dropped onto the seat. "And you might not want to continue working with me when you hear the story."

Dak started the engine and turned the truck into traffic to head back to Weaver's station, trying not to imagine the worst possible scenarios between Weaver and Cherry. She wasn't about to start playing a guessing game though. "Just spit it out. If you don't tell me, someone else at your station will at some point. Wouldn't you rather be in control of your own narrative?"

Weaver let out a small laugh. "Cool way of putting it. I would like to be in control of my own narrative, yeah. Who knows what messed-up version of events you'd get from my ex-colleagues in vice."

"Does it have anything to do with why you transferred?"

"No. I told you, I always wanted to work homicide because of my father."

Weaver shifted in her seat like she couldn't get comfortable. Which she probably couldn't given the heat inside Betty's cab. Dak had to get that damn AC installed and resolved to do it that night. Roger and Nicole were leaving on Saturday, so it'd be her last chance to have some easy help. She and Ben used to spend hours on Betty while they mulled over cases. It suddenly struck her that maybe that's why she'd been avoiding doing it with anyone else. She shook her head. Just when she thought she was straight with all that emotional baggage, it smacked her upside the head to remind her Ben would never leave.

"You should just tell me." Dak pulled up at a stop sign and looked at Weaver. "All this buildup is making it seem far bigger than it probably is."

"Okay, okay." Weaver grabbed two bottles of water from the cooler and opened one before offering it to her.

She took it and half-emptied it, grateful for the ice-cold liquid's ability to compromise the infernal heat of this city. "Thanks. Stop stalling."

Weaver emptied her bottle. "I was working vice, and my partner was an asshole." Her short laugh held no humor. "I seem to get that a lot. Maybe I'm the asshole, and everyone else is okay."

"Psychology later. Story now, please. If you want to keep working with me, you need to know that I'm not a patient woman."

Weaver saluted. "Yes, ma'am. We were working Cherry's area, and he got unnecessarily physical with her."

"What did he do?" Non-specifics were of no interest to Dak. She wanted the whole story so she could make up her mind whether she would continue to work with Weaver or not.

"He was searching her for drugs, he said. But his hands were going places they shouldn't. Cherry pushed him away, and he slapped her... But he didn't stop." She swallowed hard. "Until I stopped him."

"I despise cops who abuse their power. Why on earth would you think that would make me not want to work with you?"

Weaver shrugged. "It's made a lot of cops not want to work with me."

"I can assure you that it makes no difference to me. How did you put him down?" Appearances could be deceptive for sure, but Weaver was a skinny runt, and Dak couldn't imagine she packed much of a punch.

"A combination of my fist and a Taser."

Dak laughed. "You electrocuted him?"

Weaver gestured to her body. "Look at me. What else was I gonna do?" She reached over and poked Dak's bicep. "If I was built like you, maybe one punch would've done the job, but I'm not. So I stopped him the only way I could."

"What happened to you?"

"Disciplinary hearing and a two-week suspension without pay."

Dak shook her head. She abhorred it when stations and agencies rallied to protect their own when they were clearly in the wrong. "Please tell me that he didn't get away scot-free."

"Kind of." Weaver crunched her water bottle into a ball and screwed the lid on. "I told the hearing what he'd done to make me act the way I did. He was encouraged to take early retirement... with a full pension."

Dak grunted. "You got him off the streets so he couldn't do anything like that again. That counts for something."

Weaver gave a vague acknowledgment.

"And it made Cherry very grateful, which led her to give us some great info on this case, so it's a double win." Dak concentrated on the road, suddenly aware she sounded like some motivational mentor-type.

"I guess I've never thought of it like that." Weaver gave a short laugh. "I wish I'd met you five years ago and told you that story. Would've given me some comfort when my captain kept telling me no one would work with me."

Dak shrugged. She would've thought the benefits of getting another asshole cop off the street was obvious, but maybe that was the benefit of objective distance. Weaver had been in the eye of the storm and couldn't see the positives when all she'd gotten for it was negative. "Well, I'm happy to keep working with you. And my boss might be more inclined to make it official once we've got this new sketch. The witness who saw our guy unloading an armchair at the parking lot of the bar where Evelyn Berenger worked—do you think you can track him down and show him the sketch once we've got it?"

"Shouldn't be too hard," said Weaver. "I'll be spending the next few nights around Skid Row anyway watching out for a priest luring boys into his truck."

Though there was no edge to Weaver's words, a little guilt hit Dak. But with her mom and CJ's parents still at her home, and with her promise to find the time to stay connected, she wasn't able to accompany Weaver. "Great. With our guy likely being English, I'll get a list of British nationals who traveled from the UK to LA in the three-month period running up to our first kill."

"Three months?"

"Our killer is ultra-organized," Dak said. "I don't think he'd need much more time than that to prepare for his macabre run of murders. I'm banking on him not wasting time by flying into another city or state and driving here. And since I can't find anything like these murders anywhere else in the US, I'm willing to bet that he wasn't already somewhere else in the country. It would also be one explanation as to why his DNA isn't in our system." That and the possibility that he'd simply been too clever to be caught before.

"Huh... So you're saying he came here specifically to commit these murders?"

"It's a possibility." Dak tugged her seatbelt away from her chest. CJ might not be happy that she and Roger would be installing that AC unit when she got home, but maybe the wedding planning could take place around them in the garage. "The other possibility is that there was a triggering event which set him off." She shook her head slowly, even less convinced now that she'd said it out loud for the first time. "But I don't think the usual profiling rules apply to this guy. If Keyes *was* his first victim, we're dealing with a very calm and collected individual. That was a pristine crime scene, and the other murders have been impeccable in their detail."

"Do you know what his motive is?"

Dak waited at an intersection and didn't respond for a moment. "*That* I don't know, and I don't care. There are ten chapters in *Close to Death*, and it could be that he plans to leave once he's carried them out. Right now, all I care about is finding him and stopping any more murders. When we've got him locked up, *then* I'll ask him about his motive."

Chapter Twenty-Three

DAK CUT INTO THE park and spotted Moreno's wife on a bench by the children's play area, just where she was supposed to be according to the junior agent who'd been assigned to trail her.

"Mrs. Moreno, do you remember me? I'm Special Agent Dak Farrell with the FBI. Do you mind if I sit with you for a while?" Dak didn't wait for permission. The panic racing across Mrs. Moreno's expression told Dak that the woman knew she was in trouble whichever answer she gave.

"I...uh...I don't know. That's not a good idea."

Dak motioned to the sleeping baby in the stroller. "What's the little one's name?" she asked.

"Neve. She's called Neve." Mrs. Moreno looked like she might be about to bolt.

"That's a beautiful name," Dak said. "Do you mind if I call you Sally?"

She rested her hand on the stroller, ready to leave. "I have to go. I can't be seen talking to you."

"No one's watching you, Sally." Dak smiled gently. Garrity and the surveillance team hadn't taken long to dismantle the web of lies Moreno had fed his wife and make sure Moreno's wife wasn't being tailed. Now Dak had all the information she needed to convince Sally Moreno it was time to cut him loose.

"You don't understand," Sally said, looking around frantically. "He's got his friends watching my every move. Just because you can't see them doesn't mean they're not around." She rocked the stroller, but it seemed more like it was to pacify herself than her tiny infant. "If they see you talking to me—"

"I can tell you with absolute certainty that no one's following you, Sally. Not today, and not yesterday or the day before that. I'm sorry, but your husband's been lying to you." Dak pulled out their own surveillance photos of Sally from the past couple of days. "We've been keeping an eye on you since we visited you a few days ago. No one else has been following you. If they were, our people would have known."

Sally took the photos and thumbed through them cautiously. Dak watched her expression change as she realized her husband had been feeding her an unhealthy diet of lies and deception.

"You're totally sure that none of Ike's buddies have been following me?"

Dak handed Sally another set of images from the surveillance of Moreno and the friends he'd had contact with over the last few days. "These have been taken over the same period. Do you recognize the other two men in the photographs?"

Sally nodded. "Jeff and Tony. They're his best friends. They take turns following me around. That's what Ike told me."

Dak sighed. Moreno had made the poor woman's life a complete misery. She was a prisoner in her own mind, held captive even when Moreno was nowhere near her. "These photos were taken during the day. You can see that they both work at Costco and the Home Depot. They couldn't possibly do what your husband is saying... Do you see that?" she asked when Sally stayed silent for too long.

Sally returned the photos and put her head in her hands. A quiet sob emerged, and Dak placed her hand on Sally's shoulder gently. "It's okay, Sally."

She dropped her hands and shook her head. "It's not okay. None of this is okay. But I don't know what I'm supposed to do about any of it."

"We can help." Dak let the offer sink in without adding further detail. Sally had to meet them at least halfway for this to work.

Sally shook her head. "No one can help me. I got into this mess fourteen years ago, and there's no way I can get out of it. Well…" she rubbed a fading scar on her left wrist, "there's one way, but it didn't work last time." She took hold of the stroller and rocked it again. "Now I have Neve, and I can't try that again."

"Because you're afraid of what might happen to Neve if you did leave her?" *Leave* was an all too innocuous word for committing suicide. Dak thought of all the thousands of women who died worldwide annually at the hands of their partners or their own hands because they couldn't see any way to escape. It was a deadly global pandemic that most people chose to ignore.

Sally nodded and gave Dak a small smile. "She's my world now. I have to keep surviving to try to give her the life she deserves."

"I understand that. But what about the life you deserve? Wouldn't you like to live instead of just survive?"

Sally glanced at Dak, a look of resignation turning her pretty face into a mask of sadness and endless despair. "My life doesn't matter, Agent Farrell. All that matters is her."

"A mother's love is the strongest love," Dak said. "I guess you don't really understand that fully until you become a mother."

Sally pulled her stroller closer and ran her fingers across Neve's chubby cheek. "No. You don't. You think you do, but then they put this fragile human in your arms, and you know with all your heart that you'll do everything in your power to protect her or die trying." She looked at Dak for a moment longer this time. "Do you have children?"

"No. It was never something I wanted for myself."

"I suppose it would be dangerous with your job."

"That's not it." Dak leaned back on the bench, almost certain now that Sally wouldn't bolt and that she could settle into the conversation. "I know quite a few women in the FBI who have children. It didn't stop them. I'm just not the maternal type."

Sally nodded as if she understood but didn't add anything else. With the evolution of the family concept, women who chose not to have children weren't quite the oddity they'd been historically.

"You mentioned that you'd do everything in your power to protect Neve; do you think you'll have to protect her from her own father?"

Sally's eyes darted away.

"He hurts you, doesn't he?" Dak asked softly. Pushing hard would only end with Sally walking away. "No one's watching or listening in, Sally," she said after receiving no response. "You can talk to me."

"I don't talk to anyone other than Ike, you know?" Sally half-turned toward Dak. "I'm not even allowed to talk to people in grocery stores. I don't have any friends, and he brought me to LA to get me away from my family. I let him." She hung her head and sighed deeply. "My family let him."

There was so much more to Sally's story, and she needed far more help than Dak could offer her. But getting Moreno behind bars would gift her the fresh start she so desperately needed. Dak registered the thought that her mom would never have let anything like that happen to her and more than that, she'd been determined to maintain the connection with her daughter even when Dak had continued to pull away. When her mom returned home to their business and to Ward, for the first time in a long time, Dak realized she would miss her.

"They haven't even tried to stay in touch," Sally said and began to cry again. "I was alone until Neve came along, and she's given me a reason to stay alive. Yes, Ike hurts me. And he takes what he wants when he wants it."

"I promise you, Sally, we *can* help you." Dak took a half-breath, hoping she'd laid enough groundwork for Sally to see a potential escape in their offer, and took the gamble. "And that starts with you helping us."

"What do you mean?"

Dak relaxed a little in the absence of an outright rebuke. "Do you remember the photo I showed you a few days ago?"

Sally closed her eyes. "I can't get it out of my head."

When she opened her eyes, Dak saw the accusation clearly. "I'm sorry about that. But I had to show you. I need you to know exactly what your husband is capable of."

Sally frowned. "You're telling me that Ike killed that girl. And the others?"

Her response caught Dak by surprise. How could she not suspect him after two visits from the police? "Your husband worked at both schools that all the girls attended, and you're his only alibi, Sally." Honestly, that was all they had aside from Garrity's hunch and the accusations from the friends of the murdered girls. Now that she'd had the chance to observe him, Dak was inclined to point the finger too. They just had to hope that a search of his residence would yield some actual evidence, but they needed Sally to withdraw her alibi to convince a judge to issue a warrant.

"That's all you have?"

"The friends of the murdered girls told the police that your husband made sexually charged comments." Dak saw the doubt in Sally's eyes. She was losing her. "Why would your husband ask you to lie about his whereabouts if he had nothing to hide? I've watched him interacting with the older girls, Sally; he's a predator." Dak touched Sally's arm lightly. "You know that. You have the bruises and the scars to prove it."

Sally nodded slowly, but Dak couldn't get a read on whether or not she wanted to believe that her husband was a child-killer.

"We can protect you, Sally. We can get you and Neve out of that house and away from your abusive husband forever. You can protect her from ever having to experience your husband's violent nature. You want that, don't you?"

"I do," she whispered. "But what if you don't find anything at the house? What if you can't prove he killed those girls? I'll be left with him, and he'll be even angrier than before."

"This is a horrible situation for you to be in, Sally. There's no getting away from that. If you don't say anything, you stay in that house, getting used like a punching bag and a sex slave, and all you can do is hope that you can keep him busy enough that he never turns his attention to Neve. But if you tell the truth about him not being in the house on the night of the third murder, we can look for the evidence that will put him in jail for the rest of his life."

"But you can't guarantee you'll find anything."

"Even if we didn't find anything at the house, it would only be a matter of time before we found something else. We'd be able to turn his life upside down, search all the places he might've taken those girls—"

"He uses a workshop in an industrial area," Sally blurted. "He was spending a lot of time down there. I thought he might be taking other women there, but... He's hardly been since Neve was born."

That tracked. A storage unit was a perfect place to take his victims. The right area could be desolate at night, giving Moreno ample time to play out his sick scenarios. But their investigations hadn't unearthed any buildings owned or rented by him other than his house. "You said that he uses it; he doesn't own it?"

Sally shook her head. "It belongs to Jeff, I think."

"Do you know where it is?"

"On Via Anita."

Dak pulled out her phone and searched the street name. It was a half-mile from Malaga Creek where the bodies were found. "That's really close to the site where the girls were found, Sally. That's no coincidence. And we haven't found any more victims since you gave birth to your daughter. We think he's taking a break while he gets used to being a father, but he won't be able to keep himself from murdering more girls. Killers like this don't just...*stop*."

Sally's attention turned back to Neve, and the distress in her expression was blatant.

"Maybe you'd be safe if you'd given birth to a boy, Sally. But Neve will grow up to be a beautiful young woman." Dak paused. Was Sally ready to hear this, or would it push her too far in the opposite direction? "Just like the three young women your husband has already raped and murdered."

Sally gasped and jerked upright. She took Neve from the stroller and clutched her to her chest. Neve gurgled and woke. She had her mother's eyes. The possibility that her innocence could be tainted by her father's continued presence was like a barb to Dak's brain and heart. She couldn't allow that to happen. No matter what, she had to get them away from Moreno. Inexplicably, she thought of Ice Hamilton. She seemed like the kind of woman who could make anything happen anywhere in the world if she put her mind to it. "I need to make a call. Let's get you both out of that house. Then it won't matter how long it takes us to find the evidence we need to put your husband away. You'll still be safe."

Sally's expression flushed with obvious relief. "And for all of this to happen, I just have to tell you that I lied about Ike being home? Won't I be in trouble for lying to the police?"

Dak shook her head. "There were extenuating circumstances. It's clear you feared for your life, and he forced you to tell that story. You don't have to worry about that, I promise."

Sally cupped the back of Neve's head and lowered her away from her chest. She stared into her tiny face for what seemed like an age. Neve's cherubic chubby cheeks and bright eyes made it impossible for even the most hard-hearted person not to want to do anything they could to protect her; Dak couldn't imagine the effect that face had on Sally, whose job it was to do exactly that.

"If you can get me out of that house today, I'll tell the police the truth." Sally kissed Neve's forehead. "And I'll tell them everything about what he's done to me for the past fourteen years too."

Dak nodded and smiled, her admiration for Sally growing. Moreno's days of freedom were numbered. "Wait here while I make that call."

Sally nodded and sat back on the bench with Neve in her arms. Dak walked far enough away to be out of earshot but still close enough that she could see Sally was safe, then she made the call.

"Agent Farrell," Ice said after answering on the sixth ring. "What do you need?"

Despite the initial tension of their first meeting, Dak had decided Ice was probably someone she could get to like. Her straight-to-business attitude right now only added to that impression. "You said I could call you if I needed anything. I've got a feeling you're not one of those people who says something like that without really meaning it."

"I'm not. What do you need?"

The repetition of the question came with more than a hint of impatience and reinforced Dak's sense that Ice was someone you didn't mess around with. "I've got an abused wife and her baby daughter who need to disappear from a child-killing husband. New life, new location. The whole deal. Can you help?"

"Fuck, yeah. I'll text you the details of a hotel in a few minutes. Take them there, and I'll handle the rest. Do you need me to take care of the husband too?"

"As tempting as that offer is, no." Dak glanced back at Sally. She would probably like Ice's way of taking care of her husband, and it shed a little more light on the type of person Ice was too. "I'm pretty sure we'll find what we need to put him away once we get a warrant."

Ice grumbled. "If you change your mind, you know how to get hold of me."

"So this wasn't a one-time-only favor?" Dak asked. Not that she'd be asking Ice to kill anyone, but there might be other ways she could help in the future.

"No. You saved my brother's life. Within reason, you can light up the bat signal until I leave this mortal fucking coil."

Dak laughed, weirdly comforted by the offer. "So you are the superhero I pegged you for."

"Like I said, I've been called that before. Check your messages." Ice hung up.

Dak walked back toward Sally while she opened her messages. The coordinates for a high-end hotel in West Hollywood and the name for Sally to use at check-in were already there, along with instructions to wait there until Ice arrived. She was certainly efficient. Dak hadn't heard from Hamilton since Dak's assessment. When he called next, she'd be grilling him about his elusive and lethal sister. "Everything's arranged."

Sally looked incredulous. "One phone call is all it took?"

"It helps to have friends in the right places," Dak said. "I'll drive you to the hotel where my contact will meet us."

Sally tilted her head and blew out a long breath. "It's really that easy?"

Dak nodded. "It normally isn't, but I've pulled in a favor." She gestured toward Neve. "You and the little one deserve a fresh start, and Moreno should spend the rest of his life in a maximum-security prison. Do you need anything from the house?"

"Is that possible?" Sally looked at her watch. "Ike will be home in three hours."

Dak held out her hand to help Sally up from the bench. "He won't be coming home that soon. I'll make another call, and the LAPD will pick him up for more questioning while we arrange a warrant."

Sally smiled broadly for the first time, and Dak could see that she was already tentatively envisioning a future without her bastard husband. It would take time and years of therapy to truly recover from the horror she'd endured too long, but now she had that chance, and her daughter had the opportunity to grow up free of the same tyranny.

And Dak could put this case to bed so she could fully concentrate her efforts on the copycat killer running around the city before he completed his chapters and disappeared as mysteriously as he'd arrived.

Chapter Twenty-Four

CHARNWOOD HAD ASKED QUESTIONS Dak couldn't answer, something she was unfamiliar and uncomfortable with. No, she had no idea where Ice had taken Sally after she'd picked her up from the hotel as promised. No, she had no way of contacting Sally directly. No, she hadn't considered protocol when she'd made the call to another government operative. And no, she couldn't give Charnwood the operative's name. Dak had even been liberally creative with how she knew Ice and for how long, but she'd assured him that Sally would provide a statement and testify at the murder trial Dak was certain would happen. If Moreno turned out to be the Rodeo Killer though, there was even more uncertainty around Special Agent Kimbal's death, and Charnwood seemed particularly unhappy about that prospect.

Nevertheless, he'd given her two teams. Headed by Garrity, one was currently positioned around Moreno's home, and the second was with her at Moreno's industrial unit. They'd had to work fast, getting Sally out of the house with everything she needed while the LAPD picked Moreno up and questioned him. Dak wanted to get inside both properties before he had any time to clear out evidence or cover his tracks, and hopefully they'd find something before the LAPD released him. She had no idea how spooked he might be by their recent visit and his questioning, and she had to wonder if he'd simply run for the border.

She gave the order for both teams to breach simultaneously and stood in front of the ten-foot-wide corrugated steel shutter door while three agents used car jacks to raise it enough for a fourth one to roll beneath it and operate the access panel. The security system sounded for thirty seconds while the agent disarmed it, then the door shuddered noisily upward. Dak smoothed down her latex gloves and took a deep breath to calm her racing heart before she stepped inside with four other agents and five CSU cops, all briefed to tear the place apart—carefully.

It was unclear what the unit was supposed to be set up for. There was a workbench along one wall, with only a few tools scattered across it. At some point, it could've been used as a repair shop if the deep pit around five feet wide by fifteen feet long was any indicator. She looked over the edge and couldn't define whether she was relieved or disappointed that it was only five feet deep. Out here in the middle of the night, Moreno probably hadn't worried about his victims escaping and didn't need to deepen his pit into an oubliette. Small mercy for the young women, but what other horrors had they been subjected to in this space?

She ran her hand over the work surface and months of dust stuck to her latex-covered fingertips, lending credence to her theory that he'd been on a slaughter sabbatical since Sally had given birth to little Neve. They could only hope that he hadn't destroyed all evidence of his crimes in this place. She had to find *something* to link him to those murdered girls.

The concrete floor and walls had been painted black, lending an eerie feel to the unit and making any blood harder to see. It was obvious he'd cleaned the area; the smell of bleach was faint but still pervaded the air, hanging around in the nooks and crannies of the faux leather couch that was pushed against another wall and in the tiny cracks scattered across the ground. But Moreno hadn't counted on the new handheld infra-red camera that was capable of seeing tiny traces of blood undetectable by the naked eye. The FBI were trialing it at three field offices across the country, and Dak had theirs in the backpack slung over her shoulder.

Dak returned to the inspection pit and shone her flashlight into its depths. Light bounced off a shard of metal in the far corner. As she climbed down the ladder to get a closer look, the stench of bleach strengthened. With her Maglite beam focused ahead, she neared the wall farthest from her, and nausea bubbled in her stomach. *Those* weren't anything to do with car repairs.

Five rings in the wall. One in each corner of the concrete and one in the center about four feet from the base—neck height for the average teenage girl. This was where he'd beaten them with a bullwhip. She remembered his words when they'd met: *"I ain't seen anything on the news about any more prick-teasing jailbait being found dead."* He thought the girls deserved to die. He was punishing them for their burgeoning sexuality, for tempting him. Merely for existing. She swallowed hard and scanned the area for blood. Nothing. So she swung her backpack around and retrieved the infra-red camera. Setup was remarkably quick. Dak got on her hands and knees close to the end wall and rested the monitor on its built-in stand. She turned her flashlight off and trained the camera on the long wall to her left. Moreno was right-handed, so the impact of his whip would result in blood in the opposite corner where she was focusing.

The porous blackened concrete reflected the infra-red rays and appeared almost white on the miniature monitor. But scattered across the hardened surface were darker spots and smeared patches. *Blood*, absorbing the infra-red light and thus appearing darker. Dak quelled the resulting rush of finding the potential evidence to tie the murdered girls to Moreno. At some point, this place had been a workshop of sorts, and the blood splatter could be from a work-related injury. Though every instinct she had told her the DNA would be a match to at least one of the teens.

"O'Reilly, can you come over here?" Dak waited until the CSU forensics expert peered into the pit, then she gestured toward the potential evidence she'd discovered. "I'm going to need you to come down here."

"That is a neat piece of equipment." O'Reilly climbed down and took the camera from Dak's grasp. "Any chance you can leave this with me?" she asked.

"With how impressively this performs, I don't think it'll be long before every force and government agency in the country has one." Dak gestured to the walls. "You're welcome to give it a test run so you can collect blood samples that will nail this creep."

O'Reilly looked happy enough with that and flashed the camera farther down the left wall. She sucked her breath through her teeth and shook her head as she studied the monitor. "See how the blood traces continue to about eight feet?"

"Yeah." Dak had seen enough crime scenes to know what that meant.

"Son of a bitch must've used a lot of force for the splatter to be that far back." She handed Dak the camera and shrugged her equipment bag from her shoulder. "Do you mind focusing it over there?" O'Reilly gestured toward the corner where the trail began.

"No problem." Dak moved around O'Reilly as she spread her gear on the ground, but what she should really be doing was searching the rest of the unit. What else would they find here to prove Moreno had killed those girls? "It's going to take a while to get individual samples from all the different areas along the wall, isn't it?"

O'Reilly looked up and rolled her eyes. "Beckett!"

Her shout echoed around the pit, and it wasn't long before a bright-eyed CSU cop approached the edge of the concrete hole.

"Yes, ma'am?"

O'Reilly waved him down impatiently. "I need you down here to hold this fancy-pants camera while I collect blood samples."

The young cop frowned. "There's blood down there?"

O'Reilly pulled a bottle from the array of her gear on the floor and sprayed a section of wall closest to her. The blood spatter showed up in bright luminescent patterns before fading. "Blood." She gestured to the monitor showing another area where Dak had the camera pointed. "More blood." Then she pointed to the ladders. "Now get down here."

"Yes, ma'am. Sorry, ma'am."

"Stop with the ma'am. You're making me feel old."

Dak handed the camera to him when he'd climbed down. "Be very careful. There are only three of these in the country, and they're worth more than our annual salaries combined."

He nodded. "Yes, ma—"

O'Reilly coughed.

"Yes, Special Agent Farrell. I'll be super careful."

Dak suppressed a smile. "I'll be back to get that, so don't disappear with it, O'Reilly."

She clasped her hand to her chest. "Would I?"

Dak hadn't met O'Reilly before today, but she liked her already. A little slice of humor could provide welcome relief from the heavy burden of a raid like this. When Dak looked back into the pit after climbing out, O'Reilly had moved to the first area of blood and was spraying saline on it. The young cop stood to attention, the knuckles on both his hands white from how hard he clasped the camera. Dak watched O'Reilly work for a moment, impressed with the reverent way she swabbed the individual blood spot before wrapping it in brown paper and labeling it.

"Jackpot, Farrell."

Garrity's voice over her radio startled her from concentrating on O'Reilly. "What've you got?"

"Three items of jewelry matching the parents' description of gifts to the three girls," Garrity said.

The news lifted some of the weight of expectation from her chest. "We've got the bastard," she said. "Anything else over there?"

"The basement is decked out like a dungeon," he said. "There's a whole rack of different whips on the inside of a closet door."

"Bullwhip?"

"Afraid not, but there's an empty hook with a space large enough for a coiled bullwhip. And there are some seriously nasty-looking restraints too. Sharp barbs on the inside of them. It's little wonder his wife was desperate to escape. Hard to imagine anyone wanting to be on the receiving end of any of that."

Dak thought of the various fleeting experiences she'd had with women into that kind of kink. "I think you'd be surprised, but it's safe to say Sally Moreno didn't want any part of that sexual proclivity."

His wife certainly couldn't be blamed for any correlation between her not wanting non-consensual SM sex and Moreno mutilating and murdering those girls. He clearly had no respect for any woman's life and abusing them, no matter their age, was something he would've done regardless.

"Yeah, well, I'm glad she and the baby are out of here," Garrity said. "Anything on your end yet?"

She glanced down at the far wall where she suspected the young girls had been secured and clenched her jaw. "We've found rings on a wall that could've been used to immobilize his victims, and there's quite a bit of blood around the area even though he obviously tried to destroy the evidence."

"DNA evidence and the girl's jewelry. That's a good afternoon's work, Farrell."

She allowed herself a small smile. "Thanks to your instincts."

He grunted, sounding uncomfortable with the praise. "The CSU guys are working on the basement now. The jewelry was stowed in a box hidden under the basement stairs, so we're hoping his fingerprints will be all over it. Could be they'll find some trace evidence from the girls there too, but I don't think he brought any of them here."

Dak shook her head. "He wouldn't need to. That'd be a risk he was too smart to take."

"Huh. But he wasn't smart enough to *not* follow the cliché of almost every serial killer by keeping sick little souvenirs."

As murderous mementoes went, necklaces and earrings were probably the least sick ones she'd come across. Tugged out fingernails and forcefully extracted incisors were just a few she could mention that better fit Garrity's description. But he was right, and she knew it was a compulsion to keep mementos, even though their macabre collector's items were often key evidence in convicting them. "Lucky us," Dak said, though to talk about luck in a situation like this seemed both distasteful and disrespectful to the young girls, who'd been anything but lucky. "Keep me posted; I need to see what else we can find here."

She ended the call and looked back into the pit where O'Reilly was still painstakingly taking evidence from the wall and Beckett stood like a Venetian statue. The stacks of brown paper bags were already numerous and neatly piled. If this was Moreno's kill site, the blood samples were likely to be mixed up. Chromatography would be able to identify different blood types, but they'd have to order detailed DNA analysis to find out how many individuals' blood it was. That would take time, so she was glad Garrity had found the jewelry; that'd be more than enough to hold him on suspicion of the murders while they waited for those results. Finding the bullwhip he used to beat and strangle them with was the missing piece of this pervert's puzzle.

He'd kept the trinkets close to him so he could revisit his kills even while he was on a baby-imposed break. Dak was convinced that there was no way he'd dispose of his favorite toy. If he hadn't stashed it at home, then it had to be here, didn't it?

"Farrell?"

Dak turned in the direction of the voice and saw two agents in front of an open safe, one of whom waved her over.

"It took us a while to get it open, but it was worth it."

The other agent stepped aside so that Dak could squat down and investigate. Resting like some fine antiquity on purple cushioning was a coiled bullwhip. "Great work." She stood and patted the other agent on the back. They had everything they needed to build a solid case against Moreno, his wife was safe, and the victims' families would get justice.

Her work here was done, and Charnwood would be pacified, though they'd still need to solve Kimbal's murder. In the meantime, she could direct all her energy toward finding this damn copycat killer before anyone else died. *I'm coming for you, asshole.*

Chapter Twenty-Five

GOOD PREPARATION IS KEY to any successful endeavor. Research is also essential. Such happy coincidence that I enjoy both of these things equally. As I was planning this series of experiments, I ran through the various murderers within the book to ensure they were replicable. One of the serial killers coming up soon is Robert Berdella, and I'd already identified that his methods pose a particular problem; he was known for keeping his male victims alive in order to torture and rape them for up to six weeks. Thus far, I've had limited contact with the people I've sacrificed in the name of science, and a few hours with Keyes was the longest time I spent in anyone's company. But replicating Robert's modus operandi would involve prolonged exposure to their screams and pleas for mercy. Will I be moved by their desire to live, or will I have absorbed and cultivated the necessary detachment not to care? The problem might derive from the fact that I don't care much for the next person I've chosen anyway. I won't have empathy for their continued existence, situation, or family... But I wouldn't actively want them dead, I don't believe, which is a crucial difference. Although killing Beasley was strangely satisfying and...warming. It didn't arouse me, but I can't deny that my endorphins ran riot for several hours after I'd discharged my weapon nine times into his face, chest, and stomach.

Moreover, I don't have that kind of time to waste. I have a schedule to keep to, a set of subjects to dispatch, and my flight home is already booked. I'd come to the conclusion before I set foot on the plane to come to this land of options that I would follow through with Robert's MO but only for two days. I believe that's more than long enough to get a taste for his method and to satisfy the parameters of my experiment. While I'm fully committed to the cause, my priority must be to remain off the police radar and very much away from the FBI and their pesky serial killer unit. I hear they have quite talented individuals on their team, and I am a team of only one. I can't possibly risk keeping a victim alive for nearly a week lest I raise suspicion around the neighborhood. Not being able to complete my investigation would be a criminal, crying shame, and the scientific community would miss out on a potentially huge discovery. Imagine the savings to governments across the globe if my experiment shows that you can unmake a murderer just as easily as you can create one.

Another killer within my source text poses a problem in an entirely different manner. When I read in more detail about the Son of Sam, aka David Berkowitz, it offended my sensibilities almost too much to include him in my study. Did you know that he tried to blame a *dog* for his murderous mayhem? A dog possessed by a demon, no less. After that, he claimed he was part of a Satanic cult and the killings were his sacrifices. And then that the love of a good woman would have saved him from committing any murders at all. Utter nonsense. Own your perversion, man. This was one murderer I was not inclined to correspond with. I mean, once you're caught, especially nowadays with all this DNA evidence, CCTV, and the cell phone towers pinging your location every three seconds, you have to accept that you're pretty much buggered, and the game is up. Of course, none of that was the case back then, so he gave it a go but to no avail. So few of the states pursue the death penalty anymore, how hard can prison be? Surely not hard enough to compromise one's self-respect by claiming an animal has been controlling you. Though I have no desire to test that particular hypothesis. Jail holds no appeal at all. I expect that my size and build would afford me some protection, certainly more than might be warranted for Beasley, that tiny little excuse for a man.

Jason Beasley. He's still my favorite kill. Wait... My *favorite* kill. When did this change happen? When did I begin to rank the murders, much less have a favorite which implies a certain enjoyment of my adventures? Think... Young Evelyn. No, I didn't enjoy that. None of it. Keyes? Besting a man of his size was a challenge, yes, but did I enjoy it and revel in my overcoming him? Perhaps. Why has this development only just come to my attention? Perhaps this is it: the beginning of the slide into becoming an *actual* murderer. I'm about to embark on the adventure of my fourth subject, not even halfway through my source text, and this little nugget has rather taken me by surprise.

Should I be concerned that this evolution passed me by? Would you be? If you are, and you're inclined to embark on your own scientific slaughter, take heed and modify your own methodology accordingly. But no. I'm not worried. This is simply a realization that I shall note and monitor. Since my next subject is rather distasteful, it will be interesting to see if that hinders this evolution somewhat. I maintain that my superior intellect will remain in control of any baser drives modified by this succession of murders. Can you say the same?

Chapter Twenty-Six

Dak ended the call and turned to kiss a sleepy CJ. "I'm sorry, baby, I have to go."

"What time is it?"

"Nearly three a.m." Dak slipped out of bed and quickly got dressed. She pulled on her shoes as CJ wrapped her arms around her waist.

"Does it have to be you?"

Dak tied her shoes then wriggled out from CJ's grasp. She knelt on the floor and took CJ's face in her hands. "It's my case. Of course it has to be me."

CJ stuck out her bottom lip before pulling Dak in for another kiss. "Fine. Will you be back before I have to go to my big 'Come to Jesus' meeting?"

Shit. Dak had completely forgotten CJ and her agent were meeting with Netflix to talk about floating a replacement show after her current season of *Dead Pretty*. She hadn't promised to go with CJ, but she did want to be supportive and drive her there. "I honestly don't know. Weaver's tailing the guy, and she's called for backup. If it goes down smoothly..."

Even if it did, Dak wanted to be in the room interrogating the guy first. There was no way she could get back unless Weaver had it wrong, and all she'd witnessed was a genuine Good Samaritan offering a homeless kid a roof over his head for the night. And she didn't want to start lying to CJ, making promises she couldn't keep. She gently tucked some stray hair over CJ's ear and kissed her deeply, ever conscious that any goodbye could be their final one. "I can't see me getting back in time, baby."

CJ frowned and flopped her head back onto the pillow. "I understand. I can drive myself. No big deal."

Dak pulled the sheet over CJ's body then stroked the curve of her breast firmly. "I'll make it up to you."

"I'll hold you to that. We still haven't christened the pool table," CJ murmured and gave her a wicked grin.

Dak swallowed hard. "That's evil."

CJ shook her head. "That's motivation to come home to me safely." She gave Dak a light shove. "Go. Catch the bad guys."

They kissed one last time before Dak dragged herself away and headed out. She retrieved her gun from the safe in their office and jumped in her truck. When she switched the engine on, the cold air from the newly installed AC blasted her face, and she shivered before turning it down. No one could complain about Betty now, unless they were in a high-speed chase. She headed in the general direction of Venice Boulevard with her emergency light mounted and figured she'd join Weaver in whatever vehicle she was driving to follow their potential killer. She'd been on the road five minutes when Weaver called.

"I'm trailing him on La Cienega Boulevard. Could be that he's heading to Kenneth Hahn State Park. I've just crossed West Adams."

"Dispatch has your location?" Dak was still seven miles from the park, and she didn't want Weaver tackling this guy on her own. She floored the accelerator and ran the red light at Santa Monica Boulevard.

"Yeah, they can track my car, but I don't know how long it's going to take them to get to me."

Dak heard the slight fear in Weaver's voice. "If he leads you to the park, stay back and out of sight. Do *not* approach him before backup gets there."

"But what about the kid? He looks about twelve."

"If this is our guy, he's got plans, remember? This isn't a quick thrill kill for him." The case files she'd read on Garavito flooded back, and she pushed down the nausea with a deep inhalation. "He's in no rush, so you don't need to be either. Are you hearing me?" Dak didn't want Weaver playing hero cop, causing the whole scenario to go to hell in a blaze of bullets.

Weaver grumbled. "I hear you... How far away are you? I'm coming up to Obama Boulevard."

Perfect. Dak would be turning right there shortly. "I'm on South La Brea. Do you think the park is still his destination?"

"Yeah—uh, wait... He's pulled in at McDonald's just after Obama."

"That's great. Pull over as soon as you can. I'm almost with you." Whether the guy was buying a last meal for his victim or had just stopped to grab food for himself, Dak didn't care. Whatever his motivation, it gave her and the backup team more time to catch up with Weaver.

"Okay. I'm swinging in to the parking lot at See's Candies. I'll call dispatch so they can let the backup unit know to wait on West Jefferson."

Dak pushed Betty to her limit then took a right onto Obama before turning onto La Brea. She glanced at the McDonald's drive-through as she passed and saw the white truck Weaver had told her the homeless kid had gotten into, but she didn't slow down to look in case it spooked the perp. At See's Candies, Dak pulled alongside a battered maroon Taurus, the only car in the lot. She got out of her truck and opened the passenger door of Weaver's car to get in.

"Good choice for undercover work," Dak said as she slid into the seat beside Weaver.

Weaver frowned. "You think Miller gave me access to the carpool? This is my vehicle, Agent Farrell."

"Still, it works well." Dak could tell from Weaver's expression that she'd offended her slightly, but she didn't have the time or the inclination to pander to Weaver's ego right now. "Did you get a good look at the driver?" she asked.

"Nope. He pulled up in front of a group of young homeless kids, all male, and I was parked too far back to see into the cab. Even when the kid got in, the interior light didn't function. All I could see was the bulk of the guy in the driver's seat."

Dak shifted to the edge of her seat so she had line of sight to the McDonald's exit. "You couldn't have seen whether or not he was dressed as a priest then?"

Weaver shook her head. "But I could see the hesitancy in the kids. It was clear that none of them knew him. It took him a while to get one of them in the truck, and that was only after he handed something to one of them."

"Cash?"

"I think so. I was parked so I could take in the whole length of the homeless camp. It was shit luck that he chose a group of kids that weren't close to me." She glanced at Dak and looked guilty. "I had to keep a low profile."

"Hey, it's okay. You did great." The truck Dak had driven past was one of the models that used the tires they'd matched to two crime scenes, the timing worked for the abduction, fitting in with the schedule their unsub seemed to have set, and it looked like he was driving to the outskirts of town. That was enough to get Dak out of bed at three a.m. "You say the kid was young?"

"Yeah. Twelve or thirteen maybe. He seemed to be the oldest of the group the guy approached. He came from the south side and stopped at the first gang of young kids along the boulevard."

Dak strained her neck so she could see the back end of the truck. "He didn't cruise up and down the boulevard?" she asked.

"No. Why? You think that's important?"

Dak shrugged. "Maybe not. Our unsub is copying the MO of other killers, and I guess Garavito couldn't have taken much time to choose his victims given how many he went through. And it could be that he'd already scoped this area out as part of his research."

"Because he's such an organized killer?"

"Yeah." Dak gestured up the street. "He's on the move. Let's go."

Weaver started her engine and pulled out. There were enough other cars on the road to not arouse suspicion if the killer bothered to check his mirrors, but Dak noted that Weaver still stayed a solid distance behind the truck. It was a good sign. She'd had quite the baptism of fire since joining the homicide squad, but she was showing no signs of being overeager, something which could lead to mistakes.

"Dispatch said the unit was only a few minutes away." Weaver glanced in the rear-view then nodded. "I think that's our guys who just pulled in behind us."

Sure enough, the car radio crackled into action. "Morning, Detective Weaver. I'm Officer Deighton, and I've got Officer Acker with me. They said you got a possible kidnapping. Is that right?"

Dak picked up the comms. "Thanks for joining us, officers. I'm Special Agent Farrell," she said and gave them the bare details.

"You think he's going to do all of that at the park?" one of them asked.

Dak registered the clear disgust in his tone and hoped it wouldn't translate to him doing something stupid when it came time to move in. "I do. And he's got nearly two hundred hectares to do it in." Up ahead, the truck took the exit to Kenneth Hahn. "Looks like you were right," she said to Weaver.

"Do we know if he's armed?" Deighton asked.

"If it's who we suspect it is, the minimum he'll be carrying is a butcher's knife and razor blades. There's no evidence that Garavito ever carried a gun, but we shouldn't rule out the possibility that this guy might."

The truck took the left to the park, and Weaver slowed down considerably. Dak nodded for her to continue, and she followed the truck even farther behind than before. Another car overtook them, came up on the truck, and then zoomed past it. Dak hoped it wouldn't concern their killer, and if it didn't, all the better for their tail.

The truck didn't speed up or slow, indicating the other car

hadn't affected the killer's course of action.

"Okay. How do you want to play this?" Deighton asked after the truck pulled into the lot at the visitor center.

"Drive beyond him and pull in behind us where we stop." Dak made the bet that the killer had decided to break into the building for some privacy and a little soundproofing, which afforded them some time to circle back on foot. He'd likely already bound the boy and would leave him in the truck while he accessed the center and disarmed the security system.

"Yes, ma'am."

"Keep your eyes forward," Dak said. "Do not look his way at all." After they'd gone beyond the parking lot, Dak motioned to a spot for Weaver to pull in. The unmarked radar car parked behind them, and the two officers got out, their hands already on the hilts of their guns. "I want this guy alive, so do *not* shoot unless he draws a weapon and you feel unsafe, do you understand me?"

"Yes, ma'am," both of them said and released their grips on their weapons.

"Deighton, come with me around the left. Acker, go with Weaver around the right. Approach quietly and watch the windows. We don't want him seeing us before we want him to. Understood?" She waited until everyone had acknowledged her order. "When we can see where our guy is, we'll decide our plan of attack."

The four of them converged on the rear of the building quietly. She'd heard no sign of forced entry, and the alarm system hadn't tripped. Dak hoped they could get to him before he went back to the truck to get the kid. She held up her hand to halt Deighton behind her when she heard the slam of the truck door. Holding her breath, she peered around the corner of the visitor center and saw the boy being half-dragged toward its entrance by a guy over six foot. She couldn't see anything in his free hand but didn't dismiss the possibility that he might have a gun in the waistband of his jeans.

"Go, go, go," she called and emerged from the darkness with her weapon aimed at the older guy's head. "Release the kid and put your hands in the air. NOW."

"You're surrounded, so don't do anything stupid," Weaver shouted.

The guy swiveled his head right to left, from Dak to Weaver, then pulled the kid close to his chest. "What's happening?"

She didn't let the absence of a British accent bother her. He could've been practicing hard between kills. "Nothing bad if you let the kid go and put your hands up. Don't make me say it again." Dak edged closer, keeping her gun leveled at his head and watching for any sudden movement.

"I'm not doing anything wrong," he said. "I'm just feeding him and giving him a place to sleep for the night."

"Yeah? Then why does he look so scared?" Weaver asked and moved closer with her weapon focused on their guy.

"Tell them you're fine." He gave the kid a shake.

The kid looked up at him and then toward Dak. "Please help me."

"Don't make this any harder than it has to be," Dak said, continuing her advance. She didn't want to shoot, but she had a clear shot at his head since he towered over the kid, and the boy's safety was her primary concern. Even though the guy didn't look much like Cherry's sketch, she had to know for sure if he was her copycat killer.

The guy raised his left hand in the air. "Okay. Okay." He pushed the kid away from him and lifted his other arm in surrender.

The kid ran in the opposite direction to all of them.

"Deighton, go after the boy. We need him," Dak said over her shoulder without taking her eyes off the guy.

Deighton took off without a word, leaving Dak hoping that he was in good enough shape to run down a scared kid. Weaver and Acker had advanced at a similar pace, and they were both within touching distance of the perp.

"Turn around slowly," Dak said, and he did exactly that. "Weaver. Cuff him."

Weaver secured him in an impressively short time before she pushed him toward his truck and pressed his face onto the hood as she recited his rights.

"Acker, get your car and go after the kid and your partner. We're good here," Dak said. "Come back as soon as you have him."

"Yes, ma'am." Acker raced back behind the building, leaving her and Weaver alone with their killer.

Weaver patted him down. "No weapons or wallet, Agent Farrell. Just a credit card in the name of John Smith and a bunch of keys plus his truck key."

He wasn't in a monk's or a priest's outfit, but Dak noted the crucifix hanging on the rear-view mirror. "Make sure the truck's locked. We'll walk him back to your car and maybe CSU will be here before we leave."

Weaver tugged him upright, and they headed back to her Taurus. Dak resisted the strong temptation to question him. They'd deposit him in an interrogation room and leave him to stew while they found out as much about him as they could. The credit card was probably in a fake name, but maybe the truck was registered and could give them more information. If he was here temporarily from England, the truck could also be a dead end, but they'd be able to match the tires from the Keyes and Beasley crime scenes and see if there was any residue in the treads that could link the truck to either location. And now that they had him in custody, they could check his DNA against the sample from the empty house across from the Keyes' house.

Dak opened the back door of the Taurus, and Weaver shoved him in none too gently, though she did place her hand on top of his head before she slammed the door. In the back of her car, he looked like a giant in a kid's toy.

"Is this our guy?" Weaver asked quietly.

"I hope so." She stepped back to observe him, but he gave her nothing, staying completely still with his eyes fixed ahead intently.

"Cherry said he had a bad Texan accent. This guy sounds local."

Dak shook her head. "That may not mean anything. He was taking a risk talking to those women, so maybe he deliberately sounded strange to put us off the scent."

"And he doesn't much look like the sketch Cherry worked up either."

"People can get confused. It'd been a while since Cherry had seen the guy," Dak said, but she was already doubting too. She'd hoped that the banknotes Cherry provided would lead somewhere, but it had proved impossible to tell where the money had originated, and it was taking hours and hours to work through the list of British nationals who'd come through LAX. She shrugged and walked around to the passenger side. "We don't know if he's using his real accent even now. We'll put him in a lineup and see if Cherry can identify him as the guy she spoke to. Can you arrange that?"

"She won't like it."

"I'm sure she'll do it for you. In the meantime, let's head back to the building and make sure it's secure, then call dispatch to see how far away CSU is," Dak said. "When we're done with them, we'll need to pick up my truck, and I'll follow you back to the station." She was about to get in the car when Acker and Deighton's vehicle came into view, headlamps flashing.

He pulled up beside them and rolled down the window. "We've got him."

She let out a breath when she saw the kid in the backseat. "You haven't cuffed him, have you?" Dak asked.

"We had to." Acker gestured toward Deighton, who looked a little flushed and somehow pale at the same time. "The little shit kicked Deighton in the nuts."

Dak understood the kid's reluctance to come quietly. His interactions with the police probably hadn't been all that positive in his short life. And given that he'd gotten into the guy's truck semi-willingly, he'd likely done some awful things he didn't want to just to eat, some of which he might've been caught for already. It sickened her that his desire to survive tonight could've led to a painful and tortured death.

"Let's swap." Dak yanked open the back door and pulled their guy out again.

Without having to be asked, Weaver retrieved the boy from Acker's car and turned him around so Acker could release his wrists. "Please don't run again. No one's going to hurt you," she said.

Her gentle approach impressed Dak; Weaver was well on her way to being a detective any law enforcement agency would be proud of. The kid nodded but still looked scared out of his mind. No surprise there. He'd just escaped the clutches of an evil murderer and had four guns pointed his way.

When they'd completed the switch and gotten back in the car, Dak turned to the kid. "How're you doing?"

His wide eyes and trembling body made her question redundant, but she asked just the same. She needed to get him to relax so he'd open up and tell them everything he could about the guy who'd picked him up. He didn't need to know what had likely been planned for him. It was bad enough that he'd probably been convinced to exchange sexual favors for what he thought would be food and a roof for the night.

"You know you're not in trouble, don't you?" she asked as Weaver started the car and began to head around to the front of the visitor center. "You haven't done anything wrong, and we're only interested in the guy who picked you up, okay?" she asked when he remained quiet.

Weaver pulled up in front of the main entrance and jumped out with the guy's keys in her hand.

"We'll take you to the station to get a statement. That's all we need." Still nothing verbal, but he bit his lip as if he might be deciding whether to trust her word. "I'm sorry this happened to you, kid."

"I'm not a kid," he said. "I'm thirteen in December."

She laughed lightly at the defiance in his voice. Like him, she'd been eager to grow up faster than biology allowed, but this kid was mostly likely motivated by the need to look after himself physically. The streets were a rough place to grow up, and kids couldn't do it fast enough. Youth equaled vulnerability and exploitation. "Sorry." She held up her hands. "I'm sorry this happened to you, young man."

He jutted his chin in apparent approval. "I'm just trying to get by, y'know?"

Dak nodded. She didn't know. She *couldn't* know. Her family had always been there, and she had no idea what this kid's story was.

Weaver got back in the car. "Our guy must work there or know someone that does. These keys are for that building."

Dak checked her watch and the board with the center's operating hours. "I imagine it'll be another three hours before anyone will be here to open up. CSU needs to check the building in case he's used it for any other murders. But if he does work here, we'll be able to find out who the hell he is soon enough."

Weaver was about to set off for the station when a CSU van came into view. "I'll deal with that," she said and got back out of the car.

Dak turned her attention back to the youth in the rear seat. "Detective Weaver said that you were with a group of younger kids..."

"She saw me get in the truck?" He pressed himself against the back of the seat, retreating.

"Relax. It's okay. People like that guy are very persuasive. They offer all kinds of things to reel you in. I promise, you're not in any trouble. She said you looked like the oldest one. You were just looking after them, right?"

He nodded but added nothing else.

His caution was understandable. The LAPD had a reputation for being cruel and pistol-happy toward the growing homeless population even though there were hundreds of good cops too.

"He said I didn't have to do anything I didn't want to."

Low-level rage vibrated under Dak's skin. She'd had plenty of exposure to this kind of crime, so she was able to control the instinct to severely beat the guy. Hopefully, Weaver could do the same. Power was in flux in any interrogation room, and if a cop unleashed their temper, the perp won.

"How about we talk about something else?" Dak asked. She'd managed to strike a tentative rapport with the kid and that would be enough to get his statement at the station. She didn't want to put him through it twice, so it was best to change the subject now and engage in something that interested him.

They were talking basketball when Weaver got back in the car. Her nod indicated everything was as it should be with the CSU team. Dak was torn between staying to see what was hidden in the guy's truck and getting to the station to determine whether the guy in the back of Acker and Deighton's car was the killer she was pursuing. A quick glance at the terrified kid in the backseat put a stop to her indecision. She and Weaver would get his statement and then they'd have to call Child Protective Services. She tried not to think about what the rest of the kid's life looked like. Would he escape Skid Row? Would he end up selling himself for as long as perverts like the one they'd just caught would pay for him? Would drugs be his escape and his anchor to this desperate existence?

She couldn't know, and she couldn't do a thing about it. Objectivity and distance were states of being that agents talked about a lot, and it had always been easy enough for Dak to show empathy without getting personally involved or emotionally invested...with adult victims. But kids? That was a whole different prospect, and one she hadn't been exposed to enough to have navigated satisfactorily. Multiple scenarios ran through her mind: not-for-profits who provided shelters; adoption agencies; maybe even Ice could help. This seemed like a job for a superhero.

Dak let out a slow, meditative breath and tamped down the swirling mist of despair at the kid's situation. He was alive. At least they'd managed to save him...this time. But there were always predators lurking in the darkest shadows. She pushed the tornado of thoughts away and refocused her concentration. She was hunting those predators down, one at a time, and they'd just gotten another one. *That's* what she should be thinking about.

But was this the guy she was looking for?

Chapter Twenty-Seven

CJ THREW BACK THE sheet and cast a quick glance at Dak's side of the bed. Empty again. How was it possible to feel this alone even though she was living with the woman who'd soon be her wife? She sighed and pushed up from the bed. Before Dak had gone back to active duty, getting out of this bed had been damn near impossible. Their mutually high sex drive overrode all sense of time and responsibility, and with CJ's TV series still in its planning stages, her work hadn't suffered.

She showered and focused on convincing herself that relationships seldom met expectations, and she acknowledged her own had been unrealistic. The routine and life they'd shifted into didn't involve enough time together, but when was there ever enough time for anything? CJ realized she wanted to be with Dak more than was actually possible even if they both had regular nine-to-five occupations. Which neither of them did and probably never would. Dak's job meant that she could be called out in the early hours of morning, just like today, because criminals didn't keep regular hours. But even when Dak was home and CJ was the focus of her attention, there would always be a little piece of her occupied with her current case.

It was simply something CJ would have to get used to, because the alternative of being without Dak was inconceivable.

CJ padded out of the shower and selected a power suit for her meeting. It wasn't like her career made their relationship any simpler. She was about to leave and fly around the country, fixing the devastation of death. Which was what she needed to focus on right now. That, and negotiating a new deal with Netflix which would work for them both. She got ready quickly, skipped breakfast, and headed out.

Emily was waiting in the studio parking lot. "Your giant bucket of iced coffee to get you through." She handed CJ a to-go cup. "Paige is already upstairs talking to Pat. They go way back apparently."

CJ took the latte and hugged Emily, then they walked toward the main office building. "Is that a good sign? The way Paige is, it could just as easily be bad history as good."

Emily opened the glass door and waited for CJ to enter. "I think it's good. I was in the room when Paige last talked with her to set up this meeting, and there was a lot of laughing. I don't think you've got anything to worry about."

They signed in at reception and headed up to the fifth floor.

"Is she mad at me?" She was aware the question sounded almost childish—she was a grown woman, for God's sake—but Paige held the keys to her continued career, and she'd worked damn hard to get *Dead Pretty* back on screen. Fixing the Artist's victims and CJ's kidnapping helped her endeavors, obviously, but still. She owed Paige a lot for getting her on TV at all.

"She's not mad," Emily said.

CJ waited for more, feeling like Emily knew something else and didn't want to say it. "I know you're in a difficult position between the two of us—"

"You're my best friend, CJ."

"Exactly. And Paige is your new boss." CJ smiled. "You love this job, and it clearly suits you. What I'm saying is that you don't have to tell me anything that might compromise that, but if you could give me a heads-up about what I'm walking into..."

Emily gently squeezed CJ's forearm. "Honestly, she isn't mad. She *might've* been a *little bit* mad if you'd pulled out of *Dead Pretty* completely like you were thinking of, but she likes your new show idea, and she thinks she can sell it." She shrugged. "And that's what really lights her fire: that challenge."

CJ bit her lip. "You didn't tell her that I contemplated that, did you?"

Emily swatted CJ's shoulder. "Of course not. After we'd talked about it, you decided not to pull out, so there was no need to poke that bear."

The elevator doors slid open. Emily hooked her arm under CJ's and guided her toward the meeting room. Her nerves settled somewhat when she saw through the glass walls that the only people present were Paige, Pat Wolf, Terry Crawford, a Netflix executive, and one other person, who CJ suspected would be from the Netflix legal team.

She and Emily sat beside Paige, and the unknown person was introduced as their lawyer, Ella Deakin.

"Paige tells us you've got another show you'd like to pitch to us," Terry said.

His easy manner alleviated her anxiety a little more. Maybe this wasn't going to be as hard as she'd thought it would be.

"But first, let's talk about *Dead Pretty*. I'd like to hear your concerns direct from you."

CJ took a deep breath and gave her best TV smile. "When we started the show, I always wanted it to be deeply respectful of the people and families I worked with. I never thought that it was strange for those families to allow us to film me working on their loved ones, because I was restoring them to the people they recognized, rolling back the damage they'd sustained at the time of their death." She took a sip of her latte, and the bitter hit of caffeine steeled her courage to continue. "And that felt like a privilege and a worthwhile service to provide. Plus, I hoped that it would help viewers be less afraid of dying somehow, showing that their physical body will be taken care of even after their soul, or whatever it is that makes us human, has long gone." She had a sudden vision of the woman named Dani who'd visited her at the church for Wallace Arnold's funeral back in Salt Lake and reiterated that her work was important. CJ still believed that, but it was the exploitation of it that was disturbing her. "I don't like that people are holding back on putting their loved ones to rest just to have an opportunity to be featured on the show and that they're in competition for me to work on their dead loved ones. It felt... distasteful."

"I agreed at our first meeting to remove that element of the show," Pat said.

CJ shrugged. "It was too much that anyone ever thought that it was a good idea at all."

Pat looked like she was about to continue arguing, but Terry glanced her away and shook his head.

"Please continue, CJ," Terry said.

"With the first seasons, we weren't held to a schedule." CJ kept her focus on Terry, ignoring the white heat from Pat's glare. "I worked on people as they happened at the funeral homes where I worked. Once we had the footage for a full season, we went to air."

Terry tilted his head. "And at the time, that wasn't just unusual, it was unheard of. I've been told that was precisely why the show was canceled, CJ."

"I understand that, but I feel like that way is the only way this show works *and* maintains respect for the dead and their surviving family." CJ turned her ice-cold cup around until the mermaid faced her, wanting a moment before she finally said what she needed to. "I also get that the studio couldn't continue without a schedule and that the season we're about to film has to work the way it's been arranged for it to work for you. I agreed to that, and I'll deliver on that promise, but after we've filmed these six episodes, I don't want to do any more. I really hope that you can see why I feel that way."

Terry nodded slowly, and though CJ stared directly at him, she could still partially see Pat about to explode. CJ really couldn't believe she'd held the director in such high esteem, thinking that her art was more important to her than commercial success. Maybe she was just being naïve; ethics and profit no longer co-existed in the film industry, if indeed they ever had. And maybe she was throwing stones from a glass house. She hadn't thought too deeply about it when she'd first signed this contract. She'd been desperate to get back on TV, eager to earn money to continue the lifestyle she'd become accustomed to, and she'd ignored the quiet alarm bells at the back of her mind.

But she'd evolved since then. Being around Dak, meeting her mom and brother, even spending more time with her own family—all of those things had conspired to show her there was more to life than money and moderate fame. Her phone vibrated in her purse, and her heart jumped in the hope that it was a message from Dak to let her know she was safe. Whatever they were both enduring in their professional lives, CJ drew strength from the belief that they were solid. Figuring out a path together would take time, but she knew it'd be worth it. She knew Dak was forever.

"The audience likes *you*, CJ," Terry finally said after a prolonged silence. "I don't think they care all that much what they see you in as long as they see you. Why don't you tell me about the next show you'd like to deliver?"

CJ regaled Terry with her vision of a show that was a mash-up of *The Great British Bake-Off*, *Ink Master*, and *The Next Great Artist*. She became more and more enthused as Terry nodded and smiled while she spoke. She couldn't wait to tell Dak how she'd stood up for herself.

"I like it, CJ. I really like it. It's a hell of a departure from working on the dead, but I think it might work. When you get back from this round of filming, we'll talk again. And we'll look at working with you to build a production team you can really gel with."

Terry threw a side glance at Pat. If CJ hadn't been aware that Pat had been bad-mouthing her, she was aware now, but whatever Pat had been saying, it clearly hadn't ingratiated her to Terry. While CJ was grateful Terry hadn't been swayed by Pat's attempts to undermine her, she was well aware that their discord wouldn't make the upcoming filming very pleasant at all.

"That's fantastic." CJ looked at Paige and was happy to see her smiling too.

"It is," Terry said. "I can see this having multiple seasons and going international. I'm excited." He focused on Paige. "You and I can iron out the contract details while CJ is away."

Paige gestured to Emily. "Emily will handle all of that, Terry. I'll just take you to Domingo's for fun."

CJ nudged Emily's leg under the table. She knew that Emily had been worried about Paige taking CJ back from her client list to handle negotiations herself, particularly since she'd thought it might be difficult. Emily's answering expression broadcast her relief.

"Excellent." Terry looked at CJ. "I'm expecting great things for this final season."

She heard the subtext loud and clear: *Don't fuck it up.* "I won't let you down, Mr. Crawford."

He waved her formality away. "Call me Terry."

"I won't let you down, Terry." CJ smiled broadly, fully committed to her statement. She was already looking forward to telling Dak all about the meeting. Her belief that the studio valued CJ had been proven right, and her advice had worked out perfectly. Damn, she'd hit the jackpot. Dak's unerring support and total faith astounded her, and she loved having someone so strong and loyal in her corner. It was something she'd never had before, but it was also something she'd gotten used to and would do anything to keep. And she'd do anything to keep Dak too. It was only because she loved Dak so much that it hurt when she wasn't around. They'd figure it out though, together. CJ was sure of that.

Chapter Twenty-Eight

DAK HAD WANTED THE guy they'd just brought in to sweat for a few hours while they gathered more information, went through his truck, and raided his home. Detective Miller insisted on a different approach.

"This isn't your case, *Special* Agent Farrell. We haven't asked for your help, and you don't have enough evidence to back up your theory that this guy is a serial killer." He waved wildly toward the kid they'd brought in, who was sitting beside Weaver and another officer at her desk. "For all we know, he's just your average run of the mill pedophile. Weaver saw that kid get in the guy's truck voluntarily."

"The kid asked us to help him." She kept her tone low and even, unwilling to entertain Miller's out of control demeanor.

"Of course he did. He's a minor, and a bunch of cops were waving their guns at him. He'd agreed to provide sexual services in exchange for money and God knows what else. The kid's not stupid. He knows that's illegal. Or maybe he just changed his mind after he saw the size of the guy's dick. I don't know."

Dak frowned. "Do you have to be so crass?"

Miller laughed, and his stale, halitosis-ridden breath assaulted her nostrils. It was all she could do not to back away, but he'd see that as gaining the upper hand.

"Sorry, m'lady," he said in a poorly affected British accent. "I forgot I was in the company of federal royalty. Maybe you're used to doing things differently but here, we treat the criminals like criminals." He glanced over at the kid again. "He should be in handcuffs too."

Dak stepped between him and the young man. "Whoever the guy in the interrogation room is, whether he's the serial killer I'm hunting or not, he was still dragging that kid into an empty building against his will. So no, the kid shouldn't be in handcuffs, because he's the victim here."

"Whatever. I want to get what I can out of him before he asks for representation. You sweat him and make him wait, 'I want a lawyer' will be the first and only thing out of his mouth." Miller held up his hand. "Weaver!"

"You can't know that," Dak said.

"I know criminals," he said and headed toward the interrogation room.

Dak strode after him. It was obvious she wasn't going to get anywhere reasoning with him, but she couldn't claim jurisdiction when Charnwood still hadn't given her the go-ahead to treat the three bodies as victims of a copycat killer. She had a meeting scheduled with him later to present more evidence, and she hoped he'd make it official, then she wouldn't have to put up with this shit from Miller. Though if the guy they'd just arrested was the killer she was after, the case would be over anyway. For now, she dismissed the gnawing in her gut that told her this guy wasn't her unsub.

Miller dropped into a chair, and Weaver offered the adjacent seat to Dak. She shook her head and stood against the wall. "This is your collar, Weaver."

She grimaced and nodded almost imperceptibly toward her partner before she sat beside him and placed a legal pad on the dull metal desk, scratched from years of handcuffs scraping over it. The bright, fluorescent lights washed out the guy's features, and he looked less intimidating than he had in the parking lot. He was secured to a ring on the table too, which often helped subdue showy arrogance, though he'd been relatively quiet since his arrest.

"Let's start with something simple since no one's buying your name is John Smith." Miller leaned back in his chair, clearly expecting Weaver to make notes while he took the lead. "What's your name?"

"Lou... Lucas Robertson," he said and clamped his teeth on his bottom lip.

"Is that really your name?" Weaver asked.

Dak wondered if his hesitation or his haptics prompted her question. Either way, it was good observation. Combined with his inability to focus on Weaver or Miller, his lip-chewing indicated his anxiety. She'd bet that was his real name, and he was busy trying to figure a way out of this situation.

"Yes." Robertson drew the chain of his handcuffs back and forth through the ring.

Miller grabbed the chain and glared at him. "Where do you live?"

Robertson frowned and laid his hands palm down on the desk as if he had to work hard to keep still. It was milliseconds before he began to pick at the skin on his thumb with his forefinger. "I've already given the other officers my address."

Miller leaned forward. "And now you're going to tell *us*."

Robertson's eyes widened, and he shrank back in his chair. Miller seemed to have forgotten that he didn't want to make Robertson ask for a lawyer. Dak made sure her expression revealed nothing, but internally, she shook her head. Miller's intimidating cop act was cliché and unconvincing. Robertson's reaction was more evidence of his nerves and chipped away at Dak's idea of who her unsub was. So far, he'd confounded all her expectations. But that could easily be an act. She'd interviewed killers who'd presented multiple ways in an effort to disguise their true personality. Robertson didn't appear to be the calm, collected, and confident man she was hunting, but maybe he knew that's what she was looking for.

Robertson repeated the information twice for Weaver, and Dak pulled up the address on Google Maps. She dropped the bendy gingerbread person onto the street for a virtual view, and the location gave her pause. An area that affluent was bound to have neighborhood watch. He couldn't risk keeping strange hours or bringing home victims without someone noticing. "Does anyone else live with you?" she asked.

He looked up at her, startled like he'd forgotten she was also present. "No. I live alone. Or I have for a little while now. My partner moved out just over a month ago."

His lack of verbal control and information-dumping didn't match her profile either, but the timing of his breakup aligned within days of the first murder and could have been the triggering event.

Dak showed the image to Weaver and Miller. "Looks like an expensive place. You must have a well-paid job," she said.

Robertson shook his head. "I'm just a hiking guide. My parents bought me that house."

Miller whistled. "Must be nice to have rich parents. Do they know you spend your nights trolling Skid Row for rent boys?"

"They're dead. And I don't do that."

"Don't do what?" Miller asked.

Robertson wrinkled his nose and clenched his jaw. "What you just said. That's not what I do. That's not what tonight was about."

"What was tonight about?" Dak asked, intrigued by the hint of offense, and backbone, Robertson showed at Miller's accusation. Evelyn had been sodomized just like Bundy had often done and Garavito raped his victims. Was the sexual part of the murders something he didn't like? "Did you have something special planned? Why not take the boy back to your nice house?"

"I wouldn't take someone like that home," Robertson said, his distaste for the kid becoming more pronounced.

"Someone like what?" Weaver asked. "Didn't you want your nice neighbors to see you bundling a dirty street kid into your fancy house?"

Robertson took a deep breath. His words and body language were so conflicting, it was all but impossible to read him. But sociopaths were more difficult to read than the average person. Dak had been paying attention to his accent and to how he was talking. There was no hint of Texan or British, and despite the tension, he spoke with relative ease. She couldn't detect any trace of difficulty in pronunciation. That didn't necessarily preclude him from being the guy who'd talked to Cherry; it just meant he was using his natural voice now.

"Were you born in LA?" Dak asked when he offered no response to Weaver's more challenging question.

Robertson's wrinkled brow answered the question for her before he responded.

"Yes." He looked down at his hands and stretched out his fingers. "I've lived here all my life."

"What were you taking the kid to the visitor center for?" Weaver asked.

"I just wanted to frighten him. I wasn't going to do anything that bad."

Dak arched her eyebrow, knowing that her definition of bad would differ greatly from Robertson's. This was why they should've waited to interrogate him until after they'd stripped the truck. Then they'd have a solid idea of what his intentions toward the kid were. They were just fumbling in the dark and couldn't lead him anywhere, hoping instead that he was stupid enough to confess. "Why would you want to frighten a homeless kid, Lucas?"

Someone knocked on the door of the interrogation room before Robertson answered. Miller shouted for them to enter, and Acker, one of the officers who'd been Weaver's backup, looked in and held up a backpack.

"The truck?" Dak resisted the temptation to snatch the bag from Acker and inspect its contents. She wasn't wearing gloves, and she'd cursed too many cops for tainting evidence by virtue of their excitement overriding protocol.

Acker tilted his head back toward the corridor. "We should talk outside."

Dak pushed away from the rough wall and went out of the room. The loud and heavy scraping of metal legs on concrete indicated that Miller and Weaver were following.

Miller slammed the door shut. "What've you got?"

Razor blades, rope, candles, butcher's knife: the tools of Garavito's torturous trade. That's what she would've expected Acker to list if Robertson was her copycat killer.

"The guy works at the visitor center. That's why he has the keys. His name was on the staff board inside the building." He consulted a small notepad. "Lucas Robertson. The registration in the truck was in the same name."

"Was that bag in his truck?" Dak asked, too impatient to wait while Acker ran through his story.

Acker held it up. "Yeah."

"And?" Miller prodded at it. "What's in it?"

Acker checked his notepad again. "Twenty-five feet of brand-new parachute cord, and a Leatherman multi-tool. A pair of boxing wraps, a few carabiners, a First Aid kit, and some electrolyte packets."

Dak's hopes that they'd caught the copycat took a serious hit. The multi-tool would have a blade, but with the rest of the gear Acker had listed, it seemed more likely Robertson had intended to cut the rope with it. He'd clearly anticipated having some trouble keeping the kid in place for whatever he had planned, but he looked less like a Garavito copycat with every passing minute. "Nothing else in the truck? Nothing prepared in the visitor center?"

Acker shook his head. "A bag of cold McDonald's on the driver's seat, but nothing you wouldn't expect to find in someone's truck. A few tools, breath mints, cigarettes. We didn't find anything out of the ordinary, Agent Farrell, I'm sorry."

"You find anything at his house?" Miller asked, shifting to stand more squarely in the corridor and partly in front of Dak.

She rolled her eyes at his supposed power move, and Weaver raised her eyebrows. Like she'd said, she'd been putting up with this kind of crap since she switched from vice, and apparently Miller was stupid enough to try the same macho garbage with a federal agent.

"No word yet. I'll keep you posted." Acker nodded toward Dak before leaving.

Miller turned to go back in the interrogation room and gave Dak a smug smile. "Looks like you're wrong, *Special* Agent. If there even is a copycat—which is a bullshit theory if you ask my opinion—Robertson isn't your guy."

Dak stepped in front of him and grasped the door handle. "I didn't, and wouldn't, ask your opinion, *Detective* Miller." She opened the door, strode in, and retook her position against the wall. She focused her gaze on Robertson and ignored the glare from Miller as he and Weaver returned to their chairs.

"You were about to tell us why you wanted to frighten a homeless kid," Dak said after Weaver had straightened out her pad and readied her pen.

Robertson bit down on his bottom lip again and breathed noisily out of his nose. He looked unsure. Since there was nothing too incriminating in his truck, he had to be concerned about them having found something at his house. Souvenirs, maybe.

"He's doing stupid things. Unnatural things. For money."

Dak recalled the giant metal cross hanging on his rear-view mirror. Despite the religious garb Garavito donned to lure his victims, he claimed that he'd been driven by a "strange force." It looked like Robertson was venturing down the God's army route, but she expected the copycat killer to claim the same motivation eventually or say that he was searching for the perfect way to kill a person. "Are you a religious man, Lucas?"

"Unnatural how?" Miller asked before Robertson answered Dak's query.

Robertson looked between the two of them and smirked a little. He looked beyond Miller and directly at Dak. "I follow the word of God, yes." He glanced briefly at Miller but concentrated once again on Dak. He sat up straight in his chair as if he was about to deliver a sermon. "Unnatural, as in the tidal wave of homosexuality will drown our children in a sea of sexual perversion. If left unchecked, it will destroy America as it did Pompeii, Greece, Rome, and Sodom."

The syntax of his statement jarred against everything else he'd said so far. It was obviously something he'd read and memorized, ready to trot out when asked about his take on queer people. He'd now answered her question as to why Robertson had concentrated his attention on her instead of Miller. It wasn't because he'd pegged Miller as the subordinate in the equation. He'd just identified her as part of the problem he was battling, and he wanted her to know it.

"Do you box, Lucas?"

He narrowed his eyes slightly, clearly not comprehending why she'd asked that, but then his expression changed again. He seemed to be gaining in confidence as the interview progressed rather than them breaking him down.

He stretched out his hands and seemed to study them for a moment before he looked up again. "The wraps were to protect my hands."

Miller glanced over his shoulder at Dak and seemed confused as to the line of her questioning. How he'd made detective was anyone's guess. They must've been pretty desperate when they recruited him. But behind his questioning look, there also seemed to be a hint of something else. Acceptance, maybe.

"To protect your hands while you frightened him into changing his ways?" Dak asked.

Robertson smiled and nodded slowly. "Yeah."

She'd heard enough. Robertson wasn't her killer. Depending on what they found at his house, he might turn out to be a killer, but he wasn't the guy she was hunting. She could trust Weaver to get this guy charged and hopefully put away, and Dak didn't want to waste any more time here. "I'll leave you to it," she said and walked out the door without a backward glance.

"What the hell?" Miller shouted down the corridor as he slammed the door shut.

Dak turned to face him. "Is there a problem?"

Miller's pudgy face reddened. "You're just done with him and you're walking out?"

She tilted her head and shrugged. If he'd changed his opinion, she wanted him to declare it. "You didn't want me in there and now you don't want me walking out? What is it you actually want, detective?"

He spluttered and motioned back toward the interrogation room. "How do you know that's not your killer?

Dak frowned, surprised at Miller's inexplicable change of attitude. "How did *you* know he wasn't the killer you don't think exists anyway?"

He glanced at the floor then looked back at her. "Look, I've just been riding you to keep Weaver on her toes."

She shook her head. "Bullshit. That makes no sense, Miller. You've been obtuse since we first met, and I don't see how that helps Detective Weaver."

He sighed and looked exasperated. Whatever was going on with him, she didn't have time for it. CJ was probably out of her big meeting by now, and Dak wanted to check in and see how it'd gone.

Miller walked toward her. "Maybe it doesn't," he said and shrugged. "I'm not good at backing down. And apparently, I'm not good at working with female cops."

Dak ran her hand across the back of her head. This was a conversation he should be having with HR or a therapist. She still had no idea how he'd taken the leap from calling her theory bull to appearing somewhat contrite, and she still wanted to call CJ. "Maybe just think of Weaver as a cop and forget about her gender so you don't feel the need to pull your macho crap. That'd be a good start."

She turned and pushed open the door into the nearby restroom, confused by the whole exchange and wanting to forget about it to free up valuable mind space. She leaned her head against the full-length mirror. The chill of it on her skin did nothing to reduce the fire running through her body. She was sure her theory wasn't wrong, but Robertson wasn't the man she was hunting. His height was the only similarity, and everything he'd said and done since being arrested was contradictory to her expectations. No British accent. No priest's outfit. And no murder weapon.

She backed away from the wall and turned on the faucet to splash water on her face. Very little sleep, no coffee, and a dead-end from a promising lead combined to shroud her in a sudden fatigue. Her meeting with Charnwood wasn't for a couple of hours, so she could grab some sleep in her office after she'd talked to CJ. If Charnwood approved the investigation formally, she'd be authorized to create a task force at the LAPD and enlist the help of Weaver and a few more detectives to get on this killer's trail.

The window she'd identified for the copycat's next kill had closed unless he'd had a change of schedule for some reason. Or worse, he'd moved to continue his spree in another city. And she'd bet Charnwood would never agree to her following the case across the country. His priority for her was to solve the murder of Special Agent Kimbal, even though they now had exactly zero leads on that case. The sharp prick of normality stabbed at her consciousness, and she had to remind herself that she'd chosen to take a rooted position so she and CJ could be together. Her life as a nomadic agent was done.

She went back out into the corridor and pulled out her cell to call CJ as she headed through the bullpen to the elevator. Out of macabre interest, she glanced at the murder board, mainly to see how the department was faring with their closing rate. A murder with last night's date caught her eye, and her stomach dropped as she drew closer to read the details. *It couldn't be.*

Male and female couple shot dead in a parked car.

The Son of Sam, David Berkowitz. *He skipped to chapter five.*

Chapter Twenty-Nine

I trust that you won't judge me, but I couldn't bring myself to copy Garavito. Children are where I draw the line in the pursuit of science, as should you. Garavito's chapter reminded me of Josef Mengel, who disguised his sadism as a commitment to scientific discovery. I am not like Mengel or his ilk. I am not a monster.

Garavito admitted to killing one hundred and sixty-seven boys, though they speculate that the more likely number was three hundred. And while he is, without doubt, one of the most prolific serial killers in history, I want no association with his lethal legacy. Did you know he's likely to be released soon? Perhaps when you're reading this, he might've been out for years already, hiding in plain sight while pursuing a political career, as he apparently wishes to. I wonder though, if I do turn into a killer, a real one rather than acting as one for the sake of my area of study, will I still maintain boundaries like these? I'd very much like to think so. And if that turns out to be the case, I might well be inclined to track him down and end him before I reverse engineer myself. One little favor for mankind and vulnerable boys before I return to my usual self and my place in this vague entity we call a society.

Or perhaps I shouldn't interfere. I'm not a huge proponent of the human race—why would I rush to save a few hundred of them? And what if I got a taste for the heady mix of killing and justice? Would I venture down the path of vigilantism? Would I no longer be in control of my actions on a deeper level? It's certainly a question to ponder, but later. Such questions divert me from my current course of action.

For now, I have to consider my latest kill, or kills rather, since it was a couple. David, aka the Son of Sam, botched several of his crimes and his victims lived, though some were incapacitated in some way and even paralyzed. But he's strangely famous for attacking loved-up couples. I suppose that I could have intentionally *not* killed the two lovers, but my continued freedom is important both to me and this scientific experiment, and any subject left alive is a person with information which could lead to my arrest. Obviously, that can't be allowed to happen. I *have* to finish my work. I feel that I'm on the cusp of determining my hypothesis. I'm becoming aware of a darkness, a chilled solidity creeping through my corporeal being.

Tonight, the first pull of the trigger sent a spark through my system, a burst of hot fire similar in temperature to the explosion of the bullet from its barrel. It came to rest in that space between the edge of my stomach and the top of my genitalia. Not an area usually associated with sexual frisson, but an area that can elicit feelings of intense pleasure, nonetheless. Did I want more of that feeling for the feeling itself? Or did I want to test if the second bullet managed to manifest an identical reaction? I squeezed a second time, a first bullet for the woman, and paid attention to my physical and psychological response.

Or that's what I'd intended to do. Instead, the fire burned bright, and I fired a third into the woman and the fourth and fifth bullets into the man. I'm distantly cognizant that I continued to squeeze the trigger but David's gun of choice, a Charter Arms' Bulldog, is only a five-shot revolver. I stuffed the gun into the waist of my trousers, and the red-hot barrel seared my skin though I didn't realize it at the time. I'm inspecting it now as my body begins the fascinating healing process; a perfectly snubby three-inch, blood-blister tattoo as a relatively long-term souvenir.

Careless. Careless and stupid. I've been so methodical to this point, so very much in charge of my actions and reactions. But I was too busy pulling cool night air into my lungs to settle the fiery feeling caused by...by this kill? I was barely aware of concealing the weapon. And if I close my eyes right now to transport myself back to the scene of the crime...to watch myself... Yes, I shoved the gun away while I... while I watched the life slip slowly from the eyes of the couple, of ~~my victims~~—my subjects. The ~~emotion~~ physiological response, the rush of dopamine through my system was, undeniably, caused by observing them as they died. I was equal opportunity in this. I believe my response was comparable for both the man and the woman. Sitting here now, I admit that's a relief and hope it reflects my continued objectivity in some small way.

Are you judging me? If you are, you shouldn't be so quick to such a tedious reaction. Understand this process from the scientific basis upon which it is founded. And no, of course I'm not losing myself. I'm perfectly lucid now, and I was perfectly lucid within seconds of this kill. Based on this experience, I'm tempted to draw an early conclusion that it is indeed possible for someone with no pre-existing indicators of pathological behavior and no previous proclivity towards killing to be edged that way through repeated exposure to the... *doing* and the *feeling*. The sense of power that's like nothing else on earth. Something that is impossible to replicate via any alternative avenue.

Analyzing it objectively and at a safe distance from the scene now, the almost god-like power that soared through my veins as I watched them die was more intoxicating than any drug or alcohol or chemically induced high that I've ever experienced. And I've tried them all in the pursuit of knowledge and an enhanced life.

As I proceed with the final five chapters, I need to be hyperaware of the lure of this power and its apparent ability to render my logical mind somewhat useless. This barrel-shaped mark will scab, and scar, and eventually fade, but that will take months. And in that time, I'm exposed. Potentially I've given the police physical evidence that I've used the murder weapon. I'll need to clean the gun thoroughly to ensure it's free of my DNA. But if the police came knocking on my door, having somehow linked me to these murders, I would have a hard time trying to explain this burn.

On top of that, I can't let anyone else see it while it heals, so that puts an unwelcome end to my pleasures of the flesh with anyone other than myself for the duration of my stay. That's disappointing and leaves quite the hole in my schedule between projects. I'll go stir crazy if I stay exclusively within these walls, so I suppose I'll have to partake in regular tourist activities: a walk over the Hollywood Stars, a visit to Muscle Beach, perhaps even a studio tour or a Lakers game since I already have their hat. Many of the murderers I'm emulating had full lives around their heinous hobby, so I'm not deviating from the experiment in a way that might be negative or might alter the trajectory of the experiment's impact upon me. And doing a spot of sightseeing might make finding ~~victims~~ subjects for the next chapters easier. If anything, widening my horizons might further replicate the life of the average murderer, since they go about their daily business hiding in plain sight with no one remotely suspicious of their favorite way of spending time. I bet you didn't know that the FBI estimates there are up to fifty active serial killers in this country alone, and I'll wager that they have jobs, and go on vacations, and do average Joe kinds of things like sitting on a beach to watch beautiful people drift by on their roller skates. I think roller-skating on Venice Beach might be just where I start.

Plus I have two guns to dispose of, which I need to do in two entirely different locations. I'm not sure I'm ready to part with them just yet though. It's a shame I won't be able to take them home; I have collections from my previous experiments, but you might know that already depending on how you've come across this journal. How depressing to think that you might just be some ordinary person from a house-cleanout company who has stumbled on my experiments randomly. If that's the case, I wonder what you make of them. I wonder if you're inspired to test your own mettle in this or any of the other areas in which I've investigated.

Unfortunately, there's no way of you sharing that with me. Clearly, I'm not going to leave any kind of contact details with my work in case I have been forced to flee. That would be moronic.

God forbid that my intentions have been misinterpreted, and I've been imprisoned in a mental facility instead of lauded in the scientific community. So I suppose the chips will fall as they may, and I shall accept that I have no way of knowing what is beyond my own horizon.

I think that's always been a problem for me. Wanting to know what's beyond this horizon, and the next, and the one after that. But isn't that the affliction for all great minds?

Chapter Thirty

Dak was talking with Lawson and Aston, the detectives who'd responded to the new Son of Sam killings, when her phone buzzed in her pocket. She wanted to see if it was CJ but she couldn't focus on CJ's network problems right now; Dak was too angry with herself for wasting time and people power to look out for a copycat Garavito when she should've predicted their unsub would skip that chapter and move straight to David Berkowitz. Because of her blindness, two more people were dead.

Some young kids had managed to break through some gates and drive down into a section of the LA River for what they probably hoped would be some privacy to do what kids their age did in parked cars. She corrected herself; they weren't kids. The victims were both twenty-three, but as she got older, young people looked younger. Whatever their age, neither had deserved the abrupt end to their lives. Five bullets between them. Dak had already told the investigating detectives to expect .44 caliber bullets from a Charter Arms' Bulldog revolver. Berkowitz had chosen that gun for its compact form and reliability, and this unsub would replicate Berkowitz's MO as closely as possible. She had yet to read the full ballistics report on the nine bullets buried in Beasley's body when their killer had copied Aileen Wuornos, but she had seen that the bullets were from a .22 caliber revolver. It was more evidence Charnwood couldn't ignore, making her confident he'd approve the investigation.

"Were there any tire tracks other than the Pinto's?" Dak asked.

Aston nodded. "There was scum and algae in the water by the gate where they entered. A second set of wide tires ran behind the victim's car for about twenty-five feet." He flipped through the crime scene photographs and laid the one of the tire tracks on the table in front of Dak.

"Can I get a copy of this, please?" She recognized the treads that matched the Beasley scene. The evidence was building to prove the same guy had committed all five murders. They just had to find him.

"Sure thing." Lawson retrieved the photo and made a color copy on the machine in the corner of the briefing room. "These are significant?"

"Yeah. There was a single tire imprint from the Keyes murder at the house opposite, but we couldn't be sure it wasn't from a potential buyer. Weaver was working down a list of all the people who'd been to view the house before the owner went on vacation, but it's taking time because some of them were from out of state. Then we got tracks from the side of the road when Beasley's car was dumped, and we think the murderer got into the vehicle that he'd left there. The right tire matched the tread from the Keyes scene, but the left tire had a different tread." She tapped the scan when Lawson slipped it on the desk for her. "These are the same mismatched tires."

"They look wide," Aston said. "We're looking for a truck or an SUV then."

Dak nodded. "Something not too old but not new. He'd want something reliable, so it's not going to be an old junker. The last thing he needs is to break down when he has a victim or any unlicensed guns in there."

"Got it." Lawson tidied the crime scene photographs and slipped them back into his file. "You'll be creating a task force... We'd like to be considered for it."

Dak smiled, happy to find that not all the detectives in this unit were of the Miller mold, though even he seemed to have changed his tune somewhat. "Consider yourselves selected. I just need confirmation from my superior and then I'll talk to your captain, but we should be able to get started later today. I'll come find you both."

Lawson held out his hand. She shook it firmly, and Aston repeated the gesture. She picked up the photo of the tire tread and left the office. As she reached the elevator, her cell buzzed again, reminding her that she still needed to call CJ. Dak waited until she was in her truck before she parked thoughts of her professional shortcomings, mounted her phone on the dash and video-called CJ. As soon as she appeared with a beaming smile, a wave of peace washed over her, and her biting anger receded a little. "Hey, wife-to-be, how did your meeting go?"

CJ's smile grew wider. "So well. Terry Crawford, one of the Netflix bigwigs, really likes my work, and he wants to talk about building a team around me for my new show idea."

Dak pulled out of the parking lot and headed to her office. "That's great news, baby. Is it still all systems go for the *Dead Pretty* filming?"

CJ nodded. "I'm just hoping that the director isn't a total ass the whole time. I don't know if she saw us making lots more seasons of *Dead Pretty*, but she's not happy that I'm pulling the plug."

"You'll handle her, no problem," Dak said. "Will Emily be going with you?"

CJ stuck out her bottom lip. "Nope. Paige is letting her come out for a day halfway through filming, and then on the final day of filming to escort me home, but I'll be on my lonesome most of the time."

She was making light of the situation, but Dak knew her well enough to see that she was harboring some anxiety. It hurt to think that they were going to be apart for so long, but CJ's TV career was important to her, so all Dak could do was be supportive. "I'll miss you."

CJ arched her eyebrow. "You'll miss the sex."

Dak winked. "Of course. You'd be worried if I didn't. But I'll miss *you*."

"Yeah?"

Dak pulled up at the stop sign and frowned. "You doubt me?"

"No, not really. But you're busy with your copycat case. I don't think you'll have time to miss me."

CJ shrugged and smiled, but there was a sadness in her eyes that struck Dak to her core. "I always miss you even when I'm busy with a case, beautiful. Please never doubt that."

CJ sighed. "This is hard, Dak."

"I know. We'll figure it out, I promise." Dak pressed her fingers to CJ's screen lips. "I love you so much."

"But not enough to wear that dress your mom picked out for you?"

Dak laughed, and the uneasy tension all but disappeared. "Do you love me enough not to ask me to wear it?"

CJ rolled her eyes and shook her head. "You know that was all your mom's idea. I think you'd look like a bad drag queen, and you also know how much I love you in a suit."

"I don't know if I should be offended or not."

"I think you do know. And you should be concentrating on the road, not looking at me."

Dak drove off slowly after a whole line of kindergarten kids had crossed the street. "I wanted to see your face, and I can pay attention to the road at the same time."

"When will you be home tonight?" CJ asked. "Maybe we could work up an appetite before dinner now that the house is empty again."

"I should be back by nine." Dak briefly thought of her life before CJ. She wouldn't have left whatever office she was working from before midnight, would've taken case files home with her, and been back at work by six a.m. Things had changed massively. Dak just hoped those changes weren't negatively impacting her work. Plenty of people had a work-life balance, but maybe those people weren't responsible for getting monsters off the streets.

"You'll let me know if your plans have to change?"

"Sure."

"If you're late and it has to be a choice between food and sex, your dinner will be in the dog." CJ wiggled her eyebrows.

"We don't *have* a dog, but we're totally on the same page, beautiful. I'm hungry for some real *us* time."

"Good. Now go, catch your monsters. I'm going home to get ready for a date with a sexy hot butch." CJ kissed the screen and ended the call.

Dak let out a contented breath. As long as they could maintain their connection, they'd be okay. They had to be. She checked the time; she had just over an hour before her meeting with Charnwood, so she'd grab a quick nap in her office to refresh. That and several buckets of coffee would keep her going. It'd already been a long day, but she had no intention of turning up at home frazzled and exhausted. CJ deserved better than that, and Dak wasn't about to start letting her down.

***

Dak used the end of her pen to push down the cuticles on her left ring finger, thinking that she needed to clip her nails. Charnwood had been studying her file for the copycat killer for fifteen minutes now, and he had yet to ask a single question. She didn't know him well enough yet to decide whether that was a good or a bad thing.

She leaned over and picked up the scanned letter and envelope that El Dorado Correctional Facility's warden had emailed to her just before the meeting, just in time to add to this file.

"What do you make of that?" Charnwood finally looked up at her.

"I think it's our unsub," Dak said and placed the paper back on his desk. "Cherry, the prostitute mom substitute, said that the guy she spoke to was trying to disguise an English accent. The UK postmark supports that. I know it could've been sent from a US citizen while they were over there for business or pleasure or even a murdering spree, but the syntax and formal politeness of the letter's contents also point toward a British national."

Charnwood tapped on the letter. "It could just be seen as twisted fan mail."

She nodded. "That's a possibility. And in a way, I think that's what the unsub intended. Rader loved the notoriety and fame that his killings garnered. This letter isn't asking permission outright to copy his MO, but it is praising him. I think it's a courtesy from one killer to another. This line, 'No one could ever, or should ever, attempt to match what you achieved, but perhaps they should pay homage to your method,' is basically telling him that's what he's going to do." Dak took a calming breath.

"Look, I know you think I'm busting your ass and making you jump through hoops, but that's the way we do things around here. By the book." He placed the letter in the case file, closed the folder, and handed it to her. "I trust your instincts, and I wasn't lying when we first met; I *am* glad to have you on board. But I think that while you've been out in the field, you've forgotten how the FBI actually works. We're not the CIA, Farrell. We follow strict protocol, and I'm really hoping that you can get used to that again."

She sighed, knowing she couldn't argue because he was right. It was slightly irritating that he'd read her so easily too, but she supposed she wasn't being all that subtle. Ben had always joked that diplomacy wasn't her strong suit, and since she didn't bother to practice it, she had no chance. But she still had a good feeling about Charnwood, and she wasn't about to jeopardize that by being petulant now.

Dak nodded. "I'm sure I will. Like you said, I've been out of the office for a long time, and I've gotten used to a larger degree of autonomy than your average agent. It's just going to take a little while to acclimatize to my new environment, that's all."

Charnwood tapped his knuckles on his desk and smiled before leaning back in his chair. "You've provided more than enough evidence for me to authorize you to pursue this investigation and officially band these murders together under the same killer. I'll call Captain Grant at the LAPD and instruct him to allow you to set up the task force you need to catch this guy. Start fresh tomorrow."

"Excellent." Despite the mini-lecture, that had been easier than she'd thought it would be. She'd expected to go through every piece of evidence and talk him through her logic, even though it was clear. She tucked the file under her arm and stood to go, eager to talk to Garrity to discuss the officers they wanted to work the case. "Thank you."

"Getting this guy off the streets will be thanks enough."

"You got it," she said and headed for the door.

"And Farrell?"

Dak stopped at the doorjamb and looked over her shoulder. "Yeah?"

"I'm grateful that you brought the Rodeo Killer down, but Garrity tells me that Moreno has never been to Mexico, let alone visited Culiacán. When you close this case, I want you to find Kimbal's murderer, okay? No more finding your own cases until we find the bastard who's killed one of our own and thinks he's gotten away with it."

She nodded. "Absolutely." It made perfect sense that Charnwood wanted Kimbal's killer found as a matter of urgency, and she liked that he was so protective of his own people, especially since she'd chosen to become one of them. Dak was bringing Hamilton into the fold too, someone she already felt a strange protectiveness toward. And with his clandestine, foul-mouthed, and highly dangerous sister in the background, the more people looking after Hamilton, the better.

Dak glanced at her watch as she walked up the corridor toward Garrity's office. It was nearly six p.m., and Charnwood had told her to start the task force in the morning. A quick debrief and prep session with Garrity now would mean she could get home by eight and surprise CJ. The plan made her smile. Once she'd talked to Garrity, there was nothing else to do before tomorrow, so spending some quality time with her gorgeous wife-to-be was definitely the way to go. It was also one of the last nights for a while that CJ would be home when Dak got back after work. She had a feeling that she'd be reverting to her old schedule while CJ was filming. The house would be too quiet, too empty without CJ running around barefoot, singing random lyrics to songs Dak had never heard of. Music was about the only area where their age gap really showed. It certainly didn't figure in the bedroom, which was where Dak planned to spend the rest of her evening.

Chapter Thirty-One

WHEN DAK AND GARRITY arrived at the LAPD station the following morning, Weaver met them at the elevator.

"The captain has blocked out the conference room for your task force for however long you need it," Weaver said as she led the way to a large room with double glass doors.

Inside, Lawson, Aston, Miller, and two other detectives she'd seen around over the past couple of weeks were studying the portable boards that had been set up with each of the murders, including their names, photographs of the victims and the crime scene, plus various leads they were ready to chase down or already had. It was impressive work, and Dak nodded toward Weaver. "Good stuff, detective."

Weaver smiled widely and blushed a little. "Thank you, Special Agent."

Dak waved her formality away. "Just call me Farrell." She raised her voice for everyone else to hear. "No special agent titles from now on. I'm Farrell, and this is Garrity. The FBI is leading this investigation in name only. We're working on this together as equals." She focused on Miller. "Before we get started, I'd like to have a few minutes with you."

Miller nodded and followed Dak. She found an empty interrogation room and beckoned him in before closing the door for privacy.

"If Captain Grant put you on this task force without asking if you wanted it, tell me now, and I'll have you replaced. There are people's lives at risk, and I don't have time for a pissing contest."

Miller held up his hands and shook his head. "Hear me out?"

He waited until she indicated for him to continue. "I asked to join the task force, just like the rest of them. Look, it's always been a shit show when the FBI turns up and take over one of our investigations. They take, take, take and give nothing back." He tilted his head to the left and shrugged. "But you've shown that you're not like that, and this feels like it might be more of a collaboration than a takeover. I'm sorry for being an asshole to you up to now, and I'm sorry for doubting your theory. This guy is fucking around in my city, and I really want to stop him. So...will you cut me some slack and let me be on your team?"

Dak recognized how hard it must've been for Miller to step up and wind back his behavior, and she'd never been one to hold a grudge. She was too busy fighting toxic people to hold that kind of poison herself. "On one condition."

He rolled his eyes. "You want me to stop riding Weaver, don't you?"

"I want you to stop being an asshole to anyone without a dick. But yeah, that's a good start. Pushing her to be a better cop is fine. If she responds to a tough line because she was brought up by a hard-working cop, that's okay. But there's no need to be disrespectful or run down her confidence, okay?"

"You know about her dad?" Miller's smile seemed genuine. "He was a great captain and an even greater guy."

Dak didn't comment on how Weaver's father had negligently exposed her to images of violent crime at a young age; Miller was trying to build a bridge, and she wasn't about to throw a stick of dynamite. "You worked with him?" she asked, putting the pieces together and beginning to understand Miller's messed-up perception of mentoring Weaver. It didn't excuse his general misogyny, but maybe including him in the team would be a step in the right direction and make life a little easier on Weaver. Excluding him could make things worse.

Miller nodded. "For over twenty years. Damn shame what happened."

Dak gestured to the door, eager to get back to the briefing and not to become embroiled in Miller's reminiscence. "If you're okay with my terms, and you can be led by a woman, we should rejoin the team."

"I am."

"Good. Make sure you let Weaver know she can expect a change of approach from you." She opened the door and made her way back to the conference room with Miller a few steps behind her. Everyone seemed engrossed with studying the case files as they re-entered, but Dak didn't miss Weaver's look of hopeful anticipation fade as Miller filed in after her. The conversations ceased, and they all looked to her expectantly. "Okay, let's get started." She motioned to the table, and people took their seats.

She asked each cop to briefly introduce themselves. Lawson and Aston were the detectives who'd been called to Evelyn Berenger's crime scene, and Gray and Taylor were working the Perez murders, the young couple murdered in their car.

"This unsub currently thinks he's operating under the radar with his multiple MOs and that we've not identified him as a serial killer. I don't want to disabuse him of that notion."

Taylor raised his hand. "Why is that? Wouldn't it be good to get people on the lookout now that we've got a sketch of him?"

"This killer is very controlled. There's no way to tell if he's killed in other states or even other countries. The ordered nature of the Keyes murder points to that *not* being his first kill, but I'm not prepared to say that for sure because he seems so unusual, and I don't think he fits into any neat idea of a psychopath that we might have. Because of that, I don't know how confident he is that he could continue to evade us once we're onto him. And if he isn't arrogant, or if he's simply ultra-cautious, we risk him packing up and leaving just as suddenly as he arrived. Then the trail goes cold, and who knows if we could pick it up again via VICAP reports from elsewhere in the States. He might even run back to England or start all over again in a European country."

"It could work the other way though, right?" Gray asked. "He could be like Berkowitz and Rader and want media attention. If the public knows about him, that might encourage him to stay—"

"Or it might ramp up his ego and pull his schedule forward," Garrity said. "Farrell's right: the last thing we want to do is upset his bad apple cart and embolden him to kill his Jack the Ripper victim earlier than we anticipate. Keeping the investigation quiet gifts us a minimum of six days to get ahead of this son of a bitch for the first time."

Gray and Taylor nodded, and there were quiet murmurs of agreement from everyone else at the table.

Dak picked up her copy of *Close to Death* from the desk and flipped it open to the page she'd bookmarked. "We know his next victim will be murdered in the same way as Jack the Ripper's victims. We don't know what his motivation is, whether he's paying homage to other murderers that he admires, whether he's finding his own method by trying lots of others, or if he's got some other reason. And right now, we don't care. Knowing his motivation wouldn't help us figure out how he's selecting his victims. But knowing the motivation of the Ripper might help us identify the potential pool of people for his next murder, which, according to his pattern that Garrity alluded to, will be seven to ten days from the killing of the Perez couple."

"Is there anything we can draw from the timing of his schedule?" Weaver asked. "Like shift patterns for a particular job? Is it possible that he came here to work a contract and he's fitting his murder fix in around it?"

"Could be." Dak patted the book again. "What he's given us is a ticking clock. Ten chapters. Ten murders. And he's halfway through, even though he skipped chapter four."

Lawson folded the front cover of his copy of the book and ran his finger down the contents page. "Is it possible he might skip another chapter?"

"I don't think so. The rest of the killers in the book target women,

men, and the elderly. No more kids." Dak sighed, not wanting to sink back into a pit of guilt. "I should've recognized that our unsub wouldn't copy Garavito. He's got some kind of moral code, and that precludes him from killing children."

"How could you hope to know his moral code? Or that he's even got one?" Garrity asked. "The other three murders were all ultra-violent, and he stuck to the original murderers' MO perfectly. You could say he lost control with the Wuornos case—nine bullets is a lot of rage. He emptied the gun, stopped, reloaded, and pumped another three shots into Beasley."

Dak shrugged. "Wuornos had a lot of rage too. Seems like he was perfectly in control when he took out Beasley. He stopped at nine, which was the maximum number of shots she ever used."

"So he draws the line at murdering children, but he's more than happy to torture men and rape women?" Weaver asked, her disgust laced thick in her words.

"I don't think he personally raped Evelyn," Dak said.

"You've lost me." Weaver rubbed her forehead before she pointed toward the board dedicated to Evelyn's murder. "The M.E. confirmed she'd been penetrated anally."

"Yes, she did. But there was no DNA evidence and no trace of anaphylactic use. No residue or lubricant from a condom. There was no physical damage, so he didn't use anything weapon-like. I think he used a dildo to copy the MO without *personally* defiling her. Obviously, it's the same thing to you and me, but to him, it provided a distance. I think he's justifying what he's doing and almost trying to legitimize it. Hence, moral code. And clearly, he wants no part in slaughtering kids, which explains why he jumped to chapter five." Dak slammed her hand on the desk. "And I should've seen that instead of sending you on a wild goose chase for a Garavito copycat."

"Hey, that wasn't a waste of time though, was it?" Weaver asked. "We stopped a different kind of psycho from torturing a kid."

It wasn't lost on Dak that Weaver had turned the tables on her by reframing what she saw as a failure. But where Weaver had taken a bad cop off the streets, Dak's oversight had cost a young couple their lives. She took a breath and refocused. Guilt-tripping herself was a waste of energy for now, and it could wait until they'd found their killer and solved the case. "Anyway, there are other elements of the crime scenes that suggest he's not invested in the method, that he's just killing by numbers and checking boxes."

Miller frowned and tilted his head slightly. "How so?"

"The beer cans in Beasley's car. There was no saliva on them at all. Seven empty Buds, and I don't think anyone drank from them. The post mortem found no alcohol in Beasley's system. It's like they were just there for set dressing: popped open and poured away. I bet that if we analyzed the dirt around where Beasley's car was found or around where the body was left, we'd find beer."

"But it's possible the killer cleaned them, right?" Miller asked.

"I think the unsub is super careful. If he thought there was DNA on the cans, he would've taken them with him and dumped them far away from the scene. He left them simply to mirror the minutiae of a Wuornos murder." She walked to the Evelyn Berenger board and looked at the photograph of the young student whose life had been ripped away from her in some game she hadn't agreed to play and one Dak couldn't yet figure out the rules to. "He didn't violate Evelyn *personally* not because he didn't want to leave his DNA signature in semen but because he genuinely didn't want to partake."

"Okay." Garrity nodded. "Say that's all true; you're taking a peek into his psyche and his motivation. Like you said, that's not going to help us catch him like it would a regular serial killer."

Dak shrugged. "No. It just narrows our evidence right down. We've got the basic details from the homeless guy matching the sketch we've got from the sex worker, Cherry Bomb. We're going to need more than that. But we know his next victim is going to be a prostitute and that he's going to remove some of her organs if he's following Jack's MO to the letter. So he'll need surgical supplies, won't he? A scalpel, forceps, and—"

"Shit." Weaver pulled the unsub's sketch toward her. "Would he be stupid enough to go after Cherry?"

"Or would he think that's clever because she knows him, and he believes she'd go with him willingly?" Miller asked.

"Any prostitute will go with him willingly," Gray said. "I don't think he'd risk being seen by the same group of women."

"But it's still a possibility," Dak said and looked at Weaver, whose concern was clear. "He has no idea that she's provided us with his likeness."

Weaver grabbed her phone. "If that's the case, I need to warn her—"

"Or use her as bait," Lawson said.

Weaver shook her head and looked directly at Dak, the plea in her eyes clear. "If we lose her, we lose a witness. We can't risk that."

Dak sighed. Now she was going to find out how Weaver reacted to being overruled by someone she claimed to respect. "I think we should put an undercover unit on Cherry ASAP. If he does choose her out of familiarity, we have a head start."

Weaver clenched her jaw. "We have to tell her at least."

"No. We don't," Dak said. "She has a schedule just like our unsub. If she deviates from that, he'd be suspicious." She held Weaver's pained glare. "My instinct says he won't go there, Weaver. He struck up a kind of relationship with Cherry. In his mind, he probably thinks he helped her out. I don't think he'll want to undo that by taking her as his next victim."

Weaver broke eye contact and scribbled on her notepad. "I hope you're right."

"Me too." Dak felt for her, but Weaver hadn't helped herself by getting emotionally wrapped up with Cherry. She needed to learn how to draw the line between helping someone and getting invested in that person's life. "Garrity, can you go talk to vice? We're going to need their help on this. They know where all the sex workers are, and they can distribute our sketch to their unit.

Give them copies of the tire tracks too."

"You got it," Garrity said.

Eager to get everyone else active on assignments, Dak went to the board where there were photos of the tire treads they'd found at the Keyes and Beasley scenes, and now, the Perez murders on the LA River. "We've got a sketch of our unsub, and we've got a signature from the truck he's driving. It's likely he purchased it second-hand and cheap. And probably from a small, low-rent garage."

"Because of the tires?" Aston asked.

"Exactly. No garage worth a damn would sell a vehicle with tires that had different treads—you're not supposed to mix them because of how they interact with the road surface. The grooves, sipes, ribs, and—" She waved her hand, realizing she was falling into mechanic-speak the way her dad used to do. The memory of him teaching her all about treads at the kitchen table with chunks of shredded tires made her smile rather than choke her heart. She'd noticed the change a few times over the past couple of months, and especially since she'd been repairing her relationship with her mom. She didn't need a degree in psychology to understand the connection. She also didn't need to be thinking about it in the middle of this briefing. "Anyway, he likely thinks that buying a vehicle from a dubious garage covers his ass because the proprietor won't want to draw attention to himself either. He wouldn't respond to a police plea for information even if our description matched one of his customers."

"Could the killer have replaced a tire himself?" Weaver asked. "Maybe he just bought one the same size from Walmart without talking to a specialist about it."

"It's possible but unlikely," Garrity said. "Even if you don't know anything about tires, you know to write down all the info from your existing tire when you go to replace it. More likely that it was replaced in a hurry by an unscrupulous garage to get a quick sale."

"Those tires are found on a lot of different trucks." Aston

scribbled something on his legal pad. "And there's no way to check without hours and hours of roadblocks and visual inspections. The city is already grid-locked. I can't image the captain will authorize something like that."

"You're probably right, but it's evidence to tie our unsub to three of our crime scenes when it comes to trial." They'd think she was planning too far ahead, but Dak had heard of too many cross-agency task force investigations failing through lack of evidence. She didn't want this to be a cautionary tale the Bureau trotted out during training.

"We've got over two hundred thousand British people living in LA County, and they've got community groups," Lawson said. "Is it worth reaching out to them? Seeing if the killer's made contact? Maybe they maintain a database of people new to the city."

"Thanks for volunteering." Dak smiled, and Aston rolled his eyes at his partner. "We don't know how sociable our unsub is, or if he's trying to blend in with that community so he doesn't stand out. We don't know whether he's here to stay or, like Weaver suggested, is only here for a short-term work contract. Hell, he could even be here *just* to kill people. So yeah, it's definitely worth reaching out to British groups. They might not recognize him from the sketch if he's only interacted online, but they still might be able to give us a list of people to work on."

Lawson nodded. He clearly understood the importance of detail-oriented investigative work. It was often that kind of work rather than anything glamorous which led to nailing killers. A murderer didn't tend to be careful with the boring minutiae of their daily life, and moving through the mountains of leads and paperwork from that could easily lead to the murderer's downfall.

"What else do we have to go on?" Garrity asked.

"I've been working up a list of black-market gun sellers and pawn shops where they don't ask too many questions." Weaver opened another manilla file and handed Dak a sheet of paper before distributing a copy to everyone else at the table. "The top five are all places that are suspected of fudging the ten-day waiting period and not looking closely at ID. The second batch are pawn shops with a similar reputation. LA isn't as gun-friendly as you might think, so even if we looked at every gun store, we'd be canvassing less than fifty. I'd be happy to take that on," she looked across at Miller, "if that's okay with you?"

Miller glanced at Dak briefly, and his lips twitched into a wry smile. "Sure thing. You can even drive."

The resulting expression on Weaver's face made it crystal clear she wasn't a decent poker player.

"He could've gotten both weapons on the dark web with no questions asked," Taylor said. "I can dig around there and see what comes up. It's a physical item, so if the purchase took place on there, we'd still have an exchange of some kind. It might've even been in person if we're lucky. And I can check for sales of surgical supplies too. Maybe he got everything he needed from one supplier."

Dak shook her head. "I think he's too careful for that. He wants each of these murders to go unnoticed. You need to look for individual purchases for each of the murders. And he's just as likely to have purchased the basic items at Home Depot or Walmart. The rope he used to bind Keyes, the latex gloves he's got to be using to keep his scenes clean—he'll be getting that stuff the easiest way possible so he can fly under the radar."

Miller held up the letter Dak believed the unsub had sent to Dennis Rader at El Dorado Correctional Facility. "This is new. Do you think this is from our killer?"

"I do," Dak said. "And it fits with Cherry's assertion that the guy she talked to is a Brit. I've asked for the original envelope so we can test for saliva. There was hair that couldn't be accounted for at the house for sale opposite the Keyes residence. I'm hoping it's a match."

"There was no match on the CODIS database," Garrity said, "so our unsub hasn't been caught for any other crimes in this country. If the DNA matches, we'll send it to the Interpol DNA gateway. Like Farrell said, this is unlikely to be the killer's first rodeo, so maybe he's been caught for something in the UK or Europe."

"Okay." Dak pulled in a deep breath and scanned the face of everyone in the room. They all looked keyed up and ready to go. "You've all got your leads to follow. If anything comes of any of them, if there's even a hint that they might take you to our unsub, call it in. We go in together, we go in hard, and we take him down. No solo-hero commando shit on this team, you got it?" She waited until she'd gotten nods and affirmative responses from everyone. "Let's go."

After a few moments of paper-gathering and chair-scraping, Dak was left alone in the conference room with Garrity.

He smiled. "I think we've got a good team."

"I agree." Dak continued to stare at the images of the victims, searing them onto her brain. They had to stop this guy, and it would only be six days before he struck again. The clock was ticking, and time was always the most powerful foe.

Chapter Thirty-Two

CJ PACKED HER LINGERIE last and didn't suppress a knowing smile when she heard Dak's murmur of appreciation.

"Should I be worried that you're taking sexy underwear on a trip without me?" Dak plucked a particularly lacy bra from the top of CJ's suitcase and raised her eyebrows. "I have a scary friend now who may or may not be CIA or some other clandestine government officer; she can commandeer satellites and spy on you if I ask nicely."

CJ huffed. "The elusive Ice Hamilton? Will I ever meet her?"

Dak shrugged. "I expect she'll be at Hamilton's graduation from the Academy." She pulled the bra away when CJ made a grab for it. "Answering a question with a question of your own is evasive behavior, Callie Johnson."

CJ crawled onto the bed and straddled Dak's naked stomach, enjoying the deep sigh and half-lidded expression it elicited. She edged back and wiggled her butt into Dak's crotch. "*You* will never need to worry about me sleeping with anyone else."

Dak grasped CJ's hips and pushed up against her. "I'll always worry. A woman like you draws attention like the moon draws the ocean. What if Elodie Fontaine says she'll divorce Madison because she's desperately in love with you? Who could resist that offer?"

CJ trailed her nail along that oh-so-sexy deep line between the muscles of Dak's chest. "*I* could resist that offer because I have you." She pressed a little harder as she worked down to Dak's abs and gave a deep sigh of her own. "I have *this*."

Dak quirked her eyebrow. "You wouldn't be even a little bit

tempted?" she asked, her voice a deep whisper that broadcast her desire.

CJ lowered her head and followed the trail from Dak's pecs to her bumpy stomach with her tongue then looked up. "Not even a little." She cast a glance toward Dak's bedside drawer. "But it wouldn't hurt your case to give me a forceful reminder of your perfect rhythm and immense stamina."

Dak grinned. "I thought you wanted to talk about the wedding and family stuff?"

"We have all night." She twisted Dak's nipple lightly. "And if you wanted to talk before we reconnected, you wouldn't have stripped down to your shorts and lay down on the bed as soon as you came home, would you?"

Dak's brief glance away reinforced CJ's suspicion that she'd gotten Dak's motivation spot on.

"You know me too well," Dak said softly. "Are you sure my predictability won't bore you when we're married?"

"You mean the way you're predictability horny the moment you come home, the second you wake up, any time you see sexy lingerie, whenever you see me in heels—"

"All of which can be attributed to your glorious femme-ness that I can't get enough of. It's not my fault."

"I'm not blaming you." CJ tucked her finger under the waistband of Dak's shorts and tugged them down slightly. "I'm just listing some of the delightful ways you're predictable, and long may that continue, *especially* when we're married." She peeled off her tank top, and Dak swallowed audibly as it revealed her sheer black satin bra.

"You know just how to play me," Dak whispered.

She took CJ's breasts in her hands and squeezed with precisely the right amount of pressure for the mood she was in. CJ placed her hands over Dak's. "I'll move my case while you," she flicked her eyes to the toy drawer again, "get ready for me." She'd barely crawled off before Dak leapt from the bed and yanked open the bedside cabinet. CJ zipped her suitcase and pushed it unceremoniously onto the floor, eager to watch Dak step into her leather harness. When Dak had slipped the marbleized shaft of silicone into its ring, CJ got onto all fours and crawled across the bed slowly, so slowly, making sure she stuck her ass high in the air.

Dak's jaw worked. CJ loved how easy it was to get her so incredibly hot and how ready for sex she always was, almost without exception, even now when she was submerged in a big case. CJ made it to the edge of the bed, where Dak stood waiting. She wrapped one hand around Dak's dildo and the other around the side strap of the harness. She tilted her head back and parted her lips, licking them before taking Dak into her mouth. Dak swallowed hard, and her breathing grew shallow. She combed her fingers through CJ's hair before balling her fist into it. CJ kept her eyes fixed on Dak's, which were dark with desire, while she worked her way up and down Dak's cock, taking her all the way in and pressing the base of it against Dak's clit.

When CJ figured she'd worked Dak into a frenzy of lust, she withdrew, grabbed the other side of Dak's harness and twisted her around to push her onto the bed. Dak's smile meant she knew exactly what CJ had in mind—another great thing about their relationship—and she pushed herself up the bed, waiting for CJ to take exactly what she wanted.

For the briefest of moments, an unwanted thought intruded on their intimacy. *What if this is the last time we make love?* A plane crash, a crazed gunman, her director going crazy: so many things could go bad while they were apart.

Dak narrowed her eyes and cupped CJ's cheek. "Are you okay, baby?"

CJ nodded and shoved the ridiculous and ill-timed rumination away. No what ifs. Only right nows. "I will be." She straddled Dak's waist and placed her hands on Dak's chest, the solid muscle beneath her palm immediately drawing her back into the moment. She kissed her deeply, sucked in Dak's tongue, and let her mouth take her pleasure.

Dak gripped CJ's waist and guided her slowly down until she'd taken all of her inside. CJ used Dak's chest to steady her as she slid up and down, Dak filling her, fucking her, completing her. She pushed down hard, and Dak's hips rose and drove in still deeper, her rhythm slow and steady.

"I need you harder," CJ gasped around the intensity of Dak possessing her entirely.

Dak nodded and thrust with more force, making CJ's breath catch against the intoxicating mix of pleasure and a hint of pain. She flipped CJ onto her back, and CJ wrapped her legs around Dak's waist, making sure she was still getting all Dak had to offer.

"Oh, God, Dak." CJ moaned through the haze of pleasure from the strong thrusts. The feeling of Dak's body heavy on hers robbed her senses of all other thought and feeling.

CJ came hard, her body clenching, her muscles rippling around Dak's dildo. The orgasm stole her breath, shattering her like it was the first time all over again. How did Dak make their time together so special?

Dak rolled to the side, held CJ in her arms, and placed gentle kisses on her neck. "I love you."

"I love you too."

"You okay?" Dak asked, the concern in her voice clear.

CJ turned and rested her head on Dak's shoulder. "I don't want to leave you."

Dak held CJ to her. "And I wish you didn't have to go. I haven't wanted to say that," Dak ran her fingers through CJ's hair, "because I don't want to put pressure on you."

CJ sighed heavily against Dak's shoulder. "We both have jobs that ask a lot of each other. But that's okay, huh?" It had to be okay; she couldn't and wouldn't let go of this.

Dak kissed CJ's forehead and held her close. "We'll figure it out, I promise. Let's just enjoy tonight and this time we have together. If we bury ourselves in our work, this time will fly by."

CJ lifted her head, and the pained expression on Dak's face brought tears to her eyes. "I'm going to miss you so much," she murmured against the softness of Dak's neck.

Dak tipped CJ's head back and wiped away her tears. "Me too, baby, but you're going to do great. Just remember. You. Me. Us. We'll get through it."

CJ nodded with a conviction she didn't feel. "We will. And when I get back, we've got our wedding to look forward to." She shifted back slightly and grinned. "How about that for a segue?"

"Seamless." Dak ran her finger over CJ's lip then kissed her hard. "I'm only talking about the wedding if you promise me more of that action before we go to sleep."

"You're insatiable." CJ tapped the end of Dak's nose like she was a naughty pup.

"But you'll still keep trying, right?" Dak wiggled her eyebrows.

"I will. Forever, in fact." She stroked the strong line of Dak's jaw. "Maybe that should be in my wedding vows—which is one of the things I wanted to talk about. I'd like to write mine, but I don't want you to feel like you have to as well."

Dak shook her head. "I *want* to write my vows to you. This is forever, and you're too special for me to just recite the same words hundreds of thousands of people have already said. Though I reserve the right to call Madison for help."

CJ chuckled. She'd been thinking she'd ask Madison to read her efforts too. "Since you brought Madison up, do you think it'd be weird to invite her and Elodie?"

Dak wrinkled her brow, and her eyes narrowed slightly. "I guess that depends on how many people we're inviting."

"How many people do we want to invite? I'd like the guest list pinned down for when I get home, so we can start sending out the invitations."

"That won't take long on my end. My mom and brother, maybe Hamilton and a plus one." Her expression dimmed slightly, and she clenched her jaw. "I'd like to ask Ben's wife, Carla, but Rhodes said she'd remarried, and I don't think I could handle seeing her with anyone else. I feel like that would be betraying Ben."

"Oh, babe." CJ traced the lines of Dak's shoulder muscles with her nail. "You don't think Ben would want her to be happy?"

"It's not that," Dak said. "I'm sure he would've wanted her to make a new life, but... I don't know, I'm being crazy. I think I've healed and that my grief has subsided, but I'm not sure I could handle seeing Carla without Ben. In all the years we were partners, I only ever saw Carla with him. Seeing her on someone else's arm would just be too hard. Does that make sense?"

CJ continued to caress along Dak's arm until she intertwined their fingers. She loved that Dak was comfortable enough to share what was on her mind without CJ having to get out a pick-axe and dig her thoughts from ice like ancient artifacts. "You're entitled to your feelings, whether they make sense to someone else or not." She winked and grinned. "That's one of the nuggets that my therapist is fond of repeating. And repeating again."

Dak half-laughed, but her expression was serious and so desperately vulnerable that CJ wanted to pull her into her arms and never let go.

"I don't care if they make sense to someone else," Dak said. "I only care what you think."

CJ lifted Dak's hand to her lips and kissed her knuckles. "It makes sense, and I can only guess how hard it was to lose Ben. I've been lucky so far. No one close to me has ever died, though you had a damn good try. I hated every second of that, and I'm in no hurry to experience it again."

Dak fell silent for a long moment, and CJ wanted to draw the words back into her mouth. Dak had been robbed of her partner and her dad already. She didn't need to be reminded of her losses. "Do you have any other FBI buddies you're close to that you might want to invite?" CJ raised her eyebrows when Dak shrugged. She hadn't considered how few people Dak had in her life, but it wasn't like CJ was surrounded by a crowd of amazing close friends either.

"So it'll just be a small wedding. That's okay."

Dak met her gaze. "Are you sure? With everything that was going on last week with our families, I thought you were looking forward to a huge affair."

CJ tucked her knees up and snuggled closer, still holding tight to Dak's hand. "I'd marry you in the City Clerk's office tomorrow and still be euphoric, Dak. This isn't about that piece of paper. It's the promise of our future that I'm interested in. Because we've both been estranged from our families in different ways, I think they want to make a huge thing out of our wedding day, but as long as you make me your wife, we could do it in front of a random couple of witnesses we drag in off the street."

Dak's eyes danced, and she gave CJ a wicked grin. "Can we talk about the honeymoon?"

CJ swatted Dak's chest. "Always thinking about the sex."

"It's hard not to when I'm marrying the most beautiful woman in the world."

"Smooth, but no. Though I'm glad you think so." She swept her hair back dramatically and gave Dak a come-hither look. Dak didn't need a second invite and moved in for a deep and hungry kiss. They had plenty of time to figure out the wedding logistics when she got back from filming. And hopefully, Dak would have solved the copycat case and would be out of danger, temporarily at least.

She reached down and took hold of Dak's strap-on, still slick from their first round. "You're very hard to resist in this mood," she whispered.

Dak grinned and pulled CJ on top of her. "Long may that continue, beautiful."

CJ eased herself down and breathed out as she took Dak inside her again. As she began to ride Dak hard, she took a second to really look at Dak beneath her, the sexy and *very* sexual woman she was marrying. "Goddamn, you're handsome," she rasped and dropped down to press her mouth over Dak's before Dak could respond. CJ didn't need her words. All she needed right now was this connection, this intimacy, this intensity. She needed to soak up everything Dak could give her tonight... Two months was way too long to be apart, and CJ wasn't sure how she was supposed to endure it.

Chapter Thirty-Three

DAK PULLED OVER A few doors from the pawn shop address Weaver had texted her and turned off the engine. Weaver and Miller got out of their car a little farther down the street and walked toward them, with Weaver looking far more relaxed and comfortable in Miller's company. It seemed like he was keeping his end of the bargain, for which Dak was grateful. Weaver had the makings of a great detective, but Dak wasn't sure that she had the mental fortitude to withstand prolonged bullying, or if she did, whether she'd be able to resist reacting aggressively and jeopardizing her career progression. This way, she had the best chance of success.

"I don't know what you threatened Miller with, but it worked," Garrity said. "It's like he's had a personality transplant."

Dak glanced at Garrity and half-smiled. "No threat. Just an honest conversation."

Garrity raised his eyebrows and got out of the car. He leaned back in and said, "Then I hope we never have to have one of those," before swinging the door shut.

Dak joined him on the sidewalk. "Aside from your bitching about my truck, you've never shown even a hint of being an asshole, so I think we're good."

"Maybe we're even better now you've had the AC installed."

She laughed then they greeted Weaver and Miller. Dak gestured to the pawn shop. "What's the deal?"

"Everywhere else we've been, we've come up blank," Weaver said. "But we showed the owner of this place the sketch of our killer, and I'm certain he recognized him. The owner's name is Terrence Brown." She tilted her head toward her partner. "Miller asked to see his records, but he said we'd have to get a warrant. I'm worried that he will have destroyed his records by then."

Dak looked beyond Weaver and Miller to the shop front. It looked well-kept and possibly in the midst of a refurb, as if the owner was attempting to legitimize it by making it look more presentable. "But you think that he'll change his mind if we ask?"

"Yeah. The LAPD clearly don't scare him, but two FBI agents... I figure that should encourage him some."

Dak nodded, though it had already been just under an hour since Weaver had called, and the owner might already have begun destruction of his files. "Is anyone else working in there?"

"Not that we saw," Miller said.

"Anyone gone in and come out since you've been outside?"

"Plenty of people."

"And he hasn't closed up at all?" Dak asked.

"No. He's been pretty busy, though it's gone quiet now." Weaver narrowed her eyes and frowned. "Why?"

Dak pulled her badge from her pocket and fixed it on the front of her slacks. Then she took off her jacket and put it back in the truck. Having her credentials and her firearm on show might encourage the owner to be more forthcoming. "I'm just trying to ascertain if he's had the time to start covering his tracks and destroying any files he might keep."

"Got it."

Weaver's gaze swept over Dak's upper body, and her eyes widened. Dak cocked her head slightly and arched her eyebrows to indicate that she'd noticed. Weaver flushed and turned toward the pawn shop. Dak couldn't decide if she was just daunted by her frame or if there was something else in her expression. It had been too rapid to fully read, and it was of little consequence either way. Dak had dealt with plenty of crushes from younger agents and cops over the years, mostly by indulging them for a night once the case was over, but those days were gone now that she was happily betrothed to CJ.

Dak nodded toward the shop. "Let's see what we can shake out."

Weaver and Miller parted to allow Dak and Garrity through. Dak opened the door to the gentle sound of a metal wind chime, and the owner looked up from the seat behind the counter, where he seemed to be polishing something. By the time she'd strode across the shop floor, he'd swept it into a drawer beneath his work area and pushed it closed. He was in his mid-fifties, with white hair and a bushy beard to match. He was a relatively round guy, but he wore clothes that complemented his shape rather than drew attention to it. And there was no unpleasant odor emanating from him or the shop like there often was in places like this. From what little she'd seen of the outside and inside, her initial observation that he was working to improve the overall appearance of his business held true. Maybe Weaver was right.

He met her eyes after he'd clearly taken in her gun and badge, then he drew in a long breath. "Can I help you, Special Agent?"

There was no obvious distaste in his tone, though his eyes bulged slightly when Weaver and Miller followed in behind and one of them closed the door with more force than was necessary. She glanced over her shoulder to see Miller turning the open sign to closed.

"How long have you been in business here, Terrence?" she asked after reading the very neat little badge pinned to his shirt pocket even though Weaver had already told her his name.

"Nearly nine months." He glanced beyond Dak's shoulder as her colleagues lifted items from the shelves and replaced them noisily.

She stepped closer to the counter to block his view. "Is it working out well so far?"

He shrugged, a gesture that looked awkward and odd, and he seemed as perturbed as she wanted him to be. "I can't complain."

Dak nodded and turned to survey the shop. "It looks like you're spending a lot of money trying to improve the place, so you must be doing okay."

His eyes narrowed briefly before his face became neutral again, like he was trying to figure out what Dak was alluding to. But the sheen of sweat beginning to form on his forehead indicated that he wasn't as comfortable as he was trying to appear.

"Like I said, I can't complain."

"You stock a lot of laptops and tablets." Dak gestured toward a wall full of Apple and Dell hardware, most of which looked pristine. "Are they what you sell the most of?"

Brown nodded.

"What would you say is your next bestseller?" She tilted her head slightly and focused on the giant wall of guns behind him. An array of armaments from single shot pistols to 9mm Sig Sauers and shotguns to old MK37s. New and old weapons were arranged in decades and then size. It was an impressive collection, and a Son of Sam revolver would've been at home there.

He glanced behind him and then thumbed over his shoulder. "Guns, surprisingly."

"Surprisingly?" she asked.

"Yeah. Legitimate gun shops aren't as big a thing in LA as they are in lots of other cities." He turned toward the gun wall a little more now. "I was hoping that if I provided a wide enough range with lots of interesting pieces, I could fill a gap in the market."

Dak nodded and gestured toward the Remington Rider single shot pistol from the nineteenth century she recognized. She was by no means a gun aficionado, but she'd inherited one from her dad. "Like that one?"

"You've got a good eye. There are only about forty of those left in the world."

She smiled. "Yeah. I've got one. There are no serial numbers or barrel markings. Makes it a good gun to commit a murder with. Impossible to trace."

He frowned. "I don't stock it for that reason."

Dak turned to Garrity and beckoned him to join them. "Look

at this."

"It *is* a beautiful gun." Brown took it down from the display and placed it on a soft cloth that he'd pulled from his drawer. "All brass, with a silver plate finish. And look at the quality of the engraving on the breech."

"Nice. You've got one of these?" Garrity asked.

Dak nodded then returned her attention back to Brown. "Are out-of-production and antique guns a hobby of yours?"

He gave her a small smile, clearly beginning to relax. "They are. I sell the new-fangled fully automatic guns, but they're clumsy tools, especially in the wrong hands."

Dak raised her eyebrows. Brown wasn't presenting as an underhanded, black market gun seller, but perhaps he was simply more sophisticated than the average pawn shop owner. "Do you remember the original Charter Arms gun company?"

Brown briefly glanced at the ceiling. "Original?"

He'd looked up and to her right, like he was searching his memory, so he hadn't divined her line of questioning yet.

"Yeah. It went bankrupt and disappeared for a while. But then another company resurrected it. Then they went bankrupt." She waved her hand as if dismissing her train of thought. "Anyway, they made the .44 Special caliber Bulldog revolver. Popular gun. Have you had any of those in lately?"

His eyes flickered slightly before he picked up the Remington pistol and took his time placing it back in its designated position on the wall. Dak nodded at Garrity, and he stepped away to give her space again. She took the artist's impression of their unsub from her pocket, unfolded it, and pressed it flat on the counter.

When Brown turned back to her, he blinked and wiped his brow with the cloth on the counter. He nodded and twisted the cloth in his hands.

"But you've already sold it because it's a damn good weapon. Reliable." She waited until he nodded again. "I'll bet that you keep records of all your sales, Terrence. Am I right?"

His expression hardened slightly as he tilted his head and looked toward Weaver and Miller at the front of the shop. "I already told those two that I do, yes."

"I understand. Client confidentiality is important." Dak leaned closer to Brown. "But we believe that this man," she tapped the illustration, "is the man you sold that particular gun to, and he used it to murder a young couple three nights ago. And thirteen days prior to that, the same man used a High Standard .22 revolver to shoot a man nine times—"

"Nine times?" Brown's forehead creased in disbelief. "That gun's a six-shooter."

"It is," Dak said. "He pumped six shots into the victim's face and chest, reloaded, and fired off another three. This killer is something else." Now she was this close to Brown, she could see a family photo tacked to the top of his computer screen. Wife and two daughters. "Do you remember what Ted Bundy did to his young female victims? This killer's done that too. And in three days or so, he's going to kidnap a young woman, slice out a few of her vital organs, and then kill her. We don't have the time for formality and protocols, Terrence. We don't have time to seek warrants and talk to judges. We've got seventy-two hours before he kills again." Seeing that her logic was winning him over, she jutted her chin toward his picture. "You have young women in your life who are important to you, Terrence. Your daughters are your world, aren't they? That's why you're working this hard day after day in this shop: to build them a secure future. What if one of them was likely to be his next victim? Would you show us your records then?"

"He's already killed four people?" Brown's gaze fixed firmly on his family.

"*Five* people in four separate crimes, and we believe he's planning a further five murders over the next two months." Dak pulled her leather notebook from her back pocket, tore out a blank sheet and pushed it over the counter toward Harris. "Give us the address he gave you. That's all you need to do to stop a vicious murderer on a devastating killing spree. You'll see it on the news, and you'll know that you helped keep this city safe. Helped keep your family safe."

Brown tugged at his lower lip with his teeth and pulled in a deep breath that stretched the soft-looking fabric of his thin sweater. Finally, he took the slip of paper and pushed up from his seat. "Give me a few minutes."

Dak nodded and turned to Weaver and Miller as Brown left. "Do you have your bulletproof vests in the trunk?"

Miller nodded. "And a Remington 870."

"We're going there now?" Weaver asked.

Dak assessed her tone and body language; Weaver seemed both scared and exhilarated. As long as her fear didn't overwhelm her training and freeze her up, she'd be okay. "We don't have the luxury of time, Weaver. The address Brown gives us could lead to our killer, and we'll go in with our full task force. Miller, call Captain Grant and the rest of the team. Tell them we'll text them the location and ask your captain to get a warrant for us to search the address we're about to send him."

Miller saluted. "Sure thing," he said and left the shop.

Brown returned and gave Dak the address. "Please tell me that you're able to keep my name out of this."

She handed the notepaper to Garrity after checking it. *Benjamin Scott.* Undoubtedly, it wouldn't be his real name, and she didn't recognize it as an anagram of a famous killer or having any other significance. She gave Brown a genuine smile. "You've done the right thing, Terrence. If the man at that address isn't our killer, we won't divulge any information about the case, including your assistance. You have my word."

"And if it is the man who killed all those people?" Brown's eyes widened. "He must have faked his ID."

Dak tilted her head slightly, understanding Brown was eager to clear himself of any wrongdoing or paperwork-fudging. "Then we'll arrest him. And the city will be too busy proving he's a multiple murderer to concern themselves with where he sourced one of his weapons." She didn't know that for sure, of course, but they had what they needed, and that was Dak's priority. Pandering to a potentially questionable gun seller didn't interest her.

"Good. Good. Excellent." Brown touched his fingers to the faces of his wife and daughters. "I hope you find him soon."

Dak folded the sketch of their killer and placed it back in her pocket. "So do we." She picked up the paper with the address and drummed her fingers on the counter. "Thanks again for your help," she said and walked out of the shop, closely followed by Weaver and Garrity. Miller strolled toward them from his car, his thumbs-up gesture indicating the rest of the team were on their way.

"That was amazing to watch," Weaver said, her awe unabashed. "I'd love to learn how to do that."

"That's not something you can teach," Garrity said. He looked at Dak and nodded approvingly. "Sublime to watch though."

While she appreciated the praise and acknowledgment, her focus was elsewhere. They were getting closer to the copycat killer; she could feel it in the itch of her bones. "Garrity, do you know this neighborhood?" She passed him the slip of paper.

"Sure do." Garrity pulled out his phone, tapped away for a moment and then showed Dak the screen.

"He's close to an elementary school." Dak pointed at the location then ran her hand across the back of her head. "We don't want this going anywhere near there. We'll station Gray and Taylor at the south end of Evergreen to stem any escape in the vicinity of the school. And we'll post Lawson and Aston at the end of Inez in case our guy tries to escape through back yards. Garrity and I will take the front of the house. You two will take the back."

"You don't want SWAT?" Miller asked.

"No," Dak said. "I think the eight of us have enough experience to handle it. The remaining chapters of the book feature killers who are hands-on, so it's reasonable to assume the only weapons that he'll have will be the two guns he's already used—if he hasn't already disposed of them. I don't see this turning into a gun battle, and if it does," she tapped her Glock 17, "I like our odds."

Miller nodded and smiled. "Agreed." He glanced at Weaver. "Are you ready for something like this?"

The question wasn't unkind, but Dak suspected Weaver would rather he'd asked it in the privacy of the car, if at all. Dak noted the flicker of self-doubt in her eyes even as Weaver stood a little straighter.

"Of course I am," she said and punched Miller's shoulder. "Let's do this."

Dak and Miller exchanged a brief look, and Miller acknowledged her concern with a slight nod. It seemed that Miller had taken Dak's directive to heart and was trying to do better. His type of attitude problem couldn't be solved overnight, but at least he was trying. She could only hope that her own trust in Weaver wouldn't bite her on the ass.

Chapter Thirty-Four

MILLER, WEAVER, TAYLOR, AND Gray were already parked on the street in front of La Casa del Mexicano. Dak and Garrity arrived after a detour to switch to Garrity's car in case they had to pursue their perp. They'd just pulled up behind Taylor's dark blue Dodge Charger when she looked in the side mirror and saw Lawson and Aston pull around the corner.

Within seconds, all eight of them were out of their vehicles and congregated around the hood of Garrity's. Taylor handed her the expedited search and arrest warrant that Captain Grant had organized. She scanned it then slipped it into her back pocket. "Great work." She scanned the faces of the assembled cops to get a read on their level of calmness. Everyone seemed steady...except Weaver. Her eyes darted around the street, catching movement from birds, squirrels, and God knew what else. Dak looked at Miller, but he mouthed, "She'll be okay."

Dak shook her head almost imperceptibly, and Miller tilted his in return and shrugged. She'd told him that he had to mentor Weaver better but having too much faith in her where it wasn't warranted was dangerous. Not just to Weaver but to all of them. "Get your weapons out and your vests on. I don't want another battle scar, and I figure none of your family would thank me if I let you get your own."

As they all shifted to retrieve the tools of their trade from their respective trunks, Dak caught hold of Weaver's forearm. "A word, Weaver."

Weaver dropped her shoulders and seemed to lose six inches in stature, making it clear she already knew why Dak was taking her aside. Dak moved across the street, out of the others' earshot.

"What's going on?" Dak asked, wanting to give Weaver a final opportunity to show she was ready for this.

Weaver's eyes flitted around, scanning the area and avoiding Dak's gaze. "I'm ready, Agent Farrell. I'm on top of my game, I promise. I know what I'm doing," she said after an extended silence.

Dak raised an eyebrow, yet to be convinced. "Are you sure? You seem...jittery."

Weaver shook her head. "No, I'm good. I'm just...excited, you know? This is the kind of case I've been waiting for. I won't let you down."

Dak considered her for a moment longer. "Are you sure you can stay focused? This isn't a game, and it's not about proving anything to the rest of the cops at your station." She grasped Weaver's shoulder.

Weaver's gaze laser-focused on Dak. "You know how my dad died, don't you?"

Dak shrugged. "I did a little research after Miller mentioned him. It doesn't matter if they're comparing you to him, and you shouldn't be comparing yourself to him either. You're different cops and *very* different people. And these are different times." As well as discovering Weaver's dad had been killed in a street gun battle, she'd read that Weaver's dad had been a particularly prolific and successful detective before making captain, but the subliminal text indicated his methods weren't always sanctioned or above board and potentially included violence. There was no place for that kind of policing in the current climate. There never should've been. "What matters is you trying to be the best cop you can be. Got it?"

Weaver nodded, a hint of vulnerability disappearing as swiftly as it had arisen. She bounced on her toes. "I know, Agent Farrell. I'm ready. I promise I can do this."

Dak clapped Weaver on the back before crossing the street and going back to the others who had reassembled at Garrity's car, checking gear and tightening each other into their bulletproof vests.

"Garrity and I will take the front. Miller and Weaver will go around the back." Dak placed Garrity's tablet on the hood of her truck with a map of the area already loaded. She pointed to the vicinity of the address Brown had given them. "Gray, you and Taylor block the south end of Evergreen as best you can with your car. If this is our guy and he runs, I don't want him anywhere near the elementary school and a possible hostage situation. Understood?"

They nodded. "We won't let this asshole get anywhere near the kids, Farrell. You can count on that."

"Good. Lawson and Aston, I want you at the end of Inez." She indicated the location on the screen. "It's a dead-end, but some of the properties on that street butt up to the rear yards of the Evergreen houses. If he makes his escape out back and toward that street, you're up. Got it?"

Lawson and Aston confirmed her order then bumped their fists together. It was a little cliché, more behavior she expected from a SWAT team than two seasoned detectives, but adrenaline pumped hard and fast in situations like this, and cops did what they felt was necessary to get through.

Dak nodded, satisfied with their responses. She took one last look at her team before getting back in Garrity's car. "Let's move out."

The convoy made their way towards the target location, separating at the intersection. As they approached the house, a deep thudding in Dak's heart prompted her to realize this was the first assault she'd carried out since she'd been shot. Instinctively, she touched her vest at the site of the healed bullet wound and sucked in a deep breath. She'd trained hard to get back to active duty, and she had years of experience. The risk was part of the job, so why didn't that make it less nerve-racking right now? It dawned on her that she'd never been bogged down with these kinds of thoughts or hesitations before. She'd always been calm, ice-cool, steady. *CJ.* Dak closed her eyes briefly and recalled their last night together before CJ had gotten on a flight to her first filming location. What if that was the final time Dak would see her face? The last time she saw CJ's eyes half-lidded in ecstasy, their final kiss...

She pushed the thoughts away, barely able to contain her self-directed anger. It was hypocritical to question Weaver's readiness when Dak allowed her own mind to run riot. The air in the sedan was charged with anticipation, and Dak was glad for the silence. She couldn't deny that she'd prefer to have Hamilton by her side right now, or even his enigmatic and highly capable sister, but Garrity had proven himself to be a solid agent. She couldn't see him failing her now.

As they pulled up a few doors down, Dak could see that the house was old and a little run-down. If the place was a rental, the landlord wasn't the best at keeping the yard tidy. There were signs of improvement here and there, a partially painted fence and a small vegetable patch that looked well-tended. Two Adirondack chairs took pride of place beside the front door. They looked weathered, but it was clear they'd been stained year on year to keep them fresh. Dak suspected yardwork was the last thing a serial killer would spend his time on. There was no truck in the driveway.

She took a deep breath and looked at Garrity, who gave her a nod. They got out of the car, and without a word, she walked with him, Weaver, and Miller the short distance to 2643 S Evergreen Street. They got to the bottom of the driveway of the adjacent property, and she gestured for Miller and Weaver to make their way along the tree-lined perimeter to the rear of the property. When they reached the base of the path, she rested her hand on the hilt of her gun, pushed through the low front gate, and she and Garrity approached the front door side by side.

Dak knocked loudly on the door and waited.

***

It's so useful to have an early warning system. It can give one time to prepare, time to preen, or even time to escape. The first alarm gets my attention, and I look up at the monitor which displays live video captured from the six cameras covering the house and its perimeter.

This clearly isn't a social visit. The people walking the path to the front door aren't Girl Scouts selling sugary treats. Nor are they Jehovah's Witnesses who I can tease with an unhealthy debate about the validity of their sky god and their ridiculous restrictions on medical interventions. With whom I can proclaim myself a sinful human with no desire to reconcile myself to God and their arbitrary force.

You know, it doesn't matter whether a person is a cop or if they're from the CIA, DEA, FBI or any other three letter government organization this country has, they all walk the same. They all carry themselves in the same self-assured, almost arrogant manner. On some officers of the law, it can be quite the turn-on. But on most, it's ugly, an overcompensation for a complete lack of humility or compassion. The tall, solidly built woman approaching the front door has an intoxicating mix of butch and cop swagger that piques my interest. I can't say that she's not my type—I'm happy to fuck and be fucked by all manner of humans—but her profession alone should be cooling my blood rather than having it rush to places which are rather inconvenient in this particular situation. Her partner isn't unattractive either. *Tsk.* It's been too long since that lovely couple in San Francisco; my sexual needs are overriding my survival instinct.

That said, the skinny, androgynous officer who's slipping around the back with her much older, much chubbier partner doesn't really seem to have that strut down pat. Yet. Perhaps they're new on the job, still green from the Academy. They think they're about to cut their teeth catching someone they've no doubt deemed an evil killer, when in fact they seek a mere scientist.

I had a feeling I couldn't fully trust that Terrence fellow. He was far too accommodating, far too gracious. He accepted the address I gave with little ceremony and certainly not the vetting that's supposed to occur when one sells a firearm, another thing my home country has over this one. Here, it's ominously easy to procure a weapon with which to kill the masses. Though the masses could do with the occasional culling, I don't deny.

I glance at the two guns I used to kill Beasley and that adorable couple. They're loaded and ready for action. I've practiced shooting with my right hand, but I've never been able to get it as strong or as accurate as my left. Perhaps I should've spent more time perfecting my technique. Then I could have a gun in each hand and shoot the pair at the front door before they've even drawn their weapons. A little sneak around the back and the same to Mr. Blobby and Mx. Skinny Pants, and I'd be done with them. Though I suspect there are other officers lurking in the vicinity, perhaps on the street behind the house. Could I jump in my truck and be gone before those officers got the chance to respond to shots fired?

***

They waited for a few moments, but there was no response. Dak nodded to Garrity, and she stepped back, ready to kick in the door. But just as she was about to make contact, the door creaked open slowly. She clasped the grip of her gun, ready to draw.

A small, infirm old man stooped in the doorway and squinted against the setting sun. "Hello?"

Dak frowned and relaxed her hand. She unclipped her badge and offered it up for the old man's inspection, close to his face since the glasses he wore were thicker than the windshield of her truck. "Benjamin Scott?"

He peered at her badge, his nose almost touching it, then looked up. "Yes. Can I help you?"

Dak closed her eyes briefly and let out the tension she'd been holding in a long breath. They'd been led on a wild goose chase. "Do you live alone, Mr. Scott?" Beside her, Garrity ran his hand through his hair and shook his head, clearly frustrated too. She nodded to him, and he took a half-step back before radioing the others to let them know Benjamin Scott was most definitely *not* the man they were looking for.

Mr. Scott pursed his lips, wrinkling his skin like Venetian blinds. Profound sadness somehow overcame his whole expression, as if he were the walking embodiment of grief. The visible change touched Dak's heart, reminding her that she or CJ had that kind of loss to face. She could only hope that it was decades away.

"My wife died twenty-three weeks and five days ago," he said, his words trembling and catching in his throat.

He lifted his wrist to his nose and checked the time. Though he didn't add the number of hours, seconds, and minutes, it was clear he felt her absence acutely in those terms.

"I'm sorry for your loss," Dak said, wishing she could offer more than the rote response everyone trotted out automatically. But the grief of others was something she struggled to cope with, having experienced too much of her own.

Mr. Scott pushed his heavy glasses back on his nose and sniffed hard. Tears edged his eyes, and his chin trembled. "Thank you." His response was equally automatic, and he stepped back into the safety of his house, grasping the interior door handle.

Dak took out the sketch of their killer and held it out. "Have you seen this man, Mr. Scott?"

He chuckled lightly, and the vibration made his tears trickle down his cheek. He wiped them away and shook his head. "I'm afraid I don't see that well these days." He tapped the lens of his glasses. "Even with these bottle-bottoms." He gestured toward his garage. "That's why my truck is rusting away in there. Can't drive it anymore, see."

Dak glanced at Garrity, and he raised his eyebrows. He

wandered off to look in the garage window, and she turned her attention back to Mr. Scott. "Couldn't you sell it?"

Mr. Scott huffed. "I couldn't do that. It was my wife's pride and joy. Last thing I did with it was get my grandson to change the front tire." He rolled his eyes. "I couldn't afford a new one, so he got something second-hand from Craig's List. Edie would've clipped him 'round the ear for that." He shrugged, and his whole frame shook.

Dak inhaled sharply at the potential connection to the mismatched tires on the truck they were searching for. She looked across to Garrity, who was wiping years of dirt and cobwebs from the small windows on the garage door. She watched him peer in while using the flashlight function on his phone.

Garrity walked swiftly back toward them. "I'm afraid there's no truck in your garage, Mr. Scott."

The old man grabbed at the door jamb to steady himself, panic consuming his entire expression. "No, no, no. You're mistaken. She's under a dark tarp, that's all. Makes her hard to see without putting the light on."

Garrity shook his head. "I can see the tarp on the ground, Mr. Scott," Garrity said. "But there's no truck in there."

Dak caught Mr. Scott as his legs gave way and he tumbled toward her, distress etched on his face as he repeatedly muttered that it couldn't be. She took his weight easily and guided him onto one of the Adirondack chairs.

"No. Not that one," he said and shuffled across the arms of the chair to sag heavily into the one farthest from the door. He glanced lovingly at the seat he wouldn't take. "That's where Edie sits."

Out of respect, Dak didn't take the chair but squatted in front of him instead. She looked up at the overhang and saw something slightly out of place on the wooden boards that framed the front door. At the area where the boarding met at the corner of the door, there was a small, perfectly circular hole. And the wood around the hole was slightly lighter than the rest of it. She didn't think that it had been cleaned as such; it was more like the dirt had been disturbed.

"Have you had any work done on your door lately, Mr. Scott?" she asked.

He huffed. "Work on my door? My wife's truck has been stolen. I don't care about the work on my door."

"Of course. I'm sorry." She should've been more sensitive, but the possibility of a solid lead on their killer after this initial disappointment was all-consuming. Dak caught Garrity's questioning look, so she flicked her gaze upward to the hole and raised her eyebrows. He nodded and moved closer to inspect it. She withdrew her notebook and clicked the end of her pen. "Can you give me the license plate and make of the truck, Mr. Scott?"

"ED 1242," he said without hesitation. "It's a Chevrolet Silverado in burgundy. Edie chose that color specifically because it reminded her of zinfandel, her favorite wine. She bought it new in 2015... Sometimes I think she loved her truck more than she loved me."

"That doesn't sound likely, Mr. Scott," Dak said gently. She looked up at Garrity, who frowned as he peered up into the corner of the doorframe. It was then that Dak knew exactly what they'd find in that hole. Their killer had set up surveillance at Mr. Scott's house in case his gun purchase was tracked. She'd wager there was a tiny camera in there replete with audio capability. *Damn it.* She quickly tracked back through their interaction with Mr. Scott to see how much they'd revealed about the investigation. Thankfully, the only real piece of information was the sketch. But he would've seen it, known how closely it resembled him. Brown could've provided them with the likeness. There was no way the killer would know it was Cherry, thus alerting him to their knowledge of at least two of his murders. The question would be the size of his ego and the level of his arrogance. Was he the kind of person to bolt at the first sign of pursuit? Or did he think himself superior to the authorities and would consider this game on?

"Mr. Scott, do you have any photographs of the vehicle?" She didn't need them. She just wanted to get him back in the house so that she could inspect that hole.

"Help me up?"

Dak stood and held out her hands for Mr. Scott to steady himself as he rose painfully slowly from the hard wooden chair.

"I'll get the garage keys too," he said as he ambled unsteadily back into his house. "I want to see for myself."

When Mr. Scott was out of sight, Dak turned her attention to the corner of the door frame. "I think he's got eyes on us." She pulled one of the chairs closer and stood on it for more height.

"That's forward planning," Garrity said.

"Maybe audio too." When she was at eye-level with the hole, she shone the flashlight of her phone into it. Sure enough, a pin camera was nestled inside. She took her mini Leatherman from her pocket and used the flat screwdriver to prize the surveillance unit out before flicking the switch to off. "What do you think the range is on these things?"

Garrity shrugged. "I wouldn't have a clue. We'd have to take it to tech."

Weaver and Miller emerged around the corner of the house. "We waited around the back for a while just in case. What's going on?" Weaver asked.

Dak threw the camera unit to her. "Check the back and the perimeter for more of these. It looks like our guy set up his own warning system."

"Impressive," Miller said as he looked over Weaver's shoulder at the camera.

Dak heard a shout of anguish from Mr. Scott and ran into the house. "Mr. Scott? Where are you?" She turned into the living room to find Mr. Scott collapsed into a large wingback armchair. "Are you okay?"

He pointed to a small, hand-painted box on the side table by the wall. His hands shook, and his whole body trembled. "The keys are gone. For the truck and for the garage. That's my wife's special box. She always kept all her keys in there. I haven't touched it since she died." He shook his head. "I didn't touch it when she was alive. She didn't trust me not to lose her keys, you see. She always said I'd lose my head if it wasn't screwed on."

Dak sat on the couch opposite him after scanning the box and confirming for herself that it was empty. She nodded to Garrity, who'd followed closely behind, to head back out. "Have you had anyone other than family in the house over the past couple of months?"

He nodded. "I have my groceries delivered every couple of weeks, and they're always kind enough to bring everything into the kitchen."

"Anyone else? Utilities? Anyone claiming to be the police?"

"There was a gas leak about five weeks ago." He wagged his finger and became more animated. "That guy was here a long time. He asked about my wife, and I'll talk about my lovely Edie to anyone who'll listen." Mr. Scott pointed toward the front of his house. "You asked if I'd had any work done to my front door: he had a good old poke around the outside. He was 'round the back, down in the basement, and even at the gate. Checking gas levels, he said."

"Did he ask about the truck?" Dak could almost envisage the killer wandering around Mr. Scott's house, probably unable to believe his luck that he could procure a vehicle so easily. They needed to check the whole property for cameras.

"We got onto cars at some point, yes. I told him I couldn't drive. And I told him that I couldn't bear to go into the garage since Edie died. Even when our grandson changed the front tire, I didn't watch him. It's too painful. I expect to see her behind the wheel, and it feels like an elephant sits on my chest when I look and she's not there."

He glanced across at the second sofa under the window and became sadness personified once again. Dak could see the two indentations from years of sitting side by side and thought about her own living room. They both had specific spots on the couch, just like they had their sides of the bed. After decades of being together, how bereft must Mr. Scott be to wake up every morning and *not* see his wife lying beside him anymore? How devastated would Dak be in the same position even though she and CJ had only been together for a fraction of that time? She couldn't imagine, and right now, she shouldn't be trying to. Still, it made her want to call CJ and tell her how much she loved her. Dak had experienced enough grief in her life to know that she'd cherish every second with CJ.

"We'll find your truck, Mr. Scott," Dak said after a few moments of silence.

He nodded slowly. "I hope so. I need to hang onto every last memory of her. I can't face letting go."

Dak rose from the sofa. "We'll have a team come by today to see if they can find any prints that might lead us to your thief, okay?"

He nodded again but was clearly lost in his heartache.

"I'll close the door on the way out."

Garrity, Weaver, and Miller waited for her on the path.

"We found five cameras, but there could be more," Garrity said. "He's a clever bastard. Miller has called CSU to do a more thorough check and to see if they find any fingerprints or DNA. Maybe he cut himself when he was busy concealing these things." He shook the tiny units in his hand like he was shaking dice at a craps table. "They should be here in thirty minutes."

"Okay, let's reconvene back at the station," Dak said. "We don't need to be here for that since Miller's briefed them thoroughly."

Garrity narrowed his eyes before it looked like he followed her thought process. "Sure thing."

Dak closed the gate behind them, and they walked up the street to their vehicles. When they were at Garrity's car, and she was sure they were out of range of any remaining cameras, she pulled out the tablet and rested it on the hood. She beckoned them all close. "We're not going anywhere."

"You think he's close by?" Garrity asked.

"I do. And he knows we're onto him. He'll know CSU are on their way and will be there a couple of hours. If he decides to run, he'll wait until they're gone." She checked her watch. "It's nearly three p.m., and I guess CSU will have done what they need to by six. Miller, get an APB out on this license plate." She held out the requisite page of her notebook while he took a photo on his phone. "And let's run a check on all households on this street. We need a list of make, model, color, and plate of all vehicles registered to them." She waited until Garrity nodded then continued, "I'll radio the others and tell them to stay in position but to hang back out of sight. Garrity and I will take the north end of the avenue." She pointed to a small offshoot on the map. "Weaver, you and Miller go to this side road off Guirado that these houses back onto."

"And then?" Weaver asked.

"We wait." *And hope to God that I'm right.*

Chapter Thirty-Five

BLOODY HELL. THIS IS an egregious interference in my business. Now they know what vehicle I'm driving, what am I supposed to use to get around? I'll have to change the plate. The arrogant little cock next door has three cars. It would be a few days before he realized the plate was missing from the nondescript sedan parked at the top of his drive. That's the one he uses the least. And they've created an incredible likeness of me, though I'm sure my nose isn't quite that pronounced. That damn prostitute betrayed me; it has to be her because I only wore that garish baseball cap while talking to her. I didn't see that happening. I would have thought that me disposing of that Beasley garbage and the few hundred dollars I'd given her would buy her silence. Since when do hookers cooperate with the police? If I didn't have to damn well abort my project, I'd teach her a lesson in etiquette by making her my next victim. I'm sure Jack, or Aaron Kosminski if you believe the Edwards' research, would thoroughly approve.

But instead, I have to abandon my plans and head home, *experimentum imperfectum*. I can't even begin to put my rage into words. All the preparation. All my hard work. The subjects I've disposed of. In vain? I'm halfway in, and I feel the change. What effect will this infernal interruption have? Do I have the potential to go off the proverbial rails and self-sabotage? Now more than ever, my self-control must be at its strongest.

Small mercies that they didn't find all my surveillance cameras. I left one inside the garage just in case the old man went against everything he told me and did venture in there to see his beloved wife's truck. I expect there'll be a CSU unit along soon enough to search for traces of me. I can still listen in to glean more information should they be loose-tongued. The more knowledge I have about where their investigation stands, the better equipped I am to leave this city without detection. I don't know how long they've had that sketch of me, but no doubt, it'll be at the airports and port, so I have no choice but to drive out of the state and fly from Las Vegas, a city where I can blend in and leave with the masses without arousing suspicion.

I'll ditch the truck and set fire to it to destroy any residual DNA. I suppose it's inevitable that they'll already have some cells of my mine from the scenes of my previous victims. Though I bleached and cleaned the scenes, it's not like I wore a hazmat suit. Mr. Scott epitomized all that is good about humanity in a way that cultivated a little empathy in me. I was only ever intending to borrow the truck and would've put it back with Mr. Scott being none the wiser. But those damn FBI agents and police have scuppered that plan. They really have no idea the havoc and trouble they've caused with their heavy-handed interference. If only they knew this was all in the name of science, perhaps they would stand down and let me complete my important work. I suppose we shall never know, shall we?

I can secure the plates now while the neighbor's at work, and I'll wait until the police have gone before I make my escape. But I shouldn't let them win. I won't let this put a complete stop to my experiment. There's no reason I can't identify another city right now. Like ~~Chicago~~. No. New York. In 2022, there were eighty murders in just one month. I could continue my project there with far less pressure simply because of the volume of homicides their police have to deal with. I suppose I should've gone there in the first place, but I have to admit that the lure of West Coast sunshine appealed to my melanin-starved self. Never mind. It doesn't do to dwell on decisions one can do nothing about. The show must go on, as they're prone to say on Broadway.

So worry not. This will just be a temporary cessation. You'll soon be able to pick up from where I've been rudely interrupted, and I'll kick off my New York residency with a Jack the Ripper victim. I simply need to leave LA without detection, which, with my superior intellect and the advance notice that they're on the lookout for me, shouldn't be an issue.

Chapter Thirty-Six

Stakeouts were tedious things. Hours and hours of ass-numbing sitting and mind-numbing small talk. Dak ran her finger down the list of alphabetized vehicles when the Ford F-150 turned into S Evergreen. "That truck's registered to a Roman Bilsworthy, resident at 15823."

Garrity chuckled. "Fancy name." He held his stomach when it rumbled for the fifth time in as many minutes. "Are you hungry?"

She shook her head. "I can't eat when I'm on a stakeout. My appetite completely disappears. I'm thirsty though. If we'd come in my truck instead of this modern piece of junk, we'd have plenty of water to last us."

"Water?" Garrity wrinkled his nose. "I need coffee. And if we'd come in your truck and do have to chase the bastard, we'd have to ask our serial killer very nicely not to drive over fifty so you could keep up."

Dak arched her eyebrow and glanced at him. "This is why I usually work alone."

He laughed again. "I heard it was because people don't *want* to work with you."

She shrugged. "Could be that too," she said and half-smiled. That was certainly true in the immediate aftermath of Ben's death. "I saw a convenience store on the corner of Eagle. You should grab something before your stomach eats itself or deafens me."

Garrity checked the location on his phone. "I can be there and back in fifteen minutes. Are you sure?"

That would give her time to call CJ, who'd been on her mind more than ever since she left Mr. Scott's house. She nodded. "It's not dusk yet. Just be quick."

"Sure. Do you want anything?"

"A few bottles of water would be great."

"You got it." Garrity got out of the car and left the door open for Dak to come around the front and get in the driver's side—just in case.

She settled into the seat after sliding it back to accommodate for her height and video called CJ as Garrity jogged across the road.

CJ answered on the third ring. "Hey you. I didn't think I'd hear from you until late."

The sight of CJ's face had an immediately calming effect. "Are you okay to talk?"

"Yeah. We've just been setting up the filming location today, and I finished a couple of hours ago. Is everything okay? You sound strange, and you look sad."

Dak tried for a big smile but saw that she'd fallen short. "I miss you."

CJ narrowed her eyes and moved closer to the camera. "There's more to it than that. What aren't you saying?"

"Can't a woman have any private thoughts?" Dak asked, though CJ's ability to see her was as comforting as it was unfamiliar.

"Not my woman, no." CJ laughed and winked. "Seriously, though. What's wrong?"

Dak bit her lip. Sharing her fears with anyone meant showing vulnerabilities she wasn't comfortable with, but the emotional response that Mr. Scott's grief had initiated was something she'd never experienced before. And that was because of CJ, because Dak couldn't bear to think about losing her or being apart.

"Dak?"

She'd gone quiet for longer than she'd thought. Being open with the woman she was going to spend the rest of her life with was part of the deal, wasn't it? "We got a lead on the copycat, and it took us to an old guy out in Boyle Heights." Dak paused, but CJ made no attempt to fill the silence with a comment or question, making it clear she wasn't saying anything until she'd gotten the full story. "His wife had died about six months ago, and his grief, CJ, his grief was so...complete that it almost took a physical form beside him." She focused on CJ, who looked like she was trying to suppress a grin. "I know that you're not a heartless wench, but I'm not sure why you're almost smiling at my sad story. Explain, please."

"You really do love me, huh?"

Dak frowned. "Have I not made that clear enough?"

"You have. But that doesn't mean that I can't appreciate moments like this." CJ touched the screen and smiled, her answering love clear in her eyes. "You're sad because you're thinking about losing me. Is that right?"

Dak nodded, not sure that her voice wouldn't betray her and emerge like a croaky frog's.

"I hate being away from you too, and with your job..." CJ shook her head and closed her eyes. "The things that could happen to you terrify me. So it's vital that we make the most of the time we're together, that we don't lose sight of each other even when we do see each other every day. I think that I want to find a way–"

"Oh, shit." Dak had been keeping an eye for movement over the top of her phone, and a maroon Silverado had just pulled up at the stop sign.

"What's going on?"

"I have to go. I'll call you back." Dak ended the call, turned the ignition, and checked the road ahead, but there was no sign of Garrity. "I've got eyes on our serial killer," she said into the radio. "He's coming out of the north end, and it looks like he's turning right to head toward me."

"We'll be with you in two minutes." Miller was the first to respond. "Keep us apprised of your route."

Dak accepted the instruction without comment even though she hadn't needed it. "Lawson, I need you to call Garrity on his cell and let him know we're in pursuit."

The truck turned slowly onto her street, and she shuffled down in her seat slightly, not wanting him to identify her. She'd prefer all the units to be with her before they made him aware of their presence. She fixed her gaze ahead but kept him in her peripheral vision.

"Where the hell is Garrity?"

She caught the concern overriding the anger in Miller's voice, though she was slightly surprised by it. Dak didn't answer the question; she didn't want to raise the radio to her mouth as their killer approached.

Not that it would've mattered, because he stared directly into the car as he drew closer, and she saw the recognition in his eyes. He pressed his lips together tightly before he sneered. Cherry's sketch had caught the killer in his eyes perfectly.

He sped off, and Dak flipped the car around to give chase. "He went for food, Lawson," she said into the radio. "The killer spotted me, and he's floored it." Still no sign of Garrity but at least the rest of the team would join the pursuit.

When she pulled in behind him, she saw he'd changed out the plates, likely for a close neighbor's specifically for his evening escape. "He's switched plates. Yankee Bravo 5032."

There was a short pause before Weaver said, "That's registered to a black Taurus at 2659. Eight houses up from the Scott residence."

"We were so close," Gray said.

"Close only counts in hand grenades and horseshoes," Miller said with bitterness clear in his voice.

"I think he's heading for the Pomona Freeway," Dak said. "Best guess as to where he's going?"

"He would've taken the South I-5 if he was driving to Mexico," Miller said, "but I'll put money on Vegas. He knows we've got his sketch and that we'll have people looking for him at the airports. He's getting out of state, and Nevada is the closest border."

"That makes sense." Dak took the right onto South Indiana then swung left onto the on-ramp of the Pomona Freeway.

"We see you," Miller said. "And I've got Lawson and Taylor behind me. It's ten miles to the 605 if I'm right about his intentions." He gave a loud huff. "Once he's on the 605, he'll have multiple route options, but he should take the I-10 to 7th Street East. There's no guarantee though. He might ignore the 605 and stay on this freeway, so we've got maybe ten minutes to converge all local patrols before he hits the 605, if he maintains this speed. What do you want to do, Farrell?"

"That's not a lot of time, Miller." Dak swerved around a semi and maintained her visual on the truck.

"Enough time for at least one patrol to get a stop stick down on the off ramp. Unless you want to try for a full roadblock farther along on the I-10, but if he takes an alternative route..."

"Okay, do it," Dak said, aware that every second of delay decreased the likelihood of success. "But make sure they stay out of sight. If he sees their patrol cars, he'll just stay on this road." The ensuing radio silence allowed her to focus on their killer. Now that he knew she was in pursuit, would he simply try to outrun her? Or would he head into a recreation area, dump the vehicle, and try to evade her on foot? He'd had the chance to assess her via his CCTV at Mr. Scott's house. Maybe he'd decided he could outrun her. And he would've seen she was alone in the car. That could inflate his confidence since he was such a big guy.

Her cell rang, and a quick glance at the screen identified the caller as Garrity. She hit accept and pressed speakerphone. "How's your food?"

"All over the sidewalk on Eagle Street," he said. "I got myself a new ride since you stole mine, and I'm a few minutes behind you. Get me up to speed."

Dak repeated Miller's prediction of their killer's route and their intended action with the stop sticks.

"Sounds like our only play. I'll call for aerial back up and then I'll try to catch up."

"You better." She hung up before he responded and gripped the steering wheel a little tighter. The killer was keeping to a speed of around ninety, and his driving wasn't erratic even as he switched lanes to get around other drivers. As chases went, this one was pretty safe so far. A lot of the drivers around them were going far faster than the speed limit anyway.

"All patrols in the vicinity are heading to the 605, Farrell," Miller cut in over the radio.

She glanced in the rear-view and saw Weaver a little too well, causing Dak to question whether she'd ever been in a high-speed chase before. "Pull back some, Weaver. You're too close."

"Sure thing."

Weaver dropped back to a safer distance, and Dak allowed herself to relax slightly now that the chance of being rear-ended by her overzealous colleague had been reduced. Up ahead, their killer maneuvered in and out of lanes without making other drivers brake, and Dak had an absurd thought that the British were polite even when they were being chased by the police. She wondered how polite he'd been when he'd killed his victims.

The truck cut across two lanes to sneak in front of a semi, and Dak lost sight of him. She tried to follow, but the car in the third lane had already taken up the space. She slowed her speed to pull in behind the semi and was about to swing into the outer lane when she saw the killer's truck also slowing down in that lane. He'd assumed she would speed up the inside lane to gain sight of him again, and he was clearly trying to pull around behind her, perhaps to disappear on the next off ramp. "No, you don't."

She hit the horn to let him know she hadn't fallen for it, and the truck jerked forward. His maneuver indicated he might also be checking to see if she was the only car in pursuit. She looked in her rear-view to see that Weaver had swung into the outer lane and was about to draw level with her. She motioned for her to drop back, and Dak slipped in behind the killer once again. He'd increased his speed though and was already way ahead.

Dak pressed the accelerator hard, and Garrity's car powered forward, eating up the space between them. Now she was really glad they'd took the time to switch out Betty for Garrity's gas guzzler.

"Three units in place, Farrell. They've dumped their patrol cars on Famosa and climbed up the bank. They're ready and waiting—"

"Behind safety barriers?" Too many officers had been killed using stop sticks, and she didn't want that happening here.

"For sure. We train 'em well out here, Farrell, I promise."

Miller's words reassured her, and she eased into the same distance from the killer's truck as before. She wanted to be far enough away to allow the patrols time to pull back the stop sticks before she and the others followed. As the truck's tires quickly deflated, they would have time to surround him and, hopefully, end this without gunfire.

Just as Miller predicted, the killer switched to the inside lane ready to take the off ramp, and Dak followed. She heard the roar of a powerful motorbike before she saw the blaze of fiery red paint zip alongside her in the emergency lane. The bike zoomed beyond her and passed the killer's truck before jamming across the front of it in an apparent attempt to go across three lanes of traffic and back onto the 60. Whether the killer reacted too slowly or whether the bike hesitated, Dak couldn't tell, but the next thing she saw was the truck hitting the bike and the rider launched into the air. The truck dragged the bike beneath it and then bucked upward as the killer slammed on the brakes and tried to wrestle his vehicle under control. The safe distance Dak had disappeared, and she jerked the steering wheel to the right to avoid the snaking back end of the killer's truck. Her car skated forward and sideways at the same time until she crashed into the driver's side of the truck.

Time slowed as her car and the killer's truck became one unit, metal mashed and tangled together, and they tumbled along the road. In her peripheral vision, she saw the drivers of other vehicles swerve to miss them, and she braced for another impact. But none came.

Until they slammed into a tree on the waste ground between the freeway and the off ramp. Her airbag deployed, hitting her squarely in the face, and her seatbelt constricted against her chest as it halted her forward motion abruptly. The immediate ringing in her ears was accompanied by the smell of burning, and she fumbled at the belt release while fighting the urge to pass out. She blinked against the onslaught of black inky vision dotted with stars and grabbed at the door handle before realizing her car door was jammed against the truck.

The seat belt jerked free, and Dak scrambled across the car and out the passenger side. She used the hood of the car to lever herself to a standing position and drew her gun. She blinked again, focused on the tall figure emerging from the truck, and leveled her firearm in his direction. He stayed behind the safety of his door, his own gun pointing directly at her from just fifteen feet away.

"Lower your weapon," she shouted.

"Perhaps you should lower yours," he said and smiled even though blood ran from a nasty gash on his nose. "You're rather exposed."

Dak dropped to her knees and rested her forearms on the hood of her car, her gun still trained on the killer's head. "Not so much."

"You're fast."

She hadn't expected a compliment nor for him to sound so impressed. "And you're under arrest." She heard the whirr of helicopter blades above their heads. Garrity might not be with her, but he had her back anyway. "It's over. There's nowhere to run. You're surrounded." She tilted her head to the right to draw his attention to the number of patrol officers she'd seen advancing along the metal guard rails. Keeping her gun on him, she held up her hand to signal the officers to hold their ground.

He glanced in that direction, and she saw his shoulders drop slightly. "So I'm to become merely another foiled serial killer in your impressive portfolio, Special Agent Farrell, and I don't get to succeed where the Artist failed in killing you."

"I guess so." The twinge in her side was almost instinctive, and she took a deep breath against the accompanying flashback merged with new pain from the crash. "I wouldn't be a very good agent if you did."

"To be shot once, Special Agent Farrell, may be regarded as a misfortune, but twice would look like carelessness."

Dak frowned at his obscure phrasing. "Are you really quoting Shakespeare?"

He laughed. "Oscar Wilde. His time in jail was rather damaging. How do you suppose I'd fare given that I appear to be in the same situation?"

"That doesn't really interest me," Dak said. "I just want to stop you killing people."

"By fair means or foul?"

She shook her head, unwilling to play his word games. "I'm giving you the chance to surrender peacefully. Put your weapon on the hood of the truck and back away."

"As you wish." He sighed deeply and began to move to lay down his gun.

The sound of a single shot of gunfire was unmistakable. Blood exploded from the killer's torso, splattering all over the window of the driver's door, and he slumped to the ground.

"What the fuck?" Dak jumped up from her position, twisting and turning to find the shooter. The patrol officers to her right all shook their heads and looked as stunned as she felt.

Weaver emerged from around a tree to the left of the killer's truck, her expression one of shock mixed with triumph. *She* was the shooter. Dak ran around the collision to get to the killer. Without knowing exactly where the bullet had landed or what damage it had done, she still held out her gun. As she came around the truck's door, she saw the killer prone on the ground, his gun no longer within reach. She holstered her weapon and got to her knees beside him. The stain of bright red on the chest of his white button-down shirt seeped into an ever-larger circle, and Dak realized Weaver had issued a kill shot.

His eyes flickered open, and as he tried to talk, blood gurgled in his throat. She leaned closer to hear what he was saying, and he grasped her wrist. Dak used her other hand to press on his shoulder and ease him back. This wasn't the way this should've played out. If she'd trusted her instincts, she would've made Weaver stand down before they'd even gone to Mr. Scott's house. *God fucking dammit.* She leaned in closer and listened to what would inevitably be his last words.

"Read my scientific journal," he said, struggling to form the words. "It explains...everything. I need someone to continue my work. For science."

"Your work? Murdering people in cold blood?" she said, not holding back on her distaste for his psychotic phrasing.

"Read," he repeated, then his eyes flickered closed.

She pulled back when several sets of boots and shoes came into her field of vision.

"Is he dead?" Weaver asked.

Dak looked up. "As good as. Unless the paramedics have a miracle in their equipment bag."

Weaver nodded as if affirming her actions, but there was no mistaking the disease of uncertainty in her eyes. "He moved to shoot you, Farrell. I saw him shift."

Dak shook her head. "He was about to surrender, Weaver. He was putting his gun down." She felt no desire or need to sugarcoat it. Protecting her wouldn't enable her to learn from her mistakes.

Weaver's expression dropped. "But he—"

Miller put his hand on Weaver's shoulder. "You did the right thing, Weaver. From your position, it was impossible to tell what he was about to do." He glanced briefly at Dak. "Better safe than sorry, right? Nobody enjoys getting shot in the line of duty, especially when it could've been avoided."

Her stomach twinged involuntarily, and she tilted her head slightly. He was right about the last thing for sure. Maybe he was right about all of it. Better the serial killer dead than her. A moment's hesitation was often the line between life and death in law enforcement. Judging from the rash of emotions crisscrossing Weaver's eyes, this was the first time she'd had to kill someone. She'd have enough trouble reconciling that, whether it was a righteous kill or not. And on the plus side, Miller finally had Weaver's back.

Miller retrieved the killer's gun from the ground with an evidence bag. "Looks like we've got a .44 caliber Bulldog revolver. I'm sure ballistics won't have any trouble matching that to the bullets that killed Beasley."

The killer wheezed and coughed, and blood gurgled from the corner of his mouth. Dak heard emergency sirens in the distance and vaguely wondered if they'd be able to save him...and if she wanted them to. Serial killers were always worth studying, and from an objective perspective, this one had been particularly interesting and something she hadn't come across before. Now that they'd stopped him from killing any more people, she was eager to find the "scientific journal" he wanted her to read, and she wanted to know if she'd been right about his reason for not copying the Garavito murder.

"We need access."

The stern, deep voice jerked Dak back into reality. She got to her feet and stepped back. The area became a mill of activity as paramedics converged on the killer, who was still somehow clinging to life. She wiped the killer's blood on her slacks, pulled on a pair of latex gloves, and walked around the truck and scrambled over the hood of Garrity's car to get access to the open passenger door window. Mr. Scott would be devastated when the police returned the truck to him, though that wouldn't be for a while since it would be impounded and processed for evidence. She didn't imagine Garrity would be too impressed with the state of his car either, especially since it was his own and not government-issued.

"Haven't you done enough damage?"

She let out a small laugh at the sound of Garrity's voice, and she looked up. "I was just thinking about you."

"Don't let our wives hear you say that."

Shit. She suddenly remembered she'd ended her call to CJ in a hurry and without explanation. She'd be worried. For now, Dak had to concentrate on the scene.

"What are you doing dancing on the hood of my car anyway?" he asked.

"I need to get in the truck." She thumbed toward the multiple rescuers on the other side of the vehicle. "And this is the only way I can get in." She leaned through the opening, pulled out a nice-looking tan leather backpack from the passenger seat, and sat on the roof of Garrity's car.

"Seriously?" Garrity shook his head but then climbed up and sat beside her. "Do you think Charnwood will authorize payment for my repairs?"

Dak dug around in the multiple front pockets of the bag and grunted. "Probably. Though if you'd bought American, it might not be quite so totaled. The handling is terrible." She pulled out a maroon-colored UK passport and flipped to the photo page. The killer was slightly more handsome without a busted nose from the airbag. She passed the ID to Garrity. "Meet Oliver Kingsley."

Garrity studied the photograph then flicked through the pages. "Well-traveled. Do you think he's murdered people in all these countries? Thailand. Australia. Kenya. Mexico—the guy could've done a world travel guide."

"A serial killer's guide to murdering all over the world?" Dak sighed. "We probably don't want to know how well that would sell." She ignored the gun and withdrew a thick and expensive-looking oxblood red leather journal with marbleized page edges from an inside compartment. She untied the leather lace from around it, opened it to the first page, and began to read the beautifully executed penmanship in a forest green ink. *Have you ever woken up from one of those dreams, and an idea has been so solid, so complete in your mind, it's as if you've been God-touched, or there's been some divine intervention? Or if you're not a particularly religious person (Who can tell? I have no idea who might eventually read this), then it might feel like the Universe has conspired to work through you in some small way.*

"What's that?" Garrity asked.

"A scientific journal, if Oliver Kingsley is to be believed." She closed the book and put it back in the bag to read later, after she'd debriefed Captain Grant and Charnwood, then she'd enter it for evidence. She slid off the hood of the car and winced at the pain now radiating through her face and shoulders.

"You should go home and get cleaned up. You look like shit," Garrity said. "The LAPD can handle this, and I'll keep an eye on everything."

She smiled. "Thanks. I think I will. Let me know if he survives."

The paramedics lifted a gurney to its full height, then one of them took the folded white sheet at Kingsley's feet and laid it over his body. He seemed to hesitate for a moment before he pulled the covering over Kingsley's face.

"He didn't make it," Garrity said, deadpan.

Dak's shoulders dropped. The chase was over. There would be no more killings, and she could relax for now. The chance to study Kingsley was lost, and anything she could learn about his motives and character would be from contacting any friends and family that might be halfway across the world and from the ramblings enclosed in the journal.

She looked across at Weaver, Miller, and the rest of their task force and gave them a thumbs-up. They'd done their job well, and they'd go back to the station as heroes, especially Weaver. But Dak saw the haunting already beginning to form behind her eyes. No matter how much they prepared an officer of the law to kill a criminal, they couldn't prepare them for the real-life aftermath of being responsible for taking someone else's life. And the fact that the suspect had been about to lay down his weapon rather than die by cop wouldn't make it any easier. She had to trust Miller to help Weaver with that.

Dak swung Kingsley's backpack over her shoulder and pulled her cell from her pocket. After her near-death experience, the only thing she wanted to do was connect with CJ, with her life. CJ was her world, her everything. And although she wasn't actually at home waiting for Dak to return, her heart waited for her, and that felt precious beyond words.

CJ answered on the first ring. "Are you okay?"

The concern in her question was palpable, and Dak sank into the love it represented. For years, Dak had been in a self-enforced solitude, but CJ had taken a wrecking ball to her walls and wrapped her in a love so complete that Dak could never imagine being without her. "Everything is fine, baby. We got him." She glanced at the metal mess of Garrity's car sandwiched against Mr. Scott's poor truck. "There was a chase, and we were in a crash, but I'm okay. I promise." She didn't need to mention the likelihood that her face was a mess of bruises already, and her jaw ached from the force of the airbag. She wiped at her eyebrow and came away with a smear of blood. It would have plenty of time to heal before the wedding.

"You promise?" CJ asked quietly.

"I promise. And I'll be even better as soon as I can hold you in my arms again."

"I should come home."

"No," Dak said, though it was exactly what she wanted. "Honestly, I'm fine. I'll fly out to see you in a few days, if that's okay with you?" Watching CJ in action would be a welcome change of pace and a chance to reconnect, and she was sure Charnwood would give her the time before she began to look into Agent Kimbal's death in Mexico. With any luck, she could have that wrapped up before

CJ finished filming.

"You will?" CJ sounded excited. "That'd be amazing. I miss you. Hard."

"I miss you too, baby. My ride is here. I'll call you later."

"I'll be waiting."

Dak ended the call and grabbed a ride home with one of the patrols who'd been ready with the stop sticks. She'd try to get a couple hours' sleep, and then she'd start reading Kingsley's journal before she wrote her report for Charnwood. She glanced back over her shoulder, and Garrity gave her a mock salute. He'd turned out to be a good partner. She might even miss working with him when Hamilton finally joined her.

She settled into the patrol car and turned the engagement ring on her finger. She was getting used to LA, an office base, and a settled home life. And now she had a wedding to plan. That had to be easier than chasing criminals...didn't it?

Epilogue

Six months later

CJ's BREATH CAUGHT AT the sight of Dak as she took the first step down the aisle.

Her dad stiffened beside her and looked at her with concern. "Are you okay?"

"More than." She hadn't expected to *literally* go weak at the knees when she finally saw Dak in her perfectly fitted, classic black tux and crisp white shirt. Handsome wasn't a strong enough word to describe how amazing she looked. And she was about to become her wife. CJ's chest could barely contain her heart as it expanded with the joy of that knowledge.

All the nonsense disagreements and minor disappointments they'd had as they were organizing the wedding disappeared last night, when it really hit them that they were getting married today. When Dak had kissed her before they parted to spend the night separately—one tradition they'd both been reluctant to embrace—the promise of today, of forever, was on their lips, and that realization was beyond heavenly.

Dak's brother, Wade, grinned widely and waved, and CJ smiled when Dak batted his hand down. When she looked into CJ's eyes, their love became a physical thing in the space between them, drawing them together like two atoms of the same molecule chemically bonded and unable to exist apart. Given how fiercely independent they both were, that intensity continued to confound CJ, but she supposed that she didn't have to understand it; she only had to accept it. And with that acceptance came a love so profound and all-enveloping that it had obliterated her fear of being alone forever.

"Are you ready?"

CJ glanced at her dad and nodded just as the music began. They walked at the expected steady pace though all CJ wanted to do was run up the aisle and jump into Dak's strong arms, knowing that she'd catch her not just today but every day. She didn't take her eyes from Dak's chiseled features. The scar over her right eye from the crash six months ago only added to her overall rugged beauty, and it reminded CJ every day to cherish every moment they were together. As they made their way painfully slowly toward Dak, CJ looked around and smiled at their guests. Elodie and Madison looked gorgeous in a coordinated suit and dress in navy. They'd seen plenty of them over the last six months, and it was fair to say that the glamorous couple had become their best friends and the people they saw most often. Dak's freshly minted partner, Hamilton, grinned at her, and his dark and dangerous sister, Ice, winked.

When they reached the altar, she kissed her dad on the cheek, and he hugged her tightly.

"Thank you, CJ," he said quietly.

She didn't have to ask what he meant. He'd said it many times over the past few months as both he and her mom continued to work hard at repairing their fractured relationship. CJ had vacillated between wanting to walk up the aisle alone or on her dad's arm, and it was Dak who had convinced her to allow the latter. Dak missed her dad terribly because they'd had an incredible relationship, so it was hard for her to understand CJ's relationship with her father. Years of inattention were hard to let go of, even as an adult, but with Dak's help and her parents' concerted and consistent efforts, CJ was coming around. And this was her way of showing that she accepted the new 2.0 version of parents she now had. Didn't everyone deserve a second chance?

He released his embrace, and CJ turned to her wife-to-be. Dak squeezed her hand, and the warmth of her grasp swept away all other thoughts.

"You look..." Dak shook her head slowly and bit her bottom lip. "You look stunning."

"And you're the most handsome woman I've ever seen. It's all I can do not to kiss you before I get permission from this guy." She tilted her head toward the celebrant, who waited with a kind smile.

"In that case," he said and stepped closer to position himself between the two of them.

Dak let go of CJ's hands and smiled. "You're worth waiting for."

The celebrant quieted the church and began the ceremony. His voice faded to background noise as CJ lost herself in Dak's eyes, in the love they expressed, in her soul, until Dak took her hands again. CJ looked down to see Dak holding a perfect circle of palladium, unbreakable like their love, in one hand and her vows in her other.

"I didn't know what love was until I fell into it with you, CJ," Dak said, the paper in her hand trembling slightly. "I didn't know what it was to be fully open to another person without feeling exposed and vulnerable. I'd never been my true self one hundred percent of the time around anyone until you. To feel seen and fully accepted for all of me, all of the weakness as well as the strength, has been a revelation. I've put aside my masks because I can be *me* when we're together, with no expectation or judgment."

The beginnings of tears edged the corner of Dak's eyes, and she swallowed hard. CJ ached for Dak's show of vulnerability and wanted to reach out, envelop and comfort her, show her that together they could get through anything. Hell, they'd already survived crazed killer twins. Anything else the world had to throw at them would be child's play.

"I need you to know that I see you too," Dak said. "*All* of you, your rainbow of emotions, and your immense capacity for love. And I can't wait to spend the rest of my life as your wife, reveling in that love and giving you all the love you need and deserve. I know that sometimes it's going to be hard, and our careers will get in the way, but I'll always make all the time in the world for you, and for us. Because you are my world. You're my everything, my life. I'll be forever grateful that you chose me back then, and that you choose me every day. And I promise to cherish you for the rest of our lives." Dak slipped the ring on CJ's finger and blew out a long breath before she folded the paper and put in the breast pocket of her tuxedo. "I love you, CJ, and I'll love you forever."

CJ stretched out her hand to admire the physical embodiment of their commitment to each other and then looked up to meet Dak's adoring gaze. Her mom held out Dak's ring, a thicker version of CJ's, and CJ clasped it in her hand tightly. She had her vows on a slip of paper too, tucked inside her bra, but she'd read and re-read them so many times that she'd memorized the words, and she'd always been better on the fly, without a script. "I was lost until I met you. My life had just been turned upside down, and meeting you turned it right side up again. Aside from being smoking hot," she waited for the chuckling audience to quiet, "you're intelligent and kind, and beneath that steel exterior, you have a soul of marshmallow, and I'm honored that you allow me to see that. I had no idea I was capable of the kind of love I feel for you, that this depth of love even existed at all. Almost impossibly, my love for you grows stronger every day, and I sometimes feel like my body is too weak to contain it, and that I'm going to explode. So in case I do, I want you to know that being your wife will be the greatest role of my life, and I promise that I'll put every last piece of my heart and soul into it." She took Dak's hand and slid the ring onto her finger slowly. "I love you with everything I am and everything I'll ever be."

The soft burn of joyful tears pushed for release, and CJ let them fall. Dak gently thumbed them from both cheeks, her expression full of their shared love, unchecked and unguarded. The celebrant said whatever he was supposed to say, she guessed. She heard him talking but once again, his voice faded into background noise as CJ focused every iota of her concentration on Dak's face. She wanted to record every line, every facial feature, every tiny movement so that she could remember this moment for the rest of time. The moment they promised themselves to each other forever and always, the moment they became legally bound and CJ could now call Dak her wife.

She must've missed the part where she was finally given permission to kiss her, because Dak held her face gently and pressed her lips to CJ's: their first kiss as wife and wife. CJ sank into it deeply before remembering they were in a church and had a rather large audience. She pulled in air when Dak moved back, and she laid her palms against Dak's chest to steady herself.

"Hey, wife," Dak said and winked.

CJ took Dak's hand and kissed her knuckles. "Hi, wife."

"So you really are okay with spending the rest of your life with me?" Dak wrapped her hand around CJ's neck and played with a wisp of her hair.

"More than okay actually. I needed to take you off the market before anyone else snatched you up."

Dak laughed and shook her head. "No one but you was lining up, babe."

"Sure they were. You just weren't looking for them."

Dak ran the back of her hand down CJ's cheek. "Once I'd found you, there was no point looking for anyone else."

CJ tilted her head toward their gathered friends and family, who were applauding and sending out the occasional catcall. "How long do you think we have to entertain this lot before we can slip away to Elodie's private island?"

"I think we could lead them to the food and then disappear. That's what most people come to a wedding for, isn't it? The free food."

Their officiant tapped Dak on the shoulder. "If you're in a hurry to leave, I should introduce you to your loved ones." He proceeded to do so, and everyone cheered as they made their way back down the aisle and into the courtyard for photographs.

Outside, Ruth tugged on Dak's lapels. "Your father would have been so proud of you, Dak," she said, her eyes bleary with tears.

"Thanks, Mom."

Dak blinked rapidly, and CJ knew she was trying to keep her own tears at bay.

CJ's mom linked her arm through Ruth's and sighed noisily. "Aren't they the most beautiful couple you've ever seen?"

"Absolutely," Ruth said. "I'm a very lucky mom."

"And I'm a very lucky wife." CJ pulled Dak in for another deep kiss, getting more desperate by the second to blow the celebration off and drag Dak to Elodie's yacht to get their honeymoon started early.

Dak looked deep into CJ's eyes as if she was trying to divine what was in her soul.

"You'll only find more love for you in there, no matter how long you look." CJ tugged on Dak's tie, remembering what Dak had said she was going to do with it as soon as they were alone on the boat. She shivered with delight at the thought.

"But I won't ever tire of looking," Dak said. "Thank you for marrying me, wife."

CJ leaned closer and whispered in Dak's ear so their parents couldn't hear. "You know *exactly* how you can thank me, wife, and you better not stop doing *that* for the rest of our lives."

Dak grinned and kissed CJ's nose. "You can count on that, baby," she said and squeezed CJ's butt.

CJ sighed into Dak's neck, peaceful down to her very soul to a degree she'd never thought possible. Whatever their future held, she knew it would be exponentially better because she had Dak by her side to share it.

THE END...

...of this story, but not the end of their story. Dak Farrell will return in *Dead Right*.

Other Great Butterworth Books

Dead Ringer by Robyn Nyx
Three murders. One killer. No motive.
Available on Amazon (ASIN B0CPQ8HFK7)

Medea by JJ Taylor
Who will Medea become in her battle for freedom?
Available from Amazon (ASIN B0CK2FB7GW)

Virgin Flight by E.V. Bancroft
In the battle between duty and desire, can love win?
Available from Amazon (ASIN B0CKJWQZ45)

Fragments of the Heart by Ally McGuire
Love can be the greatest expedition of all.
Available on Amazon (ASIN B0CHBPHR6M)

Here You Are by Jo Fletcher
Can they unlock their hearts to find the true happiness they both deserve?
Available on Amazon (ASIN B0CBN935ZB)

Stunted Heart by Helena Harte
A stunt rider who lives in the fast lane. An ER doctor who can't take chances. A passion that could turn their worlds upside down.
Available on Amazon (ASIN B0C78GSWBV)

Dark Haven by Brey Willows
Even vampires get tired of playing with their food...
Available on Amazon (ASIN B0C5P1HJXC)

Green for Love by E.V. Bancroft
All's fair in love and eco-war.
Available from Amazon (ASIN B0C28F7PX5)

Call of Love by Lee Haven
Separated by fear. Reunited by fate. Will they get a second chance at life and love?
Available from Amazon (ASIN B0BYC83HZD)

Available on Amazon (ASIN B0994XVDGR)

Let Love Be Enough by Robyn Nyx
When a killer sets her sights on her target, is there any stopping her?
Available on Amazon (ASIN B09YMMZ8XC)

Dead Pretty by Robyn Nyx
An FBI agent, a TV star, and a serial killer. Love hurts.
Available on Amazon (ASIN B09QRSKBVP)

Nero by Valden Bush
Banished and abandoned. Will destiny reunite her with the love of her life?
Available from Amazon (ASIN B0BHJKHK6S)

Warm Pearls and Paper Cranes by E.V. Bancroft
A family torn apart by secrets. The only way forward is love.
Available from Amazon (ASIN B09DTBCQ92)

Judge Me, Judge Me Not by James Merrick
One man's battle against the world and himself to find it's never too late to find, and use, your voice.
Available from Amazon (ASIN B09CLK91N5)

Scripted Love by Helena Harte
What good is a romance writer who doesn't believe in happy ever after?
Available on Amazon (ASIN B0993QFLNN)

Call of Love by Helena Harte
Sometimes the call you least expect is the one you need the most.
Available on Amazon (ASIN B08D9SR15H)

What's Your Story?

Global Wordsmiths, CIC, provides an all-encompassing service for all writers, ranging from basic proofreading and cover design to development editing, typesetting, and eBook services. A major part of our work is charity and community focused, delivering writing projects to under-served and under-represented groups across Nottinghamshire, giving voice to the voiceless and visibility to the unseen.

To learn more about what we offer, visit: www.globalwords.co.uk

A selection of books by Global Words Press:
Desire, Love, Identity: with the National Justice Museum
Aventuras en México: Farmilo Primary School
Times Past: with The Workhouse, National Trust
Young at Heart with AGE UK
In Different Shoes: Stories of Trans Lives

Self-published authors working with Global Wordsmiths:
Steve Bailey
Ravenna Castle
Jackie D
CJ DeBarra
Dee Griffiths
Iona Kane
Maggie McIntyre
Emma Nichols
Dani Lovelady Ryan
Erin Zak